WAR OF THE ARCHONS

A DEMON IN SILVER

ALSO BY R.S. FORD AND AVAILABLE FROM TITAN BOOKS

A Demon in Silver
The Hangman's Gate (June 2019)
The Spear of Malice (June 2020)

BOOK ONE of WAR OF THE ARCHONS

A DEMON IN SILVER

R·S·FORD

TITAN BOOKS

A Demon in Silver
Paperback edition ISBN: 9781785653063
Electronic edition ISBN: 9781785653070

Published by Titan Books
A division of Titan Publishing Group Ltd
144 Southwark St, London SE1 0UP

First edition: June 2018
2 4 6 8 10 9 7 5 3 1

A CIP catalogue record for this title is available from the British Library.

Printed and bound in the United States.

What did you think of this book?
We love to hear from our readers. Please email us at:
readerfeedback@titanemail.com, or write to us at the above address.

To receive advance information, news, competitions, and exclusive
offers online, please sign up for the Titan newsletter on our website:

www.titanbooks.com

THIS BOOK IS DEDICATED TO JOHN JARROLD...
MAY HE NEVER RETIRE. ONWARDS!

PROLOGUE

S IFF wept as torn banners fluttered in the breeze. The tattered remnants of a dozen armies lay scattered and broken on the once lush plain, and broken armour shone lambent in the sun, where it wasn't spattered red.

Durius had seduced the guardians of the Blue Tower, twisting them to his will. He had made them promises, given them a new eidolon to worship, and for their loyalty they had been swept aside like dust.

Siff knelt amidst the carnage, Bezial's body cradled across her lap. He had been her most loyal disciple – captain of her guard, high priest, lover. Now he was dead. Her finger traced a furrow that marred his bright armour. Where her tears fell upon his breastplate it displaced the red as though the blood feared her grief.

Bezial had led the vanguard, bellowing her name, riding forth on a black steed with its hooves aflame, sword aloft. Now he lay still, his voice forever silenced.

Siff felt the loss deeply, and her tears fell until her black hair was abruptly swept about her face by a gust of turbulent air. She looked up to see a creature of unparalleled beauty; a beauty only matched by its cruelty.

Innellan swooped down on nightingale's wings, landing amidst the shattered landscape with a feather-light touch. Her pure white hair billowed in the breeze, her robe black as a starless night, hands slick with crimson. She paused, surveying the scene of carnage before stepping forward, bare feet treading lithely through the scattered weapons and fallen pennants. The hem of her robe trailed through the gore and the viscera, and soon her feet were stained as crimson as her hands. She smiled, revelling in the butchery.

'Was all this worth it?' Innellan said, surveying the scene before settling her eyes on Bezial. 'All this death?'

Siff recognised the insincerity in that question. Innellan's lust for slaughter was legend.

'It has to be,' replied Siff. Despite her sorrow, she knew the death of Bezial was a small price to pay for the catastrophe she would avert – if they had been in time. 'And now we have to scale the tower. Who knows what damage has been done.'

Innellan silently nodded in agreement, making for the tower in the distance. It soared up into the darkening sky, blue walls sheer and roiling like the sea.

Siff looked longingly at her First Knight, before gently laying him down on the grass to his final rest. She followed Innellan across the devastated field, eerie in its silence. The battle had been costly but it was a price that had to be paid. The Blue Tower had held the Heartstone in its lofty prison for millennia. When it had come under threat there was no alternative but to fight.

Siff spied Armadon sitting amidst the carnage, wiping his giant blade with one of the worthless banners. He was covered in gore from the top of his horned head to the bottom of his cloven hooves, but he kept his weapon clean. His brutality turned Siff's stomach, but allying with him had been a necessity. She needed all the Archons she could muster, and Armadon was the most ferocious of their number. If it was to be war, she needed him at her side.

'The tower awaits us, brother,' Innellan said.

He looked up, regarding the white-haired Archon with disdain.

'I am no brother of yours. Once this is done with our alliance will be over—'

'And we can return to the fight like we always have.' Innellan smiled as though relishing the thought.

Armadon rose wearily. Naturally, of all the slaughter today, the lion's share belonged to him. He tilted his huge head to one side, cracking the joints and sinew of his thick neck.

'Let's see an end to this,' he said.

The three of them walked slowly towards the tower, blue marble stretching to the sky. Dread built within Siff as they walked in through the huge carved archway. Seraphs were hewn into the stone, silently trumpeting their entrance.

Marble stairs spiralled upwards into blinding light and Siff took every step with reverence. Behind her Innellan trod the white stairway, leaving bloody imprints in her wake. Armadon brought up the rear, his tread surefooted despite his hulking frame.

When Siff reached the summit, the sky was black. Some might have thought that ominous, but she had come too far to be put off by signs and portents. The Heartstone stood in the centre of the huge gallery, its light shining forth toward the four cardinal points like a beacon.

It was as old as the Archons. The source of their power. A conduit through which they could travel to the plane of mortal men and meddle in their affairs. It had been a century since Siff had sought to banish its power, shattering its core and exiling it to this high and forbidden place.

For a time she had succeeded.

Durius had harboured other plans.

Though the twelve Archons had agreed to an accord — making a pact that none of them would ever again abuse the Heartstone's power — the Archon Durius had sought to mend the artefact and use it to pass through to the mortal realm. There he would reign as a single monarch, unchallenged by his peers.

If not for Siff, and her alliance with Innellan and Armadon, then Durius may well have succeeded. Now it looked as though his plan had failed.

'It was a mistake to raise this tower,' said Armadon. 'We should have hidden the Heartstone away, deep beneath the earth where none of us could find it.'

'It would have changed nothing,' said Siff, remembering how this tower had been her idea. How she had thought it would solve millennia of war. The Archons had left it defended by a legion of warriors they had thought incorruptible. How wrong they had been. 'It would always have come to this. Hiding it would have done no good. We would all have been drawn to it eventually. It calls to us even now.'

The three approached the glowing jewel. Energy pulsated

and roiled within as though a storm was brewing inside. The power at its core churned with the need to be released.

As they drew closer Siff could see hairline cracks on the veneer, myriad imperfections marring its surface.

'It is still incomplete,' said Armadon.

After all these years Durius had still not managed to remake the Heartstone anew.

'But complete enough for us to pass over to the other side,' said Innellan.

Siff could sense longing in her voice and was unable to quell the sense of foreboding it inspired.

Siff held out a hand toward the Heartstone. The air grew thick as though the burgeoning clouds outside were growing heavy.

'Durius has not fled,' she said. 'He has not gone through.'

'And the gate?' Innellan said. 'Is it repaired?'

'It is imperfect,' said Siff. 'But it could still provide a pathway.'

They stood in silence, waiting. Listening. Then Siff heard it, and she knew the others heard it too.

A prayer from across worlds.

A call to the Archons.

Worship.

1

Canbria, 100 years after the Fall

STARING at the back end of a carriage for mile after mile was no one's idea of theatre. But it beat watching the back end of a horse, so Josten had that to be thankful for.

His right hand loosely held the reins of his mount, his left gripping the scabbard of the sword at his hip. Idly he flicked the cross-guard with his thumb so the blade popped out of the sheath with a steady rhythm, as though counting the beat of their ride. It kept the weapon loose in its scabbard, ready for action. It was a habit Josten had fallen into when he was young, and the oldest habits were the hardest to break. But a sword stuck in its sheath was about as much use in battle as a broken tree branch, so he reckoned some old habits were worth keeping.

'This is a shitty detail,' said Mullen, riding close beside him.

Josten didn't have to look to know Mullen would be scowling in distaste at the carriage in front of them. Mullen Bull was given to scowling a lot, and you were never in any doubt as to what was on his mind at any moment of the day. If it could be moaned about, Mullen was sure to be the one doing the moaning.

'How can you say that?' Josten replied. 'We have the

bright beautiful day above us.' He gestured to the grey skies that hung over them like a pall. 'Good company.' Josten patted the sweating, stinking nag that had carried him for gods knew how many miles along the same muddy track. 'And best of all we're being paid a king's ransom for the pleasure.'

That last raised a smile from Mullen. They both knew there were a lot of shitty things about this shitty detail but the pay was far and away the shittiest.

'I had dreams about being in the duke's personal guard,' Mullen said, raising his big eyes and long stubbly face to the cloudy skies. 'Visions of prestige. Of travel and adventure. Of a tight uniform, and the women it would bring flocking to me. This is not what I had in mind.' He wiped the back of his neck with one broad palm, glancing briefly at the sweat and grime left there before cleaning it on his thigh.

'If it's any consolation you've managed to get yourself the tight uniform.' Josten nodded at Mullen's prominent gut, which, despite several days on the road and the meagre rations that went with it, still stuck out like he was smuggling a pig under his hauberk.

Mullen ignored him. 'And it's not as if we're even protecting the duke. Don't get me wrong, the duchess is a much prettier duty to perform, and who wouldn't want to guard that body, but—'

He stopped as Josten swiped a hand across his throat in a *shut the fuck up* gesture. The carriage in front of them might be a solid wooden box designed to deflect a well-aimed arrow, but he was sure it wasn't soundproof.

The rhythmic beat of galloping hooves cut short any

chance of more conversation, and Josten twisted in his saddle, staring down the road behind them. His right hand was on the hilt of his sword, the thumb of his left pushing the cross-guard clear of the scabbard's locket.

A rider came into view, driving his horse like all the demons of hell were after him. The steed was breathing hard and heavy, mud spattering its legs and flanks, eyes wide with panic just like its rider.

Mullen's sword was out of its sheath and he spun his own horse to face their pursuer.

'Steady,' said Josten. 'He's one of ours.'

The rider's livery was clear to see now. Duke Harlaw's red eagle clutching a black rose, visible through the mud that caked the rider's chest.

'Hold!' Mullen shouted toward the front of their column as the rider reined in his horse in front of Josten. He was gasping hard and Josten gave him a moment to catch his breath.

'Bandits,' he finally managed through heavy gulps of air. 'Quarter-mile back down the road.'

'How many?' Josten asked, trying to stay calm. There was no reason to panic just yet.

'Twenty? Maybe a few more. But it ain't the numbers we should be worried about.'

All right. Still no need to panic. 'Who is it?'

'It's Tarlak Thurlow,' said the rider, his voice almost cracking with fear.

Now was the time for panicking.

'Bollocks,' said Mullen. 'Shitty fucking bollocks!'

Bollocks didn't even begin to cover it.

'The duke's at Ravensbrooke, ten leagues north of here,' Josten said to the scout. 'Get word to him we're heading for Fort Carlaine.' The scout nodded, reining his horse around and setting off at a gallop the way he'd come from.

'Fort Carlaine's a ruin,' said Mullen. 'Why the hell aren't we going to Drinsport?'

'We'd never make it before Tarlak caught up with us. We've got more chance defending a ruin than getting caught on the road. Now get to the head of the column and get us bloody moving.'

As Mullen spurred his steed forward, cursing to himself about their inevitable deaths, Josten moved up to the side of the carriage. He rapped his fist against it three times, feeling the solid oak, but knowing it would be no defence if they got caught by Tarlak and his men. A shutter slid back, showing the face of one of Duchess Selene's handmaids.

'Tell her ladyship things are about to get a little bumpy,' Josten said, as the handmaid's eyes widened in concern. 'And please pass on my apologies.'

He tried to make the last comment sound as sincere as he could, though the duchess's comfort was the last of his concerns. If they didn't get to safety before Tarlak Thurlow caught up with them, a sharp piece of metal in his guts would be a big concern and the duchess would find herself on the wrong end of a hefty ransom demand. If Tarlak's reputation was anything to go by she'd be lucky to get out of it with her honour intact, so he was damned sure she could stand a bruised arse.

Mullen's voice cut the quiet of the afternoon air, the

sound of birds tweeting replaced by choice language and hooves clapping on the forest path. The column quickened its pace and Josten reined his horse towards the rear of the carriage once more.

They rushed on faster through the forest. Josten could see the carriage bouncing along the path in front of him, imagining the scene within as the duchess and her entourage were flung around the wooden interior. The thought of it brought a smile to his face; but the unwelcome thought of their pursuer quickly wiped it away.

Tarlak was only a quarter-mile behind them. If he was riding at pace he'd catch up in no time. Tales of the Red Forest's most notorious bandit were legion. Josten had always had a strong stomach when faced with stories of torture and dismemberment but there was no way he wanted to find out if any of them were true. If it came to it he wouldn't be taken alive.

Before he could start to let the thought of that freeze his insides, Fort Carlaine came into view through the trees ahead.

It wasn't so much relief that washed over Josten as despair. Mullen had said the place was a ruin. It was in slightly better shape than that, but not by much. Fort Carlaine had been a famous outpost in its time – a watchtower used by the Wolf Brigade during the Age of Penitence. Brave deeds had happened in this place, as well as murders and a royal wedding. Now it looked barely decent enough to take a shit in.

The column trundled over the decrepit drawbridge and at any moment Josten expected it to give way, the carriage plummeting into the moat. Not that it would have been a problem since the moat was only about a foot deep.

He rode in through the gatehouse, thinking it might collapse on his head, before pulling up his horse beside the carriage.

'Get the duchess inside,' he barked at the duke's men-at-arms as the door to the carriage swung open. A handmaid stepped down looking suitably dishevelled after the brief but uncomfortable journey. Selene stepped out after her, helped down from the carriage by two men-at-arms. Despite being buffeted like a flag in the wind she still looked immaculate, hardly a hair out of place on her beautiful head. She gave Josten a glance that was impossible to read before allowing herself to be led up to the keep.

'What now?' said Mullen, jumping down from his horse.

'Now we secure the portcullis and wait to be rescued,' Josten replied. 'No point putting ourselves in needless danger, is there?'

'I'm afraid that won't be possible,' said a croaky voice behind them.

Josten turned to see an old man, who looked every bit as derelict as the fort surrounding him, standing in the courtyard.

'Why not?' Josten asked, dreading the inevitable answer.

'Portcullis don't work. Hasn't for years.'

'And you'd be?'

'Gerrard. The castellan of Fort Carlaine. I've been here for—'

'All right, we don't need your life story,' said Josten, jumping down from his saddle. 'Listen up, you lot!' he shouted, voice ringing out across the courtyard. 'We're going to have company any time now, and it's not the polite conversation and cakes kind of company your mother likes. Secure the gate, check your weapons, and if any of you pray I'd start right about now.'

As men-at-arms went about securing the rickety gate that looked ready to fall off its hinges, Mullen came to stand beside Josten.

'So, what do you rate our chances?' he asked.

Josten thought about it for a short while, rubbing the stubble on his chin. 'Well, Tarlak Thurlow, the most renowned brigand in the Red Forest, is on his way with twenty of his dirtiest bastards to kill us all and kidnap the duchess. We've got six men-at-arms, me, you and a couple of handmaids to defend her with. Oh, and that old man there.' Josten pointed to the frail-looking castellan as he limped across the courtyard, making himself busy with nothing in particular. 'We're in an ancient fort with a gate that would blow down in a stiff wind and the only help we've got coming is ten leagues away.'

Mullen nodded at the news. 'So, what you're saying, in a nutshell, is that we're royally fucked?'

'Something like that,' replied Josten.

'Great.' Mullen turned to the men-at-arms and started barking orders of his own as they piled barrels and hefted a broken cart in front of the main gate.

Josten took the stairs up to the roof of the gatehouse, surveying the keep. Its walls were crumbling, of that there was little doubt, but they still had a solid perimeter to defend. The drawbridge and portcullis were out of action but at least there was only one way in and that was through the gate. If they could defend it long enough for help to arrive, they might make it through this.

It was a slim hope.

For a fleeting moment Josten thought that he should just run. That he should grab Mullen and get the hell out of there. But he knew that wasn't an option. There was one reason this had become more than a job. There was more than just gold keeping him here, and he'd most likely get killed because of it.

'Everyone gets what they deserve,' he said under his breath.

The sound of beating hooves echoed through the forest and Josten saw a score or more horses break the tree line. At their head was a fearsome-looking brigand, his beard unkempt, tall even in the saddle. Josten had heard of the man but never seen him in the flesh. Tarlak Thurlow's appearance was every bit as formidable as his reputation.

With a renewed sense of urgency, Josten moved down the stairs to the gate. The men had done a good enough job of shoring up the defences and it now looked like it might take more than a stiff breeze to knock the gate over. There were gaps in the wooden timbers and Josten could see Thurlow and a couple of his men jump down from their saddles.

'Who's in charge?' Tarlak shouted across the drawbridge.

Mullen glanced at Josten with a shrug.

'That would be me,' Josten replied through a gap in the gate.

'A name would help,' said Thurlow, like he was talking to an idiot.

'Josten Cade. Guard Captain of her ladyship, the Duchess Selene of Ravensbrooke.'

'Cade? I've heard of you, son. I'm—'

'I know who you are.' Josten could see Thurlow's mouth twitch into a smile, pleased his infamy preceded him.

'Then you know why I'm here and what I'll do if you don't give her to me. We're not interested in you, Cade. You and your men can walk away from this. Just hand over the duchess and no one has to die. What do you say?'

Josten had already taken a loaded crossbow from the hands of a man-at-arms. There was a big enough gap in the gate for him to aim and fire through. Unfortunately, his aim wasn't all it could have been. The bolt crossed the drawbridge before Thurlow could make any more demands, the man to his right taking it full in the chest and dropping without a sound. Josten had been aiming for Thurlow but he'd always been better with a sword than a crossbow. Either way, he'd made his point.

'Does that answer your question?' he shouted, as Thurlow and his men scrambled to safety.

Josten handed the crossbow back and looked to Mullen, who just stared in disapproval.

'So much for negotiations,' Mullen said.

'I think I've made our position clear,' Josten replied.

'And I reckon Thurlow is glad you were so straight with him. I'm sure he'll return the favour and make his position just as clear while he's nailing our heads to the nearest tree.'

'That's what I like about you, Mullen. There's always a bright side.' Josten turned to the rest of the men, who looked a fine mixture of brave and shit scared. 'Right, lads. Time to earn your coin. It's going to be a busy afternoon.'

He looked back through the gap in the gate as Thurlow began to muster his men for the fight and realised that busy didn't even start to cover it.

2

'Put your backs into it!' Mullen shouted for the umpteenth time as he and the men-at-arms braced themselves against the gate.

The gate bowed inwards as Tarlak Thurlow's bandits battered against it, screaming in rage, desperate to get inside. A spear shot through a gap in the timbers, slicing one of the men-at-arms across the shoulder and he screamed as he backed away.

'You'll live,' said Josten, pushing the man back towards the gate to add his weight to the press.

He finished loading a crossbow, aiming it through the gap and pulling the lever. The bow snapped and Josten grinned at the scream that told him the quarrel had found its mark.

The gate bent in once more as the bandits assailed it with renewed vigour.

'You're just making them madder!' Mullen shouted over the grunting and yelling.

'What do you want me to do? Start negotiating again?' said Josten, adding his own shoulder to the press.

'I think it's a bit late for that,' Mullen had time to reply, just as an axe came hacking through the wood in front of his face.

One of the men-at-arms slid a sword back through the gap the axe had made, looking pleased when it hit something solid. The look of satisfaction didn't last long as an arrow came flying through the breach and lodged in his neck. He staggered back, gripping the shaft, gagging and choking. There was nothing any of them could do but keep pressing themselves against the gate as he died.

'Where the fuck is Duke Harlaw?' growled Mullen.

Josten was thinking the same thing, but he knew there'd be no rescue yet. Even if Duke Harlaw rode like Aethel the Stallion God, he wouldn't reach them before the gate fell and they were slaughtered to a man.

'All right, enough of this shit,' Josten said, his patience all but lost. The gate was going to fall eventually; there was no doubt of that now. Better to go down fighting than stuck like pigs in a pit.

He picked up a shield, drawing his sword and bracing himself behind the gate.

'Open it up,' he shouted.

One of the men-at-arms said something about him being a mad bastard, but Mullen just nodded. They'd been together a long time, and if anyone knew what a mad bastard Josten Cade was then Mullen Bull was the man.

But he also knew what this mad bastard was capable of.

Josten braced his shield as Mullen pulled open the gate. He almost laughed when he saw the look of surprise on the first brigand's face. Josten brought his sword crashing down through the brigand's skull. He fell without a sound and Josten slammed his shield into the face of a second brigand before the rest came at him in earnest.

With Mullen holding the gate half shut they could only reach him one at a time, and Josten went to work as they tried to squeeze through. He felt his heart pumping, violence welling up inside as he braced behind his shield, feeling the thump of sword and axe against it, biding his time, waiting for his moment. When it came, he swung, the keen edge of his sword connecting with a brigand's arm, slicing flesh and severing sinew to the bone. The brigand screamed, dropping his axe and trying to retreat, but the press of men behind him meant he had nowhere to go but down.

Josten raised his shield again in time to catch another blow, the strength of it jolting up his arm. He gritted his teeth, taking a second strike, before he ducked down low, sweeping his sword against an exposed leg. Another slicing of flesh and muscle, another scream. Another brigand hit the ground.

There was the snapping of a crossbow from over Josten's shoulder and he felt the cold rush of a quarrel hiss past his cheek. A brigand in front of him took it in the jaw and fell back, eyes wide, not quite understanding what had happened.

Josten pressed in again. This time the shield was forgotten as he hacked at the brigands, not giving them a chance to raise their weapons. One went down as Josten's sword smashed through his shoulder. Another tried to back away, desperately fending off Josten's relentless attacks.

'Retreat!' someone shouted from the back of the crowd.

The brigands needed no further encouragement after

seeing half a dozen of their lads cut down in no time at all.

Mullen watched them retreat for a moment as Josten rushed inside, before he slammed the gate shut. A couple of the men-at-arms gave a little victory cheer, clapping each other on the shoulder at a job well done. Josten almost felt like joining in, but one of them screamed before he had the chance, an arrow buried in his back.

'Bastards,' said Mullen, regarding the parapet that ran around the fort.

Josten turned to see a group of brigands had managed to scale the wall on the eastern side of the fort, the last of them still pulling himself over the crumbling merlons.

'Stay on the gate,' Josten shouted at the men-at-arms as he raced towards the steps leading up to the battlements. 'Mullen! On me.'

He could hear Mullen grumbling behind him about how it was always him had to do the following as he mounted the steps. An arrow clattered against the wall at the side of Josten's head, reminding him to keep his shield up. He felt the thud of a second arrow embed in the wood before he'd taken another two steps.

The walkway was only wide enough for two men abreast and Josten rushed forward, glad that the brigands up here would be funnelled in much the same way they'd been at the gate. Another arrow lodged in his shield as he charged forward, not slowing as he barged into the first brigand who grunted at the impact, the whiff of his bad breath hitting Josten's nostrils for the briefest of moments before he swung his shield, taking the brigand across the side of the head and toppling him from the walkway. The bandit fell into the keep, slamming onto the cobbled courtyard with a sickening thump that had a finality all its own.

Josten crouched low as the next brigand came screaming at him. That was always a giveaway – if they came at you with a scream on their lips they were shit scared, using noise to hide how terrified they were. The brigand's axe came down in a desperate hack, and Josten easily caught it on his shield, countering with a quick stab to the groin. The scream of fear rose in pitch to a squeal, the brigand darting back, dropping his axe and grasping a crotch that was fast soaking with blood. The man behind pushed him out of the way, sword held high and Josten rushed to meet him.

This one was silent, not afraid but determined, and their weapons clashed. The pair of them struggled, slamming against the edge of the battlements. Josten saw more brigands coming on behind. Caught up as he was in a wrestling match, there was nothing he could do to defend himself.

Relief washed over him as Mullen squeezed past, a growl coming from his throat as he bowled into the brigands, his sword chopping down relentlessly, each blow punctuated by a word of profanity.

'Fucking. Bastard. Shit...' he barked, battering the brigands.

Josten was still struggling with the enemy in front of him. He was wiry but strong, spitting his desperation through gritted teeth. A knee to the bollocks freed him as the bandit squealed and Josten stepped back, his sword flashing, cracking the brigand's skull.

As his enemy fell he stepped forward, ready to help his friend, but Mullen had already pushed back the rest of the attackers and they now stood alone on the battlements.

Josten glanced back down towards the gate, half expecting the brigands to have attacked anew and the remaining men-at-arms to be fighting desperately for their lives, but they simply stood watching pensively. Then one of them pointed through a gap in the gate.

'Look,' he shouted.

Josten moved across the battlements towards the gatehouse, half expecting Tarlak Thurlow to be leading his men across the drawbridge once more. Instead what he saw made him grin the widest grin he'd ever mustered. A column of horses was galloping down the forest road. Even from this distance he recognised the eagle and rose banner carried by the rider at their fore.

'Well, that's a bloody relief,' said Mullen, as Josten rushed down the stairs.

The men-at-arms had already opened the gate, laughing and shouting abuse at Tarlak and his brigands as they desperately leapt atop skittish horses to make their escape. Josten couldn't help but laugh along with them as he watched from the open gateway.

'I'll fucking have you, Cade,' shouted Tarlak Thurlow, as he reined his horse around.

Josten couldn't resist firing him a wink in the absence of a loaded crossbow. Thurlow only had time to blow a gob of hateful spit before digging his heels into his horse's flanks and galloping off to safety.

'Stand aside,' came a voice from behind them, and the men-at-arms' sniggers turned to loud guffaws as they saw the old castellan staggering across the courtyard. He was weighed down by an oversized breastplate and helmet, and a huge halberd slung across his shoulder in an unwieldy manner. 'I'll show these bandits what for. I fought with Lord Blodwin at the Battle of Silak Moor. I'm not afraid of common thugs.'

Josten couldn't help but add his own laughter to the crowd, looking up and seeing Mullen grasping his knees, bellowing his glee to the ground. This was the kind of victory he liked – the painless kind where he didn't have to have anything stitched up or bandaged.

As he turned back to watch Tarlak's retreat something hit him in the chest, knocking the wind out of him.

The next thing he knew, he was lying on the cobbles of the courtyard staring up at the grey sky. Mullen was by his side, saying something that Josten couldn't hear. It was all so confusing, right up until he looked down at his shoulder and saw the flight of an arrow sticking up like someone had planted a flag right through his hauberk.

So much for painless victories.

3

H<small>E</small> was groggy from the herbal tea he'd been given and now his mouth tasted like the inside of a tart's chamber pot. At least he was still breathing.

The arrow lay in pieces beside the pallet bed he sat on. Thankfully he'd not been conscious when they removed it. There was nothing like the pain and humiliation of being awake while your wounds were treated and he was glad to avoid it whenever possible. Intense agony always had a funny way of changing a man's demeanour. There was no way to look tough and cry your eyes out at the same time.

Fortunately for Josten, one of Duchess Selene's retinue was a former Priestess of Maerwynn and fully proficient in battlefield surgery. She was none too gentle, and he grunted in pain as she tightened the bandage that bound his shoulder and chest.

Mullen stood in one corner of the room, arms crossed over his gut, smiling in amusement at his comrade's discomfort. Josten stared back as the handmaid continued to minister to him, gritting his teeth and doing his best to pretend he wasn't in excruciating pain. The handmaid tightened his bandage with a final tug and Josten grunted. Mullen opened his mouth and laughed silently. As the handmaid turned to leave Josten offered him a two-fingered gesture.

'Don't move around too much or you'll tear the stitches,' she said as she reached the door. 'Drink plenty of water. Boil it first.'

'What about wine?' Josten asked.

'No wine,' said the handmaid, as though he were an idiot.

'Ale?'

She shook her head despondently as she walked through the door.

'Is he allowed spirits?' Mullen called after her, before sniggering at the lack of an answer. He looked Josten up and down. 'How are you feeling?'

'How am I looking?' Josten replied.

'I'll admit, you've looked better. Still a lucky bastard though.'

'Strange then, that I don't feel it.' He tried to adjust himself on the pallet bed and winced at the twinge of pain in his shoulder.

'Another inch or two and that arrow would have made a serious mess of your collarbone. Then you'd have something to moan about.'

'Coming from you, that's a bit rich.' Josten tried moving his arm. It felt like he was being stuck with a hot needle.

'Apparently, I'm in charge of Duchess Selene's guard detail while you recover – so it's not all bad news.' Mullen grinned from ear to cauliflower ear.

'At least something good's come of this,' said Josten, raising an eyebrow as high as he could. 'I'm so pleased for your sudden turn of good fortune.'

'Thanks.' Mullen couldn't seem to lose that grin. 'I thought you'd be happy for me.'

The door to the chamber opened before Josten could tell his friend exactly how fucking happy he was.

A tall knight appeared, the eagle and rose livery of Duke Harlaw on his chest. The knight was young but still had an imperious look to him. He gripped a helmet in one mailed hand, the other on the pommel of his expensive-looking sword.

Despite his youth, the young man walked in like he owned the room. Josten had seen it often amongst the duke's retinue. He was most likely from the gentry, his knighthood bought for him, his good name seeing to it he wasn't challenged by the lower orders. As much as Josten had dragged himself up from the gutter to reach his position he couldn't bring himself to be resentful. These were hard times, and you had to grab what you could and cling onto it, no matter if it was handed to you on a gold platter.

'Josten Cade,' said the young knight, staring straight ahead as though he were on the parade ground. 'I am Sir Percel of Jallenhove. Second Sword in the retinue of Duke Harlaw of Ravensbrooke.'

He paused, as though the information might provoke a reaction. Josten and Mullen merely sat and looked on. They found it was always best to seem unimpressed, especially with young officers in the duke's entourage – it never failed to put them off their stride.

'I… er…' Percel continued.

'Arrived just in time,' Josten said, sparing the young knight any more discomfort. Mullen looked disappointed at his friend's uncharacteristic graciousness. The knight smiled and nodded in that self-assured *yes, I did indeed save your arse* type manner.

'Well, almost,' Mullen said, nodding to Josten's bandages. 'There's two dead men-at-arms could have done with you here a bit earlier.'

Percel bristled at the notion he was to blame for the deaths. 'We came as quickly as we could. If the scout hadn't found us on the road and notified us of your predicament you would have all been slaughtered.'

Mullen inclined his head as though that were questionable, but Josten couldn't be bothered with would-haves.

'And the duke? Where is he?'

'Still to the north in Ravensbrooke,' said Percel. 'Word has been sent and he should be on his way as we speak.'

'That's a relief,' said Mullen. 'There was me wondering how we'd manage without him.'

Josten gave his old friend a reproving glance. Percel looked annoyed at Mullen's insinuation, opening his mouth to speak. The door opened before he had a chance.

Her entrance silenced the room.

Duchess Selene had been on the road for days and spent the night in a decrepit fort under siege, yet she was still the most beautiful thing Josten had ever seen. Her black hair was tied up in braids, loose ringlets caressing her neck. She regarded them with piercing green eyes that could hold a man's breath in his throat until she saw fit to let him breathe. Behind, her handmaids stood fidgeting in the corridor, sensing their mistress's ire. Josten could sense it too, and it only made him smile.

'Captain Cade,' she said, staring at him. All Josten could do was meet that gaze. 'Still alive I see.'

'Not quite kicking, milady, but I'm sure I'll be dancing the rondel before you know it.'

'And would you like to explain exactly what you were doing risking your life, and those of my honour guard, by opening the gate and allowing those bandits the chance to enter?'

An uncomfortable silence descended on the room. From the corner of his eye, Josten could see Mullen chewing his lip as though fighting back the need to snigger at his friend's dressing down.

'It was a tactical decision, milady. The gate would have been breached eventually—'

'And you thought it best to open it and allow Tarlak Thurlow to stroll in, rather than keeping him out?'

'Well, I—'

'And I am also led to understand Tarlak was willing to negotiate? An option you thought it best to answer with a crossbow?'

'Milady,' said Sir Percel. 'I can assure you, Tarlak Thurlow would have honoured no bargain. Captain Cade's actions—'

'When I want your opinion, I'll ask for it,' said Selene, not even deigning to look at the young knight. 'As for you—' She fixed Josten with a firm gaze both withering and thrilling. '—my husband will hear about your actions.'

'Milady, I must protest,' Percel pressed, despite Selene's admonishment. 'Captain Cade acted with the utmost bravery.'

'It's true,' said Mullen, in an unexpected show of support.

'Cade only had your best interests at heart, milady.'

Silence once more. Selene didn't take her eyes from Josten. It was all he could do to hold her gaze.

'Give me the room,' she said quietly.

Sir Percel didn't hesitate, bowing low even though she had her back to him, and opening the door. As Mullen followed her out he offered the same throat-slicing gesture Josten had given him on the road earlier. Maybe it was intended as a sign of solidarity. More likely it meant *you're fucked*.

When the door closed behind him, Duchess Selene walked slowly towards Josten. She held him in that inscrutable gaze of hers, black pupils like pinpricks in an ocean of green.

'Does it hurt?' she asked as she stood not two feet in front of him.

He could smell her, the scent of some perfumed oil, a heady musk that made him grow faint.

'Only if I move,' Josten replied. His eyes no longer held hers but slid down, taking in the perfect contour of her left shoulder, just visible above the neckline of her dress.

'Shame,' she said, reaching out a hand to run her finger lightly over the bandage that bound his shoulder. Without warning, she pressed her thumb into the flesh above his wound.

Josten grunted at the sudden pain. He reached out and grasped her hips, pulling her towards him so that she straddled his thighs, pressing his face into her chest and breathing deep.

Selene grasped a fistful of his hair and wrenched his head back, forcing him to look at her. She stared intently into his eyes, searching for something in them.

'I thought they were never going to leave,' she said, before kissing him hard on the lips.

Josten grasped her buttocks, pulling her close, grinding himself against her. She moaned as she kissed him, one hand still clutching his hair, the other caressing his cheek.

The pain in his shoulder burned like hellfire but Josten ignored it. No torturer in the world could have distracted him from this. The smell of her consumed him, the feel of her in his arms driving him mad.

Selene's tongue teased the end of his and he felt himself growing hard in his trews as she moved on top of him.

'You've made me wait too long for this,' she breathed.

Damn right I have, he wanted to say, but he was suddenly too busy fumbling for the hem of her skirts. She leaned back, reaching down to undo the drawstring of his waistband. As she moved against Josten's grip, his shoulder screamed, but he gritted his teeth. There was no way an arrow through the shoulder was going to hold him back.

He dragged her skirts up, his hands feeling the bare flesh of her thighs. Selene tugged at his trews as he lay back on the pallet bed. No sooner were they round his knees than she was on top of him, easing him inside her so slowly he almost screamed.

They both gasped gently, and for the first time the duchess closed her eyes, fingers grasping at the muscles of his arms, pulling him deeper. Josten grunted against the discomfort in his shoulder, trying his best not to cry out from lust and pain.

Selene opened her eyes again, smiling as she pressed her hips down against him. Josten could stand it no longer, grabbing her around the waist with his good arm and tossing her onto the bed. Again, she grabbed the back of his head, pulling him close and kissing him so hard their teeth clashed.

Josten didn't care about the danger anymore; he was already lost deep inside her. As always, the last thing that went through his head before he forgot himself was that he'd probably be executed for this. It would be neither quick nor painless.

4

THEY stood in the courtyard, waiting as a breeze rushed through the ageing stones of Fort Carlaine. Josten watched the road, seeing movement in the distance. Mullen was by his side along with the four surviving men-at-arms and Gerrard the old castellan, still wearing his scratched and dented armour. Sir Percel and twenty knights stood behind them, unmoving in the afternoon air, like statues standing in ancient reverence. It seemed apt in such a venerable place as this.

Josten loathed this kind of pomp. Ceremony for ceremony's sake. They were only waiting for Harlaw, not crowning a new king.

He looked up to where Selene stood with her handmaids. She glanced back, catching his gaze and raising her eyebrow a touch. Josten wasn't sure how to take the gesture. Was she agreeing this was all horseshit? Or was she remembering what they'd done the day before? Josten was struggling to get that out of his own head, feeling the familiar stirring in his loins the memory of her always induced.

The sound of galloping hooves shook Josten from his thoughts and he turned his attention back to the road. Dust was in the air, horses racing toward the gate, Duke Harlaw's flag raised high. Sir Percel and his knights seemed to stand yet more stiffly to attention, if that were possible. Even Mullen seemed to puff his chest out that bit further as the first of the riders clattered over the broken drawbridge and into the courtyard. Old Gerrard saluted, his rusty gauntlet clanking on his helmet.

Duke Harlaw was a handsome man well into his fifties. His beard and flowing locks had more than their share of white, but the blue of his eyes shone like crystal. He steered his huge white charger into the courtyard, scanning the waiting honour guard before looking to his wife. As his retinue reined up their horses behind him he leapt down from the saddle with the vigour of a much younger man, mounting the stairs to where Selene stood.

'My lady,' he pronounced, his voice echoing for all to hear. 'It lifts my heart to see you unharmed.'

He reached out and took her hand, brushing it gently with his lips before turning back to Josten and the rest of the men. Selene looked unimpressed with his gesture.

'And here are the men of the hour,' said Harlaw, striding back down the stairs towards Josten, Mullen and the men-at-arms. 'The brave heroes. Defenders of Fort Carlaine.' He stood before them now, white teeth shining from amidst his lustrous beard. 'There'll be reward aplenty. Tales told. Songs sung. I'll see to it.'

Under the barrage of compliments Mullen couldn't stop himself. 'It was nothing, my lord,' he said. Josten felt like slapping him around the back of the head.

'Nothing?' said Harlaw, grasping Mullen by his broad shoulders. 'Without you my wife would have been taken by brigands. Who knows what would have become of her.'

Josten glanced up to see Selene and her handmaids moving back inside the keep. He knew all too well that she had little enough patience for Harlaw's blether.

One of the duke's captains climbed down from his horse and began barking orders. As he did so Harlaw turned to Josten, moving closer.

'And I've heard about you, old friend,' he said.

Josten nodded an acknowledgement, trying his best to sound modest. 'Just doing what you pay me for,' he replied.

Harlaw shook his head. 'Walk with me.' He turned and headed toward the weathered staircase that led up to the battlements.

When they'd mounted the wall Harlaw paused, planting his hands between the crenels and taking in a deep breath.

'I can't begin to tell you how grateful I am,' said Harlaw. 'Without you, only the gods know what might have happened.'

'I think Thurlow's reputation might have been slightly exaggerated. He's not as dangerous as he makes out.' A sudden twinge in Josten's shoulder reminded him what utter shite he was talking.

'Well, I'm still grateful,' said Harlaw. 'And so is my wife, I'm sure. I hope she showed her appreciation in a suitable manner.'

A fleeting memory of pale breasts and sweet lips flashed through Josten's head.

'Yes, her thanks were more than adequate.'

Harlaw nodded, still staring out onto the surrounding forest. 'And how's the injury?'

'I'll live,' said Josten, rolling his shoulder, feeling the stitches.

'Good.' Harlaw turned to look at him. 'I'll need you fighting fit in the days to come. And more men like you. Tough times are coming. I need real warriors beside me if we're to survive them.'

'I'm yours to command, my lord.' Josten felt a twinge of guilt.

'I know.' Harlaw smiled. 'You always have been. The most loyal soldier I've got.'

That made the guilt burn hotter. Josten had served Harlaw for years, fought beside him during the Mercenary War, and had a lot to be grateful to him for. His and Selene's betrayal hurt, but despite his desire for the man's wife it didn't mean he would serve Harlaw any less faithfully.

'If it's roaming bandits that worries you, I'm sure a few more patrols should see them off,' said Josten, desperate to change the subject.

Harlaw shook his head. 'It's not the likes of Tarlak Thurlow that concern me. The Mercenary Barons across the Crooked Jaw are mustering their armies, ready to take advantage of our war. The Blood Lords of the Ramadi are long dead, but their servants still vie for power to the north. As soon as their civil war is over they'll be looking to expand their influence. These are trying times, Cade. If I can't unite the kings of the Suderfeld we could well be done for.'

Ending the War of Three Crowns seemed an impossible task for one man, but if anyone could do it, it was Harlaw.

'You can rely on me,' said Josten. He meant it. For all of Harlaw's bluster and pomp it was obvious the man was in need of help.

Duke Harlaw smiled. 'I know I can,' he said, clapping a hand on Josten's shoulder. 'But enough of this. We need to celebrate. There must be a banquet table somewhere in this old ruin. I'll have some of the men hunt us some meat and I've brought wine from the Kellden Flats. The best there is!'

Josten nodded with enthusiasm. He was more than happy to drink Harlaw's wine. But then, he was more than happy to fuck the man's wife when it would most likely lead to his death, so a little wine seemed the least of his troubles.

As night fell, the sounds of revelry rang out from Fort Carlaine. Harlaw's men had found tables and placed them end to end in what used to be the main hall. Candles of a hundred different lengths and shapes lined the walls, bathing the dark room in winking light. A buck turned on the spit in one corner and the welcome smell of roasting venison filled the room, making Josten's mouth water. Mullen clearly felt much the same, as his stomach sang a song like a thousand frogs croaking.

By the time the night sky darkened, Josten had sunk enough ale to make the sting in his shoulder subside to a dull ache. Harlaw's retinue were drunk for the most part, but the duke himself was clearly making a fashionably late entrance with his wife. Sir Percel sat at the far end of the table sipping at a goblet. He didn't seem to be enjoying proceedings. Josten could only think he was still sore from missing the action earlier. He seemed the type who craved recognition, and capturing Tarlak Thurlow would have been just the right amount of heroics to secure his reputation for life.

'I'm fucking starving,' Mullen tried to whisper, though with the ale and the noise filling the rest of the hall it was almost a shout. 'When's the meat being bloody carved?'

As though answering his question the main doors to the hall opened and two of Harlaw's knights walked in, turning half a step then standing to attention. Josten could only think how much Harlaw loved his pomp as the duke walked in, Selene by his side, her hand on top of his in the courtly fashion. Every man in the hall was on his feet with the scraping of a score of chairs. Josten felt a slight tug of jealousy. As much as he wanted her, as much as he'd tasted her, she was married to Harlaw. She was the duke's in the eyes of the gods and the law and she could never truly belong to a man like Josten Cade. And if it were discovered they had lain together, Josten would be strung up from the nearest tree. It didn't make his desire, or his envy, burn any less bright.

The duke and duchess took their seats at the head of the table, with Harlaw giving a casual wave of his hand to signal that everyone should sit.

'About bloody time,' said Mullen, as two of Harlaw's men started to carve the venison.

More meat and ale were served but Josten couldn't take his eyes off Selene. Idle chatter buzzed around him, laughter filled the hall, but all Josten thought about was her. Selene did not once try to catch his eye, but neither did she engage

Harlaw in conversation. Their marriage was a political one. She had never loved him. If she loved anyone it was Josten bloody Cade, of that he had little doubt.

Mullen's meaty hand slapped against Josten's shoulder and he was thrust from his dreams of Selene.

'We should drink,' said Mullen, his breath almost unbearable in Josten's ear. 'To us. To you. And especially to me.' He clapped a hand against his new jacket that denoted him as captain of the duchess's honour guard. 'We're going places, Cade. You and me.'

Josten lifted his tankard without enthusiasm. As he did so he caught Harlaw staring at him. Harlaw raised his own goblet, silently joining in the toast. Josten smiled, giving the duke a nod.

Selene suddenly stood, making to leave, but Harlaw grasped her hand. She stopped for a moment, not deigning to look at him before she wrenched her hand free of his grasp and walked quickly from the room.

Josten made to stand, seeing an opportunity, but Mullen thrust him down in his seat.

'Dicing with death, old mate.'

Josten looked at his friend quizzically. 'What's that supposed to mean?'

Mullen leaned in close. 'I might be ugly as a donkey, but I'm not stupid as one.' He raised a knowing eyebrow.

Josten stared at him for a moment before nodding in defeat. He'd known for the longest time that his late-night trysts with Selene could never stay a secret. He was just glad it was Mullen who knew – a man he could trust.

'Look,' Mullen filled his tankard from a jug, 'you know me. I'd fuck a snake if someone held its mouth open for me. But sometimes you've got to stop your loins leading you round like a sheep at market. Especially when it'll get you killed.'

'It's not like that,' said Josten, trying to convince himself as much as Mullen.

'Whatever it is, it's got to stop. So, sit here, drink until you can't speak, go and puke, and sleep safe in your bed for another night.'

Josten opened his mouth to argue, but he had no idea what to say. He knew Mullen was right. Instead he picked up his tankard and nudged Mullen's with it.

'That's the spirit,' said Mullen. 'Now, let's get pissed.'

Josten could only laugh, and once he started he couldn't stop. As the night wore on his shoulder hurt less and less, along with his desire for Selene. This was probably for the best anyway. He'd been kidding himself. Their affair had been doomed from the start. If they got the chance to be alone again he'd be sure to tell her so. It was over; this was no good for either of them.

The ale was drunk and songs were sung till long into the night and Josten could barely remember his own name. Harlaw had already left, along with most of his retinue, which gave Mullen plenty of opportunity to point out what lightweights they were. It wasn't until Mullen threw up a bucketful of puke next to the fire that Josten thought it might be time to get some sleep.

The corridors swirled as he made his way up through the

fort's twisting staircases. Luckily the passages were tight, so he couldn't have fallen over even if he'd wanted to. When he made it to the small room put aside for him he was pleasantly surprised to find someone had lit a couple of candles so he could see what he was doing.

Josten stumbled inside, trying to stay focused on his bed until he realised someone was in the room waiting for him. His heart suddenly leapt, thinking it was Selene, but as Sir Percel walked into the light his hopes were dashed.

'You lost?' asked Josten, trying his best to not stagger too much.

'No, Captain. I'm afraid I'm not.'

Josten stared for a moment. Percel's face was serious. In his drunken haze the thought process took its time, but eventually he worked it out.

'Fuck,' he said, just as two more of Harlaw's knights entered the room.

One of them hit him before he could move, the ale dulling his reactions. Josten fell to his knee as the second knight kicked him in the ribs. He floundered, too drunk to fight back.

As the blows rained down, he could hear Percel saying something about how sorry he was.

5

His head was pounding and there was no light as he opened his eyes. Josten had no idea how long he'd been out – it could have been an hour, could have been a day.

He tried to move but his hands were bound, the wound in his shoulder screaming as he did so. He gritted his teeth, stifling a shout of pain. What came out was a low hissing moan. A tooth was loose at the back of his mouth and he moved his head up from the floor, feeling his skin peel from the sticky stone beneath him – could have been blood, could have just been the damp of the floor.

Even in the dark he could tell one of his eyes was swollen shut. His ribs had taken a kicking – whether any of them were broken only time would tell. Once on his knees, he managed to lift his head, realising how groggy he was. The room span and he wavered slightly before willing himself to stay still. He worked his jaw, tongue probing the side of his mouth to tease at the tooth loose in the gum.

This didn't feel good. It didn't feel good at all.

Voices outside the cell. There were footsteps. Someone laughed.

Fuck them and their laughing. He was as good as dead in here and someone still had the stones to find mirth in it. If he managed to get free of these bonds he'd...

What? What would he do? He was beaten to shit. Unarmed. There was nothing he was going to do. Right now, all Josten Cade was good for was hanging till dead at the end of a rope. Best to face these things head on. When there was no hope there was no use in pretending.

The cell door creaked open behind him, letting in a little light. Something scurried into the shadows in front of him as someone entered behind. They left the door open as they walked into the room and slowly Josten turned his head. Harlaw stood there, half hidden in shadow, just watching.

'I never wanted this,' said the duke. 'But you left me no choice.'

Josten heard the words and knew the truth of them. Tied up and beaten as he was, they were still hard to accept. He wanted to tell Harlaw that there were always choices. That he could always untie Josten's hands and let him go.

Instead he worked his tooth loose from the gum with his tongue and spat it onto the cell floor. There was no way he'd beg.

'I wanted to avoid any unpleasantness,' Harlaw continued. 'But my men are loyal. They may have been a little... vigorous, in the execution of my orders.'

'Loyal?' Josten said, then spat a gob of blood from his mouth. 'You talk about that a lot. Wasn't too long ago you were saying I'm the most loyal soldier you've got. I'm not sure I want the job anymore.' He laughed a gallows laugh.

Harlaw didn't see the funny side. 'Were you loyal when you were fucking my wife?'

Josten let the condemnation hang there. He knew there was nothing else to say, no excuses that might see him get out of this alive. He had always known his infatuation with Selene would see him dead. It was only ever a matter of time.

'Best just get it over with then,' Josten said, looking at Harlaw through the dark, staring at his executioner with as much defiance as he could. Not that it mattered; you could be as defiant as you wanted but when you were beaten and bound it still wouldn't save your life.

'I won't be the one to kill you, old friend,' said Harlaw. 'We go back too far for that. But you'll die, of that there's no doubt. What is it you always say? "Everyone gets what they deserve"?'

'Still none too keen to get your hands bloody?' said Josten, wanting this over as soon as he could. There was never any sense in drawing these things out.

'Oh, I'd like to kill you, Cade. I'd like to throttle you with my own hands. But Selene hates me enough. If she knew I was the one that killed you, things could go badly for me.'

Josten smiled at that one. 'Frightened of your own wife?'

'No.' Harlaw shook his head slowly. 'But I need her and her family onside. There's no reason to make her hate me any more than necessary. Don't worry yourself though. I've got men willing to do the job for me.' He took a step towards the door before stopping. 'Rest easy that it'll be quick. I owe you that much.'

He walked back through the door and closed it, plunging the room into darkness.

Josten knelt there for gods knew how long. The pounding in his head subsided but the cold and damp seemed to creep into his bones, resting there like a maggot in a peach, squirming into his marrow and making him shiver till he wanted to piss himself. When the door to the cell opened again, Josten was more than ready for them to take him.

He recognised Percel in the warm lantern light. The other two were Harlaw's knights; big fuckers, the kind you sent into the vanguard where the fighting was bloodiest. The kind that showed no mercy. Not that Josten expected any.

They picked him up and led him out of the cell. It was still night. Harlaw obviously didn't want his prisoner paraded around Fort Carlaine like a prize. That was something for Josten to be thankful for. But then Harlaw probably didn't want the fact he'd been cuckolded getting around the duchy. Reputation was everything to a man like that.

Josten had to grit his teeth as they led him out. The knights were none too gentle and the aching in his ribs and the sting of his shoulder made him want to weep. There could be no weeping though. He'd not show weakness now, even at the end.

They took him through the courtyard, Percel leading the way, but there was someone else waiting in the dark. Josten squinted through his one good eye, seeing Mullen standing there, watching. For a second his heart beat that much faster. For the briefest moment, there was a surge of hope that his old friend might be there to save him. It was dashed when Percel said something and Mullen stood aside.

Josten knew then. Mullen had known all the time he and Selene had been lovers. It was Mullen who stood to benefit with Josten out of the way. Gods' blood, he'd even admitted he knew during the banquet. No one else could have told Harlaw.

'You fucker,' Josten spat as they dragged him towards the gate. 'I would have killed for you! Died for you, bastard!'

Mullen shook his head, guilt written all over his long ugly features.

'I'm sorry.'

Josten couldn't hold back the rage. 'Fucking sorry?'

With a surge of strength Josten struggled free of the two knights. His hands still tied behind him he charged at Mullen, a low growl escaping from his throat. There was little he could do but give one last show. For his part, Mullen grabbed him around the neck as they both skidded on the cobbles.

'I'll fucking kill you,' Josten snarled, but he knew it was empty bluster. He wouldn't be killing anyone ever again.

'Calm it,' Mullen said. Then, 'Just accept what's coming,' in a low, calm whisper.

As Mullen spoke, Josten felt his friend place something in his hands, just before the knights grabbed him and pulled him away. Josten grunted as he felt the tug in his ribs and shoulder, staring at Mullen as he was dragged through the gate. He clung tight to what Mullen had given him and hope crept back in as he felt its sharp edge.

They led him off into the woods. There was no use

struggling now; he'd been given his chance, and he just had to hope there'd be an opportunity to use it. The further into the woods they went the more the dawn light encroached through the trees. Josten realised the piece of steel Mullen had given him was an arrowhead, a little piece of the shaft still attached. Most likely it was the arrow they'd cut from his shoulder. Josten couldn't help but smile. That bastard Mullen. Maybe he hadn't been the one to betray him after all.

'Here's far enough,' said Percel after they'd walked for a good mile. The young knight drew his sword. The other knights drove Josten to his knees. They stood watching.

'Do we need an audience?' Josten asked, already going to work on the rope binding his wrists, feeling the arrowhead slicing keenly through the fibres.

Percel looked at the other two men and nodded. 'All right. Leave us alone. This won't take long.'

Behind him, Josten heard the two knights walk off into the woods.

'You don't have to do this, you know,' said Josten. 'It doesn't have to be this way. You could let me go and no one will ever hear from me again.'

Percel shook his head, doubt on his youthful face. 'I have no quarrel with you, Cade. But Duke Harlaw has ordered you dead. I have no choice.'

Josten felt the rope at his wrist suddenly give.

'There's always a choice,' he replied.

'I've always admired you,' Percel said. 'This gives me no pleasure.'

He took a step forward, raising his blade. The rope at

Josten's wrist fell away. He surged up, the arrowhead gripped tight in his fist. Percel had no time to make a move before it was buried in his neck.

The lad stared Josten in the eye, surprise on his face as his sword fell to the ground with a soft thud. His knees gave out and Josten twisted the arrow in his neck, feeling the blood gushing over his fist.

'I'm sorry,' he said, as he slowly lowered Percel to the forest floor.

The knight tried to speak, choking on his own blood. Josten glanced back, hearing the other knights growing restless through the trees. He stared through the dark, at any moment expecting them to rush at him through the night, but they didn't come.

Percel was quiet now, the little choking noises stopped, tears welling in his eyes. Josten wanted to stay, to wait until the lad was dead. No one should have to die alone, but if he stayed there would more than likely be two corpses in the woods rather than one. Josten had done wrong, but he was damn sure he didn't want to die in this dark wood because of it. But then he was sure neither did Percel.

Trying not to think too much about what he'd done, he picked up Percel's fallen sword and stumbled off through the dark as quick as he could.

The oceans had barely ceased to boil, the mountains just risen to splay their jagged fingers to the sky, when the hundred tribes of men fell upon one another. They came from the skies on wings of threaded fury, crawled from the ground bringing all the darkness of the pit, dragged themselves from the sea with gnarled and barnacled hate. For ten thousand years did they do battle, until their blood and tears ran in an endless river. Until the names of the tribes and their wrathful kings were forgotten.

When the skies had turned a perpetual grey from the funeral pyres, and the ground was blackened with rot, did the elders meet on the Mountain of Gaiessa. For twenty days and nights did they parlay. Through blazing sun and freezing dark. In rain and hail and wind. But none would relent, for an accord had to be met lest the future of man be trapped in an endless cycle of woe.

And on that twentieth night did the elders settle on a pact: that they would harness all their sorcery and channel it to a single purpose. That they would take all the aspects of man that led him to war and seal them away so that there could be healing across all the nations of the world.

Every tribe gathered to erect the eleven dolmens. Men from all continents and across the churning seas. Each vast stone was the span of thirty horses and stood as tall as a mountain, yet by their colossal labours the great circle was finally erected.

And for a year and a day the elders of each tribe stood

in vigil, imbuing their power into the stones, turning them into vessels that might hold every facet of man that had driven him to an everlasting state of conflict. Then did they fill the stones with all the elements of life. The flesh; fire, water, blood and bone. The desire; pride, lust, vengeance, honour, wrath. Then one vast stone they filled with wisdom and another with sin.

As the eleven dolmens began to consume these energies a twelfth grew at their centre. A stone of union. A stone of peace.

Across the lands and oceans an era of harmony settled. Suffering ended, subsumed by a period of culture and education. Vast cities were built and sciences developed. Knowledge and philosophy were spread across all nations during a time of peace.

But it was not to last.

As the elders had poured into the standing stones all the facets of man's warlike nature, so had they stirred all his malice and spite and hate. And when the dolmen of peace had risen from the ground so another, darker obelisk had begun to grow beneath the earth. This malevolent seed hid itself away, watching, waiting. It grew, feeding, infecting the hearts of men, until it could wait no longer and after ten thousand years it emerged.

For the first time in an age, malcontent and discord were sown throughout the realms of men. Brother once more turned on brother as jealousy and avarice consumed harmony and charity.

The vast shrines created in a time of majesty were torn

asunder, cities reduced to ash until no more monuments remained. Only the twelve dolmens stood as testament to an age where war was unknown. And so, the ravenous populace, twisted by a nameless evil, turned its attention to them.

A swarm of warped souls stormed the mountaintop on which stood the dolmens. Armies that had once battled one another united in their hatred of the ancient stones, bent on reducing them to rubble. One by one they were brought down, and as each toppled the power held within was unleashed once more. But as the aeons had passed this power had become quickened. Had become deified. And when it was released, each dolmen claimed a human avatar for its own – each taking one of those wicked children come to strike it down and making it one with its own purpose.

These children of Gaiessa vowed never again to be bound. Never would they be locked away from the worlds of men. And a game of supremacy began that would never end… and mankind would play as its pawns.

☥

6

SHE fell burning from a crimson sky, lungs bursting with soot and flame, her breath coming in short desperate gasps. Plunging from the heavens wreathed in fire, she was a flaming arrow of torment. Her scream was lost, fear manifesting as frigid paralysis, the pain engulfing her so completely she became one with it.

The hair burned from her head, disintegrating in enervating strands, her flesh blackening and sloughing as she fell, fluttering away like burned parchment.

Winds whipped her face, fire crackling in ears burned to hardened stubs. Something tore from her back in a fury of flapping debris, taking flesh and bone with it. Agony clutched her in its relentless grip.

The fall was long and hard, ending in a final tumult, dust and sand erupting around her as she smashed into the hard ground. The impact rocked through her body, crushing the life from her in a crescendo of deafening violence. Yet still she could see. Still she could hear a ringing and crackling as the last of the fire died down.

Breath came in a sharp wheeze, what little air she could process through her blackened lungs spilling out in wisps of dust.

She could not move. Every bone broken, her flesh charred, her joints atrophied. And yet she lived, her mind still reeling from the nightmare, desperate to grasp some memory. She reached out, yearning to remember. It opened with visions of horror and she was not quick enough to close it.

Howling beasts from the pit tore at her as she fought, her spear twisting in her grip, ripping flesh asunder, spilling demon blood. She howled as she fought, eyes dripping red fury, every movement precise, every thrust piercing black flesh.

As she lay, body broken, her mind reeled with the memory of it…

They came at her in myriad numbers, dark claws grasping. She fought unendingly, her strength perpetual, black blood coating her spear, running in rivulets across the haft until it drenched her hands.

The vision was haunting and revitalising all at once, imbuing her shattered limbs with a last vestige of power. She drew in breath through collapsed lungs, filling them so her chest expanded, the shattered ribs cracking back into place, the scorched flesh binding once more. Seared hands, no more than blackened bone, pressed flat against the desert floor as she raised her head, her body wracked with pain. A howl issued from inside her, a sound as alien to her ears as the nightmare was to her mind. Across the desert, as the red sky turned to yellow, there was no one to hear her scream.

In the still of the desert her dead flesh cooled. She shivered as she lay there, grasping onto life, willing herself to move as night turned to day and the blazing heat of the sun began to bake the ground.

The first attempt to stand filled her body with unholy

agony and she whimpered, crying out, though no tears would fall from her scorched eyes. She rose, only to collapse to the earth. On her second attempt she managed to remain standing for a moment, squinting cracked brows into the searing sunlight before falling again. The third time, gritting her smashed teeth, feeling blood fill her mouth and the scabrous flesh of her body cracking in the heat, she managed to remain standing.

The desert rolled to the horizon in all directions. She had no means to determine which way she might find help or if any route would provide succour. With no notion of where to go, she took her first step.

As the sun beat down she placed one foot relentlessly after the other. The baking sands eroded the flesh that remained on her feet and blood pooled thickly between her toes. The pain numbed her senses and with every step she issued a moan. Misery enveloped her but she would not give in. She would not die in this place. Whatever the state her body, her spirit was still intact. She would not let the wretchedness of her torn and rent flesh defeat her will to carry on.

As the day wore on, the heat became oppressive. It was curious that she could feel it despite her blackened flesh, her charred nerve endings still able to react to the vagaries of the sun. But she paid it little mind. Better that she focus on finding help, rather than questioning why she could still feel, or why she still lived.

Despite her wounds, she walked inexorably on, the pain relentless. Her cracked skin began to weep, drying instantly in the sun, leaving a sheen over her body. When she moved, her skin would break open again, the torment unbearable, and yet she bore it still with every tortuous step.

Scorching day turned to freezing night and back to day. Still she walked with relentless tread. Refusing to stop. Refusing to die. When she saw hills begin to rise in the distance she almost wept. How would she ever go on? Even were she not grievously injured, crossing those hills would be a task that required immense effort. But what other choice had she? Turn back? Pick another direction?

No. She had come this far. She would move ahead or die. Those were the only options open to her.

The ground hardened below her feet the higher she trod. The boiling sand of the desert replaced by scorching rock. Every footstep left a bloody imprint behind her. In places she had to crawl, her hands burning on the sharp surface.

Above her the sun had risen high, taunting her with its unyielding rays. She ignored it, not allowing it to leach the strength from her. One step at a time.

A noise made her stop. She stood in the silence of a gorge, ears straining, but there was nothing but her heart beating in her chest, her breath coming short and shallow.

As she took another step the noise came again, the low growl of an animal. In the gorge, there was no way to tell how close the creature was and she slowly turned, feeling the atrophied sinew crack and whine in her neck as she did so. Her breaths came faster, her heart pounding. She saw nothing, but it did little to stifle her panic.

One more step and she heard the tinkling of shale behind her, the scrabble of paws on rock. Without looking around she burst into action, the pain of movement agonising, the rock tearing the soles of her feet as she moved faster.

She was surprised by her speed, the impetus of panic, or fear, imbuing her with an inner strength she thought had waned. Despite her newfound vigour she would never be able to outrun the beast pursuing her.

But she would not stop before it took her.

Would not give in to the hunter.

The gorge dipped and she slipped down a sheer slope, feeling the broken and cracked flesh shred from her palms and feet and buttocks. The jolt of landing at the bottom sent her broken teeth clashing together, every joint screaming in protest. As she continued her flight she dared a glance back, seeing her pursuer standing at the top of the rise, feline eyes staring in hunger, its shoulders bunched, huge paws gripping the edge of the rock as it prepared to follow.

Fear was replaced with the instinct to survive. She had to try, to make one last show of defiance.

She ran on, the gorge narrowing at either side, before opening up. Ahead was a dead end; a wall of sheer rock barred any hope of escape. And as she stopped before it, the pain in her body returning more keenly than ever, all she could do was laugh.

The noise echoed around the gorge. She turned to see the mountain lion approaching slowly. It knew there was nowhere for her to go. It was a lean beast, ribs showing starkly through the tan fur that covered its flesh. It padded forward on dusty paws, claws drawn as it moved silently toward her.

All she could hope was that the end would be quick.

Or perhaps she should fight?

She almost laughed again at the thought. Her body was broken. There was nowhere to run. The lion would have little trouble bringing down prey much larger and in infinitely better condition. And yet…

The lion was within ten yards now and she took a step forward to meet it. There was no doubt in its eyes, and it did not falter in its approach despite her defiance. Why would it? She was easy meat.

A victim.

But she would not be a victim. Not of this beast. Not here, in this place.

Her fists clenched as she took one more step. A crimson flood descended over her eyes. *Blood. The screaming of demons. A flash of a silver spear. A flurry of feathers.*

The mountain lion bared its fangs, leaping at her. Her hands caught the beast's jaws. Its fetid breath blew in her broken face as she felt its teeth pierce her hands, tearing flesh and muscle to the bone. The lion roared.

She screamed back, defiant, as the crimson haze turned to black.

The scream carried her through the darkness. Through the silence where there was no pain. An endless limbo into which she would have gladly submerged herself forever.

Her eyes opened, seeing the sky above the gorge had turned to dark grey.

She was lying on the ground. For how long she had lain there she could not say. Turning her head, she saw the mountain lion on its side, dead eyes staring, jaws unnaturally wide, split apart.

Gingerly she raised her hands, bracing herself to see palms torn to shreds. They were still cracked and broken, scabbed from the fire that had consumed her, but they were whole. Black blood covered them, dried and crusted, falling away as she clenched a fist, sending dull pain through every digit.

With some effort, she managed to stand. The dead beast before her looked pitiful now, all ferocity stripped from it. Just a corpse in the desert – as she soon would be if she did not start moving.

Still wracked by pain she began her journey, retracing agonising steps back along the gorge.

There was no time to question what had happened. She had to survive, that was all she could think about. Not where she had come from. Not how she still lived after being so horribly burned, after falling from the heavens, after killing a beast that should even now be feasting on her immolated flesh.

She could not even ask her own name.

The desert cared nothing for it.

7

The Cordral Extent, 105 years after the Fall

'DON'T choke the hammer.'

The echo of those words rang in Garvin's ears. Advice his father had given him, what seemed a hundred years ago. Garvin Longfeather had long since learned to swing a hammer with deft ability but still his father's advice came back to him every time he raised one.

His mule snorted as Garvin hit the nail. Once, twice, and it was in. He took the waterwheel in his strong hands, flexing the spoke to see if there was any give. The nail had done its job and Garvin stood, hefting the wheel into an upright position. With a grunt, he lifted it back onto the axle, knee deep in water, feeling the sun blazing off his shoulders. When it was fixed on he took a step back and looked at the waterwheel. Without it they were lost. Without it nothing would grow in this place. It was their most precious possession and one Garvin cherished.

In the distance, he could hear the boys laughing. He had always regretted bringing them here, to this harsh and merciless land, but he knew there was nothing he could do about it now. Best teach them well and raise them right. They'd grow strong at least, in this arid place. Garvin wouldn't have to worry on that score.

He paused to cup a handful of water from the stream and douse his sweating head, feeling momentary relief wash over him. Then he stepped from the water and tethered the mule to the counter-axle. It tried to bite him, swinging its dolorous head, but Garvin had learned to be quick when dealing with the mangy animal. Many a bruised arm had taught him that much. Despite the beast's bad temper, it began to walk anyway, turning the axle and moving the waterwheel attached to it.

Garvin paused to watch as the blades cut through the water, depositing it in the trough that flowed from the shallow stream. The gutters began to fill, running down the hill towards the field, and Garvin felt relief wash over him just like those waters.

He allowed himself a rare smile. He hadn't smiled much in the five years since Tilda had died giving birth to their son, Fenn. There had been little reason for it, and Garvin took whatever simple pleasures he could. A working waterwheel and well-irrigated fields were about as much pleasure as he'd find today.

Suddenly one of the boys screamed. The smile drained from Garvin's face as quick as it had appeared. He was moving before he even knew which direction to run, the hammer dropping from his hand before he realised he might need to use it as a weapon.

'Da!'

Garvin recognised Darrick's voice. His older boy sounded panicked. It was rare Darrick succumbed to any emotion, not since Tilda had died.

He moved down the ridge, feet slipping on the loose gravel. Darrick shouted for him again. Garvin slipped at the bottom, falling on his arse and tearing his trews on the sharp shale. Stumbling to his feet he raced along the valley floor, following the sound of his son's shouts. They weren't so loud now but he could still hear them. As his feet stamped along the dusty ground and the breath came short in his throat he realised they were no longer in alarm. In fact, they were squabbling as usual.

Garvin slowed, turning the corner to see his boys looking at something on the ground.

'Leave it!' said Fenn, grabbing his brother's shirt.

Darrick pushed his younger brother aside, a stick in his hand.

'It's dead, ain't it,' said the elder brother. 'Doesn't matter if I give it a poke or not. I wanna know what it is.'

'No,' said Fenn, clearly in distress. 'Leave it.'

Garvin moved toward them, unable to see what it was they were looking at. Darrick was threatening something on the ground, holding his stick out like a broadsword.

'Darrick,' Garvin said.

Both his sons jumped, turning as one to see their father approaching. Fenn immediately ran towards him.

'Da. We found an animal. It's all burned.'

Garvin moved forward, gingerly. He could see now what they were fussing over. Something lay dead at the bottom of the valley, blackened by fire. Some hair was charred and matted to its head and there was blood on its hands and feet. Garvin couldn't tell if it was man or beast and from the smell he didn't fancy getting close enough to find out.

'What are we gonna do with it, Da?' asked Darrick, still brandishing his stick.

'Well we can't just leave it here to rot,' said Garvin, looking the thing over and wondering how it had managed to get itself in such a state. 'We'll have to bury it.'

Gingerly he cupped one hand beneath the corpse and turned it over. It was human – but whether man or woman he couldn't tell.

'Ugh, Da! It stinks,' said Darrick.

Garvin couldn't argue with that; it stank like someone had set fire to a pile of donkey shit.

'Fenn, run back to the house and get my shovel—'

Eyelids flipped open in the charred face, two pools of white amidst the blackened flesh. Fenn and Darrick screamed, Garvin scrabbling back from the body, holding his arms out to protect his boys, not that they needed protecting from the burned and broken thing that lay before them.

The corpse sucked in a long wheezing gulp as those eyes stared, searching the sky for something. Blue irises glared like clear water in black earth, searching until they came to rest on Garvin.

He and the boys could only stare as the corpse raised a hand. Garvin at first wondered if it was a hand of accusation, if this was some messenger of the Scorpion god Vermitrix come to send him through the Bone Gate. It took him too long to realise that this was no corpse. That this was a soul in pain, begging silently for succour.

'Darrick, get water from the well, as much as you can

carry,' he said. 'Fenn, run back to the house and find as many blankets as you can.'

As always, both boys obeyed without question.

Garvin stared down at the body. He knew there was little he could do to save the waning life in front of him, but he couldn't simply stand by and let it die. That was not Garvin Longfeather's way.

Carefully he knelt and took the burned body in his arms, lifting it gently. It weighed hardly anything, but the stink almost made him gag. As he began the long walk back to his house all he could think was how useless this was. Even the most skilled apothecary would be able to do little but alleviate the pain. Whoever it was he held in his arms, they needed no healer. A priest would be more apt.

Garvin walked with growing despair as the wheezing body stared up at him. The eyes still gaped but they no longer pleaded. There was a resignation there now – as though this life had held on for the longest time, waiting for another human to find it in the desert before it could succumb to the mercy of the All-Mother.

When he finally made it back to the house both his boys were waiting for him on the doorstep. Garvin didn't pause, carrying the body inside and laying it on his bed, the filth and burned flesh instantly dirtying his clean sheets.

He took up one of the blankets Fenn had laid out in a pile and tore it into a strip. After dipping it into the bucket of water Darrick had fetched, he approached the body. Still it stared up, the eyes the only thing that seemed untarnished. Garvin had no idea where to start. Fenn walked forward and Garvin could see he was fighting his fear. Gently, the boy raised one of the body's arms so Garvin could wrap the bandage.

'Darrick, get a knife from the kitchen and cut the blankets into strips.'

Silently, his son obeyed.

As day turned to night Garvin Longfeather and his sons bandaged a broken and burned body they had found in the desert. With the grey moon rising over the desert, he doubted the stranger would last till morning.

8

GARVIN had expected the stranger to die overnight. But as he stood in the doorway, watching the dull red light of morning encroach on the room, he saw it breathing, stronger than the day before.

It was hard to believe the All-Mother had not come — it would have been a mercy — but it was obvious she was busy elsewhere.

He stepped into the room. The body's chest moved up and down in a steady rhythm. Garvin could see he and the boys had done a good job. Almost every inch of their patient had been covered, hiding the charred flesh beneath. If he'd possessed balm he would have used it. There was every chance his blankets would cause an infection, but it had seemed the right thing to do at the time. Besides, this soul could well be bound for the Bone Gate whatever they did; it was unlikely it would survive long enough for infection to set in.

Slowly he reached forward, touching one of the bandages on the body's arm. It had dried in the night, become encrusted over the flesh beneath. The smell that had assailed him the day before had relented slightly and the windows to the room were open, the fresh morning air chasing the stench away.

Garvin peeled back the dried material, hearing a sickening sound as it came away. He stopped, half expecting the body to convulse in pain as the flesh was torn away from bone but still it made no sound. The underside of the bandage was encrusted with dirt and blood and the scab had come away from the body to reveal… healed skin. The flesh was raw and livid but it looked healthy.

He frowned, staring at the arm that had been miraculously renewed overnight. Unable to believe his eyes, Garvin peeled away more of the bandage, seeing yet more blackened skin and dirt slough away with it to reveal whole flesh beneath.

With careful tenderness, Garvin reached out a hand, his fingers gently brushing the skin of the body's arm. How was this possible? Magic?

No. There was no magic. Not anymore. There hadn't been magic for a hundred—

The arm snatched out, grasping Garvin's wrist. The eyes flicked open, regarding him with that cold blue stare. He opened his mouth to speak. Maybe the body could hear him; maybe he could offer some words of comfort.

Before he had a chance to say anything the hand tightened on his wrist. He issued a grunt of pain, the grip so tight he felt his bones grinding.

Garvin snatched at the hand, the bandages that bound it cracking and peeling under his own clawing grasp. It felt as though his arm would break and he almost shouted for mercy.

As quick as that arm had snatched out it weakened, falling back to the bed. The eyes closed, and Garvin staggered back, knocking over a chair.

He stared down at the body. This corpse-like figure that had seemed on the threshold of the Bone Gate, possessing so much power in its grip.

Horses' hooves tramped the ground outside, diverting his attention before he could even begin to comprehend what had just happened. Garvin backed out of the room, unwilling to take his eyes from their guest until he reached the front door and warily stepped out into the yard.

Hedren sat atop his chestnut mare, smiling down at him.

'Garvin,' said the old man, reaching into his jacket and taking out a kerchief to wipe his wrinkled brow.

'Hedren,' Garvin replied, nodding and flashing an uncertain smile at the alderman. Old Hedren did his rounds every week, checking on Kantor's outlying farmsteads. Garvin's was one such farm. Not that there was much beyond the city-state's border than empty desert.

'Hot today,' Hedren said, banal conversation being his speciality.

'That it is.' Though Garvin could scarcely remember a time when it wasn't. 'Any news from Kantor?'

Hedren shook his thin head. 'None to speak of. The aldermen still argue over trade prices. The traders still argue over fees and everyone argues over taxes.'

'I've no doubt of that.' Garvin scanned the edge of the farm for the boys, but he couldn't see sign of them. With any luck, they were about their chores as always.

'Word is, the mountain bandits plaguing the eastern trade routes have stepped up their attacks. Nothing for you to be worried about, I'm sure.'

'I've nothing for them to steal,' Garvin replied, hoping against hope Hedren didn't ask to come in for a cup of water. The waterskin by his hip looked full enough though, so this was most likely just a stop-off before he headed back to the city.

'How are the boys?' said the old man.

'Oh fine. Growing fast. You know how it is.'

'That I do.' Hedren smiled a toothless smile. 'I remember how fast mine grew. They'll be men before you know it.'

Garvin just smiled back. The last thing he wanted was to engage Hedren any further. He didn't want him in the house. If he discovered Garvin's patient it would only lead to trouble. Officials would be informed back at Kantor. The council might want a full report, which would mean more aldermen coming to investigate. And if they discovered what Garvin had seen, that the victim was healing unnaturally fast and appeared to possess abnormal strength, they might well send the militia. Garvin was a man who valued his privacy. He could do without any intrusion from the aldermen of Kantor. Best they kept their beaks out of his business.

'Anyway, good talking to you.' Hedren tugged his wispy grey forelock. 'Guess I'll see you when the harvest's ripe.'

'Guess you will,' said Garvin, reaching to tug his own hair, but Hedren had already put heels to horse and spun it from the yard.

Garvin breathed out slowly as he watched the alderman riding off, just as Fenn and Darrick came back from the field. Fenn struggled with the water bucket as he came, and Darrick carried the empty bag of feed he'd given the mule.

'Is it dead yet, Da?' Fenn asked, placing the bucket down on the ground and letting some of it slop over the side. Garvin almost smiled at his son's morbid curiosity.

'No, Fenn. It's not dead yet.' Whatever *it* was.

'Can we go see?'

Garvin shook his head. 'No. Neither of you are to go near it.' The memory of how tight that grip was on his wrist made him say the words more harshly than he might otherwise.

'Was that old Hedren?' Darrick asked. Garvin nodded. 'What did he think of it?'

Garvin shook his head. 'Hedren didn't see, and I didn't tell him. And neither of you should either.'

'But why?' asked Fenn, disappointed he wouldn't be able to brag about their find to anyone and everyone who happened past.

'Because it's no one's business but ours. And there's nothing to tell.' Garvin paused, doubting his own words. Perhaps he should have told Hedren all about it. But there was something about the stranger that made him want to protect them and nurse them back to health. Something in the back of his head that told him this was the right thing to do. 'Just stay away from it and don't speak to anyone.'

He scanned the horizon, for once glad of their isolation. Sometimes they had no visitors for weeks on end, and they didn't need to do another supply run to Stafkarl for days yet.

With any luck, they'd be safe enough from prying eyes.

Before the boys could argue any further he sent them off on more chores – Fenn to pick wild berries, Darrick to sharpen the tools for the fields. If they were both occupied hopefully it would keep their minds off their new guest long enough for Garvin to decide what to do.

In the kitchen he stood in silence. The wounded body in his bed could well be dangerous. Something strange was going on; the Blood Lords to the north and the Crown Sorcerers to the south were long dead. There had been no miracles for a hundred years. Magic was a myth, stories of ancient rites and raging demons they used to scare children away from the fire. And yet...

A thump from his room made Garvin jump, memories of childhood tales fraying at his nerves. He rushed to the room, opening the door, half expecting some raging demon to have emerged from the bandages, licking its slavering maw, hungry for his children.

The body lay on the floor, one bandaged arm pawing at the bed sheets. Garvin watched, unsure of whether to help or not. He was afraid, but he would not simply stand there and watch a wounded soul struggle in vain.

He took the figure under the arms, gently lifting it as best he could back onto the bed. This time there was no struggle; the body didn't try to grab him and the eyes in that bandaged head were hidden beneath heavy lids.

Once back on the bed the figure began to claw at the bandages covering its face, breath coming in short panicked gasps.

'No,' said Garvin, trying to take hold of the clawing hands. 'You shouldn't—'

But the bandages had already peeled away, to reveal mended flesh beneath. Instead of stopping the figure, Garvin gently began to help. Strip by strip he peeled off the makeshift binding. The hair atop the skull was short and singed but the skin was fresh. With each layer, more of a face was revealed until eventually Garvin stood back, regarding the woman that lay on his bed.

She looked up, her blue eyes regarding him with confusion.

'Water,' she croaked.

Garvin continued to stare before coming to his senses. With a blurted, 'Yes,' he rushed out to where Fenn had left the bucket. After filling a cup, he ran back into the room, offering it gingerly to the woman.

She took the cup greedily, pressing it to her lips and gulping down every last drop. He wanted to tell her to take it steady, not to drink too fast, but all he could do was stare. The flesh of her face was raw, filthy, and yet he couldn't take his eyes off her. Garvin had not seen a woman so fine since Tilda had died. Silently he chided himself, guilt at his unfaithful thoughts filling him with sorrow.

She placed the cup back down by her side, then stared at him and smiled.

He smiled back.

'What's your name?' Garvin asked. 'Where did you come from? What happened to you?'

She regarded him for a while, mulling over his words,

and he could see the confusion on her face grow as she turned them over in her mind.

'I don't know,' she answered finally, voice gravelly and strained.

Garvin had no idea what else to do, until she offered the cup to him once more. He took it with a nod, and walked back to where the bucket stood.

As he filled it he knew he had to help this woman recover. Had to get her back to fitness. It was not in Garvin's nature to simply hand her over and make her someone else's problem. But he also knew that once she was well enough she had to go.

There could well be trouble here. If Garvin Longfeather knew anything, he knew that.

9

SHE stared at her hand in the wan morning light. It was all but healed. The flesh having hardened, the nails of her fingers almost fully repaired.

Memories came in fleeting bursts of violence, of despair, but they were distant… unlike her dreams. Every night she dreamed of the rage. Of the violence and blood as though she had been a part of it. Every morning she woke gasping for air, drenched in sweat.

Garvin had been kind, but distant. He had fed her, brought her water and cleaned her as best he could. But he seemed wary of her. Almost afraid.

Elsewhere in the house she had heard the sounds of children but so far seen nothing of them; they never ventured into the room. One of them was called Fenn, the younger of the two from what she could gather. The elder was Darrick. Garvin had cause to talk to Fenn often, chiding him for his unquenchable curiosity. Darrick, it seemed, had little interest in her.

Still she had no idea what her own name was, or where she had come from. For now, she would have to satisfy herself that she yet lived, that she had not died anonymous and broken in the desert. The rest would have to wait.

The door to her room opened, gently as usual, the quiet creak of the door hinge bringing her back to focus. She was wary, though she knew it could only be Garvin come to check on her. As he entered, she also knew that from her position in the bed she could rise faster than he could react and kill him in any one of a dozen ways.

That was the most frightening thing of all. Her knowledge of his anatomy, of his vulnerable points; weak as she was she could still kill him with her bare hands if she chose to.

He stopped in the doorway, the light from the room beyond causing her to squint.

'How do you feel today?' he asked. The same question every day.

'Better,' she said, giving the same answer.

He entered, moving to her bedside, but remaining out of arm's reach.

'Do you think you can stand?'

She nodded. For the past two days, she had known she was able to stand, but had also known she needed to rest. Her recovery had been fast but still she had much healing to do.

'Would you join us for breakfast?' he said.

She could sense the unease in his voice, the uncertainty at his own words. He was afraid. More for his children than himself, and yet still he asked.

'I will,' she answered, pushing the blankets aside. She had to show him she was no threat – that he and his children were safe with her in the house.

She swung her legs gently over the side of the bed, her bare feet touching the floorboards. For a moment, she remembered the pain she'd felt walking through the desert but now there was nothing. She was eager to stand, to walk unaided.

Garvin took a step forward to steady her but she held up a hand, feeling the cool of the morning air through the trews and shirt he had given her.

She managed to stand, at first a little unsteady, but as her balance returned she surprised herself at the strength in her legs. Garvin stepped back as she moved forward, then opened the door and led the way into the kitchen.

His two boys sat at the breakfast table waiting for them. Both were silent. The elder, Darrick, glanced at her, then down at the plate sitting before him. Fenn, a child of no more than five summers, stared at her as though she had just risen from the grave rather than his father's bed. Self-consciously she ran a hand across her stubbly scalp, before taking the nearest chair.

'Fenn, bring the eggs. Darrick cut the bre—' Garvin stopped when he realised the bread was already cut on the table before them.

Young Fenn brought a pan of cooked eggs to the table and Garvin began setting out the plates. Darrick offered her some bread, and without a word she took it.

The four of them ate in silence. The food tasted wonderful and she drank water from a pewter cup, realising she had wolfed down the eggs and bread while the others had barely started.

Fenn stared at her, his own meal ignored.

'What's your name?' asked the boy. She stared back at him as he looked at her expectantly. She shook her head.

'Where you from?' he continued.

All she could offer was a shrug.

'Is she staying, Da?' he asked, still staring at her.

'Eat your eggs,' Garvin said.

Fenn glanced down at his plate, then back at her. 'She could be our new ma.'

Garvin glared across the table at the boy. 'As soon as she's able she'll be leaving. Now eat your eggs.'

Fenn would not leave it alone. 'But she could stay here and help around the house. Where else is she gonna go? She don't know where she's from. Bet she don't know where she's going neither.'

She couldn't argue with the child's logic, but it was clear Fenn's concerns weren't shared by Garvin.

'Fenn, eat your eggs.' Garvin's voice was raised and this time the boy went back to his meal. She could see tears welling in his eyes. 'She's not staying. She's not... one of us.'

That much was true at least. She had no idea who she was, and she couldn't blame Garvin for his concern. Already she had noted where the three knives in the kitchen were and how quickly she would be able to move to them. She knew it would only take two heartbeats to kill everyone in the room.

Fenn stuffed eggs into his mouth and chewed as though they tasted like dirt. When he'd finished, he slammed his fork down, looking up furiously with tears in his eyes.

Garvin stared across the table at him; he was desperately trying to stifle his anger. Before his father could speak, Fenn jumped up from the table and rushed out of the kitchen, leaving the door swinging and letting the morning light lance into the room.

When they had finished, Darrick cleared away their plates. She sat and watched as Garvin clenched his hands, showing the whites of his knuckles.

'I should leave,' she said to him.

'No,' said Garvin without much conviction. 'You aren't well enough to travel. Anyway, Fenn's right – you don't know where you're headed.'

'It doesn't matter,' she replied, standing. 'I still need to leave. I am not your responsibility.'

Garvin didn't argue. Instead he nodded, ordering Darrick to pack some dried meat and water for her journey. He gave her shoes, a change of clothes, and a cloak to guard against the cold desert night.

'Kantor is two days' walk westwards. You'll be able to see it on the horizon after one,' he said as she stood on their porch.

'Thank you for all you have done,' she replied.

Before she turned to leave she could see a look of regret on his face. He was torn, but he had his family to think of. She could not blame him for that.

As she walked from the farm, she could feel him watching her. She did not look back.

Out in the desert air she felt invigorated. She was alive, and there was much to learn. Once she reached Kantor she would try to find out who she was. Where she had come from. Perhaps her memory would return. Perhaps she would…

Darkness shrouded her vision. Black wings cut across her eyes – a fluttering of birds. A vulture's squawk. A dark pit. Panic. A young boy's fear. His desperation as the blackness yawned before him and his screams of terror. He was alone. There was no one to hear. North.

She staggered, the pack Garvin had given her sliding from her shoulder to hit the ground, and she was running, sprinting northwards. Up ahead she could see the ground rise to become rocky hillocks. That was where she had to go, she was sure of it. In the face of the hills there was an opening in the rock wall, shored up by brittle wooden beams. An old mine from the look of it.

Her legs pumped, muscles straining; too long lying in bed, not long enough training herself, restoring her strength. She mounted the rise, slowing as she strained up to the steep entrance, pulling herself inside, feeling the wooden prop give, dust spilling from the lintel. As she raced into the dark she knew this place was dangerous, but Fenn was in here somewhere. How she knew that she could not say – another mystery for her to solve in the fullness of time. For now she had to find him.

'Fenn!' she cried, her voice still fragile and croaky. Her eyes strained through the black. 'Fenn!' she called again.

A faint echo emerged from the dark and she moved towards the sound. She felt panic begin to well up until, somehow, her eyes began to adjust. Down here, with no ambient light, she could still make out the shape of the corridor, twisting to the right up ahead.

Turning the corner, she saw him, grasping the edge of a pit, his lantern spilled and useless on the ground. She ran forward, seeing his face in the dark, his panic. His despair lifted for one moment before his grip gave way and he plunged into the black.

He fell.

She moved fast.

His wrist was in her grasp as she teetered at the edge. One-handed she lifted him from the pit and held him close. Fenn buried his head in her shoulder, quivering in shock and fear. She cradled him as she walked him back through the abandoned mine and out into the sunlight. Held him as she walked the desert back to the farm until Garvin saw them approaching.

When they were within a hundred yards Fenn struggled from her grip, sprinting off towards his father. By the time she reached them she could hear Fenn finishing his story, Garvin down on one knee listening intently.

She stopped some way in front of him as he looked up, gratitude in his eyes.

'I've warned him about the old mine a thousand times,' Garvin said. Darrick had come out of the house now to see what the commotion was about.

'She has to stay now, Da,' said Fenn.

Garvin stared at his son, then up at her.

'If that's what she wants,' he said.

She could only nod.

'You should have seen her,' said Fenn, running up to his brother. 'She was quick as silver. Snatched me out of the mineshaft like an arrow.'

'Silver?' asked Darrick, clearly unimpressed. 'Guess that's what we'll have to call her then. Until she remembers her real name.'

Garvin looked back at his boys, then at her apologetically.

For the first time she could remember, she smiled. 'Silver it is.'

10

THE cart trundled along the desert path behind them. Garvin strained in the heat, grasping tight to the leather strap attached to the yoke. Silver walked beside him, her breath coming steady and even, barely feeling the cart's weight. She tried her best to take most of the strain but Garvin was determined not to be outdone. That brought a smile to her face.

It had been thirty days since they'd found her in the desert. Now she was unrecognisable from the husk they'd discovered. The muscle had returned to bulk out her shoulders and her hair had grown over an inch. Despite Garvin's subtle questioning about her past, Silver still had no recollection of where she had come from or who she really was. She had thought that given enough time the memories would return but so far they continued to elude her.

In turn, Silver had learned that Garvin lost his wife in childbirth and raised his sons alone. The pain of that loss was obvious, despite his attempts to hide it. She would catch him now and again staring toward the distant horizon with pain on his face, memories of a past that he would never regain. Silver could only envy him that. Memories of her own, no matter how painful, would have been a blessing.

But there was nothing. Only her nightmares of a life she could not possibly have lived, fighting an endless battle against impossible foes.

Perhaps her memories would return to her. Perhaps not. Either way, she was happy with this life, alongside Garvin and the boys, and that would be enough for now.

The eastern outpost of Stafkarl came into view, the path gradually becoming easier to pull their cart along the closer they got. It wasn't much of a settlement – a few ragged huts arranged in two rows, but Garvin said it was the closest thing to civilisation until Kantor, twenty miles further along the road. Once they had pulled their cart along the street and up to the trading post, Garvin dropped the strap from his shoulder and leaned back to stretch his tired muscles.

'Nothing to it,' he said to her with a wink.

She smiled back at him, taking the strap from her own shoulder and flexing her arm, more for show than because it ached.

He threw one of the bags of corn over his shoulder and walked up the creaky wooden steps to the trading post. Silver was tempted to take two bags, it would have been easy enough, but she had to spare Garvin. He was proud, of that Silver had no doubt, and she would never have thought to shame him by showing her true strength.

Inside, the trader and his wife gratefully took the corn, exchanging it for the essentials they'd need to see them through the next season.

Back out in the street, Garvin finished packing the cart for the return journey.

'Longfeather,' said a voice behind them. Silver turned to see an old man looking at them with a wry smile.

'Hedren,' Garvin replied.

'Supplies for the winter?' Garvin opened his mouth to reply but the old man was too quick with his next question. 'And who's your friend?'

She could see the subtle look of discomfort cross Garvin's face. Whoever this old man was it was clear Garvin was none too keen to let him know the truth.

'Her name's Silver. Traveller helping out on the farm. She's just passing through.'

Hedren nodded. 'Just passing through?' He stared at her and she held his gaze. 'It's dangerous on the road. Especially for a woman travelling alone. You must have the Fool's own luck with you.'

She gave no answer, just stared at the old man. But then what would she have said? There was no way she could have explained her survival even had she wanted to.

'She's lucky for me, anyhow,' said Garvin, before the silence became too uncomfortable. 'Been a great help around the farm. I'll be sorry to lose her when she moves on.'

'I'm sure.' Hedren gave her an appraising look up and down. 'Anyway, I won't keep you. I'm sure you've a long walk ahead.'

Garvin tugged his forelock and Silver continued to watch the old man as he said his goodbyes and wandered off down the street.

They finished packing the cart and made their way out of Stafkarl. Silver noted Garvin's haste as he did so, clearly none too keen to answer any more questions.

When they were halfway back, and Garvin was sweating heavily once more, she felt the need to ask.

'What are you trying to protect me from, Garvin?'

He continued to pull the cart and she wondered if he'd heard her at all.

'People don't need to know our business,' Garvin said. 'Especially not Hedren. If the aldermen knew the truth there'd be all hell to pay.'

'Because I know nothing of my past?'

'And because you're the strongest woman I've ever seen. Because you heal faster than anyone has a right to.'

'If I'm causing you trouble, you should tell me. If I'm just passing through there's no reason I can't be gone tomorrow.'

Garvin stopped, letting go of his side of the cart. Silver still held up the load on her own. 'There's no reason for you to go. We need to be careful, is all.'

'So you want me to stay?' she asked.

He smiled at that. 'Do you want me to say it? All right then, I want you to stay. I need you. The boys need you.'

She smiled back at him. 'That's settled then.'

He picked up the strap once more and they carried on the rest of the way in silence. The smile stayed on Silver's face all the way. She was relieved. Where would she have gone had Garvin asked her to leave? Besides, she had grown fond of him and his sons; she wanted to stay with them for as long as she could. It was obvious Garvin was fond of her too, and wanted to protect her. That made her happier than anything.

The boys were eagerly awaiting them back at the

homestead. Fenn ran to greet them, hugging his father tightly, then Silver, before he shook himself free of her grip and peered into the back of the cart to see if they had brought him any treats. He was disappointed with the drab supplies of dried meat, oil, fabric and other sundries, but if he had expected new books or the occasional sweet candies Garvin sometimes brought he made no complaint.

Darrick merely stood and watched as they began to unload the cart. He was wary of Silver, that much was obvious, but now he seemed much less afraid. She knew it would be a hard task to make him fully trust her.

Later they prepared dinner. Fenn filled the kitchen with his usual chatter and it took Silver some time to realise that, for the first time since she had walked out of the desert, she felt comfortable. She felt safe.

After they had eaten, Garvin read to them from a book he had procured from the market, an old tale of ancient heroes which the boys loved. As they sat, Fenn leaned against Silver, his head nodding until eventually he was asleep on her lap.

Garvin eventually finished his tale and told Darrick it was time to go to bed. Silver expected him to take Fenn's sleeping form from her but instead he looked at her expectantly. Gently she picked the boy up and carried him to the room he shared with his brother.

After putting Fenn to bed and closing the door, she turned to see Garvin watching her in the dark. He gave her a strange look she couldn't read before averting his eyes.

'Goodnight, Silver,' he said, moving into his room and pushing the door to.

She went to her own room, undressing and donning the plain linen gown Garvin had given her. It belonged to his wife, one of the few things of hers he had kept, and Silver appreciated the gift. Such a thing must have held much sentiment for Garvin.

As she sat in the dark on the edge of her bed she glanced at the door. Longing was building inside her. Garvin was a good man, a strong man. She realised how much she wanted him. How much she had become used to his boys and the protection of this house.

Silently she stood, moving to his room. The hinge creaked when she opened his door and she saw him stir in his bed as she entered. Garvin looked up as she moved forward and in the scant light of the room she stood for a moment. He made to speak and she reached out a hand, placing her finger on his lips, the other moving to slip the linen strap of her nightgown from over one shoulder.

Garvin sat up slightly as the nightgown slid to the floor and she moved forward, sitting astride him as he lay in bed. Gently she leaned forward, kissing his lips before he could try and speak again.

He reached up, his fingers tracing her lean hips and she could feel him growing harder beneath the covers. She kissed him firmly, her tongue sliding into his mouth and he moaned with excitement as she pushed herself against him. His hands grasped her buttocks, pulling her closer and she let out a moan of her own, pulling back from his kiss and tearing the blanket from him.

His body was lean, hardened by the desert and years of

labour on the farm. She breathed faster, her hand pushing against his firm chest as she eased herself atop him, feeling him deep inside.

Garvin grasped her wrist and she realised she had raked his flesh with her nails, leaving track marks visible in what moonlight encroached into the room. It only served to stir her further as she let out a sound from deep within, grinding her hips down against him.

Red flashed in a spatter. Warm on her cheek, the taste of it coppery on her lips. Roaring in her ears, a cacophony of inhuman noise. Rage. The spear reassuring in her fist. Its song rising above the screams. The crimson thirst of battle had overcome her. A frenzy of blood hunger taking control. Her own infernal roar carried across the field, striking at the hearts of a thousand enemies.

Silver opened her eyes to see Garvin staring at her. She was breathing heavily, gasping in the quiet aftermath of her lust. He breathed deeply too, the sweat on him gleaming, and for untold moments they simply stared at each other as though neither of them could quite fathom what had happened.

Eventually she settled into the crook of his arm as he was overcome by sleep. She watched him in the dark, matching her breathing to his as he slept, her fingers tracing the scratches she had left on his flesh.

When eventually she succumbed to sleep it was unspoiled by nightmares for the first time since she could remember.

All the Thirteen went to war,
The Jackdaw and the Raven King,
Magpie with its gilded claw,
A purple stripe upon its wing.

Cormorant was quick at hand,
A golden fish within its beak,
Owl and Falcon swept the land,
Their talons drawn for prey to seek.

Carrion Crow and Vulture soared,
And stripped their meat from out the dead,
Rook came hunting with its horde,
A crown of blood about its head.

Jay and Dove and Nightingale,
Raised songs of peace to quell the fight,
None were heard above the hail,
And could not stop the fall of night.

As they fought, in secret lay
The thirteenth of them with no name,
Still it watches to this day,
Till it can soar and end the game.

'The Thirteen', a Canbrian rhyme

11

Canbria, 105 years after the Fall

LIVIA led the horse diligently. Ben watched her from behind the plough, his gnarled hands gripping the handles for all he was worth. Occasionally he'd glance back down to watch the share cutting a furrow in the soft earth, but Livia kept their old dray steady and straight. It made his job that much easier.

As he watched her black hair blowing in the breeze, her skirt trailing in the mud all spattered and frayed, he felt that old guilt again. She was seventeen summers. Clever. Beautiful. She was worth so much more than this. But what would he do without her? Ben Harrow was an old man now, and every year the work got harder. Work he'd been doing most of his life, which had seemed so easy in years gone by. Work he'd been suited to when he was a younger man. If she left – if he let her go and pursue some other life she deserved – the farm would collapse.

Not that she'd ever leave him. It wasn't in her nature. She was the kindest girl he'd known in all his days, and he didn't just think that because she was his blood.

Livia wasn't his daughter, not even his granddaughter, but he'd brought her up as his own since she could just about walk. When the Mercenary Barons had come looking for war Livia's father, Ben's nephew, had answered the king's call. He'd never returned. Livia's mother had lasted a whole season before the grief had gotten too much and she had taken her own life, flinging herself from Cutler's Point like so many others over the years. There was just the two of them left. Them and the farm. It was all Livia had ever known.

She turned as he watched her, face all muddy but her brown eyes big and shining out from the dirt. Her smile was warm and white in the midst of that filthy face. It filled Ben with a joy he'd never be able to express. He smiled back, his own face all cragged, teeth broken where he had them. Then she patted the dray and turned back, looking on at the horizon, leading him ever on.

In a way she'd always led him; she'd always given him hope. When she'd been a child he'd had to stay strong for her. Now she was a woman grown he needed her more than ever. More than she'd ever needed him. It hurt, but that was the reality of it. If Ben had been a braver or stronger man he'd have given her enough coin, sent her off to Gadingham or Mountgale to learn a craft, to use her cleverness for something more than farm labour. But Ben had never been much for bravery, and his days of being strong were long behind him. Best to stick to what you knew and not think too long and hard on what you couldn't change. With the smile fading from his face, old Ben turned his attention back to his plough.

The days were growing lighter but the dark still fell far too quickly. They'd only managed half a field before it got too dark to work anymore and Ben and Livia unharnessed the horse and began to make their way back to the farmhouse.

'Good day's work, while it lasted,' Ben said.

'I know,' Livia replied, leading the black horse beside her, running one hand along his neck and mane as though thanking him for the work he'd done.

'We can start the sowing—'

'Tell me one of the old stories again,' Livia asked.

Ben smiled. As much as he wanted to talk about farm work she was always more interested in the tales he told. Ben knew the labour bored her. She was far too bright for it and it was the least he could do to humour her.

'All right. Which one do you want?'

She pursed her lips, chewing the inside of her cheek like she always did when she was thinking.

'The Fall,' she said with a smile.

Ben shook his head. 'It's always about the Fall,' he replied, looking at her in the hope she'd change her mind. She just stared back. There was no changing Livia's mind once it was made. 'All right. Which story?'

'The Blood Lords, I think.'

'Very well. The Mage Lords of Ramadi. Masters of the Seven Deserts. Keepers of the Eternal Eye. For five thousand years they ruled in the north, building vast cities in the sand where no city had any business to be. It was said they could eat men's souls and talk with the dead. That each would live a span of nine hundred years before—'

'Eight hundred,' Livia interrupted.

'Who's telling this?' said Ben, raising an eyebrow at her.

'Last time it was eight hundred.'

Ben nodded. She was probably right; he could barely remember the details and Livia most likely knew the stories better than he did. But she liked the way he told them, so there was no arguing the point.

'All right. It was said each would live a span of eight hundred years before they would have to be reborn in their foul blood rituals…'

At the mention of blood rituals he could see Livia smiling in the waning light. The stories used to scare her when she was younger but now they just filled her with a grim mirth.

Ben went on with his story, describing how the Blood Lords had ruled with steel and flame. How they held the northern half of the continent in their demonic fist and spread their influence throughout the kingdoms to the south. How wars were fought to stem their bloody tide and how they bred fearsome warriors to do their bidding. About how they planned to conquer all of the known lands and they might have succeeded, had it not been for the Fall, when in a single night all magic was inexplicably drawn from the world, leaving the Blood Lords powerless. Many of them crumbled to dust, their unnaturally long lives coming to a sudden and gruesome end. The rest vied for what little power remained, starting a civil war that would be fought perpetually until the present day.

Livia listened intently all the while. How she loved Ben's stories of foreign lands. How her eyes lit up at the thought of far-off places and grim warriors. It was no surprise – the girl had never been further from their farm than Bardum Market and the grimmest warrior she ever saw was Cabul the Blacksmith. And he was hardly the square-jawed hero of legend.

When they were within a half-mile of the farm they could hear Jake barking into the night. He raced towards them through the dark. Livia laughed as their dog jumped up between them, licking Ben's hand and pawing at Livia's skirts. He whined like they'd been away for weeks and not just since dawn. Their dray whickered at the excited dog.

Jake raced around them as they walked the rest of the way to the farm. Ben stabled the horse, giving him a quick brush down and some feed while Livia started a fire and put the remains of yesterday's stew onto heat.

When Ben walked out of the stable he saw Livia had lit every lantern in the garden, as she always did. He'd already chided her about it being an unnecessary luxury, but she'd insisted on making sure he could see where he was going in the night. 'Last thing I need is you tripping in the dark, old man,' she'd said. He'd scowled at her for that one, but deep down he knew she had a point.

As he made his way back to the cottage he glanced mournfully down at the flower patch he'd seeded. Not a single bloom was poking through the soil. No matter how he'd tended and watered it, nothing seemed to grow. Ben had been an expert in growing crops all his life, but when it came to flowers it was like he'd been cursed. No one needed flowers on a farm, but he'd wanted something pretty for Livia to look at. The house was full of wildflowers she'd picked from the hedgerows and it might have been nice for her to have something of her own.

'Not this year,' Ben said to himself as he made his way back into the house, leaving the dead flowerbed behind him.

It smelled of simmering stew as soon as he entered through the door. Stew was always better the second day, when the meat and stock and veg and herbs had had a chance to fashion their magic. Ben's stomach grumbled in anticipation.

They ate in silence. Jake, as ever, sat in front of the hearth, watching hungrily.

Livia cleaned the dishes as Ben's eyes began to droop. The fire warmed him through and before long he was nodding off.

'Come on then, old man,' Livia whispered. 'That field won't plough itself tomorrow.'

He'd heard her say that a thousand times but he still never got bored of it. Ben let her lead him to bed, undressing him and pulling the blankets over his tired body. She kissed her finger and pressed it to his lips, then left him in the dark. Wasn't long before the sleep took him.

Ben dreamed every night. Not all the stories he told Livia were ones he'd learned from the travellers passing through Bardum Market. When he'd been younger Ben had travelled. And he'd seen war; more than most men. Every night those old memories came back to haunt him; every night he fought old battles as only a young man could. That night, he fought harder than he ever had, and when his eyes finally flicked open there was a sheen of sweat on his brow.

He pulled back the covers, feeling his heart beating fast in his chest. Light lanced faintly through the shutter of his window, even though it was well before dawn. His first thought was that Livia had forgotten to extinguish the lanterns.

'Bloody waste of oil,' he grumbled as he eased himself out of bed.

Then Jake began to bark.

Ben stumbled through the house, eyes adjusting to the scant light. He bumped into the kitchen table, staggering to the door, Jake at his feet, jumping as though there was a rabbit just beyond. Light encroached beneath it, bright enough to light Ben's feet and his muddy boots sitting on the mat. He didn't pause to put them on, but wrenched the door open, stumbling out into the night.

Jake ran out beside him but they both stopped dead in the cold mud. Some distance away Ben could hear the dray, its high-pitched whinny cutting through the night, the rhythmic pounding of its hooves as they smashed against the stable door.

Livia was on her knees in the flowerbed. It was dead no longer.

As she knelt in her nightdress, black locks flowing around her as though she were submerged in water, it seemed that every seed Ben had planted had flowered at once. But they weren't sprouting from the ground – they floated about Livia like faeries on the breeze, each one glowing with its own light. Yellow hawkbit, pink foxglove, red poppy, blue cornflower and all the rest, shining through the dark so bright Ben had to raise a hand to shield his eyes.

The old man's mouth dropped open, and at first all he could do was look on in awe.

Magic.

Not seen in these lands for a hundred years.

Panic gripped him.

If the tallymen heard of this they'd take Livia away from him. Duke Gothelm's law keepers would take her to gods knew where to do gods knew what. No one could ever find out about this.

Ben ran forward. Jake didn't move, just stood at the door all panicked and whining. As Ben got closer, bare feet tramping through the cold of the flowerbed, he felt a pressure in his head. It got hard to breathe as he neared Livia and his hand shook as he reached out to her.

His trembling finger touched the sleeve of her nightdress, feeling her flesh cold and clammy beneath.

Then the lights went out.

12

A CHOIR *sang. They were somewhere in the cloud, voices like sweet fragrant flowers, lulling her. Livia walked through the haze toward the sound, the white silken dress she wore soft against her skin. She barely noticed how beautiful it was, so intent was she on the song.*

As she walked, the cloud began to part and she suddenly held her breath in anticipation of the sight. Thrilling at the prospect of a host of seraphs singing their melodious canticle just for her.

Though the cloud parted she still couldn't see. The white mist around her darkened, turning a pallid grey. Through the miasma the choral song grew discordant, voices rising and falling in pitch, out of tune. The beauty suddenly infected with ugliness.

Livia felt panic rising within her. The grey cloud surrounding her darkened further. A scream in the distance made her shiver. A sudden clang of metal like the chiming of a bell... Was it the clash of weapons?

She tried to back away from the noise, stumbling through the haze, but wherever she went the sound only got louder. The ground beneath her feet grew cold and she looked down.

Blood.

Covering her feet, soaking the hem of her dress, turning the white silk a lustrous black.

Something ran past her but she couldn't quite see what. Then behind her: a figure sprinting through the smoke. Livia raised a hand to her mouth, stifling the choking mist as much as her sobs of panic.

Without warning the cloud lifted.

Livia stood agape at the sight it revealed, her screams stuck in her throat.

The host battled.

A thousand thousand winged warriors fought amongst the heavens. Blood spewed from horrific wounds. Cries of fury and pain lanced the air. Breastplates were rent asunder. Spears thrust into ribs. White wings torn from perfect bodies.

The battle grew ever more brutal — acts of violence reaching tumultuous heights. Livia could not draw her eyes away from the slaughter. Transfixed by the ferocity. And as she watched the fighters, so perfect in their beauty, they began to change.

Each took on a demonic visage — teeth became fangs, eyes reddened to spiteful slits, white feathers turned to horned leather, forked tongues lashing.

Livia wanted to scream. She tried to open her mouth and cry out in terror for all she was worth but there was no sound. Her throat was closed and all she could do was stare at the horror.

Until every baleful eye suddenly turned to look at her...

†

Her room was cold.

Livia looked at the ceiling, still reeling from the vision. As she stared, the memory of it began to fade. A dream.

Only a dream.

Her hand moved across the blanket that covered her until

her fingertips were consumed by Jake's soft fur. She breathed easier as she felt his chest moving up and down rhythmically as he slept. Her throat was parched and she felt as though she hadn't eaten in an age. Livia hadn't realised a nightmare could take so much out of a person.

Ben opened the door. Jake jumped up, scrambling from the bed and running up to him. The old man looked relieved to see Livia awake and she smiled, raising a hand in greeting.

'How are you feeling?' he said, coming to the bed and taking her hand.

'Thirsty,' she croaked. 'Have I been ill?'

Ben smiled, filling a cup from a jug beside the bed and handing it to her.

'You don't remember?'

Livia took a drink, feeling the cool water relieve her parched throat. 'I remember waking in the night. I dreamt...' But what would she tell him? That she had dreamt of a war in the heavens? That was just the fever dream of illness; the details didn't matter, and besides, Ben would most likely think her mad. 'How long have I been asleep?'

'Almost two days,' said Ben, placing a hand on her brow and sighing with relief at what he felt there. 'But that's not all I was concerned with.'

He looked down at his lap, face marred with worry.

'You're worrying me,' she said. 'What is it?'

He looked at her gravely. She sat up, taking his hand, and he smiled.

'Nothing to worry yourself with.'

'Tell me.'

He took a deep breath. She could see the emotion marring his already troubled brow.

'I've told you my stories of before the Fall. When the world was filled with magic. When the Blood Lords ruled the north and the Crown Sorcerers advised the rulers of the Three Kingdoms and beyond.' He paused.

'Yes. What's that got to do with me falling ill?'

'You're not ill. At least, not with any malady you can be treated for.'

'Then what is it?'

Another pause as Ben's brow creased yet further.

'Two nights ago I found you outside. You were...'

'What? What is it?'

'I don't know.' Ben almost laughed but his face turned grim. 'Somehow you have magic within you. I found you in the flowerbed in some kind of trance. You'd brought every seed to life all at once. They floated around you. It was...'

Livia laughed. It was shrill and sounded odd. She didn't know who was madder, old Ben or she.

'What are you talking about?' she said with a nervous giggle.

'I think you have sorcerer's blood.' Ben stared at her. He wasn't joining in with the laughter.

'But there's no such thing as magic anymore.'

He shook his head. 'I think we can safely say there is.'

What he was saying was impossible. But Ben wasn't a man who made idle jests, and it was clear that he was deeply concerned.

'So what do we do?' she asked.

'Nothing,' he said, too quickly. Clearly he'd thought on it long and hard. 'You must tell no one. If the tallymen find out they'll take you from me. I don't know what they might do once they have you.'

Livia placed a hand on his arm to calm him.

'It's all right,' she said, trying to soothe the old man, though she was pretty sure it was her that needed the nursing. 'We won't speak of it again. I'm sure it was nothing, Ben. I'm sure we have nothing to worry about.'

He smiled at her. 'I'm sure you're right.'

Livia could see the worry that remained behind that smile, but they spoke no more about it.

After a week they both acted as though nothing had happened. The days grew a little longer and between them they managed to plough and sow their fields. Livia thought on what Ben had said but she couldn't recall anything about the experience. Neither did she have any more dreams, and by the time the annual fayre at Bardum Market came around she hardly thought on it at all.

'I might get us a pig,' said Ben, as they walked the road into town.

Livia smiled. 'Just the one? Or have we not got enough to do in the fields?'

'They say every farmer should have at least one pig.'

She laughed out loud at that. 'Says who?'

Ben chewed on that one for a while. 'They,' he said finally, before flashing her a broken-toothed smile.

The fayre at Bardum Market was a busy event, some might have said the highlight of the year; for Livia it was a rare opportunity to meet up with people she hadn't seen for a season or more.

Mara and Gilly were waiting by the apple stand, talking idly, Gilly twirling the ribbon in her hair. Livia left Ben to size up his pig and rushed to join them. The girls embraced as though they hadn't seen one another for years, rather than months.

They talked long and loudly about what they'd been doing in the months since they'd last seen each other. Mara's father had insisted on her learning to read and had paid for a tutor to come from Jallenhove to teach her – apparently it would help her find a suitable husband – but she had grown bored of it and didn't really see the point. Gilly talked about her chickens, but there wasn't much else she was interested in, and the other girls took pains to change the subject. It was the usual idle banter Livia was used to but she welcomed it. As much as she loved old Ben he was about as talkative as their dray horse unless she pushed him to tell her his tall tales.

'Afternoon, ladies.'

The three girls ceased their chatter and turned at the voice. A boy stood there smiling, just like Livia remembered him.

Cal Redfen was taller than any other lad his age. His blonde hair flowed down to his broad shoulders and his eyes burned green. He had the cutest dimple in the middle of his chin that grew bigger every time he smiled that wide, toothy smile.

'Hello, Cal.' Gilly was the first to acknowledge him, twisting the ribbon in her hair with renewed vigour.

'Good day to you, Redfen,' said Mara, flashing her own smile, but Cal only looked at Livia, waiting for her greeting.

She was damned if she'd give it. Cal Redfen was the most eligible young man in the county but she'd not give him the satisfaction. He had girls chasing him from Wenchest to Luddop Hill. Livia Harrow wasn't about to be just another admirer in a long, long line.

'I just wanted to ask,' he said, trying not to appear ruffled by her indifference, 'if you weren't busy tomorrow, whether you'd like to join me and the Brunner boys for a picnic?'

He was still looking straight at Livia. She opened her mouth to refuse him but Mara was at her shoulder before she had a chance.

'Of course we would, Redfen. Where do you want us to meet?'

Cal smiled, still not taking his eyes off Livia. 'Noon. At Crow's Cross.'

'We'll be there,' Mara beamed as she pinched Livia's left buttock.

'Can't wait,' said Cal, turning to leave.

Livia had to stifle a cry of pain as Mara pinched harder. There was no way she wanted to look a fool in front of Cal Redfen, even though she had no intention of showing any interest in him whatsoever.

Once he was far enough away she slapped Mara's hand.

'What are you doing?' she said.

'I'm fixing your future, Livia Harrow.'

'My future doesn't need fixing, thank you very much.'

Mara looked at Gilly and they both giggled. 'Don't be

ridiculous. If it were up to you you'd be living on that farm with Ben until you were an old maid. Who's going to want you when you're all old and crusty?'

Livia took a step forward, determined to point out if she wanted to find a man before crustiness set in she could do it all on her own, but a commotion from across the fayre stopped her before she had a chance.

Voices were raised and someone shouted for everyone to get back. Livia instinctively moved towards the ruckus. Mara and Gilly called to stop her going but she barely heard them.

A crowd had formed by the time she reached the source of the noise and she pushed her way through. Once at the front she saw an old woman on her knees surrounded by half a dozen men dressed in black.

Livia recognised the woman as Bett. A hag, some called her, who lived on the outskirts of Bardum Market, selling salves and tinctures. It was also rumoured if a girl suddenly found herself in the family way and out of wedlock it was Bett who could fix the problem.

The men in black Livia knew immediately. Tallymen – the keepers of Duke Gothelm's peace, and men not to be crossed if you valued your freedom or your life. They carried out the will of the duke with a ruthless efficiency, and in most cases to be taken by the tallymen was to never be seen again.

'You're coming with us, old woman. No point making a fuss over it.' The tallyman's voice was cold. Livia was sure she recognised him – a man in his thirties, long greasy hair streaked back across his head – but she couldn't be sure of it.

'But I haven't done nothing,' pleaded Bett, still on her knees, eyes wet with tears.

'These are sorcerer's brews, you old trout,' said another of the tallymen, picking up one of the tinctures on a table behind her. 'You're selling potions, you witch.'

'I'm no witch,' Bett said, voice rising in panic. 'You all know me.' She directed her panicked words at the crowd now. 'You know I'm no witch.'

'You can tell that to the duke,' said the tallyman, throwing her tincture to the ground and grabbing her arm.

'Please,' she sobbed. 'Somebody please...'

Livia couldn't stop herself. She knew interfering with the tallymen's business was tantamount to suicide, but surely Bett didn't deserve this. She'd done no harm to anyone.

She took a step forward but before she could grab the tallyman and try to make him see reason a hand grasped her arm, pulling her back.

Livia turned, about to unleash a tirade, when she saw it was her uncle Ben standing there, holding her tight in his grip. She made to speak but he just shook his head.

There was nothing she could do as the tallymen picked Bett up and dragged her away through the crowd. The tallyman with the greasy dark hair watched them go, before turning back to the crowd.

'Nothing more to see,' he said, almost apologetically. 'Carry on with your business. Enjoy the day.'

As he made to leave he saw Ben holding Livia. For a moment she thought he was about to ask what was going on, but instead he simply nodded at her uncle.

'Ben,' he said.

'Randal,' Ben replied, before the tallyman disappeared into the crowd.

Slowly the onlookers dispersed, some of them talking about how they'd known Bett was a witch all along. Others that it was a shame the tallymen couldn't leave innocent folk alone.

Livia stood there all the while, Ben still holding her arm. Once the crowd was gone she shook free of his grip.

They didn't speak the whole way home.

13

IT was a beautiful day, the sun beaming in through the cottage windows, but Livia was still angry. Angry that Ben had stopped her and angry that she'd let him. Bett had been dragged away by the tallymen to gods knew where and no one had lifted a hand to help the old woman. Livia could have accepted that of the rest of Bardum Market – they were weak and fearful people. But she had honestly thought better of Ben.

Perhaps she was angry with herself too. Maybe if she'd kicked up a fuss she could have done more for the woman.

Her excitement at the prospect of a picnic was dulled by the experience, but she still dressed quickly, then slipped on her shoes and made her way out of the cottage.

Jake yapped at her heels as she went but she shooed him away, eager not to draw any undue attention. The last thing she wanted was to wake her uncle up and explain what she was doing.

'Where are you off to?'

Livia stopped at the sound of Ben's croaky voice. So much for not drawing attention.

She turned to see him standing in the doorway of the

cottage, nightgown down to his knobbly knees, what little hair he had left mussed up atop his head in a white brush.

'I'm out for the day,' she replied, as though daring him to question her.

Ben just stared back, a look of sorrow on his face that made her almost feel sorry for him, until he said, 'All right then.'

That only made her more furious. He should have at least asked what she was up to so she could tell him to mind his own bloody business.

'Don't you want to know where I'm going and who with?'

Ben shook his head slightly. 'I reckon that's your own affair.'

'Just don't bloody care, do you?' she snapped. 'Don't bloody care about anything. Like you didn't care about old Bett.'

Ben's gaze drifted to the ground. 'Weren't nothing could be done about that,' he said quietly.

'Like hell.' She almost shouted the words. 'There was plenty could be done by anyone with enough guts to say something.'

'And what would you have me do, girl?' Ben seemed to have found some fire from somewhere that almost shocked Livia. 'Take on the tallymen on my own? You stand up to the tallymen and you're standing up to Duke Gothelm himself. I'm just one old man, and you're a slip of a girl. Weren't nothing to be done.'

'What about the one you knew? What was his name? Randal? You could have made him see reason.'

Ben shook his head, looking sorrowful. 'Randal's not the boy he was. If there was ever a time he could be reasoned with it's well in the past.'

Livia's fists were clenched in frustration. She wanted to go on at Ben but she knew it wasn't his fault. He was talking sense and she knew it. She should have said sorry for shouting, should have told him she was just angry with herself because of the injustice of it all. Instead she turned and walked away from the farm as quick as she could. Ben said nothing to her as she went.

The day was bright enough to calm her a little by the time she got to Crow's Cross. She was still angry, but seeing Mara and Gilly waiting by the old milestone helped her forget what had happened and think about what was to come.

'Hello there, Livia Harrow,' said Mara with a big grin.

Gilly didn't say anything, just offered a smile, blue ribbons in her red hair flapping in the breeze.

'Hello, you two,' Livia replied. She tried on a smile of her own and found it was easier than she'd thought it would be. Maybe this was the best thing for her after all, to take her mind off the guilt.

They spoke for a while of the weather and the usual farm gossip. Not one of them mentioned old Bett or what might have become of her and they didn't have to wait long before the three boys arrived.

Cal led the way, striding up all tall and windswept, and Livia found she couldn't take her eyes off him as he approached. She barely noticed the Brunner boys, Mack and Jock, as they brought up the rear. They were big, broad-shouldered farm stock, just like Cal, but neither was anywhere near as handsome. It was well known they fought one another like cat and dog, and the years of brawling had given them both faces to prove it.

'Shall we?' said Cal as he arrived.

'We shall,' said Mara, moving forward and taking his arm before he had a chance to offer it to any of them. For all her bluster the day before about making sure Livia didn't end up a crusty maid, Mara was certainly making sure Cal paid her some attention. But then, Mara was prone to flirtation. It shouldn't have bothered Livia one bit – after all, she wasn't interested in Cal. Or at least that's what she told herself as she followed with Gilly, the Brunners taking up the rear, one of them slapping the other on the arm as they went.

The six of them walked up the hill to Canter's Point. The sun was bright but the breeze took the heat out of it. Before Livia knew it they'd reached the crest and could see the massive old oak standing there.

Cal unpacked the bag he carried over one shoulder and Livia saw he'd stuffed it with fruit, cheese and a meat pie. He had also purloined two bottles of wine from somewhere. One of the Brunners unfurled the blanket he carried and they all sat in the shade of the oak.

The conversation flowed and Livia found herself laughing often. They each took turns swigging from the wine bottles and before long they were empty. Mara sat closest to Cal, and Livia found herself growing quite envious. As much as she hated herself for it she couldn't help but stare in admiration at him.

Evening came all too quickly and a chill steadily crept into the air. The Brunner boys became increasingly boisterous with one another until Livia knew she'd had enough. Whatever designs she might have had on Cal had clearly been usurped by Mara and so she stood, ready to announce she was heading home.

'Are you going?' said Cal, rising to his feet.

Mara was stopped mid-sentence and she looked up at him, clearly offended.

'It's getting late,' Livia replied. 'I have to get back before dark.'

'I'll walk you,' Cal said before anyone else could say goodbye to her, or either of the Brunners offered in his stead.

Livia shook her head, seeing the sudden look of anger on Mara's face.

'It's fine, Cal, really. I'll be home before nightfall.'

'But I insist,' said Cal, walking forward to stand beside her. 'Boys. Make sure Mara and Gilly get home safe.'

Before Livia could protest further Cal placed a hand on her back and led her down the hill. She glanced over her shoulder as they went, in time to see Mara glaring as Gilly twirled her ribbons for the Brunner brothers.

They walked some way in silence, Cal close beside her as though she might need guarding from the dark. His arm occasionally brushed against hers and she tried her best to ignore it and convince herself she didn't like him. But then she'd wanted Cal Redfen from the first moment she'd laid eyes on him.

The fact that she hated her attraction to him didn't change it. Cal Redfen had all the depth of a puddle. He was pretty and dumb, so why did she find him so attractive?

'So… you and Mara seemed to be getting along,' she said, sick of the uncomfortable silence.

Cal smirked. 'Mara's a silly girl,' he said as they came to a fence. A stile was cut into the centre of it and Cal began to help her over.

'She comes across that way,' said Livia. 'But she's very clever really. She can read at least.'

'Being clever is more than just book reading and numbers,' he said as he climbed over behind her. 'She's silly in the head. I want someone with some sense.'

He looked at her and grinned at the gobsmacked expression on her face. It looked like Cal Redfen had some depth after all, but Livia couldn't bring herself to say anything in reply.

They crossed a bridge over a shallow stream as the sun began to drop toward the horizon. As they reached the centre, Cal took her hand gently.

'I'm talking about you, Livia Harrow,' he said.

She looked up at him, raising an eyebrow. 'How romantic, Cal Redfen. It's not that I'm beautiful or have the manners of a princess. I'm sensible? Quick, let me ask old Ben's permission to marry.'

Cal looked embarrassed. 'No, that's not what I meant either.' He moved closer. 'Of course I think you're beautiful. I'm no good with words but…'

Livia almost giggled at his clumsiness, until he began to move closer. His head dipped, his eyes closed and before she knew it he was kissing her. His lips were shut tight at first but suddenly he opened them.

For a brief moment Livia experienced a jolt of panic, but as she felt his tongue against hers she found her own eyes closing and she reached up to put her arms around his neck. He gripped her tight about the waist, pulling her close and she could feel him hard within his trews. Any other day that would have made her squeal and run for the hills, but not this day. Now it only made her heart beat faster as she pressed her lips harder against his.

Cal moved one hand down from her waist, his fingertips stroking her buttocks and then moving around to her upper thigh. She grasped him tighter, feeling the firmness of his body against her breasts. His left hand moved lower and she gripped the back of his neck with one hand, the nails of the other caressing his chest…

Black wings fluttered across her eyelids. Veined and leathered. Claws raked at white porcelain flesh, leaving lines of crimson in their wake. A flawless voice screamed. A howl from the gates of hell followed…

Livia opened her eyes. Cal was leaning back against the other side of the bridge, his head thrown back, mouth gaping open in a silent cry. In the twilight she could see his eyes had rolled back in his head and every inch of him shook fitfully.

'Cal?' she said, moving forward but too scared to touch his convulsing body. 'Cal!' she shouted, but he didn't hear as a line of saliva dripped from his open mouth.

Livia ran in a panic. She had to get help. Had to reach Ben; he'd know what to do. He always knew what to do.

Her feet clattered across the bridge then padded through the grass. She sprinted in the dark, her breath coming in ragged gasps. The memory of a nightmare flitted through her head as she ran. In every shadow something waited with dark wings and blood in its eyes.

Livia crossed a shallow stream, stumbling at the opposite bank, her skirt drenched as she clawed her way up. When she crested the rise she saw a tree silhouetted in the dark. She made to run past but what she saw hanging from it made her stop, a cry of anguish caught in her throat.

Bett hung by her neck, the rope that held her there creaking in the breeze. The old woman stared blankly, tongue sticking out from one side of her mouth as though she had just tasted something vile.

Livia stood and stared, feeling her heart thundering in her chest before she managed to drag her eyes away and run the rest of the way back to the farm.

14

THE Redfen farm was only eight miles north of the Harrows'. Still, by the time Ben reached the gate sign identifying the place the old dray he rode was huffing with fatigue.

He dismounted, leading the horse down the path that led to the cottage standing at the centre of the farm. It was by far the biggest Ben had ever seen, but Morgen Redfen was said to be the best woodworker in the county. It was only natural he'd have the finest house. Not that Ben was envious of that; he'd never coveted what other men had, although if he admitted it to himself he was a little jealous of all Morgen's pigs. Every farmer should have a pig. Morgen Redfen clearly abused the privilege.

Before he'd even tethered the dray to the rail, the door to the cottage opened. Molly Redfen stood on the threshold, as though guarding it, her eyes glaring at Ben like he'd come to do her and her kin harm. That was the last thing on Ben's mind and he tried a smile and a nod of greeting to show it. Molly just glowered.

'Good day, Molly,' he said, walking up onto the porch. She stood there barring his way. 'Is Morgen home? I think we need to speak.'

She opened her mouth, clearly not about to say anything nice, when a deep voice from inside said, 'Is that Ben Harrow?'

Molly frowned, still staring at Ben.

'Who do you bloody well think?'

'Let him in then. Don't leave the old geezer standing out in the cold all day.'

Reluctantly Molly moved aside and Ben walked in. Morgen Redfen sat at his kitchen table, spooning broth from a wooden bowl. The smell of it made Ben's stomach grumble.

'Been expecting you, Ben. Take a seat,' Morgen said without looking up.

Ben took the chair opposite, keeping one eye on Molly in case she decided to grab a rolling pin, or something more lethal, and give him the good news with it.

'Leave us, Mol,' Morgen said before spooning more broth into his mouth. He was grizzled, maybe mid forties, and he ate with the same purposefulness as he farmed.

'Leave you? Alone with this freak? Gods know what he and that witch have been brewing on their farm. I'll not leave him—'

'Get out, woman!' Morgen shouted, broth spilling from his mouth.

Ben jumped at the sound. Everyone knew about Morgen Redfen's temper. He was rarely crossed in the county and never by anyone twice. Not even his formidable wife.

Molly fell silent, wringing her hands on her apron before heading for the door.

Morgen sat for a moment, calming himself before he

wiped broth from around his mouth with a cloth and ate another spoonful.

'How's Cal?' Ben asked. Trying to sound as concerned for Morgen's son as he was for himself.

Morgen still didn't look up. 'He's fine.' Then went back to spooning that broth.

Ben glanced around the Redfen kitchen. Everything was in its place. Everything meticulously cleaned. He felt more envy that his own small place wasn't so tidy. The longer he sat there the more he felt like he was visiting with Duke Gothelm rather than a fellow farmer.

'Look,' said Ben. 'We need to talk about—'

'I know what we need to talk about,' said Morgen, placing his spoon down by the empty bowl. 'We need to talk about your girl.' He picked up the cloth and wiped his mouth again.

'Livia's not sure what happened.'

Morgen regarded Ben blankly. 'I'm sure she's not.'

'She slept for most of the day after she got home. Says Cal maybe had some kind of a fit.'

Morgen nodded slowly. 'Yes. That would be one explanation for it.'

'What did your boy have to say?' Ben braced himself for the answer. Gods knew what Cal had said.

'Not much. And when he's been able to speak he's wept.' Morgen's expression turned grave. 'Do you know what that's like, Ben? To have your boy crying like a girl?' Ben shook his head. 'He hasn't cried since he was teething. And there he is weeping like the world's ended.'

Ben glanced down at the table, cleaned and polished like

the Redfens had been expecting nobility to come round.

'It must have been a frightening thing for him. To have an affliction like that come on all of a sudden.'

Morgen stood, picking up the bowl and spoon and placing them next to a washbasin by the window.

'An affliction? Cal Redfen with an affliction?' He let that hang there.

'It's the kind of thing that could happen to anyone.'

'Not my boy, Ben.' Morgen turned to him, eyes blazing. The one on the left gave an unnerving twitch.

'We've known each other a long time, Morgen,' said Ben, trying and failing to sound like he wasn't intimidated by Redfen's rage. 'I came here to—'

'You came to see if I'd already told the tallymen about your girl.'

Ben stared at him, all hopes of not being intimidated fleeing like a craven from his body. That was pretty much the reason, though he hadn't intended to say it. If there was the slightest rumour that Livia had been showing signs of magic they'd be shouting 'witch' from one end of the county to the other. Molly Redfen had already used the word. Ben needed to stamp out any spark of a rumour before the flames took and burned the Harrows' farm down around their ears.

'And have you?' he asked.

Morgen gave a little snort of mirth through his nose, then returned to the table and took his seat.

'We've known each other a lot of years, Ben. And when times were hard back in that grim winter I remember how we helped one another. It's how things have always worked around here. Before Gothelm let his tallymen run rampant through every farm from Vallen Kale to the Eldreth border.' He reclined in his seat and smiled. 'I'm sure Cal's affliction is only something mild. He's a strong boy. He'll be fine. No reason to get the tallymen all riled over it.'

Ben let out a sigh as silent as he could without showing Morgen how relieved he was.

'I appreciate that,' said Ben. 'And I'll take no more of your time.'

He stood, ready to leave, when the door to the kitchen opened. Ben was expecting Molly to come rushing in, railing about how this wasn't good enough and how she'd cry 'witch' from every hill she could climb.

He wasn't expecting Cal Redfen.

The boy's eyes were drawn, his skin pale. He was stripped to the waist and Ben could see three scratches in a tight row on his chest as if a wolf had mauled him.

'Hello, Cal,' he said, when the boy appeared, not really knowing what else to say.

Cal didn't give an answer. Just walked in and stared out of the window.

Morgen looked at him. Then at Ben. It was clear to anyone with eyes in their head that Cal was far from 'fine'.

'It's misty in here,' Cal said, as though he were locked in a dream while he wandered around awake. 'But I can still see their wings. And the noise they make. So...'

Molly rushed in before either of the men could say a word, taking her son by the arm and leading him out. She shot Ben a hate-filled glance.

'Thanks for coming round, Ben,' Morgen said, opening the door hurriedly and letting some of the cold air in.

Ben felt that cold air chill him for a second before he thanked Morgen for taking the time to see him and walked out. The door slamming behind him was like a coffin lid shutting over him.

He could barely remember the ride back. The dray clopped along the path as Ben's mind raced. The Harrow farmhouse appearing over the horizon was the only thing that brought him out of his stupor, and as soon as he saw it he urged the dray on to greater exertion.

Livia was waiting for him when he returned, her face careworn.

'Well?' she asked before Ben had even shut the door behind him. 'What did he say?'

Ben looked at her, desperate to give good news – that they would be all right, that everything would be just as it was.

'I spoke to Morgen. We go back a long way, he and I. He told me there was no need for the tallymen to find anything out.'

Livia smiled, breathing out in relief and raising a hand to her chest.

'I'll make tea.'

Ben almost laughed. How Livia loved her tea. But instead he laid a hand on her arm as she reached for the kettle.

'Pack your things. We have to leave. Be quick about it.'

He moved to the bedroom as fast as he could, breathing heavily. It was all he could do to suppress his panic.

'What are you talking about? You said he wouldn't tell the tallymen.'

'And I wish I could believe him. But if you'd seen...'

He wanted to tell her about Cal. About the blankness in his eyes and how he looked as though he was walking in a dream and the strange words he said. There was no way this would stay a secret for long. And once the word was out...

'If I'd seen what?' Livia said, still standing in the doorway of Ben's room.

'Just pack!' Ben raised his voice. Livia stared at him, shocked at his anger. In all the years he had cared for her Ben had never shouted at her, not even when she'd been up to mischief or sung the same song over and over until it grated on his nerves. But now all that mattered was that they ran as far from this place as they could.

She stared at him with hurt in her eyes.

He took a step towards her. 'Look I—'

Jake began to bark in their yard outside.

Whatever Ben had been about to say was forgotten as he stumbled past her to the front door. His hand went to the handle but he paused before turning it. Jake's barking stopped suddenly.

Ben glanced back at Livia. She shook her head a little, almost imperceptibly. There was no way out.

He opened the door.

Half a dozen tallymen stood in the garden. At the threshold was Randal, hair greasy and slicked back, a smile on his narrow face.

'Hello, Ben,' he said. 'Can I come in?'

15

BEN moved aside and let Randal walk into their kitchen. Livia could only stand and watch in fear as the dark-haired man came inside. Out through the front door she could see more tallymen standing just beyond their front porch, one of them holding Jake in his arms, hand clamped over the dog's mouth. She wanted to run out and snatch Jake from the tallyman's arms but her legs wouldn't move; she knew it would be futile.

Randal sat in a chair in their kitchen, crossing his legs and reclining back in his seat. Slowly Ben closed the front door.

'Would you like some tea, Randal?' Ben asked.

'That would be lovely, Ben. Thank you,' replied Randal with a smile.

Ben looked at Livia. 'Would you boil the kettle for us?'

Livia stared as the old man calmly took the chair next to Randal. They sat in silence while she stepped forward into the kitchen and picked up the kettle. It was full of water and she placed it over the fire that crackled quietly in one corner.

'How've you been, Ben?' Randal asked. 'How's the farm?'

'Things are good. Mild winter always makes things easier

in the spring. Harvest looks like it'll be good this year. I wouldn't mind a pig though. Every farmer should have a pig.'

Ben was babbling; he always did when he was nervous. It amused Randal, who carried on smiling at the old man. There was a degree of affection in his smile, which Livia took some solace in.

'That's good news, Ben. So many farms are struggling. The duke will be pleased you're doing so well.'

'These are difficult times,' said Ben. 'We can only do what we can.' Then as an afterthought, 'And I'm sure Duke Gothelm wishes only health and happiness for the folk who work his lands.'

'He does,' said Randal. And though Livia wasn't looking at him directly she could tell he was still smiling. But the affection had faded away now, and it seemed as though he was deriving some small sadistic pleasure from Ben's discomfort.

The water in the kettle began to boil and Livia lifted it from the fire, covering the red-hot handle with a clean towel. She'd bought it from Bardum Market the year before from a trader; white cotton with red silk flowers woven into the fabric.

Livia filled the teapot with the hot water and placed the lid on to allow it to brew. As it steamed, giving off a warming aroma, she turned back to the two men.

'Is everything all right, Ben?' said Randal, sitting unmoving in his chair.

Ben was wringing his hands on the worn table-top, not able to look Randal in the eye.

'Everything's fine,' he replied.

'Only you haven't asked me why I'm here.'

Ben looked up. Randal's smile wavered.

'I reckon you'll tell me when you're good and ready.'

Randal nodded at that. 'Aye. Reckon I will.'

Livia was under no illusions – Ben knew exactly why Randal and the tallymen had come. They were here to take her off and hang her from the nearest tree, and there was nothing she or Ben could do about it.

Fighting to keep her hand steady, Livia reached for the teapot and then filled two cups through a strainer before bringing them to the table.

'Tea,' she said as she placed them down, her hands shaking.

One of the cups spilled, and tea dripped off the edge of the table onto Randal's black trews. In a panic she grabbed the towel and made to dab at his lap. Randal grasped her wrist before she could touch him, a flash of annoyance in his eyes before it was gone. Then he gently took the towel from her grip and cleaned himself off before placing it back on the table.

Silently, Livia backed away to the window once more as Randal stared at Ben.

'How's your mother?' Ben asked suddenly.

Randal raised an eyebrow at that, a brief moment off his guard before his face returned to that haughty expression.

'She's fine, Ben.'

'I've not seen her for so long. Does she know you're here?'

Randal inclined his head. 'No, Ben. I never mentioned it to her.'

Ben was looking straight at the tallyman now, eyes pleading.

'I remember once, when you were little, me and your mother collected pears from Farmer Gant's orchard. It was unseasonably hot. You had a rash that year, on your belly, but it went away all on its own. Anyway, we made cider and it was awful, worst I've ever tasted.' Ben smiled at the memory. 'Your mother, she made more pear pies than I'd ever seen. Bardum Market's never been so fat on pear pie since. It was a good year. Almost feels like it was yesterday.'

Randal sat and listened like Ben was his own uncle. When the old man had finished he let out a long sigh that filled Livia with dread.

'I have to take her, Ben,' he said.

Livia felt sick to the pit of her stomach.

Ben nodded. 'I know you do. And you know I won't allow it.'

'I know. You've always been a stubborn old man. I always liked that about you.'

Randal's smile was filled with regret. A moment of sorrow before he moved, quick as a snake, hand coming out of his sleeve almost too fast for her to see.

The knife was in Ben's neck before Livia could even think to scream. By the time Randal drew the blade across Ben's throat Livia's voice was lost. She could only stare, her hand clamped over her mouth as Randal withdrew the weapon, letting blood gush from the wound.

Ben's head lolled back, opening up a yawning red mouth in his neck, his eyes wide, staring at the ceiling. Randal stepped back calmly, picking up Livia's towel, her favourite one with the red flowers, and wiping his blade clean with it.

As Ben died before her, gurgling his last, Randal picked up his cup of tea and drained it.

Then the door burst open.

The rest of the tallymen rushed in, grabbing Livia where she stood. She heard the fabric of her dress tear as they dragged her outside. One of them grasped her hair, pulling her along by it, and she heard herself screaming as they threw her to the ground. As she lay there she saw Jake lying on the flowerbed amongst a host of dead petals. He wasn't moving.

'Who's got the rope?' said one of the tallymen.

'Fuck the rope. This one we'll have to burn,' said another.

Livia's panic overcame her fear, the need to survive crushing all else, and she tried to rise to her feet. There was no way she could fight them but she could run. Before she was even able to stand one of them kicked her in her side, another slapping her so hard on the side of her head her ear began to ring. She fell again, sobbing in the mud.

'We're not to kill her.' That was Randal, talking as casually as he had with Ben. 'Duke Gothelm will want to see this one. She's no mere brewer of potions. The Redfens said she has real power.'

At his words Livia felt anger boil within her. There was still a ringing in her ear, her face stinging, her side numb from where she'd been kicked. Whatever power she had, whatever had happened to make this nightmare come true, she willed it into being.

Livia closed her eyes, calling on the foul magic that had

afflicted Cal, the magic that had manifested itself in this very garden. With every fibre she summoned her powers to strike down the tallymen and eviscerate them where they stood.

Nothing happened.

No angelic voices sang in her ears. No demons on wings of leather came swooping, horned and bloody, to her aid.

There was just her, and the dirt, and the men who had come to take her.

As she looked up, tears stinging her eyes, she saw Randal kneeling beside her.

'Try not to be afraid,' he said. 'You won't be harmed. Duke Gothelm has business with you.'

With that the tallymen grabbed her, one of them binding her hands behind her back.

As they led her off the only solace she had was Randal's promise that she would not be harmed. But all she could see when she closed her eyes was that dark vision of old Bett swinging from her tree, and Ben dead in the kitchen they had shared, a yawning wound in his neck.

16

Her tears had stopped several miles back along the road, but she still had plenty of reasons to cry. Livia's shoes had fallen off hours ago and her wrists were raw from the rope. One side of her face throbbed and she could feel her eye starting to swell.

A vision of Ben's empty death-stare flashed across her mind's eye again, and Livia did her best to quell the image before it made her sob. No amount of sobbing would do her any good now. The tallymen would take no heed of it, and if she were to get out of this alive she needed a clear head.

'We need to head north through Ballenheim,' said one of the men at the front.

'No, you fucking idiot,' said another, his wispy dark hair doing a shit job of covering the scabby pate beneath. 'If we go west by the River Clavern we'll be in Ardenstone in less than three days.'

Randal stepped forward before either of them could argue anymore. 'We go north,' he said. 'It's the quicker route.'

No one questioned him, and the tallymen continued on their way. Randal wasn't the biggest of them, and he certainly didn't look the meanest, but he commanded a respect among these men that was undeniable. Livia wanted him dead more than anything in the world.

She'd never hated anyone in her life, though there were plenty of people to choose from in Bardum Market. But this man – this murderer – made the bile rise in her throat and her stomach knot with rage. Still she remained as helpless as a lamb being dragged along to the sacrifice. If Randal was going to die it would have to wait.

They dragged her further north as the sun began to slide down toward the horizon. At the back of the group she could hear a couple of tallymen whispering out of Randal's earshot. They were questioning him, convinced they should have strung Livia up from the nearest tree. Witchcraft was much feared in Canbria, and it seemed these men were more superstitious than most. Luckily for her it was all bluster. Neither of them seemed to have the courage to go against their leader. As much as she hated Randal, Livia was suddenly grateful for the sway he held over his men.

It eventually got dark – so dark that Livia couldn't see where she was going, treading on sharp stones on the shadowy ground. By the time they stopped she was gritting her teeth in pain.

'That'll do,' said one of the tallymen.

Livia strained her eyes through the murk, spotting a light from down a shallow drop. The tallymen led her toward it. As they moved down the hill, the smell of a chimney fire reached her nostrils and dread welled up inside her.

Another homestead. Another innocent farmer at the mercy of the tallymen. What would they do to this poor wretch? Leave another old man sitting in his kitchen with his throat open?

When they reached the farmhouse Livia realised she needn't have worried.

A grey-haired farmer answered his door in the dark, candle in hand. A quick exchange of words and he invited them into his house. Livia felt a well of relief rise up in her as she entered the warm confines, but the feeling was fleeting.

'Siddown,' said one of the tallymen, after dragging her to the corner of the room.

She dropped to the floor obediently, watching in silence as the rest of them took up positions around the sparse cottage.

'I don't have much,' said the old man. 'But you're welcome to whatever—'

'We only have need of shelter.' Randal spoke with the usual authority. 'You have nothing to fear, old man.'

The grey-haired farmer nodded, but his eyes flitted toward where Livia was sitting. It was clear he had doubts about how honest Randal was being. These were tallymen, and if they strung the old man up for the slightest provocation it would hardly be the first time.

As the evening wore on, Livia's head began to nod, but she was determined to stay awake. The tallymen surrounded her and she wanted to be ready for what they might do.

As she sat, one of them quietly began to sing. It was a song of the ancient woodmen; a verse told in a language little used nowadays. It seemed odd – such a sweet tune from a man in such wicked company.

Though she fought it, Livia couldn't help but be lulled by the soft song, as though the tallyman were singing a lullaby just for her.

She was flying on ethereal wings. The rush of the air in her face matched the rush of the blood through her veins. Her senses were keen; she could hear her own heart beating, taste every drop of moisture in the air.

In the distance was the Blue Tower, rising up towards the clouds. Before it ran a plain of green, dappled with blue and red and yellow. As she banked she could see that the colours made a mosaic, overlaying something beneath.

With a sweep of her massive wings she halted her flight, descending to the earth amidst the sea of colour.

It was a battlefield.

But where there should have been carrion crows feasting on the dead men and horses, there were millions of butterflies, decorating the corpses with a myriad of colours. They were a soft blanket laid over the carnage, wings fluttering in the breeze.

She could feel herself smiling – no lament for the dead, only awe at the beautiful spectacle. Two of the creatures fluttered before her, dancing with each other in mid-air. When she reached out her hand they came to rest on her palm, one with wings of vivid gold, the other one bright cerulean. She closed her fist, crushing them in her white-knuckled grip, and when she opened it again the insects had turned to shining jewels: one topaz, one sapphire.

The light from those precious stones darkened as the sky turned from blue to black in an instant. A crack of thunder pealed across the heavens but she did not fear it.

An arm surged from the ground, red-skinned and thickly

135

muscled. *At the same time there was the sound of beating wings as something else swooped down from the sky.*

As one, the myriad butterflies took flight, lifting like a veil from the earth. Before they had risen ten feet they began to disintegrate, flowing off into the ether like pollen on the breeze.

From the earth climbed a vast being, horns curled from its temples to its jaw, eyes dark, shoulders and chest like boulders. Dark wings carried another figure to the ground, impossibly thin but beautiful, hair shining gold, feathers across her back trailing into a multicoloured tail.

Both these beings greeted her with a name she couldn't quite hear. She returned the greeting, but the names she uttered were lost as soon as they had passed her lips.

'It is time?' said the horned monstrosity.

'Shall we, sister?' asked the winged beauty.

She did not answer, but spread her own wings and took to the air. The Blue Tower seemed impossibly far, but still she knew she would reach it with ease.

At the top of the tower was a marble pagoda, open to the elements. The winged woman and the beast were already awaiting her as she reached the summit and swept down to the marble tiles with the most delicate touch.

In the centre of the floor stood a thin podium of steel; sat atop was a giant crystal. She could see it was cracked, but still contained a thick mist, like the storm writhing overhead was mirrored within the crystal.

'They are calling to us,' said the beast.

'Calling to all of us,' said the woman.

Deep within the crystal it was clear there was something to fear.

'But it has been so long,' she said. 'And it is still broken. How will we? How can we?'

The woman smiled as the beast placed his hand upon the crystal. Above them, the clouds began to open; unleashing rain at first, then hail, crashing upon the roof of the Blue Tower, shaking it to its core.

The woman placed her hand upon that of the beast. 'Do not be afraid,' she whispered.

But there was so much to fear... and perhaps gain.

She stepped forward, gently placing her own hand upon the crystal, feeling the cracks and imperfections in its surface.

No sooner had she touched it than something gripped her insides. Pulling at her soul. Dragging her down. Ever down...

She woke not with a start but a simple opening of her eyes. The singing had stopped. From the wan, pre-dawn light she could see the outlines of the tallymen as they slept. One snored gently in the dark. Another murmured quietly.

'Early riser?'

Livia started at the whisper in the dark. She slowly turned to see Randal looking at her. He sat in an armchair that looked wholly out of place in the small room. It wasn't the only thing.

'That's not surprising for a farm girl, I suppose,' he finished. When she did not answer, Randal continued to stare.

'You're a monster,' whispered Livia, before she could even consider that it might be a bad idea to insult her captor.

'Many people in the duchy are saying the same thing about you.' She saw the hint of a smile play on Randal's face through the shadow. 'Have you seen Cal Redfen recently? Only a witch could do that to a strapping young lad in his prime.'

Livia felt a wrenching pain in her gut. She had never meant to hurt Cal. She didn't even know how she had done it, but the guilt stung.

'I never meant—'

'Save it,' whispered Randal. 'It won't help you.'

'Just like it didn't help Ben?' she spat. If she had intended to move Randal with her words it didn't do the trick.

'That was unfortunate. I wish I could have avoided that but Ben would have shouted from the rooftops that you'd been taken. If word of what you'd done reached King Stellan he might well have wanted you for himself. Gothelm can't have that. Ben just had to go.' Randal glanced into the embers of the fireplace, as though they showed him a picture of a past he could never reach. 'He was good to me, old Ben. After my father died he did his best to look in on us. If things had been different he and my mother might have wed. I might have been his son.' He looked back at Livia. 'But things aren't different. Things are as they are. I am fatherless. Ben is dead. And you will face Duke Gothelm's judgement.'

Livia hunkered down in the silence, fighting back her tears. She was determined not to show him any further weakness but she felt like she might break at any moment.

'I used to see you often at Bardum Market when we were children,' Randal continued. 'I doubt you even noticed me. You were always smiling. Always ready with a kind word. All the old hens making a fuss of the orphan girl. Where are your hens now, Livia Harrow? No one cares for you and no one is coming to help.'

She was about to snap back at him. To tell him she didn't

remember him. To tell him she had no idea who he was and would never have noticed such a snivelling toad, when one of the tallymen stirred.

Randal stood. 'On your feet,' he said, his voice filling the room.

Without complaint the tallymen stirred, each silently rising, stretching, and gathering his bedroll. Without another word the door to the cottage was opened and they began to file out. One of them grabbed the rope that bound Livia's wrists and pulled her to her feet.

As she was dragged outside she could feel Randal's eyes on her. In the cold of the morning, as she was pulled along the muddy road to her fate, she wondered how many times those eyes had regarded her while she walked the fayre at Bardum Market.

Whatever the answer, she was not in Bardum Market now.

She doubted she would ever see it again.

✝

For centuries the three great kingdoms of the Suderfeld had been at war. A succession of warrior kings rose and fell as the lands were riven with strife. The rulers of Canbria, Arethusa and Eldreth were at once noble and merciless — their codes of chivalry as widely respected as their ruthlessness was feared.

With their Crown Sorcerers at their sides — twisted and venal to a man — there looked to be no end to the conflict. For as each king rose and fell their advisors and puppet-masters would still be lurking, ready to pick up the pieces and perpetuate the never-ending war of attrition.

This might have gone on endlessly had the Fall not come and snatched power from every sorcerer in the Three Kingdoms. With their magic gone the glamour they had placed upon their kings vanished. Those that did not flee were slaughtered — strung up as an example to any who might try and usurp power from the rightful rulers of the Suderfeld.

Though antipathy still reigned amidst the Three Kingdoms, it was soon overcome by a common enemy. From across the Crooked Jaw rose the Mercenary Barons, their fear of Suderfeld gone after the demise of the Crown Sorcerers.

They came as a great horde, united under a dozen banners, bent on seizing the rich lands of the Suderfeld and slaughtering its rightful rulers. The Three Kingdoms had to unite or die to face this new threat and quickly drew up the Treaty of Iron — an accord that would seal their alliance and allow them to face the Mercenary Barons as a unified force.

The Mercenary War was a brief one. The invading

forces were sent scurrying back over the Crooked Jaw where they licked their wounds and thought long on their folly. When the war was over, the Treaty of Iron was honoured by the rulers of the Three Kingdoms.

Harald of Canbria, Craggen of Arethusa and Leonfric of Eldreth became friends over the intervening years, raising their sons in the noble tradition and guaranteeing peace through an annual tourney, where any rivalries or disputes could be resolved on the field in a battle to first blood.

It was on the night of one such tourney that the champion to Leonfric of Eldreth was said to have poisoned his rival, the champion of Canbria, to dull his senses for the following day's match. Some say the dose was too high. Others say that the champion of Arethusa had also poisoned the knight of Canbria and the combined cocktail was too much for the man's heart. Either way, upon finding his champion dead Harald declared the Treaty of Iron void.

Without the treaty binding their realms, the kings of the Suderfeld soon regressed to their baser instincts. Their wars began anew. A conflict that would outlive Harald, Leonfric and Craggen and pass down to their sons. A war that seemingly had no end...

— A Treatise of the Suderfeld Wars,
Brother Hephestus Baal,
Third Penitent of Halbor the Wise

†

17

Canbria, 105 years after the Fall

IT was a dingy inn. Not quite the worst Josten had been in over the years but somewhere close. The dim candlelight revealed the filth surrounding them, a thick layer of dust and grease that seemed to cover everything – even the old man asleep with his head in his arms at one table. Maybe the guttering candles made this place look more of a shithole than it was. Maybe in daylight it could be considered quaint.

As he spied a rat run beneath a nearby bench Josten realised he couldn't blame the candles.

'What a fucking shithole,' said Mullen, loudly so all could hear.

Josten couldn't argue. This place was an insult to shit.

'Well? What are you having?'

Mullen's frown of disdain turned into a welcoming smile as he turned to the serving girl who stood behind them. She was every bit as greasy and careworn as the inn, but that didn't stop Mullen.

'Two flagons, my dear,' he said with his massive horse-faced smile. 'And is that chicken I can smell roasting somewhere, my beauty?'

'Two coppers a flagon. Three coppers a chicken,' she

answered, seemingly impervious to Mullen's charms. Not that Josten was surprised – most women were impregnable to his friend's advances, unless Mullen was paying for it.

'The two flagons will do then,' Mullen replied. Chicken was out of their budget.

'Coins,' she said, holding out her hand wearily.

Mullen looked like he was about to argue the price then thought better of it, fishing in his coinpurse for the money before depositing it in her outstretched hand. She looked at Mullen like he'd just pissed on her palm, before turning and stomping off without another word.

'She's desperate to fuck me,' said Mullen.

Josten couldn't even be bothered asking where he'd got that impression, he was too busy wondering how his life had come to this. He was cold, filthy and they could only afford ale instead of chicken. They were warriors in a kingdom riven by war and couldn't find anyone to pay them for their services. Over the years they'd both managed to kill, betray or abandon their way to being the most unpopular mercenaries in all the Suderfeld. Anyone would be desperate to employ them now. But then, these were desperate times.

'If I were you I'd concentrate on finding work for the weapon people might want you to use, rather than the useless one hanging between your thighs,' said Josten, only half-joking.

'It wasn't me who fucked Duke Harlaw's wife,' Mullen shot back.

Josten couldn't argue; this was his fault and he knew it. Under Duke Harlaw they had both lived a blessed existence.

Josten's desire had ruined all that and Mullen's loyalty meant he was now knee-deep in the same mire. For the thousandth time since they'd fled Ravensbrooke he made sure Josten knew it.

He could only hope things would pick up, but in the five years since Josten had escaped execution, times had got harder. They'd both been forced to take work where they could with the foulest mercenary bands in all the Three Kingdoms of the Suderfeld. Josten had a lot of regrets, and dragging his friend down with him was up there among them. He could only take solace in the fact the fighting was escalating. Surely they'd find work soon.

'Two flagons,' said the serving maid, banging the drinks on their table. The ale was frothy with what looked like a layer of scum riding at the top. Still Mullen beamed up at her.

'Thank you kindly,' he said as she walked away and he took a long draught. 'She definitely wants to fuck me.' He wiped his mouth on the back of his sleeve.

Josten contemplated his own flagon for the longest time. Then the door to the inn opened before he could put the drink to his lips.

Four men walked in, two of whom he recognised. They were dishevelled from the road but keen of eye, glancing warily around the inn looking for signs of trouble. Their eyes fell on Josten and Mullen. They knew that if there was trouble to be had, then Josten or Mullen was where they'd find it.

The one at the front gave a nod of recognition. Thierry Chulders was well known throughout Canbria. Rumour was he'd been a Mercenary Baron in his day but had fallen on hard times. Whatever the truth, he fought hard in battle and was never short of work. He was a man to be respected, if not liked.

The next two Josten had never seen before, but the one at the back made him sigh deeply.

'Fucking Beckan,' Mullen said under his breath. This time he was quiet enough that only Josten heard him.

Dirty Beckan they called him. A bastard if ever there was one, but a hard bastard who carried a big axe. He was also connected, having fought for almost every mercenary crew in the Three Kingdoms. Not a man to be messed with.

'Cade!' Beckan shouted across the empty inn. 'And Mullen, of course. Where there's one there's always the other. Just like horse shit and the stink it brings.'

He spoke through the gap where his front teeth should have been and Josten only wished he could find the man who'd knocked them out and buy him a barrel of ale.

Chulders and the other two took a table and waited for the serving girl, but Beckan continued to look on, leering across the inn like he was on heat and they were the tastiest whores he'd ever seen.

'What you two doing here anyway?' asked the big man. 'Still looking for a company to take you on? Like anyone's gonna want two washed-up old fucks.'

Mullen reached down ever so slowly for that axe he always kept at his side nowadays, but Josten gave him the *don't do anything stupid* glance.

'Sit down, Beckan,' Chulders said.

Beckan kept smiling like an inbred before moving to sit with his three companions.

'Don't even start to tell me he's not worth the hassle,' said Mullen.

Josten was about to do just that when Beckan leaned back on his chair for one last dig.

'Killed any fucking babies this week, Cade?'

This time it was Mullen's turn to give an expectant look. Josten just stared back, easily reading his friend's intent. Any move he wanted to make and Mullen would back him. But two against four wasn't fair odds in anyone's book.

They went back to their ales in silence. The first swig was bitter to Josten's lips but it didn't taste as bad as it looked. By the time he was halfway down the tankard he'd got the taste for it, but before they could order any more, Thierry Chulders moved from his table and came towards them. Mullen was his usual wary self but Josten knew they were in no danger from Chulders, as long as they weren't facing one another on the battlefield.

'Gentlemen,' Chulders said, taking a seat at their table. 'I see business could be better.' He looked both men up and down with a wry grin.

'Business is fine,' Mullen replied. It was obvious to all three of them that was a lie.

Chulders signalled to the serving girl that he wanted another drink and she gave him a disinterested nod.

'It's just that we're headed east to Tarrandale. To fight for King Ozric. He has the best chance to win this thing and he's also the richest patron in the Three Kingdoms. Men like you would be valued assets to any company. I'd like that to be my company.'

'No thanks,' said Josten. He didn't need time to think on it.

'We're choosy about the company we keep,' added Mullen, glancing over towards Beckan, who was noisily talking of past deeds to the two men he sat with. Neither of them looked particularly interested, but neither did they tell him to be quiet.

Chulders leaned in close. 'We all know that's not true,' he said. 'We all know the company you've kept. The things you've... been involved in.'

Josten wanted to argue that one but he knew Chulders was right. He might be no baby killer but he'd run with men who were. And who'd done much worse.

'The War of Three Crowns is almost over,' Chulders continued. 'Anyone not fighting for Ozric will be on the losing side. Where else will you go? Across the Crooked Jaw? The Mercenary Barons are a spent force; you won't find riches there. Or you could always head north. I hear the death cults are looking for good men but you might have to sell them your soul before you get any coin in your pocket.'

'We'll work something out,' said Josten.

Chulders shrugged. 'Well, work something fast. It looks like you both need the money.'

It was a decent offer, and one Josten was close to accepting. Instead, he said nothing.

With a nod, Chulders stood and returned to sit with his companions.

'You know he's right,' said Mullen.

'He is. But do you want to run with him and men like Beckan? We've done enough pillage. We're fighting men, not murderers.'

Mullen snorted. 'We used to be fighting men, and well respected ones. Now we're mercenaries, in case you'd forgotten. And Ozric's gold is as good as anyone's.'

Josten fixed his friend in a serious gaze. 'The Battle of Han Tor? The Massacre of the Calamites? King Ozric is far worse than the others. And Chulders is talking out of his arse. There's no guarantee he'll win this war.'

'So where does that leave us?'

'I'm working on it,' said Josten before draining his tankard. 'And sitting around here's not going to solve the situation.'

He stood, grabbing his gear, and Mullen followed his lead. The ale had gone straight to his head as he made his way to the door, and when Beckan walked in from taking a piss outside he felt all the anger and frustration build.

Just ignore it, he told himself, *not worth the hassle.*

Mullen was behind him; he didn't need to worry about anyone watching his back. All he had to worry about was—

'Off to find some more babies to fucking kill?'

The words weren't even out of Beckan's mouth before Josten had reached for the knife he kept hidden at the small of his back. It was out of its sheath and buried to the hilt in Beckan's guts before Josten could even think it was a bad idea. He pushed Beckan back against the wall and blood spilled from the mercenary's mouth instead of more bullshit.

'No,' Josten said through gritted teeth, looking into

Beckan's dying eyes. 'I haven't killed any babies today. But I have killed one cunt.'

He could hear chairs scraping on wood behind him but couldn't bring himself to tear his eyes away from Beckan's, taking that unique pleasure you could only get from watching a man die and knowing you'd been the one to kill him.

'Ain't no more trouble lest you want it,' he heard Mullen say behind him.

Beckan's life ebbed and Josten pulled out the knife, letting the big mercenary slide to the floor, his eyes still pleading. He turned to see Mullen standing with his axe in his hands. Chulders and his two were also standing, weapons drawn.

'We're gonna walk out,' Josten said. 'You gonna try and stop us?'

Chulders thought on it a moment, then shook his head, lowering his blade.

'I reckon not,' he said.

Mullen and Josten backed out of the inn. Once outside they moved as quickly as they could down the street without running.

'And they say I'm the one without any brains,' said Mullen, when they were far enough to slow to a walk. 'As if enough people don't want us dead already.'

Josten could only shrug. 'What's a few more in the queue?'

Mullen looked at him, raising that bushy eyebrow of his. Then they both laughed so loud anyone passing must have thought them mad.

18

THE rain had turned Ballenheim into a mud-spattered mess. Everything was brown and black, and dour like the town's mood.

'What did we come to this craphole for?' said Mullen. Josten gritted his teeth against telling him to shut the fuck up. It had been his idea to come here after all. Back when King Stellan had been putting down Carnus Bollem's rebellion this had been a main hub for mercenaries to come and trade their services. Now it looked like the only thing traded here was horseshit and cabbages.

They hunkered under an awning that looked out onto the dead street. No one had come and told them to piss off, so for now it was theirs.

'We'll move on when we know which direction to move in. Do you want to spend another week walking the bloody hills?'

'I want to spend a night in a bed. That would be a start.'

Josten had to agree, but without any coin to pay for an inn, sleeping under the stars would have to do.

'We'll hear word on what's happening soon enough. We just have to wait a while until we do. Once we know who's best to fight for, and who's paying what, we'll head out.'

'There's war in all three fucking realms and we're stuck here shivering like shitting dogs. I knew we should have taken Chulders' offer.'

Josten was starting to think Mullen was right about that. Maybe they should just pick a direction and move off. Surely they'd find someone to take them on eventually. He was about to give in and tell Mullen to grab his gear and they'd get the hell out, when he caught sight of something down the road.

A group of dark-clad men moved up the street. There were five of them, all dressed the same, and in their midst was a woman. Her hands were bound behind her, and a gag was over her mouth. As they drew closer, Josten could see tears had streaked clean tracks across the filth on her face and she had a yellowing bruise over one eye.

He and Mullen watched as the men tramped past them through the muck and led the girl into the inn opposite.

'What do you reckon all that's about then?' Josten asked.

'Fuck do I know? Probably a criminal,' Mullen replied with disinterest.

'She doesn't look much like a criminal. What could a girl like that have done?'

'What does a criminal look like? Maybe that's why she's so good at being a criminal – she doesn't look like one. Unless you want me to go and ask? Or we could just mind our business and concentrate on what's gonna earn us some coin.'

Josten stood slowly. Mullen glanced up at him, frown creasing his bushy brow.

'Oh no,' he said. 'Not that look. That's the look that generally lands us in the shit.'

'I just want to see what's going on, is all.'

Before Mullen could tell him what a bad idea that was, Josten had walked from under the awning and across the street. He didn't even stop to kick the mud from his boots before stepping into the inn. It was filled with the usual dreck he'd come to expect from a town like Ballenheim – mostly pig farmers and turnip growers – but in the corner sat the men in black with their captive on the floor.

Josten stood in the shadows, avoiding the eyes of anyone bothered enough to take an interest in him, and watched as the innkeeper approached the men. One of them, with greasy hair and a nose like a hawk, spoke for the group. From what Josten could gather he wanted rooms for the lot of them and food. When the innkeeper tried to argue, maybe to say he was full, maybe to ask what they were doing with a helpless girl gagged and bound amidst them, the man in black mentioned Duke Gothelm. Josten saw the innkeeper grow more uncomfortable as the word 'tallymen' was used.

Josten found himself getting excited. Whoever this girl was, and whatever she'd done, it was Gothelm's business. And Gothelm was well known to be one of the richest dukes in all the Suderfeld. There was money here. Josten wasn't exactly sure how, but that girl was the key to it. That was all he needed to think about.

Still unseen in the dark, he waited until the man in black had finished telling the innkeeper what was what.

The old man grabbed a set of keys and led them up the staircase that ran up one side of the wall. Josten watched just long enough to see which room they put the girl in before he slipped out of the inn as quick and quiet as he'd slipped in.

'Satisfied, you nosey bastard?' asked Mullen as Josten took his place back beneath the awning.

Josten didn't answer. He watched the door to the inn. The more he thought about it, the more it made sense. He and Mullen had done some shitty things over the years but kidnap hadn't been one of them.

No better time to start than now, he reckoned.

'I'm starting to get worried,' Mullen said.

'Don't,' Josten replied. 'I think I've found the answer to all our problems.'

'Someone wants to hire us? Or you've just found a purse full of coins?'

'Better. I've found out who wants that girl.'

Mullen shifted uncomfortably. 'I know I'm going to regret asking this, but who?'

'Old Duke Gothelm.' Josten turned to Mullen, his grin beaming out of his face.

'No. You're not thinking what I think you're thinking? There's enough people trying to kill us as it stands. Now you want to go up against his tallymen and steal a prisoner from right under their noses?'

'That's pretty much the long and short of it, yes.'

'No. That's suicide. And even if we manage to spirit her away without getting stuck with cold steel, who's to say

153

Gothelm's going to pay us any coin for her? We don't even know what she's done.'

'Whatever it is, Gothelm's sent five of his best to collect her. I'd say he's pretty keen to have her. Maybe keen enough to make us rich.'

'Of all the stupid fucking things you've thought up over the years, this is by far the stupidest.'

'And it could well make us rich.'

'Well I'm out.' Mullen folded his arms in a determined fashion.

'No you're not,' said Josten.

'There's no way I'm doing this.'

'Yes there is.'

'I thought we were mercenaries, not kidnappers,' said Mullen sullenly.

Josten knew Mullen was right, but this just seemed too easy. And that girl looked like she was in for a rough time whatever they did. May as well try and make some coin from her before Gothelm did whatever Gothelm was going to do to the poor wretch.

They sat there in silence for a while as the sun went down. Josten kept his peace, just watching the door to the inn as Mullen grumbled about the growing cold and how empty his belly was. As night fell Josten stood, pulling the scarf from around his neck and tying it tight over his face to cover nose and mouth. He looked down at Mullen.

'You're gonna be the fucking death of me,' said the big man, rising and tying his own scarf tight about his face.

They moved across the muddy street, hidden in the dark.

Josten waited at the door, listening. There was no sound from inside and he tried the handle. Locked. He drew the knife at his back, sliding it between the door and the frame until it found the latch. With a twist he released it and the door gently swung open.

Inside, the inn's candles were burned down almost to the nub, but there was still enough light to see by. The place looked deserted as Josten and Mullen stepped across the floor as silent as the creaky floorboards would allow. They took the stairs, Mullen bringing up the rear, axe in hand. For his part Josten had no weapon in hand. He wasn't willing to kill anyone if he could help it. There was no point trying to persuade Mullen of the same; if someone pulled a blade on him they'd be taking a gamble on their lives – one that Mullen would prove a mistake.

Josten paused at the door he'd seen them take the girl into, listening in the dark. Someone was snoring inside. Nothing else.

He turned the handle gently, pushing the door open and letting the sound of snoring fill the inn. As his eyes adjusted to the dark he saw two men on the bed asleep. On the floor was the girl, hands bound, mouth gagged. In the dark he could see she was awake, staring at him. She looked at him fearfully, and Josten raised a finger to his lips before entering the room. When he was close enough he took her by the arm and lifted her gently to her feet.

Mullen was still standing in the doorway, wringing the haft of his axe nervously in both hands as Josten led the girl out. She made no move to stop him even though two masked men had just come to take her off in the night. He could see she was scared and didn't look a bit dangerous – not that it mattered. She was a way for them to get rich; dangerous or not they were taking her.

Josten led her into the dim light of the inn. He almost allowed himself a smile beneath that scarf – this had been easier than he thought – until he kicked something across the floor of the room.

It skittered with a metallic clang. A discarded tankard? Whatever it was it rang out like a bell, destroying the silence in an instant.

'Take her,' Josten said as the two tallymen stirred, rising from their beds.

Josten was on them before they could work out what was happening, his fist smashing one back onto his bed in the dark of the room. The second went for a sheathed sword but Josten was quicker, kicking it away before the man could grab it and smashing a knee into the side of his head.

With both men down, Josten ran out of the room. Mullen was already at the bottom of the stairs, dragging the girl after him. As Josten moved to the top of the stairwell, a door opened beside him. A tallyman appeared, eyes bleary, beard all bushy and black. There was a sword in his hand and Josten grabbed at the hilt before he could use it. He barged the man with one shoulder, slamming him into the doorframe, and wrested the sword from his grip, spinning it deftly. As he smashed the pommel into the tallyman's head it gave a hollow woody echo before he went down.

Mullen waited at the bottom of the stairs, brandishing his axe as Josten came after.

'Fucking move,' Josten said before he reached the ground floor.

Mullen pulled the girl towards the front door as Josten raced after him. He was almost across the bar when a tallyman jumped down from the balcony above, sword drawn, eyes keen – the hawk-nosed one who had done all the talking earlier.

Josten stopped before he ran straight onto a yard of sharpened steel. For a second he thought about going for his own blade but held his hands up instead. This man looked fast and serious. There was no doubt he'd go for a killing blow if Josten made a move.

Before either of them could think what to do next Mullen rushed in, axe flailing. The tallyman ducked, swinging around and backing up against the wall. Josten moved at the same time, grabbing his wrist and banging the blade against a wooden post. The tallyman looked in no mood to give in, gritting his teeth and glaring in fury. Josten's headbutt wiped the anger from his face, flattening his hawk nose as blood burst across his lips.

As the tallyman went down Mullen ran for the door, dragging the girl with him. Josten stuck close to their heels as they rushed out onto the muddy street.

'That went well,' Mullen said as they ran, and started laughing between his huffs for breath.

Josten stayed silent as they dragged the girl with them, in no mood to congratulate himself. Not yet, anyway.

19

THE sun had come up on the rough land somewhere north of Ballenheim, far enough into the wilderness that they'd be next to impossible to find. It was good enough for now.

Josten and Mullen sat next to one another watching the girl. She was sitting under a tree, hands still bound, gag still on. In the cold light of day Josten was beginning to think this had maybe been a stupid idea, but it was too late to turn back now. Best see this through to the end, whatever that might bring.

'What now?' Mullen asked, still staring at the girl.

Her black hair was matted, face a mess of blood and dirt. Josten was trying to convince himself she couldn't be dangerous, but then why else was Gothelm so dead set on getting his hands on her?

'I don't think she needs to have that gag on, do you?' Josten said.

Mullen glanced at him. 'So take it off then,' he replied.

'You take it off.'

They both sat in muted stalemate until Mullen eventually huffed and rose to his feet.

He approached the girl cautiously. Seeing him there,

big Mullen, not afraid of a thing in the world, treating this bound and gagged girl like a snarling dog, Josten realised the stupidity of it all. Mullen reached out gingerly and pulled the gag free from her mouth. Spit dribbled from one corner as she continued to stare. Josten couldn't tell if she was afraid or not. She looked more watchful than fearful, like she was done with terror and had moved on to assessing who'd taken her prisoner this time.

Mullen backed away and Josten rose to his feet. They both looked down at her again, with no idea about what to do.

'What now?' Mullen asked for the second time.

Josten took a step forward, feeling a little ridiculous for the fear he'd felt. He knelt down in front of the girl and looked into her eyes. Her face was blank.

'What's your name?' he asked. All he got in reply was that stare. 'Your name?' he repeated slowly. 'Do you understand the words I'm saying?'

'Maybe she's deaf,' Mullen said.

'Maybe she's foreign,' said Josten, trying to spot anything in the girl's expression that might give away she understood. 'She could be from beyond the Crooked Jaw.'

'She doesn't look foreign. Maybe she's just picky about who she talks to.' Mullen had clearly given up on trying to help.

'Why were you a prisoner?' Josten said to her. 'Why does Gothelm want you?'

Nothing.

'I don't think she's in much of a mood for chit-chat,' Mullen said, rubbing his hairy chin.

Josten stood, the feeling he'd made a massive mistake consuming him.

'Maybe we should just let her go?' he said.

Mullen looked at him, brows creasing into a single bushy mess. 'Are you out of your fucking mind? After what we went through to get her. What happened to getting rich?'

Money didn't seem massively important anymore as he looked at the girl, who mutely stared at him. 'We don't need to worry about the tallymen; they didn't see our faces. And there's no guarantee Gothelm will pay anything for her. Then what?'

'Then what nothing. We'll cross that bridge when we stumble onto it. Let's find out if he's willing to pay first, before making stupid decisions. I didn't risk my neck for a payday just to see it run off into the hills. We should at least eat before we make any rash decisions.'

Josten didn't want to argue. As Mullen went off to try and snare them a rabbit he built a fire. The girl watched him in silence all the while. It made him uncomfortable. He had no idea what the hell was going on with her, but whatever it was it unnerved him.

Mullen returned as the sun rose to its zenith in the pale sky, carrying a brace of coneys. He slumped down next to the fire and started to skin them. Josten constructed a makeshift spit from the wood that lay strewn beneath the tree and began to cook the rabbits. It was a well-drilled routine – only difference now was their silent audience.

When the rabbits were done they snapped the wooden spit in half and took one each. Mullen didn't hesitate, falling on his like a voracious bear. Josten paused, looking at the girl and seeing her lick dry lips.

He stood, tearing a leg off his rabbit, and moved towards her. She watched him approach, or rather watched the rabbit he brought within her reach. He moved to the back of her, pulling his knife and cutting the rope that bound her hands.

'Eat,' he said, offering the rabbit.

She stared at the meat all blackened by the fire, then looked up at him.

'Take it then.'

Still she stared.

Josten wasn't about to have a battle of wills with a young girl. It looked like she'd been through it but that wasn't his fault. If she didn't want to eat he wasn't about to waste good food.

'Suit yourself,' he said, taking a bite from the leg and moving back over to Mullen.

'Maybe it's your cooking,' Mullen said.

They both ate their rabbits in silence with the girl watching them.

Later, as they sat before a pile of bones, Mullen gave a deep sniff.

'What now?' he said.

Josten shook his head. It was the third time Mullen had asked him and he still had no idea. There was only one way tricky questions like this could be answered.

'Let her go or hold her for ransom, that's what,' he said, reaching into the purse at his side and pulling out a copper coin. It was the last one they had between them. With a flick of his thumb he sent the coin spinning.

Mullen snatched it from the air before it landed back in Josten's hand.

'No,' said Mullen. 'Not in the hands of the gods. There's a reward out there for her, one way or another. I reckon it would be a good idea to claim it.'

Josten stared at the girl who acted as though she couldn't understand a word they were saying.

'All right. Gothelm it is.' Josten rose to his feet. Mullen stood with him and they started to pack up camp.

'How are we doing this?' Mullen asked, kicking out the fire as Josten packed their meagre belongings. 'Send him one of her fingers?'

Josten frowned. 'What is wrong with you? We'll find Clancy. He was tight in Gothelm's court a few years back. He can send a message for us.'

'Yeah,' Mullen replied as though he'd just worked out a tricky sum. 'That would probably make more sense.'

Josten approached the girl. 'On your feet. There's a long walk ahead.'

She stood without complaint, a little unsteady.

'So she does understand,' said Mullen. 'Maybe she's just got no tongue.'

'I've got a bloody tongue all right,' the girl said.

Both men stopped in their tracks and stared at her. She stared back, defiant.

'What's your name, girl?' Josten said.

She paused, as though weighing the value of telling them.

'Livia Harrow,' she said.

'Well, Livia Harrow, there's a long walk ahead. And you're gonna wish you'd eaten some of that rabbit before we're halfway there.' He then gestured for her to start walking along the road.

She turned solemnly and made her way down the embankment towards it.

'That rabbit was overdone,' she said as she walked away.

Mullen barked a noisy laugh. 'See! I told you it was your cooking.'

Josten just shook his head. He could only hope Mullen would still be laughing after Gothelm received their message.

20

THEY hadn't got much more out of her on the walk north. Josten had asked what Gothelm wanted from her, why he'd sent five tallymen to bring her to him, but she remained tight-lipped. Either she didn't know or wasn't saying. What were they going to do, beat it from her? Josten and Mullen had done some questionable shit in their time but beating a young girl for information wasn't among it. Besides, it didn't matter. They were in deep now and whatever this girl had done wasn't the problem. Their main concern was sealing the deal without getting killed.

'How do you even know Clancy's going to be there?' said Mullen as they both kept an eye on the hedge.

'I don't. But last I heard Gothelm had ordered border keeps built all along the edge of his duchy. If we work our way along them we're bound to find Clancy eventually.'

Mullen nodded. 'That's as good a plan as any you've had in the past ten years.'

Josten wasn't about to get complacent. Gothelm's border ran for another forty miles northward. If they had to walk all that way before finding Clancy they'd be all but exhausted. That would be no good if they ran into trouble, or more tallymen, on the way.

'Right, let's move,' said Josten, keen to get on with business.

They set off down the road, Mullen bringing up the rear. The day brightened but it did nothing to bring up their spirits any. Despite the girl's poor condition she managed to keep up the pace and Josten found himself admiring her resilience. They passed one of the forts marking the border of Gothelm's duchy, keeping out of sight – it wouldn't do to get questioned before they'd had a chance to get paid for their prize, but the place looked all but deserted. Further on there was a farm that looked burnt-out. A lone donkey stood in a field. Mullen couldn't resist.

'Look at its face,' he said laughing. 'Reminds me of that ugly whore I banged in Cullington.'

Josten wasn't in the mood to reply that there'd been more ugly whores than either of them could count.

'Takes one to know one,' Livia said quietly.

Josten stopped, turning at the unexpected comment. Mullen stopped too, staring at her. Then Mullen burst out laughing.

Shaking his head, Josten led them on.

The next of the border forts looked like it had been besieged for a week. The walls were blackened; loose masonry lay all around a gaping hole in its midst. The three of them paused for a while to look for any signs of life. When they were confident enough that there was no one alive, Josten moved towards the fort, his curiosity getting the better of him. If there was trouble on the road ahead they needed to at least get an idea of what they faced.

The fort was gutted. A fire had raged through it, burning

165

the wooden floors up to the third storey. A discarded helmet and several weapons lay strewn about but there were no bodies.

'What do you think?' asked Mullen.

'I think we shouldn't hang around,' Josten replied, about to lead them off when he saw a wisp of smoke rising on the horizon. The road ahead would lead them right to it.

'That doesn't look good,' Mullen said, following Josten's line of sight.

Josten stood and looked. His initial reaction was to go around, but that could well add a day onto their journey.

'We don't have time to worry about it. Most likely just an old campfire. Let's press on.'

With that they set off, with Mullen grumbling all the way about how this was going to get them killed. Josten had heard that grumble a thousand times and they were both still alive. For now.

When they eventually reached the source of the fire they slowed, keeping to the hedgerow as they moved. The village was blackened; not a splinter of wood stood untouched. It must have been like a tinderbox when aflame, but now it was a silent, charred mess. There was no sign of who'd set the fires.

Josten moved from the bushes, walking slowly towards the carnage.

'What the fuck are you doing?' Mullen hissed, louder than most people shout. Then he followed, but then Mullen always followed.

Josten drew his sword, Mullen pulling his axe as they walked through the smoking remains of the village. There was a dead dog in the road; then a horse, entrails strewn, tongue lolling.

They moved to the centre of the village, not a sign of anyone until they reached the central square. It was a slaughterhouse. Men, women and children lay all about. Flies buzzed around staring eyes and wounds lay open, the blood long since dried to a thick black crust.

'Who do you think did it?' asked Mullen.

Josten shook his head. 'Castor Drummon to the east has been harrying Gothelm's territory. But it could be anyone. Maud Levar. Lorac's crew. Take your pick. Every one of them is bastard enough to leave a place in this state just for the hell of it.'

He looked around for as long as he could stomach. It wasn't the slaughter that bothered him, he'd seen plenty enough of that in his time. It was the memories it brought back. There was a time, not too long ago, when Josten Cade was part of a company that would have left a place in the same state as this and not thought twice on it. Even if Josten hadn't joined in with any of the slaughter, he'd still run with men who had. It was a time he'd sooner forget.

'Let's get out of here,' Josten said.

Mullen didn't need any further encouragement, picking his way northward through the bodies. Livia just stood in front of the village well. Josten hadn't even thought what she might feel about this. It was doubtful a girl so young had ever seen such horror.

'Let's go,' he said to her after moving closer.

Josten could see her eyes were fixed on an old man sitting with his back to the well. Someone had opened his throat and his head lolled back, eyes white and blank.

Just as Josten was about to give her a shake she moved after Mullen without a sound. He wasn't sorry to leave the dead village behind.

The road north continued to wend its way alongside the river that marked Gothelm's border. The sky grew ominously dark as though the rain were about to pour its misery on them but the clouds managed to hold out long enough for the next border fort to come into view. Josten allowed himself a smile of relief as he spied a scaffold constructed on one side of the circular building.

'This could be it,' he said.

'Right,' said Mullen, gripping his axe. 'Let's get down there.'

'No. I need you two to wait here.' Josten could see Mullen's disappointment. 'I'll handle Clancy. We need to approach this carefully.'

Mullen raised an eyebrow. 'Because you've done a great job of that so far.'

'We're still here, aren't we? We're not fucking dead yet?' Mullen had nothing smart to say to that. Josten moved on down the road towards the half-built fort.

As he got closer he could hear the clang of the mason's hammer and see men placing stone and levelling off mortar. Two spearmen wandered around the site, vigilant for anyone who might come and disturb the work. If whoever had levelled that last village passed by he doubted two men would be much defence.

When he was within a hundred yards, Josten felt his

heart beat that much faster. Clancy was there, reviewing parchments on a small table. His head was bowed, covered by a grey skullcap. Wispy beard dangled from his chin and his hessian smock looked filthy at the hem. Clancy had never put much store by his personal appearance.

Josten managed to walk within an arm's distance of Clancy before either of the two guards noticed him. They rushed over immediately, shouting their warnings, and Clancy turned, a comical look of surprise on his lined face. When he saw it was Josten he clutched his chest as though his heart had given out.

'It's all right,' said the old builder. 'I know this man.'

The guards lowered their spears, still eyeing Josten warily.

'Hello, Clancy,' Josten said. 'Long time.'

'Not long enough,' Clancy replied, shooing the guards away with one wrinkly hand.

'Don't be like that. There's a lot of water under the bridge since Hagenworth.'

'I almost got my neck stretched because of you.'

Josten smiled at the memory. 'And yet here you stand. Neck still the length it should be.'

Clancy smiled with him. 'How've you been, Cade?' He looked Josten up and down. 'Not had a great run of luck from the state of you.'

'No. But I'm hoping to change all that. And you can help.'

The smile fell from Clancy's face. 'Why do I have a bad feeling about this?'

'You have Gothelm's ear. I need you to pass a message

169

on. I've come into possession of something he wants. For a price I'm willing to give him what he's after.'

The colour in Clancy's face drained away as Josten spoke.

'You were the one who took the girl?'

Josten was surprised the news had travelled so fast. 'You've heard about that already?'

'Everyone this side of Eldreth has heard. If the tallymen catch you you're a fucking dead man, Cade. Are you bloody insane?' The builder thought on that for a moment. 'What am I saying – of course you're insane. Everyone knows that. But this time you've bitten off more than you can chew. Stealing a prisoner from the tallymen? Gothelm will see you swing for this.'

'That's why you have to persuade him what a reasonable man I am. There's a burned-out fort a few miles back along the river. I'll be waiting there in two days' time. Two hundred pieces of silver and she's his. Any sign of an ambush and she's dead, and so is anyone he sends. Is that simple enough, Clancy?'

'I can give him the message, Cade. Whether he goes for it—'

'Just do your best, old friend. That's all I ask.'

Clancy nodded. 'Two days. Two hundred silver. Seems simple enough.'

Josten gave the old man a nod before turning to leave, then thought better of it.

'Out of interest, why does he want the girl? She seems pretty ordinary to me.'

Clancy just shrugged. 'I have no idea. But he's willing

170

to kill to have her, I know that. So watch your bloody back.'

'Always do,' Josten said with a wink. Then he turned and took the road back towards Mullen and Livia.

The dark sky opened up before he was halfway back, peppering Josten's cloak and soaking it by the time he found them. When he reached the spot he'd left them in he could hear Mullen's deep voice resonating through the brush at the roadside. Then the girl laughed; a high giggle. It was the last thing Josten had been expecting.

As he drew closer he could see them sitting under a tree just off the road, Mullen holding his cloak over both their heads. He was treating her to one of his many bawdy stories – not the kind of thing you'd tell a slip of a girl, but she seemed to find it as funny as any mercenary.

Josten stepped out into the clearing and Mullen stopped his tale. Livia looked up, the smile dropping from her face.

'A word,' Josten said.

Mullen offered Livia an *I'm in the shit* expression, before leaving her his cloak and following Josten into the rain-spattered undergrowth.

'What the fuck are you doing?' Josten asked when they were out of earshot.

'Just a few stories to pass the time,' said Mullen innocently – he could be thick as a tree trunk sometimes. 'Where's the harm?'

'Where's the harm? You're laughing with her like she's the local serving wench. She's not someone for you to have a giggle with. She's two hundred pieces of silver. She's leverage. And if things don't go to plan we might have to slit her throat and leave her to bleed in the fucking road.'

Mullen frowned at him. 'I didn't—'

'No, you cocking didn't, did you? So I'm telling you – don't get attached. Whoever she is she'll be gone soon. The last thing I need is your judgement being dulled any more than it already is because you've developed a liking for her. I need you sharp. Is that understood?'

Mullen's face turned grave. 'I'm not a fucking idiot. Was just a couple of stories, that's all.'

With that he walked back to the clearing.

Josten watched him go with the feeling this wasn't going to be as simple as 'two days and two hundred silver'.

21

THERE was a feeling you got before battle. Dread, deep in the pit of your stomach. An overwhelming sense that this would be the day you died. It was something you always had to push aside, to stop you pissing in your trews or fleeing to the hills, screaming for your mother as you went. It was a feeling every man wrestled with before he had to take up arms and fight for his life.

Josten had that feeling now.

No great battles were being fought here today though.

He stood alone in the shadow of the derelict fort. A crow cawed in the distance. Josten's thumb flicked up the cross-guard of his sword – a sharp click as it was released, a smooth metallic ring as it fell back in place. Over and over his thumb worked as he stood in the damp air, waiting for their riches to come riding from the gloom. But was he just waiting for death?

Josten tried to put that thought out of his head. Best not to dwell on the bad. Better to think on how much coin he was about to make; better to keep a hand close to his blade. Thinking about the worst would shred a man's nerve.

Before he had the chance to properly consider what he

was doing, he heard riders coming through the mist.

Five horses trotted into view, slowing to a walk when they came within a few yards of the fort. Josten took a breath as they approached; black cloaked riders all staring at him. Josten recognised the one at their fore – the one whose nose he'd flattened back in the inn. His hair hung down in greasy locks, eyes blackened, a bandage across his face. He must have been pissed off at Josten, but there was still no reading his expression as he nudged his horse forward. The other four riders spread out, hands close to their weapons. One of them had a small casket resting on his saddle.

'That's close enough,' Josten said. Best to let them know who was in charge early on. He needed to lay out his terms and keep control. 'Is that my silver?'

'Where's the girl?' said the one with the bandaged nose.

Josten regarded him carefully. Obviously he was in charge, though he looked the youngest of the group. It was clear none of the others would make a move unless this one said so.

'What's your name, son?' Josten asked.

The young man regarded him for a time before relaxing a bit in his saddle.

'I'm Randal Weirwulf. And you are?'

For a moment Josten wondered if it was worth the lie, but chances were Clancy had already told Gothelm whom he was dealing with. That was why he hadn't bothered covering his face with a scarf.

'Josten Cade. I'm guessing you already knew that.'

Randal nodded. 'That we did. Thought I'd ask anyway. Now where's the girl?'

'She's not far. Do you have my silver?'

Randal glanced across at the tallyman with the casket, then back at Josten. 'I'd really like to see the girl.'

'I'm sure,' said Josten, thumb hovering beneath the cross-guard of his sword, ready to flick it up at the slightest provocation. 'And you will. Just as soon as I've got my silver.'

Randal smiled, his eyes shining. 'You really have no idea what you've got, do you, Cade?'

'I was hoping I had two hundred silver, but right now I only see a closed casket.'

Randal glanced around, searching for something. He took in the derelict fort, the river in the distance, and then looked back at Josten.

'Where's the other one?' he asked. 'There were two of you.'

'Where do you think? He's taking care of our prize. So hand over my silver and we can get this done with.'

Randal stared at him, a wry smile on his face. Josten hardly knew this little fucker and he already hated him.

'So I hand over your pay and let you walk away, and trust you to just send her back to me?'

'That's the only way this goes. If I don't return in one piece my associate opens her throat and no one gets anything.'

Randal nodded knowingly. 'I see.' He looked to the tallyman with the casket on his saddle and nodded. The tallyman lifted the casket and threw it on the ground in front of Josten. By the way it bounced it didn't seem quite as full as he'd hoped.

Carefully Josten stepped forward, kneeling down and

flicking the clasp on the casket. The lid creaked open and Josten held his breath all the while. He exhaled in a panicked huff as he saw Clancy's severed head staring up at him.

A sword rang from a scabbard, heels kicked a horse and it galloped forward, but Josten was already moving. The thud of hooves on the damp earth followed him as he ran towards the fort.

'Mullen!' he screamed as he ran, at any moment expecting to feel the hard impact of a sword against the back of his head.

There was the crisp *thwap* of a crossbow being fired. The bolt shot from within the broken confines of the fort, whipping past Josten's head. He heard the dull strike, the whinny of an animal in pain, before he reached the edge of the fort and dived over broken masonry and into the dark.

He looked up to see Mullen already cranking the string of the crossbow, eyes scanning for the next target. No one came. Josten scrambled to his feet, wrenching his sword free, his breath coming hard.

'Again, things haven't exactly gone to plan,' said Mullen.

Josten resisted thanking Mullen for his unfailing ability to point out the fucking obvious.

They waited in the shadows of the fort, scanning the mist, waiting for the tallymen to come running. Nothing. The wind blew in, swirling the grey fog, and Josten caught sight of the horse Mullen had shot lying dead, the quarrel pointing up from its neck. He gave silent thanks for the lucky shot.

'Cade?' Randal's voice rang out through the mist.

'There's nowhere for you to go. Five against two is poor odds. Just send out the girl and we'll let you live.'

Josten glanced at Mullen, who just shrugged his big shoulders. Even if he believed Randal would honour his proposition, they didn't have Livia with them.

'Why don't you come in and get her?' Josten shouted back.

There was no reply.

'What now?' Mullen asked.

Josten glared at the morning mist. The longer they stayed the more chance Randal had of sending for more men. Maybe they were already coming. Maybe they were already here, waiting out there in the mist ready to strike. Either way, he and Mullen were dead if they stayed here much longer.

'We make a run for it,' Josten said.

Mullen nodded, his eyes going wide as he wound himself up for the fight.

'So much for your old friend Clancy,' Mullen breathed through clenched teeth.

'I don't think this is Clancy's fault,' Josten replied, remembering the waxy face staring up at him from within the casket.

'On three?' Mullen said.

Josten tightened his grip on his sword. 'On three.'

'One,' said Mullen, fingers clenching on his crossbow.

'Two,' said Josten, bouncing on the balls of his feet as he prepared to leap through the breach in the fort.

Before they could get to three there was a cry of rage. Three tallymen burst through the mist with swords raised.

An arrow flew past them both, narrowly missing Josten's head and clattering off nearby masonry.

Mullen aimed his crossbow, trying to track one of the charging tallymen in his sights. He wasn't quick enough, blurting a curse as he stumbled back from a sweeping sword, his quarrel flying off into the misty morning.

Josten braced himself behind the crooked masonry as the first swordsman came running. The man growled as he jumped over the wall, and Josten ducked his sword, dipping his shoulder and tipping the tallyman over his back. The second attacker came in from the side and Josten struggled to parry his incoming blow.

More arrows came flying, missing friend and foe alike. Josten parried two more blows before planting his fist in the tallyman's face, knocking him back over the wall of the fort. He turned in time to see the other one rising to his feet. The tallyman looked up, eyes widening, before Josten hacked down, splitting the man's skull and sending blood spurting down his face.

Mullen had grappled his opponent up against the wall of the fort and was headbutting him despite the man already being unconscious.

'Let's get the fuck out of here,' Josten barked, grabbing Mullen's coat at the shoulder and pulling him away. Mullen let the tallyman drop, his face a bloody mess, and they both vaulted over the broken wall of the fort as more arrows rained down.

Josten staggered through the mist, trying to find where the arrows were coming from. Suddenly he spied another tallyman on horseback, bow in hand. An arrow whistled past them as they ran and Josten made straight for him as the bowman desperately pawed at the quiver on his saddle. Before he could nock, Josten had a hold of his leg, dragging him from the horse. Mullen was at his side, axe drawn. Josten didn't look as he mounted the horse, but he heard the dull crack of the axe against the bowman's skull.

Mullen jumped up behind as Josten pulled on the reins, showing the beast who was in charge before it could become skittish and bolt. With a last look around for more enemies he dug his heels in and the horse galloped off, hooves making slick divots in the soft earth.

They galloped as far as they could, following the river, the horse snorting plumes and struggling under the strain of two riders. At any moment Josten expected that bastard Randal to come tearing at them through the mist, sword held high, but no one appeared. When he was satisfied they weren't being pursued he slowed to a trot.

They were a mile away from the fort now, not far from the small copse where they'd left Livia. The men dismounted and walked the horse to within the tree line. Livia was still there, tied to the trunk of an oak.

Josten stopped them some yards away, letting go of the horse's reins and letting it breathe deep as it whickered in the shadows.

'What now?' said Mullen.

Josten turned on him. 'I wish you'd stop fucking saying that. Like I've got all the answers. What do *you* think we should do now?'

Mullen took Josten's anger with a blank expression. Then looked over to where the girl was. 'Maybe we should be rid of her and then get the fuck out of here.'

He placed a hand on his axe, stained with blood.

Josten glanced over to Livia. He could just see her through the trees, filthy and bedraggled, her hair hanging in dark strands, face a bruised mess. His thumb flicked up the cross-guard of his sword. Then he let it fall back into the sheath.

'Go on then,' he said.

Mullen pulled his axe free. Josten felt something tighten in his gut. A hundred memories of what he'd seen, of what he'd done, came flooding back. For a moment he almost reached out and grabbed Mullen's arm, but he didn't need to. The big man just looked over to where the girl was tied. Then shook his head.

'Do your own shitty work,' he said, putting the axe away and turning back to where the horse was grazing.

Josten left him, moving through the trees to the clearing where Livia waited. He pulled the knife at the small of his back, considering the keen edge of the blade for just a moment before he cut her free.

She looked at him as though she were about to ask why they weren't laden down with silver. Instead she stayed silent.

'Let's go,' Josten said, as Mullen led the horse into the clearing.

With that the two men started to walk off northwards. Josten stopped before they'd made it ten yards and turned. Livia was staring at them.

'You coming?' Josten asked.

A smile crossed her dirty face. 'What the bloody hell else am I going to do?' she said, before following them through the trees.

The nomads of the Cordral Desert began worshipping the constellations millennia ago, relying on them to navigate the oceans of sand. This tradition endured, even after the Fall, and though the introduction of agriculture has meant the Cordral is no longer the perilous wasteland it once was, their observance is still maintained.

Each constellation represents one of the ancient gods of the desert, making up an ancient pantheon that circles the world, locked in an eternal struggle for dominance over the heavens. The constellations themselves are grouped into Cardinals containing three celestial bodies that exist coterminously.

The gods of the Northern Cardinal are Sol, Lilith and the Unnamed. Sol shines brighter than any other star, a yellow beacon perpetually pointing north. Lilith is a tiny blue star and the Unnamed a distant red, constantly circling her. Legend tells that Lilith was the most beautiful being in the heavens, admired by all men, but jealous Sol forced her to wear a mask so that no other could covet her splendour. Despite her hidden beauty, the Unnamed took her as a lover, until Sol stole her away. Still, the Unnamed pursues Lilith across the heavens in an endless, but ultimately vain, quest to claim her heart.

In the Eastern Cardinal sit the Scorpion Vermitrix and her sister Essena the Serpent. They are a constant plague on Halbor, the wise old wanderer shining yellow and bright in the eastern sky. It is said the sisters infect Halbor with their venom each night, stopping him from *showering his wisdom on the earth, keeping the lands of men in constant ignorance.*

The Western Cardinal is home to the Fool and the Fallen King, their names lost in the annals of time. These twin stars are often mistaken for each other, so closely do they sit amongst the heavens, often appearing as a single star. In legend, the Fallen King allowed the Fool to sit atop his throne but so alike were they that the court mistook the Fool for their liege, and now the King must forever watch his usurper make a mockery of his celestial kingdom. Around them both revolves Anural the Cup Bearer, serving both Fool and King with equal reverence.

Finally, the Southern Cardinal consists of the white stars Vane the Hunter and Karnak the Reaver, separated by the All-Mother. As Vane and Karnak fight in their eternal battle, so does the All-Mother try and bring peace. But distracted by her squabbling sons' fight, the All-Mother's task to bring harmony throughout the lands is a futile one.

– *A History of the Cordral Extent*, Sebastius Hoight

†

22

The Cordral Extent, 105 years after the Fall

SHE had slept for too long. The bed was empty, the sheets crumpled and sweat-moistened. Silver ran her hand over the mattress where Garvin had left an indent of his broad back. She should have smiled at the memory of him, of how they had become entwined in each other the night before, their breath coming in heightened gasps. But that memory was overshadowed by the nightmare, as always.

It still fluttered on the periphery of her mind, teasing her like a fly she couldn't quite catch, although this morning it was more vivid than the previous. Every day Silver had realised she remembered more – *the violence and blood, the screaming in rage, the ecstasy...*

It should have horrified her. Should have brought her to tears but it didn't.

It thrilled her.

To Silver's shame she knew that thrill was more intense than anything Garvin could give her, their bodies as one, him inside her, her legs wrapped about his hips, pulling him deeper. A nightmare she could barely remember stirred her more than being in her lover's arms, and for that she could never forgive herself. Not that she would ever have told him.

She shared her bed and her body with Garvin, but the passion of her nightmares was hers and hers alone.

Silver took a breath before rising from the bed, stretching the sleep from her limbs, feeling the strength in them. She clenched her fists, tensing the muscles of her arms and shoulders, delighting in how healthy she felt. Her first memories had been of weakness and pain before Garvin and the boys had found her. That weakness was now distant, ephemeral. It was as if she had always been powerful, always as strong as she was in her dreams.

She dressed quickly and walked into the kitchen, smiling at the eggs Garvin had left for her on the skillet. Despite how strong she had become he always cared for her as though she was some kind of timid maiden. It was why he had allowed her to sleep. He knew her nights were troubled and he let her lie in long after she should have been awake and helping in the field. She could only love him all the more for that.

As she ate the eggs and washed them down with a drink from the pail, more memories of her dreams came back: a field of carnage, angels and demons battling before a great cerulean tower. Silver had cut a swathe through them, fighting her way towards the massive edifice. There was a yearning within her to reach that tower, but whatever its origin she had no idea. Even now, in the quiet of the kitchen she still felt that need.

She was suddenly glad of the banality of the day, of the ordinary house and the tedious work she did. It served to ground her from the elation of her dream state; a remedy for her nightly communion.

Somewhere she could hear the boys laughing. It made her smile; usually they only bickered. As much as she would have liked to join them Silver knew she couldn't leave Garvin to the field on his own. He would never have complained had she decided to spend a day with his sons, but there was something about the field, and working it by his side, that she looked forward to. More of that banality perhaps? Knowing that the violence of her dreams was make-believe, that this was reality and she should embrace it. This was her life now, whatever her dreams showed her – whether visions of a stark future or distant memory.

Silver left the house. A basket sat on the porch and she placed it over her shoulder, picking up the sickle that lay beside it.

Garvin waved as she approached the field. She waved back, watching as he held the sickle loosely in his hand and stretched out his back, flexing his broad shoulders.

'Hello,' he said when she came closer, his white teeth seeming to glint in the sunlight.

'Hello back,' she replied.

They looked at one another for a moment. Mutual appreciation. Neither seeming embarrassed of their attraction to the other. They were past that now. The previous night she had felt closer to him than ever, and she knew he felt the same.

'You let me sleep too long again,' she said.

'I know,' Garvin replied. 'But you seemed to be so settled this morning. It wasn't right to disturb you.'

Silver knew that was only a half-truth. Lately her dreams

had become so intense that they took something from her. Stripped her of vigour if she rose early with him. It was sweet that he would allow her the extra hours in bed.

'Did I wake you in the night again?' she asked.

'Only once. You spoke but I couldn't understand you. I'd love to know what makes you so animated.' He raised an eyebrow suggestively.

'I don't know,' she lied. 'I never remember my dreams.'

'Shame. It would be nice if you could share them with me.'

Nice? Silver thought that was the last thing they would be. Best if Garvin was ignorant of what she dreamed. He might think her insane if he ever found out.

'Anyway,' he said, hefting the sickle. 'This field won't tend itself.'

'Indeed not,' she replied, moving alongside him.

For the rest of the morning they worked the field side by side, making a deep furrow in the lush flora. Each time they filled a basket they would tie it into a sheaf, leaving it standing on the shorn ground. It didn't take long for Silver's row of sheaves to be almost twice as long as Garvin's, her energy seeming to know no end. It was always the same, but if this ever dented his pride he never showed it.

They worked long into the afternoon until their bodies were slick with moisture. Something about the sweat on his body and the smell of his labours made Silver want Garvin all the more. She could have taken him right then and there in the field, but she knew Fenn and Darrick might not be far away.

When they had finished they collected the sheaves into bails, strapping them to their backs and carrying them to the farmhouse where they were stored in the shed. Inside the house the boys were waiting, Darrick busying himself with his chores while Fenn greeted Silver with a wide smile.

'Hello, Ma,' he said.

'Hello, Fenn,' she said, returning his smile and ruffling his hair as she went to wash.

It had not taken long for Fenn to start calling her 'Ma'. At first she had felt awkward with it, the naming seeming even more unfamiliar than 'Silver'. But Garvin had not seemed to mind and she had grown fond of Fenn – a fondness that left an ache in her chest. If it brought a smile to the boy's face she was happy for him to say it.

For his part, Darrick gave her a nod as she passed by. Garvin's eldest son had been somewhat less ready to accept Silver as his mother. He made no complaint, showed her no disrespect, but it was clear he was not ready to open up to her. He was a guarded child, never showing any feelings other than when he snapped at his younger brother.

When she had washed the dirt of the field from her body, Silver set about making them all a stew from goat and dried fruit they had purchased from a farmer at the trading post. The smell filled the small kitchen and made her stomach grumble in anticipation. She had become quite the cook in the past weeks, or at least she thought. Garvin and the boys had made no complaint. In fact Garvin had commented several times on how they ate better now than they ever had. Silver could only doubt the truth of that.

When the boys had eaten and taken to their beds, Silver cleared their dishes as Garvin slumbered in a chair. Afterwards she opened the door to the farmhouse and stepped outside into the balmy night, feeling restless.

The stars shone brightly, a million lights in the sky, fires burning in the distance. Garvin put little store by religion but he had told her they were the souls of the gods; twelve beings set in the sky to watch over the world, but who were so preoccupied with their own squabbles they ignored the lands of men, for the most part. He had laughed when he told her that story. They both knew it was nonsense. Whatever those stars were they were not gods. Silver knew the gods still lived, she saw them every night in her dreams.

'You must be tired.'

Silver turned to see Garvin watching from the doorway.

'A little,' she replied. She wasn't tired at all.

He walked forward, standing close behind her and wrapping his arms around her. She held his forearms, feeling the muscle there, knowing his embrace was a gesture of love, to reassure her. To keep her safe. Silver knew there was nothing for her to fear out here. The only danger this night, in this desert, was her.

'Your dreams have become... more intense,' said Garvin.

That took her by surprise. He had never made a point of discussing her nightmares beyond the odd casual comment.

'How so?' she asked.

'I had to rise early – you were thrashing in your sleep. I thought you were going to attack me at one point.' He

189

grinned, an attempt to laugh off the comment but she could tell he was concerned.

'I'm sorry, you should have woken me,' she replied. 'Why didn't you tell me earlier?'

Garvin shrugged, gazing up at the stars with her. Perhaps he was thinking about an old legend regarding the All-Mother or the Fallen King or some other dead god. Perhaps he was wondering what he had allowed into his home. Into his bed.

'We've never talked about where you came from,' he said. 'I've been avoiding it. Maybe your dreams are the key to finding that out.'

Silver grew uncomfortable in his arms. It felt as though he was judging her for the first time. She felt guilty; he had every right to question her origins, but she couldn't help but feel anger well up within her.

'I thought the past didn't matter. I thought this was our life now and that was all that mattered.' She turned to him and could see his brow furrowed in the light of the moon and stars.

'It is all that matters,' he said. 'But I want to help you.' He was staring into her eyes now, an intense look she had never seen before.

'I don't need help,' she said, placing a hand on his chest and pushing him away. Too hard. Garvin stumbled back, looking shocked at her strength.

He stared at her, fear and hurt playing across his strong features before he shook his head and turned back towards the door.

'I'm sorry,' she said, rushing forward and taking his arm,

careful to hold it firmly but gently. He stopped and looked down at her.

'I understand how you feel,' he said. 'I understand how confused you must be. I understand why you're angry.'

'I know,' she said, placing her hand gently on his chest. She smiled at him, knowing that Garvin did not understand. How could he know what she saw in her dreams? How could he ever understand the thrill? How she fed off the feelings of might, of power? She could never tell him of it, could never make him understand. And even if she tried it would only make him think her more inhuman than he already did. That was the last thing Silver wanted.

He stared into her eyes, as though seeing something in them he had never seen before. 'You know I've fallen—'

She grabbed the collar of his shirt and pulled him close, kissing him firmly before he could say anything else. There was no reason for him to say the words. No reason for either of them to speak.

23

Fᴇɴɴ sat on Silver's lap, reading from one of Garvin's tattered books. She marvelled at his skill with the words – only six summers and able to read so quickly and deftly. Silver could hardly decipher a single word. Whatever she had been before she arrived at the Longfeather farm it had not been a scribe.

Though the boys would always be farmers out in this grim land, Garvin had still seen the importance of them learning their letters and sums. Less chance they'd be swindled when they made the trip to the trader's post in Stafkarl. If it was known the Longfeather boys were educated, even just knew how to read, it would put them above most of the other farmers and traders in the Kantor region.

'Do you want a go?' Fenn asked suddenly, stopping his story and looking up at her curiously.

Silver smiled. 'I'm no good with the letters,' she said. 'But I like listening to you.'

'I could teach you,' he said. Silver found herself giving him a tender squeeze at that. Fenn's nature was sweet, an oasis in this harsh, unforgiving place, and it filled her with a warmth she would never have been able to describe even if she'd known all the words in all the books of the world.

Before she could tell Fenn how pointless it was, he climbed down off her knee and hurried to a chest in the corner of the room. It opened with a creak and he began to rummage inside. Finally he found what he was looking for and turned. Silver saw he held a piece of parchment in his hand along with a tattered feather and a bottle of ink.

'Fenn, I'm not sure that—'

'It's all right,' he said, hurrying back to stand beside her. 'Da doesn't use it for nothing.' He placed the parchment before her on the table. 'He'll like it if you learn your letters.'

Fenn twisted the lid off the bottle of ink and placed it down carefully, afraid of spilling the precious black liquid. Silver could only imagine how expensive it was, feeling a sudden flash of admiration at Garvin's investment in his sons.

'Start with 'A'. Then we'll go through the rest.' He carefully dipped the quill and handed it to her, staring in anticipation.

Silver felt the futility of this in her gut, but she took the quill anyway. She stared at the parchment, realising she had no idea what an 'A' looked like.

Fenn picked up the book they had been reading and pointed to one of the letters.

'That one,' he said helpfully.

Silver replicated it on the parchment as best she could, feeling a sense of satisfaction when she had it almost right.

Fenn made an encouraging noise and said, 'Do a 'B' now.'

Again he pointed at a letter in the book, and again Silver drew the sigil on the parchment. On they went, working their way through the alphabet with Fenn growing more eager with every letter. For her part, Silver found it easier as they worked through the letters, focusing on replicating each one. And with each letter she seemed to glean some kind of strange understanding... perhaps a memory, perhaps a knowledge she had kept hidden.

When they reached the final letter, Fenn gave a little clap of his hands. 'Now try a word,' he said. 'Try writing "cat" or something.'

He took a seat at the other side of the table as Silver stared at the parchment. Then she closed her eyes, taking a deep breath, thinking of the letters that would make up the word.

She dipped the quill in the ink once more and pressed it to the parchment. Her hand seemed to move of its own accord, the ink marking sigils, swirling across the page as though the quill had a mind of its own. Silver wrote from instinct, the words coming fast, the quill scratching its way across the yellowed paper, the script spidery.

When she had finished, a verse was written on the parchment in no language she could understand. She very much doubted it said 'cat'.

'What's that?' Fenn asked, frowning at the strange words on the paper.

'I—' she stopped at the sound of Garvin's footsteps on the porch.

Silver stood, grasping the parchment and its strange verse and crumpling it in her fist. There was no need for Garvin to see what she had done – he was curious enough about her past without this adding to his confusion. And besides, she had no answers; the words were a mystery.

Garvin entered, his face grave. Fenn stood to greet his father.

'Da,' said the boy. 'You should see what Silver—'

'Fenn, go and play,' Garvin said.

The boy turned to look at Silver but she said nothing, glad that Garvin had stopped his son before he could say anymore. Without a sound Fenn walked from the kitchen and out into the sunshine.

'What is it?' Silver asked, reading Garvin's troubled expression.

'The crop is failing,' he said, the gravity of it clearly weighing heavy on his shoulders. 'We might be able to sell about half, but the rest is rotten. We'll need to burn it all. I can't tell if it's some kind of pestilence, but we're in trouble.'

Silver crossed the kitchen, putting her arms around him. 'It's still early in the season,' she said. 'We could plant another crop.'

'It'll be hard work,' he replied.

'Neither of us is a stranger to that. And the boys will do everything they can to help.'

Garvin nodded. 'Maybe if we can sell what we have in Stafkarl there'll be enough grain to plant a new crop.'

'It'll be all right.' Silver raised her hand, placing her palm against his cheek. Her other hand held tight to the parchment crumpled within it.

Garvin smiled. 'You're right,' he said. 'It'll be all right. As long as I have you.'

They kissed, and she felt him relax as her lips touched his.

'I'll take what we have to market,' she said. 'We both know I'm the strongest.'

Garvin opened his mouth to argue but thought better of it. He knew she was right.

'I'll pack the cart,' he said. 'You should put some supplies together for the trip.' He made to walk away then turned back to her. 'Just remember not to let Oynar swindle you on the price.'

She smiled at him as he made his way towards the barn. She still held the crumpled parchment in her fist, but there was no time to wonder about the mystery of the foreign words she'd written.

There were more pressing matters.

⁜

Stafkarl was busier than Silver expected. As she pulled the cart into the street, piled high with maize, there was a bustle about the place that surprised her.

Men and women rushed across the main thoroughfare, kicking up dust in their wake, seeming not to see Silver as she made her way towards the trading post. Several times she had to stop rather than trip over a panicked settler. And everywhere she looked there seemed to be militia roaming the streets. No wonder brigands were roaming free to pillage outlying settlements when all the fighting men were here, guarding the dust.

Silver left the cart and its payload – with everyone in such a panic it was doubtful someone would make the effort to steal a pile of crops. The door to the trading post creaked open as she pushed it, and a bell jangled as she entered then let the door sweep shut behind her. She waited in the quiet, but the traders who owned the place didn't appear.

'Hello?' she shouted.

There was movement somewhere, before a small man appeared, red-faced and flustered.

'What do you want?'

Silver guessed this was the 'Oynar' Garvin had warned her about.

'I have wares to trade,' she said.

The man seemed to grow angry. 'Are you mad? You want to make a trade now? Everyone's leaving the outpost. You should do the same.'

'Leaving? Why?' she asked.

'You haven't heard? Raiders are abroad,' said the old man. 'Reports from all along the eastern extent, from the foot of the Crooked Jaw to Ardenstone. Half a dozen farms burned to ash.' He paused, eyes growing weary. 'No survivors.'

Silver stared. A feeling of sickness rose up within her. The Longfeather farm was on the eastern extent. She took a step back from the counter, the periphery of her vision blurring.

White wings flecked with blood, a scream of pain matched by one of triumph. Her throat was hoarse with the effort of it. Red eyes burned with hate. Death lay all around, carcasses pledged in victory.

Silver inhaled sharply, staggering back.

'Are you all right?' asked the old man.

'I'm sorry,' she said, her breath coming quick.

She staggered back further, fumbling at the door handle

before wrenching it open. The little bell jangled once more in her wake as she tumbled out onto the porch and stumbled down the stairs.

The street was still busy as she took a deep breath. No one gave her a second glance.

Her head throbbed with a burning pain, as though blood ran molten behind her eyes. Vision blurred at the edges, a scene of violence she couldn't quite focus on.

'You there.'

Silver turned at the voice, squinting to see who had spoken. A grey-haired man atop his horse, staring angrily. She recognised him through the cloud of fog at the edge of her eyes... Hedren.

'What are you doing here?' he said. 'Where are Garvin and the boys? They need to get to safety.'

'I... They...'

Silver staggered, steadying herself against the cart.

'What's wrong with you?' asked Hedren, struggling to keep control of his horse. The beast seemed agitated in Silver's presence, its eyes wide, nostrils snorting its disquiet.

Blackness.

There was a scream in Silver's head. The pain of it was so intense she grasped at her hair with numb fingers.

Garvin. The boys. A feeling of cold dread piercing her like a spear.

'What's wrong with you?' barked Hedren. 'I asked you a—'

Silver reached forward, the pain in her head relenting in that instant of motion. She pulled Hedren from his saddle, the cloth of his shirt tearing as he was sent crashing into the cart behind her.

The horse reared, squealing in panic, ready to bolt. Silver grasped the reins, dragging the beast's head down. She stared into its eye and they were locked in each other's gaze. The stallion stopped its mewling, muscles quivering in fear, letting out a single snort from its nostrils.

Then she leaped up onto its back, her feet finding the stirrups, heels kicking its flanks. It bolted along the street and Silver felt herself relax into the rhythm of its run as though she had ridden a thousand horses through the desert. It was a memory she could not quite grasp, as though it floated in her periphery.

But the mystery of it didn't matter now.

Her family was in danger.

She had to reach the farm in time.

24

THE horse was faltering, snorting and stumbling beneath her, but she urged it on. Her heels dug deep into the creature's flanks if it tried to slow and she could see the fear in its wide-open eyes, sense the terror at having her atop its back.

Silver could not relent, could not allow the beast any respite, even if she rode it into the dirt.

As she saw smoke drifting on the horizon her panic and fear intensified. The Longfeather farm was aflame. Garvin and the boys were in terrible danger.

Silver kicked frantically at the horse. She could hear every one of its laboured pants and smell the stench of its salty hide. The animal was close to falling but its fear of her kept it moving. Silver could barely understand the power she had over the beast but she was not about to question it.

As the horse crested the rise to the Longfeather farm it gave a last pained whinny, forelegs buckling. It tumbled to the ground and Silver deftly rolled clear, coming to her feet and sprinting over the rise.

A scene of horror confronted her. The farmhouse and store

shed were still burning, though the embers were low. On the hill, beside the recently ploughed field, lay their mule, its entrails strewn about, head half lopped off, blood drying in the dust.

Silver reached the bottom of the hill and in her panic she lost her footing, stumbling to her knees. She stopped, pausing for air, her breath coming as short and sharp as that of the steed that had carried her from the outpost.

Despite the horror, she had to stay in control. The bandits could still be in the area and still be eager for a fight. If the boys were still alive, if there was any chance she might rescue them, she had to keep her head.

Slowly Silver rose to her feet, hands shaking as she looked around the devastated farm. She walked past the farmhouse, and didn't have to go far before she spotted Garvin's body.

All thoughts of control suddenly fled. A cry of anguish left her throat as she rushed forward, crossing the hard earth until she was within five yards of him. Then she stopped.

He lay on his front, head skewed to one side, the blood having pooled, then dried, beneath him in a dark halo. Silver felt her jaw clamp shut as she took a step toward him, his once-shining eyes staring at her blankly. She knew he was dead, there was nothing she could do for him now, but still she had to touch him.

As she crouched down beside her lover's corpse all she could think was that she would never feel him against her again, never hear his impassioned whisper in her ear, and she reached out her hand towards him.

Memories flashed through her mind as she touched his bare skin; not her memories, or memories of a dream of battling demons in a distant land. These were something else…

Garvin brought the scythe down in a steady rhythm, sweeping the sheaf of maize in two, every stroke at the same level. He looked out over the field, the mid-morning sun beating down, making him squint. Not far to go and he would be finished. One more row and the field would be done.

A footstep through the scythed maize. Garvin turned: a bearded face, pocked skin, eyes wide and dark. A weapon, raised high.

Garvin brought up the scythe, catching the blade on its haft with a dull clank. His attacker hissed. Garvin clouted the wild man against the jaw, sending him reeling and he stumbled, losing his footing on the uneven earth and tumbling to the dirt.

He lay on the ground, staring up, angry and desperate, all yellow teeth and viciousness. Garvin thought about letting him run away, letting him live. He had never killed a man before and didn't want to start now, so late in life.

On the ridge above his farm, Garvin saw more figures coming… running. Raiders.

Garvin raised his scythe high and brought it down. The blade sheared through flesh, burying itself in the bandit's chest. He abandoned it, turning, desperate, sprinting back towards the farmhouse.

The boys came running at his panicked cries. He screamed at them both, howling at them to flee. It crushed his heart to see the looks on their faces but they had to run. Their fear might be the only thing that could save them.

As his sons ran in the opposite direction, Garvin stopped. They would not be able to run far enough through the desert before the bandits caught them. Garvin knew he had to buy his boys time.

He turned; even with no weapon he was determined to harry the bandits as much as he could, even if it meant his—

The blade cut deep into his side. The bandit stared at him as he twisted the knife and Garvin's breath came out in a long pained sigh. This raider did not look wild or manic. His face was shaved, one eye glassy from the scar that ran down from forehead to cheek.

He drew out the blade slowly, and Garvin felt every last inch. He wanted to fight but all the strength had left him. On his knees he could do nothing but watch as the bandits raced after his sons, two of them stopping to kick in the door to the farmhouse.

Up on the ridge he could just see his boys running before he pitched forward into the dirt. The blood ebbed from his body. There was nothing he could do to stop it...

Silver reeled from the vision, sobbing into the dirt. Her hand trembled over Garvin's body but she dare not touch him again lest it show her more.

Tears streamed down her cheeks as she stood. She had to find the boys.

Garvin had last seen them fleeing towards the ridge and she turned, seeing the sun about to drop beyond the rise. Her feet stumbled through the dirt as she moved. In the wan light she could just make out tracks in the dust, tracing a path where the boys had run.

Her stumble steadied, turning into a run, then into a sprint, as she raced up the rise. Silver could only hope there was some sign the boys had escaped, but deep in her heart she knew that was impossible. As she crested the rise, Darrick's body lay on its back staring up at the darkening sky.

Silver's hand clamped to her mouth to stifle a cry of

anguish. She advanced slowly then crouched beside him, the tears running freely. All thoughts for her own safety had fled. All she had left was grief.

Darrick was dead. But what of Fenn?

She scanned the hilltop. There was no sign of the youngest Longfeather. Then she looked down at Darrick.

Kneeling beside him she reached out a hand to touch his cooling flesh…

Fenn's hand was hot and clammy but Darrick grasped it tight all the same. He'd never seen such fear in his father's eyes, never heard him bark so angrily, so desperately.

His breathing was fast and hot as he pulled his little brother up the hill. A quick look over his shoulder and he could see the bandits coming after them. He had lost sight of his father, but surely he must—

The ground gave way underfoot. Darrick yelped, pain lashing through his ankle. He fell on his face, knees and elbows, taking the brunt as Fenn came down with him. His little brother was on his feet quick, pulling Darrick up. Darrick tried to stand, tried to put weight on the twisted ankle but it was no good. He would only slow Fenn down.

'Go,' he said, staring into Fenn's tear-streaked face. 'Go now.' He tried to instil the same command his father had.

Fenn shook his head.

'Now!' Darrick screamed, slapping Fenn across his cheek.

The little boy stumbled back. Darrick felt something break in his heart as his little brother turned and ran towards the shallow river.

Hands grasped at his throat, the thick fingers tightening. Raiders ran past him, chasing little Fenn, and there was nothing he could do as a fog began to close around his eyes…

Silver's hand was shaking. She trembled as the cool of evening began to envelop her.

Fenn.

She looked over toward the river, staggering to her feet, stifling the sob in her throat.

Just let him be alive. Let them at least have spared Fenn. Her boy.

She could hear the tinkling of the river. The waterwheel had been smashed. Bloodstains where they had wounded the mule, a trail leading away.

His body lay face down in the river, shirt and trews sodden. She rushed into the water, feeling it chill her to her thighs. Fenn's body was so small and weighed almost nothing as she picked him up, holding him tight as she staggered back onto the bank and fell to her knees. With one trembling hand she pushed his sodden hair back from his face. His eyes were half closed as though he were pretending to sleep but couldn't quite manage the ruse.

Perhaps his death had been quick. Perhaps despite their savagery the bandits had granted that one small mercy to a little boy. Silver's hand shook as she pressed her fingers to his cheek…

His father was gone. His brother was gone. Fenn ran. Ran towards the river. Ran as fast as he could. He was quick, had always been quick. Almost as quick as Darrick—

A hand grabbed his arm as he reached the bank of the river. It raised him into the air, and his shoulder screamed in agony. He would not show them fear. His father would not have wanted that.

From the corner of his eye he saw the mule. Saw the bandits fall on him, cutting him free of the axle, cutting his belly, slapping his rump with their bronze blades and watching him run with guts hanging out.

The bandit dragged Fenn into the river. He could hear laughing; first one man, then more. They spoke, but as his head was rammed beneath the surface of the water he couldn't make out what they were saying.

Fingers were curled tight in his hair. As much as he fought there was nothing he could do. Once he was pulled up for just long enough to gasp a breath of air before being plunged back under. He could still hear the laughing, even under the surface.

The water tasted filthy in his mouth. He tried not to swallow but couldn't help it. They weren't going to let him up this time. There was nothing he could do. Fenn stopped fighting...

She screamed. Cursing at the sky as she squeezed the body of a drowned little boy to her breast. She screamed until her cries turned to whimpers in her throat.

When the sun had dropped below the horizon and the chill of night stoked her she finally placed the body of Fenn Longfeather on the ground.

She should have buried them. But burying them would not quell the fire in her chest. Would not scratch the itch in her palms. Would not give her the blood she yearned to taste.

Jaws ripped at pure white flesh. A crimson gout as sinew tore. The taste of triumph. Screams of victory drowned out by the pumping of blood in the ears. And still the feel of the spear in her palm, still the need for more slaughter. It was never enough. Could never be enough. An unceasing need.

Silver looked eastward into the dark. She could see no tracks but still she knew that was where they had gone. Even had there been no stars she could still have found their trail.

In the dead of night she followed.

25

TALBAT struggled over the ridge, bringing up the rear as usual. He was by far the youngest of their band, but since he had to carry the cooking pot, the bedrolls, the spare weapons and what loot the other lads had given him, it was always going to have been a struggle. This was what you got if you were the newest member of the gang. He could only hope there'd be new meat soon and he could pass on some of his quite considerable load.

'Come on, boy,' shouted Jerral. He glanced back with a grin before taking another bite from one of the heads of corn he'd been demolishing for the past half-mile.

Talbat didn't have the breath to answer and just gave him a wave of acknowledgment.

How had it come to this? How had he fallen in with a band of brigands?

Talbat knew full well how he'd fallen in with them. His sticky fingers were how he'd fallen in with them. The choice of fleeing the town, or to stay and face losing a hand for thieving. With nowhere to go and no friends he'd been forced to make new acquaintances. Before long Talbat had found himself part of Kai Farrand's band of brothers. And what a bunch they were. He couldn't have picked a meaner pack of bloodthirsty cunts if he'd tried. But Talbat hadn't really had much choice. It was either fall in with this rabble or starve. And there was no way Talbat was about to let that happen – no matter how many villages and farms he had to ransack.

It had all been going so well. They'd made a camp at the foot of the Crooked Jaw, and had set up half a dozen ambush points along the trade pass through the mountains. Things were good. Back then, they didn't resort to killing unless it was completely necessary. That had all changed after the warlord had risen in the east. The Iron Tusk, they called him. Come out of nowhere, attracting men to his cause from every shadow and cranny from the southern edge of the Ramadi to the northern tip of the Suderfeld. Hard and fearsome men for the most count, and the smaller bands of brigands had been forced to join or die.

Not so for Kai Farrand, their eponymous leader.

'Fuck this warlord,' he'd said. 'We'll make our own way.'

An inspiring, if somewhat short, speech. All one hundred of his men had followed him. Talbat had gone along with them. So they'd made their way west, coming out through the desert, raiding as they went. And with every farmhouse sacked and village burned they'd become more vicious, more desperate. Murdering and raping and burning like they'd been born to it. Talbat had watched with growing dismay, wishing he'd taken up some simpler career, wishing he'd not been so keen on thieving, but he guessed this was his lot now and he'd best get used to it. There was nowhere else for him to go and no other trade he knew but theft.

Their band was small. Kai had split his men into groups, sent them raiding all over the place. 'Keep the militia guessing,' he'd said, and so far it had worked. Talbat was part of Jerral's crew, seven of them at the start but now they were down to six. Trust Talbat to end up alongside the five maddest bastards in the whole of Kai Farrand's band.

Howel had been the meanest. He was a proper savage; all bearded and ragged. Even Talbat had known he'd end up dead sooner than later. When he'd run across that field ahead of the rest of them, and the farmer had stuck him with his scythe, none of them were surprised. Talbat wasn't going to shed any tears over him.

The rest of the lads clearly thought more of Howel than Talbat did. They'd chased down that farmer like he was prey, tearing across the field. Jerral had been the one at their head, knife in hand, moving faster than any of them despite his size. He'd stuck the farmer deep and quick before he had a chance to fight back. Then things had gotten crazy.

Talbat had ransacked farms before. He'd seen innocent men and women killed, but this time his group were like men possessed, taking delight in hunting down the children. As Rey and Yedrig ran up that hill after the young boys, whooping and cawing like animals, it was all Talbat could do not to be sick. He followed them just the same, chased them up onto the ridge and witnessed what happened.

Yedrig had been the one to catch the first lad. The poor little fucker had hurt himself and was lying on the ground. The other one, the younger one, ran like a desert rabbit even though there wasn't anywhere to go. Yedrig grabbed the fallen boy round the neck and squeezed so tight his own eyes bulged and his tongue stuck out almost as much as the boy's, like he was mimicking the lad's final death stare.

The rest of the crew ignored him. All four of them were chasing the little boy.

Talbat had played his part, but he hadn't been the one to catch the boy in the river. It was Munro who'd held that lad under the water as the rest of them laughed. He'd been the one to let him up once for a gulp of air before pushing him back under till he stopped squirming. And they'd all carried on laughing as Talbat stood in the midst of them, wondering how in the hell it had come to this. Knowing he was just as guilty as the rest for what had happened here.

No point thinking on it now though. What was done was done. Before long they'd be back at Kai Farrand's encampment and have to explain to him why their loot could be carried by one young lad. Talbat could only hope there'd be no repercussions – especially repercussions focused on the lad carrying the loot.

As the day waned, Jerral ordered them to stop and make camp. They were in a tight ridge that would hopefully mask the light from any fire they built. The last thing they needed was the local militia finding them.

Jerral ordered Munro to go and hunt them some scrub rabbit while the rest lounged around, carrying out their usual camp rituals. Yedrig pulled off his boots, picking at his feet with a knife like he was whittling something from wood. Whatever it was Yedrig was trying to dislodge must have been long gone or in there for good, but still he picked away. Talbat couldn't stand to watch him for long.

211

Rey lay on his back, hands crossed over his stomach, snoring as usual. If he wasn't walking, fighting or shitting, Rey tended to be asleep.

Barton lurked at the edge of the camp, hand not far from his axe. He stared into the dark like something was going to come crawling out of it. Talbat was glad of Barton being constantly on the watch; one of them had to stay vigilant.

As the night drew in and the fire sputtered with nothing to keep it fed, Jerral started to get pensive.

'Where the fuck is that wanker Munro?' he said to himself as much as the rest of them.

No one had an answer anyway. Talbat just stared into the fire, his belly growling in hunger.

'You. Go have a look for him,' Jerral said.

It took a moment for Talbat to realise their leader was talking to him.

'Me?' Talbat replied.

Jerral looked at him as if to say, *yes of course you*. Talbat didn't think it wise to argue.

He stood, looking out into the dark desert, wondering which way to start walking. It was pitch black out there and he'd most likely get lost. And then what? Wander the desert alone in the dark? The thought of it filled him with such dread he suddenly needed to be sick.

Before he could take a step, something came flying out of the dark. It bounced once in the midst of the camp, rolling near to the fire before coming to a stop.

Yedrig shouted when he saw what it was, scrabbling backwards, looking stupid with just the one boot on. The object glaring at them was Munro's severed head.

'Fuck!' shouted Jerral, ripping the knife from the sheath at his side and turning to stare out into the dark.

Barton had his axe in hand, facing the other way in case they were surrounded. Yedrig gave Rey a kick and he woke with a start. On seeing the other lads standing defensively, then noticing Munro's head next to the fire, he scrambled to his feet and grabbed his blade.

'Who's out there?' Talbat asked, suddenly wishing he had a weapon to hand, but his knife was on the other side of the fire.

'How the fuck should I know,' growled Jerral, as though reminding Talbat what a stupid question that was.

'Could be militia,' said Rey.

'Where the fuck's Barton?' said Yedrig, tottering on his one boot.

They all turned. Where Barton had been standing at their rear, axe in hand, there was no one.

A sound issued out from the dark. A growl, the sound of rending, and what might have been a muffled scream. Something sprayed out from the black, hitting Talbat in the face. At first he panicked, reeling back and lifting a hand to his cheek. Moisture. Had he been wounded?

Something dripped into his lips and he tasted blood. Not his. The thought made him want to be sick again.

'Show yourselves,' Jerral shouted at the dark.

A woman walked into the camp, shirt covered in blood. In one hand she held Barton's axe, blood dripping from it, all shiny and fresh.

Talbat took a step back from her but Rey wasn't so shy.

213

He screamed, its echo filling the little canyon as he raised his blade high. The woman moved so fast Talbat could barely see her, stepping to the side of Rey's sweeping blade and then swiping his head right off his shoulders. She didn't pause, sending the axe spinning through the air where it ended up buried in Yedrig's chest up to the stock. He stared down at it for a second before pitching back. Talbat looked down at him, axe stuck in him, one foot still bootless.

Jerral moved forward slowly, that knife held out at the ready. The woman just waited, the fire flickering, lighting up her face beneath that blonde hair and making her look like a wraith.

'Come on then, you fucking bitch,' Jerral snarled running forward, drawing the knife back to strike.

She moved at the last instant, stepping aside and grabbing Jerral's arm, faster than anything Talbat had ever seen. Her other hand grasped his throat and he made a choking sound before she pulled him off his feet, snapping the arm that held the knife over her knee.

Jerral screamed and Talbat almost covered his ears at the awful sound. When the woman picked up Jerral's knife and plunged it into his eye, Talbat was almost relieved at the sudden silence that fell on the little canyon.

Talbat took in a couple of breaths, realising his hands were shaking. During all that violence he hadn't moved an inch to help. Hadn't even had the guts to make a run for it.

The woman stood, letting Jerral's body fall to the dust. Talbat felt his hands shake even more as she stared at him over the fire.

'I didn't have anything to do with it,' he said. Talbat had no idea exactly what it was she thought they'd done, but there was plenty to choose from.

She walked forward, right through the fire, flames licking at her legs. Her trews smouldered but she didn't seem to notice the heat as she came.

'Please don't kill me,' Talbat said, backing away, but the wall of the canyon was right behind him. He should have run when he had the chance.

She stopped in front of him and for the first time he saw her eyes. Two black oily pits. As she spoke in a language he didn't recognise he felt the words squirm into his ears and heard himself mumble pleas for mercy.

Whoever she was, whatever she was, she couldn't hear him...

The disparate folk of the Suderfeld kingdoms worship a pantheon steeped in fable. Though the names and archetypes might vary from nation to nation, and even county to county, there is a constant theme to Suderfeld's twelve gods.

At opposite ends of the pantheon sit Aethel, the stallion, and Waernoth, the dragon or great wyrm. These two, more than the others, seem to be locked in a constant struggle within the various myths surrounding the Suderfeld gods. Both vie for supremacy, seeming bent on anointing themselves as father or leader to the others.

At varying times Osred, the knight, is seen to be allied to Aethel, in one legend riding him into battle against Waernoth. But in others he is also allied to the dragon, often relying on him as a faithful mount (see The Tale of Osred and the Boggart King).

Also at odds are the hag, Juthwara, and Maerwynn, the healer. Oftentimes in legend they stand opposed to one another as Juthwara tempts innocent souls into one trap or another, appearing as both hag and temptress, while Maerwynn is sent to the victim's rescue. Again, contradictory tales arise that pitch these goddesses against a common enemy, and united they are a formidable couple.

Closely linked with Maerwynn is Cwen the maiden, and in many areas these two are one and the same. The Tale of Holst the Fisherman sees the love-struck angler come into contact with a goddess who bears the name Maerwynn or Cwen, depending on the region in which it is told.

The final common juxtaposition is Elwyn the seer and Urien the trickster. In legend it is Urien who is sent to tempt mortal men into sinful and lascivious acts, with Elwyn always giving such victims wise council to put them back on the straight road.

The rest of the pantheon is made up of nature gods, represented by animals, though in some tales they manifest in human form. Vadir the wolf, Frith the songbird, Tancred the bear and Kenelm the raven are worshipped to varying degrees throughout Suderfeld, mostly appearing as avatars of both war and peace, depending on the area and its religious traditions.

— Introduction to the Pantheon of Suderfeld, Friar Mollen Rand,
Year 34 after the Fall

†

26

LIVIA had never dreamed of travelling so far north. Her life had been the farm, had been Ben. All she had hoped for was to marry and live out her days raising a family, like everyone else. She could never have imagined this: what the tallymen would do, seeing her uncle murdered before her eyes, being beaten and dragged off to some unknown fate at the behest of Duke Gothelm.

But here she was.

The way had been hard and her clothes were muddied and torn from the journey. Still she gave no complaint, despite her travelling companions. 'Rescuers' wasn't an appropriate word for them. They had taken her with the intention of selling her to Gothelm themselves, and she gave thanks to whatever gods might still watch over her that Mullen and Josten had been betrayed. Not that it was likely any gods were watching. It was clear she was cursed.

Josten Cade was a surly man. When he wasn't sullenly watching the northern horizon he was barking at her to keep up, to sit down, to go to sleep. She obeyed him without question. There was no doubt Josten was intimidating, but there was something else about him… a sadness behind his eyes. Occasionally she would catch him staring with a haunted look, as though he was plagued with regret. It was a sorrow she would have deeply liked to ask him about, but she knew better than that. The last thing she wanted to do was make him any angrier.

If not for Mullen, she would most likely have tried to escape. For all his bluster and vulgarity, she could tell Mullen had a big heart in that broad chest. Yes, he talked of bedding wenches and cracking skulls, but beneath it all he was like a child. A bad-tempered child on occasion, but Livia was able to soften him. A sweet smile in reply to his scowl always brought a huge grin to that ugly face of his.

'Another day in the beautiful Arethusan countryside,' said Mullen, inhaling deeply through his nose.

The countryside was anything but beautiful. In another time perhaps the rolling hills and sparse copses might have been considered striking, but not now. The further north they travelled the more the signs of war became apparent. Carts were overturned beside their slaughtered owners. Men stripped down to their socks and left dead at the side of the road. Women and children strung up from trees, seemingly for no reason. The more they had travelled the more horror they had seen. Livia thought her heart might eventually harden to the sights but it didn't. With every new mile a new revulsion, and she felt her stomach lurch at the prospect of what lay ahead.

'Carrot?' asked Mullen, holding one out to her.

Livia never ceased to be amazed by his thick skin. No matter what they encountered Mullen took it all in his stride.

'No thanks,' said Livia.

'Suit yourself.' Mullen took a big bite and began to crunch loudly.

'We're not far,' said Josten. 'Just over that rise I reckon.'

'You've been saying that for miles,' Mullen replied with a mouth full of chewed vegetable.

'I recognise that tree. I'm sure of it.' He gestured to a windswept oak standing atop the hill ahead of them.

'You've been saying that too,' ventured Livia. She had to say it before Mullen. The threat of prodding Josten's ire was far less intimidating than seeing what Mullen had in his mouth for a second time.

Josten gave her that look of his. She smiled back and after a short pause he shook his head and wandered off.

'Why is he always so dour?' she asked Mullen quietly, as Josten forged ahead.

Mullen watched his friend walking up the hill as though reminiscing. 'You wouldn't think it to look at him, but Josten Cade was once an important man. Respected. Admired. Feared.'

Livia looked at the muddy, bedraggled man ahead of them. 'Really?'

'I know, it's hard to believe,' laughed Mullen.

When he reached the oak, Josten turned and flashed a rare smile.

'See,' he said, pointing down the other side of the hill.

There was a small town lying in a wooded valley. It wasn't much to look at but it appeared more hospitable than anything they'd found in the past five days. The town was alive with movement and a large encampment had been erected to its eastern side. Even from this distance she could see troops moving among the range of tents; men in armour marched in regimented drills, soldiers cleaned and sharpened their weapons.

'Who do we think?' asked Mullen.

'Canio Delloch,' Josten replied, gesturing to a flag with a burning wheel upon it, which fluttered from one of the tents.

'Just remind me, does Canio like us right now or not?'

Josten cocked his head, as though he was unsure. 'After last time? I doubt it.'

'So, should we steer clear, or try and make amends?'

'Only one way to find out,' said Josten, before leading them down the hill towards the town.

No one paid the three of them much mind as they wandered into the close grouping of shacks. With so many people coming and going they went unnoticed among the constant train of tinkers, whores and mercenaries. The ground beneath Livia's feet had been churned up and her shoes were caked in mud as they plodded along.

As they made their way through, Livia caught sight of a young man with close-shorn hair moving parallel to them down an adjacent street. He limped heavily on his left leg and his face bore livid scars. She was unnerved by his stare and it became obvious he was following, but before she could tell Josten or Mullen the man disappeared.

When they reached the tented area at the town's eastern extent they were stopped by one of Canio's company.

'What's your business?' the mercenary asked.

'Josten Cade, come to look up his old friend Canio Delloch,' Josten said, with as much confidence as he could muster.

The mercenary must have recognised the name, nodding in recognition and pointing them towards the command tent at the centre of the camp.

Josten grinned at Mullen, but the big man didn't seem to share his confidence.

'You sure we're going to be welcome?' asked Mullen.

'Canio Delloch's a reasonable man,' Josten replied. 'I'm sure he'll let bygones be bygones and all that.'

'What did you do?' asked Livia.

Mullen laughed as Josten regarded her awkwardly.

'We might have changed sides during a battle,' he said.

'Ah,' she said. 'I take it you ended up on the opposite side to this Canio fellow?'

'Yes,' Josten replied. 'But it happens all the time in war. One day you're watching a man's back, the next you're trying to stick a knife in it. Day after that you're fighting side by side again. It's the way it's always been in the mercenary companies. Besides, nobody got killed after we changed sides.'

'What about the standard bearer?' asked Mullen. 'Didn't he die?'

'All right,' said Josten. 'Almost no one died. Canio never liked that standard bearer anyway.'

'How very reassuring,' said Livia.

They continued in silence until they reached the tent with the burning wheel flag atop it. Josten approached and the guard outside seemed to recognise him.

'Look what the cat dragged in,' he said. The sentry held

a spear but he didn't appear threatening. That did little to put Livia at ease.

'Is he here?' Josten asked.

'He is. Not sure if he's gonna want to see Josten Turncoat any time soon though.'

'Why don't we let him decide?'

The guard looked the three of them up and down before ducking inside the tent. He reappeared a moment later and held the tent flap open for them.

'Guess he's in a good mood,' said the guard with a sly smile.

Josten led them inside and the guard gave Livia a suggestive look as she passed by.

The inside of the tent was sparse. Dark coloured rugs had been thrown on the floor and weapons hung from the rafters – Livia guessed trophies of war. Two men stood at either side of the tent as the three of them entered, hands not far from the swords at their waists. At the far end sat a handsome man behind a dark wooden table. Scrolls of parchment were laid out before him, one of them a map, though of which region Livia couldn't tell.

'Josten,' said the man, as they entered. 'And Mullen. Naturally. Not sure I'm familiar with your new companion though.' The man ran a hand across his stubbly jaw as he regarded her.

'I pick up friends everywhere, Canio. You know that.'

Josten smiled as he spoke but even Livia could tell it was forced. He was nervous, and by the way Mullen gripped the handle of the axe at his belt, so was the big man.

'Oh, I know,' said Canio. 'Maybe I should warn her about the company she's keeping. I wonder if she knows about your habit of swapping sides when the mood takes you.'

'About that,' said Josten, looking awkward. 'I hope there's no hard feelings.'

'If you thought I was still sore about that battle you wouldn't have come here,' said Canio. 'Unless you're about to make me such a good offer that you thought I wouldn't care about the time you betrayed me and the rest of my company?'

'Well…' There was that awkward look again, and for a moment Livia thought she was about to be used as a bargaining chip for the second time. 'I was about to offer you Mullen and I. At a bargain rate, of course. For old times' sake.'

Canio rubbed his chin once more, mulling over the offer.

'Josten Cade and Mullen Bull? In my company? For cheap? I'd be a fool to refuse.'

Josten couldn't hide his look of relief. 'I always knew you were a man of sense,' he said.

The flap opened behind them, and three more men entered. Mullen slowly manoeuvred himself to face them.

'Be with you in a moment,' said Canio, before regarding Josten once more. 'And what about your friend?' he asked. 'What does she have to offer?'

Josten looked a little thrown. 'Nothing,' he replied. 'She's just with us. You know how it is.' Livia didn't appreciate his suggestive wink. But then Josten and Mullen hadn't laid a finger on her during their whole journey, so she could appreciate the subterfuge.

'Right.' Canio smiled. 'I see. Like that is it?'

'Yeah. It's like that.' Josten fixed Canio with a hard stare and his thumb flicked up the cross-guard of his sword.

'It's just that I've heard things. From the south. Tales of kidnappings, and money being put on heads, and rewards for safe returns.' Mullen slowly pulled the axe free of his belt. 'Please. None of that.' Canio waved at Mullen to lower the weapon. 'You're surrounded. There's no need for this to get messy.'

'Messy?' said Josten. 'You've got no idea how messy this could fucking get.'

'Josten. Come now.' Canio reclined in his seat. 'You think after everything we've been through I'd give you up to Gothelm and his boys? Just hand over the girl and you can be on your way. Though where you'll go I have no idea. Gothelm wants your head something awful, and I hear there's a crew after you for killing Dirty Beckan. Good job on that bastard, by the way. I never liked him.'

Josten looked at Canio, then glanced over one shoulder, weighing up exactly how much trouble he was in.

'That seems like a fair offer,' Josten said, his thumb still pushing his sword out of its sheath an inch. 'But you know... I've got quite fond of the girl. Just wouldn't seem right handing her over like that. Not without a fight at least.'

'Always were the mad one,' said Canio. Josten just stared again. 'There's no way she's worth it, Cade. Look what happened the last time you went all mushy over a woman.'

'This time it's different,' said Josten.

Canio shook his head. 'I doubt it.'

There was silence. Livia tried to see where might be safe

to hide when it all kicked off, but realised there was nowhere to hide from this.

Mullen was the first to move, bellowing as he swung his axe. Josten's sword was out of its sheath before anyone else could move and Livia thought Canio was done for, but Josten turned away from the mercenary captain, hacking at the wall of the tent and cutting a vertical furrow along its length.

'Go!' he said, grabbing Livia's arm and flinging her through the hole.

She landed on the ground outside, mud spattering her face as she sprawled in the dirt. More of Canio's men stood outside, looking down in confusion. Clearly they had been expecting Josten or Mullen to come out fighting, not some dishevelled girl.

Inside the tent she heard the quick sharp sound of clashing weapons and men barking in anger. One of the guards ran towards the furrow but was thrown back before he had a chance to enter. Mullen burst out, axe in hand, spit on his lips, teeth gritted in fury.

'Come on, bastards!' he screamed, running at Canio's men.

They looked like veterans, each one tougher than the next, but Mullen was like a bear facing wolves. One went down clutching his head as the flat of Mullen's axe clanked off his helmet. The next fell back, face full of headbutt, and the third took a kick to the balls so hard he fell squealing.

Mullen grabbed Livia's arm and pulled her to her feet. It was all she could do to keep up with him as they ran back towards the town.

Men began to take up the chase, but Mullen was faster than he looked.

'What about Josten?' she said as they fled.

'Don't worry about him,' said Mullen, jinking through the tents. 'Worry about us.'

Livia glanced over her shoulder as they entered the tight streets of the town. Canio's men were almost on their heels. It was all the incentive she needed to keep on running.

They turned down a narrow alley, skidding on the slick ground and running like all the demons of hell were after them, until Mullen came to an abrupt stop at a dead end.

'Shit,' he said, turning to face their pursuers and pulling her behind him.

Livia watched the end of the alley, listening to Canio's men approach. As they advanced, Mullen's fingers gripped the haft of his axe so tight his knuckles were white.

There was the sound of a scuffle. Someone shouted in surprise. Then nothing.

Mullen glanced at Livia in confusion as he edged his way to the entrance of the alley. Peering around the corner, they saw three of Canio's men lying unconscious on the ground, their weapons strewn about the street. It seemed there were no witnesses to whatever had happened.

'What's going on?' she asked.

'No idea,' Mullen replied, glancing down at the men who had been beaten by some unseen phantom. 'Let's not hang around to find out.'

He grabbed her arm again and pulled her along the muddy street. Before they turned into another alley, Livia glanced back. For a second she saw the man with the limp who had been following them earlier. He stood watching as they ran, face scarred, his eyes staring intently.

Then he was lost from sight.

27

HIS jaw ached like mad and blood was caked in his hair, but Josten was too angry to let that bother him. All he wanted was to smash Canio's deceitful face to mush; but his hands were tied behind him. The post he was bound to irritated his back and his shoulder throbbed from an old ailment. If only he had his sword – then there'd be fucking trouble. He loved that sword. It had got him out of more scrapes than he could remember.

Not this particular scrape though. That sword hadn't been much bloody use at all when he'd been surrounded by half a dozen of Canio's best. But he was still alive, that was something at least.

'I didn't want this to happen,' said Canio.

They were alone in the tent. Canio sat on his desk picking at his fingernails with a short knife.

'That makes two of us,' Josten replied. 'But here we are.'

Canio placed the knife down beside him. 'We're mercenaries, Cade. It's what we do.'

They stared at each other until Josten started to laugh. Canio joined in and the tent was filled with the sound of them bellowing.

'Everyone gets what they deserve,' Josten said.

'You always say that,' Canio said, finally stifling his laughter. 'And you're right.'

'Remember that job in Annavale we took?' Josten asked. 'That prissy little lord wanted us to sack a village. What was his name?'

'Lord Borran,' said Canio.

'That was it. And when we got there to carry out the contract it was just some old man and his goat.' Josten laughed. 'I remember your men wanted to go through with it and kill the poor old fucker. And his goat.'

'Yeah,' said Canio. 'They always were a dedicated bunch. I can't remember who changed their minds.'

'That was Mullen. I think he said the first one who hurts the old man gets a taste of the bull's horns.'

'Ha! I remember,' said Canio, the memory obviously a good one. 'That was the first time I thought there might be a heart in that big old chest of his.'

'He's full of surprises.'

'Surprises? He surprised Lord Borran all right. Didn't he make him eat that contract in front of everyone?'

'And made them all stay and watch till he shat it out the other end.'

Canio laughed. 'Yes. Strangely we never got another contract from Borran. I always knew you and Mullen were trouble. Always costing me money.'

'We were good for some things,' Josten said with a wink.

Canio nodded at that. 'Yes you were. And not just to swing that blade of yours.'

Josten realised what Canio was referring to. The mood turned sombre.

'She was a good girl,' said Josten. 'It's a shame what happened to her.'

Canio nodded. 'I hated you for the longest time. Just because it was you who introduced us. I needed someone to blame when she went, and if not for you I'd have been spared the pain.'

'Is that what this is all about? Revenge because your wife died?'

Canio smirked, shaking his head. 'You seriously think this is because you introduced me to her? Josten, this is all because you're the stupidest, nastiest cunt I've ever met.'

They laughed again and only stopped when one of Canio's men entered the tent.

'They're here,' he said.

Canio nodded. His look of mirth turned solemn.

'You understand this is just business, Cade,' he said.

Before Josten could answer, more men entered the tent. They wore black and Josten recognised the first one immediately. His hawk nose was still flattened but the bruising had gone from his eyes. Randal, he'd said his name was. Randal Wolf, or somesuch. He regarded Josten with a blank expression but the rest of the tallymen looked like they wanted to hack him to pieces.

'The other two escaped?' Randal asked, still staring at Josten.

'They did, but they won't be far away,' Canio replied.

'Very well.' Randal signalled to one of his men who

threw a purse at Canio. The mercenary caught it, and it looked heavy. Canio wasn't giving him up for a pittance.

'Goodbye, Cade,' Canio said as they untied Josten from the post. He almost sounded regretful.

'Be seeing you,' Josten replied, knowing it was a lie.

The tallymen dragged him outside and bound his hands again before they led him through the camp in silence. Canio's men watched with hatred as they passed by. It had taken half a dozen of them to bring him down; two of those men were wounded badly. He imagined they wanted to be the ones to get a little payback, but the tallymen had handed over their coin so he guessed it was their honour by right.

Randal led the way through the miserable little town. No one seemed to give a shit what their business was and Josten doubted any of them would have the guts to ask. He wouldn't get help here.

At the southern end of the town was the hill Josten had first looked down from. The oak sat waiting for him at the top, and he suddenly started to feel sick. He'd been in fixes before, faced execution and certain death, but he couldn't see a way out of this one.

They dragged him up to the tree and one of the tallymen threw a rope over a thick overhanging branch.

Randal turned to face him as the tallymen tightened the rope about Josten's neck.

'I see you've taken on some more recruits since we last met,' said Josten. He'd never been one to pass up an opportunity to take the piss. Begging would do no good. 'Though let's face it – the last bunch you brought were about as much use as a broken cock in a brothel.'

Randal regarded him without emotion. Clearly he didn't see the funny side, but then it was obvious he was a man who took himself very seriously.

'Yes, I brought more men,' said Randal. 'That one is called Deren,' he gestured to the man holding the other end of the rope. His arms were as thick as the oak's branches. 'You killed his brother a few days ago.'

Before Josten could say anything, Deren and one of the others pulled hard on the rope. Josten was in the air, that rope tightening around his neck, squeezing his throat shut. He tried as hard as he could to grit his teeth – there was nothing more stupid-looking than a hanged man with his tongue lolling out – but it appeared there wasn't anything you could do about that when there was nothing under your feet.

His neck stretched. His eyes bulged. His tongued poked out of his stupid bloody head.

It seemed to go on for an age. Josten felt the world go hazy at the edges. Then he was on the ground, his throat open just enough to let a little air in, which he wheezed greedily into his lungs.

Randal was kneeling down next to him now, still looking on impassively.

'Where has your friend taken her?' he asked.

Josten looked up at him, trying to fill his lungs enough to speak. 'How the fuck do I—'

The rope was yanked again. Josten was off the ground before he could think to draw a breath in. This time he kicked his legs, doing the dance he'd seen a dozen times before. He danced that jig for as long as he could until the rope loosened again and he hit the ground before blackness completely enveloped him. It hurt to inhale, but somehow he managed to fill his lungs.

'Where has your friend taken her?' repeated Randal.

Josten stared at him, trying to breathe.

'If… he has any sense… they'll be miles away by now.'

Randal scanned the horizon, then looked back at Josten. 'I don't think so. Your friend won't be far away.'

'Then… you don't know my friend… very well at all.'

Josten felt the noose tighten at his words but Randal held up a hand.

'No. We might need him.'

'But he killed my brother,' said Deren.

Josten might have apologised for that if he'd thought it would do any good. He didn't bother wasting what breath he had.

'And there'll be plenty of time for your justice, my friend.' Randal rose to his feet. 'Take him back to the town and make sure he's well guarded.' He glanced into the distance once more. 'I reckon we'll have company sooner or later.'

As they dragged him back down the hill towards the town, Josten could only hope Mullen wasn't stupid enough to try and save him.

28

THEY watched from the copse as the tallymen strung Josten up by the neck. Livia could feel Mullen growing more agitated as his friend dangled from the oak.

He took his axe from his belt and began to move towards the edge of the small wood. Livia grabbed his arm before he could break the tree line.

'No! That's what they want, don't you see?'

Mullen didn't look at her but continued to watch his friend being tortured. 'I don't give a shit. If that's what they want I'll fucking well give it them.'

'They're hanging him from that tree to draw us out. It's the highest point for miles. They want us to see.'

Mullen stopped and stared, his teeth grinding. Livia could see how white his knuckles were. 'Am I supposed to stand here and watch him die?' he growled.

Livia still gripped his arm, watching as the rope loosened and Josten fell to the ground. 'You know this is the only way, Mullen. Unless you give me up to them.'

Mullen nodded and looked at her. Clearly he was considering it. Of saving his friend by sacrificing her to the tallymen. Instead he shook his head. 'You're one of us now.

We don't abandon our own,' he said, before moving back further among the trees.

Livia watched as they hung Josten up once more and let him fall. From this distance she could recognise Randal. He had brought more men with him this time — eight of them in all — as rough and ruthless as the last bunch. Gothelm was determined to have his prize.

'I'll go to them,' she said.

'What?' Mullen replied.

She turned to face him. Her mind made up. 'I'll go to Randal tonight and offer myself to Duke Gothelm if he sets Josten free. It's the only way. There are too many of them to take on, even if we set up an ambush.'

Mullen smiled. Then he laughed. 'You're sweet,' he said. 'And brave, I'll give you that. But as soon as those bastards have you, Josten is dead. Fuckers like that keep no bargains. They wouldn't deal two hundred silver for you, they're not about to let Josten free.'

'But we can't fight them. There are too many.'

Mullen put his axe back in his belt. 'We'll see about that, lass.'

With that he sat and rested his back against a tree trunk. Livia saw that the tallymen had taken Josten down now and were marching him back towards the little town. She felt helpless. Desperate. But Mullen was probably right. Their only option was to fight.

Night came in quick and cold, and Livia found herself pacing in anticipation. Mullen rose as it grew dark, his face grim and determined as he strode toward the town. He looked quizzically as Livia began to follow him.

'Where the hell are you going?' he asked.

She looked up at him, setting her jaw and doing her best to stare him down. 'Fucking going with you,' she replied. Livia had to admit the curse word felt good as she said it.

Mullen furrowed his brow as he looked down at her but it was gone as quick as it came. Livia had made it clear she was in no mood for being ordered around, even by her former kidnapper.

'All right,' he said. 'No need to be rude about it.'

They made their way down the hill to the small town. She almost tripped over her skirts twice, making her wonder why she thought this was a good idea, but she was determined to help Josten. Livia should have held little loyalty to him, but over the past days she had seen a side to both men she liked. Besides, she knew she was no longer their captive. It might have been a bit of a stretch to say she was their friend, but she liked to think she was somewhere close.

The pair made their way into the narrow streets, keeping to the shadows as they went.

'What now?' asked Livia. Neither of them had any idea where the tallymen were holding Josten.

Just as she asked, one of the town's night watch strolled into view. In the dark Livia saw a smile creep across Mullen's face.

He moved surprisingly quietly for a man so big, and the night watchman had no idea he was being hunted until it was too late. Mullen grabbed him, lifting him bodily and dragging him into the dark. He stared at the man, hand clamped over his mouth.

'The tallymen have a prisoner. Have you seen them?'
The night watchman nodded, eyes staring fearfully. 'Where
are they holding him?' Mullen slowly removed his hand
from the man's mouth.

'Grain store,' said the watchman, his voice a high squeak.
'Two streets over.' He pointed a trembling finger.

'Thanks,' said Mullen, hammering the man's head off
the nearest windowsill. It gave a dull thud that made Livia's
stomach tie in a knot.

As Mullen moved on she whispered a pointless 'sorry' as
she crept past, hoping the watchman would still have all his
wits when he eventually woke up.

When they reached the grain store, Livia could see there
was light coming from beneath the double doors. Mullen
crouched in the dark, watching the building.

'They'll be expecting us,' she whispered.

'I know,' said Mullen, still staring at the grain store.

'We need a diversion… or something.'

'What did you have in mind?' Mullen asked.

Livia glanced around for something, anything they could
use to draw out the tallymen, but she could see nothing.

Raised voices and a cry of pain echoed within the
building.

'Fuck this,' said Mullen, standing up and striding towards
the door.

Livia wanted to shout for him to wait. Wanted to grab
him and make him stop, but there was no point. Mullen
wasn't going to stop for anyone now.

He planted a foot against the door and it gave with a

crack. Light streamed out onto the street from within the grain store and Mullen charged inside.

Livia crept forward as the sounds of violence ensued. Weapons clashed and someone shouted out in pain. She heard Mullen growling. Heard another thud. Through the open door she could see black-clad tallymen rushing to join the fray.

She should have run, taken the opportunity to flee this place, but something within forced her to stay. She couldn't just leave Josten and Mullen. They had risked their lives to save her. Yes, for their own venal reasons, but they had rescued her from the tallymen and neither had done her any harm. Not like Randal and his thugs.

Instead of running, Livia moved closer. More shouts. One of the tallymen fell in the doorway, dead or unconscious.

'Bastards!' shouted Mullen.

'Have him!'

A last cry of anguish. Then silence.

Livia paused outside the door. She could hear several men breathing heavily, no one speaking. She wanted to move closer, to peer inside and see what had happened. Before she could decide what to do, someone appeared silhouetted in the doorway.

She tried to run, to flee into the night, but the figure grabbed her arm and dragged her inside. Livia looked up desperately at a face she recognised.

'Hello, Livia,' said Randal. There was a gash on his cheek and his brow was moist from his recent efforts.

Livia glanced around the room. Josten was tied to a

support beam, his face beaten and bloody. Mullen lay on the ground, blood running from his head. He obviously hadn't gone down easy as two tallymen were on the ground too, one in the doorway, another next to Mullen. Neither of them moved. Another tallyman lay on his back nearby, grasping at a slash in his thigh, gritting his teeth against the pain.

'Someone tie him up,' Randal said, motioning to Mullen as he pulled Livia into the centre of the room.

Josten looked up at her, clearly in pain. He said nothing.

'You have me now,' Livia said desperately. 'You can let them go.'

Randal looked at Josten and Mullen, who was being tied to another post. 'Why would I do that?' he replied.

'Randal,' she pleaded. 'There's no need for any more of this. There's been enough killing. Just take me to Gothelm. Let them go.'

He looked at her with a pained expression. 'These men are criminals. They have to be punished as such.'

Mullen was coming round now, his eyes groggy, and he shook some sense back into his head.

'Which one first?' asked one of the tallymen, a broad and brutal-looking man.

'What do I care?' said Randal.

The tallyman smiled, fished a coin from the purse at his belt and flipped it. Livia could only look on with dismay as the rest of the tallymen eagerly awaited the outcome. The broad one caught the coin and slapped it onto the back of his hand. With a sly glance he checked which side it had landed on, then grinned wider.

'The fat one,' said the tallyman, moving towards Mullen. None of the other men argued as he drew a knife from his belt.

'Wait,' Livia shouted. 'The duke might want them for questioning. You can't just—'

'Livia.' She turned to see Mullen looking at her. He was smiling, despite the grogginess. 'Let it go, girl. They've made up their minds.'

She could only watch as the tallyman with the knife approached Mullen. Tied to the opposite post, Josten squirmed helplessly against his bonds. As the tallyman plunged his knife into Mullen's gut, Josten shouted a cry of rage that hurt Livia's ears.

She watched in a daze as the tallyman drew his knife across Mullen's belly. Mullen spat blood between gritted teeth, trying his hardest not to give the tallymen the satisfaction of seeing him scream.

Josten bellowed on till it numbed Livia's ears. She couldn't drag her eyes away from the sight as the tallyman plunged a hand in, pulling out a sausage-string fistful of guts.

Mullen could resist no more, crying out in pain as the tallyman stepped back, laughing as he did so.

Livia felt rage burn inside her. Felt the cruelty of these men wash over her, purging her of fear. Even as the tallyman plunged his knife back in, this time into Mullen's chest, Livia felt no fear. Only the need to bathe every one of them in a cleansing fire…

Wings teased at the corner of her vision. A spear of vengeance, hot in her hand. The taste of righteousness burning red on her lips.

The tallyman pulled his knife free, turning to Josten, who was still raging, spitting the blood from his lips at the death of his friend.

'Don't worry, mate,' said the tallyman. 'Your turn now.'

'No,' said one of the others. 'He's mine.'

That one drew out a length of rope and moved forward. Livia strained against Randal's grip but he held her firm as the second tallyman moved behind Josten and secured the rope tight about his neck. She watched helplessly as he pulled on the rope, throttling Josten against the post.

No. Not *helplessly*.

The heat of a thousand suns filled her with might. The holy purity of a god's wrath gave her succour. The white flames of fury filled her soul…

Randal was screaming. Livia held his wrist now, crushing it in an iron grip. His scream of pain was like a pig at slaughter, only serving to stoke her fury.

She flung him across the room and he smashed into the wall, wood cracking and dust flying. Another of the tallymen raced towards her but she moved faster than she could think, planting her hand into his chest and knocking him back a dozen feet through the air.

Two of the tallymen panicked, fleeing from the grain store through the open door. The others stood back, fear marring their once-cruel faces.

Livia looked towards Josten where his would-be executioner had also backed away, his rope forgotten.

'Cut him free,' she ordered, hearing a voice that wasn't her own.

Immediately the tallyman obeyed, and Josten stumbled forward.

Livia looked at Mullen's body, still lashed to the post. She wanted to cut him down too but before she could order it, Josten grabbed her arm.

'Let's go,' he said.

She stared for one last moment at the big man hanging there, his guts dangling to the floor, before she let Josten drag her from the building and out into the cold night.

29

A T least now Josten knew why Gothelm wanted the girl so badly. But that was for worrying about later. He dragged Livia through the town, staggering on his weak knees. Those tallymen had given him a beating all right – beaten him like they were tenderising a slab of meat.

And they'd killed Mullen. Strung him up and gutted him like they were butchers at market.

He wanted to stay and make them pay, but Josten knew that would mean he'd end up like Mullen. As furious as he was, as much as he needed his reckoning, he still had enough wits to know when to make an escape and when to hang around for a fight.

He glanced at Livia as he ran, dragging her along behind him. She looked pale, in a daze, like she'd just been drugged. Far from the raging creature she'd been back in that grain store, throwing men around like rag dolls.

But later. Think about all that later. Now we just have to get the fuck out of here.

Josten limped to the western extent of the town. Somewhere a bell started ringing, chiming into the night and filling him with more dread. He didn't pause, striking out towards the wood that lay just outside the town.

Livia kept pace with him as he fled, staggering behind like she was half asleep, and he felt relief wash over him as soon as they reached the trees. He stopped for a minute, pausing to look behind and watch for any sign of pursuit.

No one came after them, though the bell ringing carried on, and was soon joined by voices raised in alarm.

In the scant moonlight Josten looked at Livia, trying to see if she recognised him. He waved his hand in front of her face but she stood like she was in a trance, eyes staring without focus.

Josten clicked his fingers. 'Can you hear me,' he asked.

She didn't reply.

This was just perfect. His oldest friend was dead because of Josten's dumb plans, and now this girl – a girl he'd kidnapped for his own greed – was catatonic.

If he'd known what trouble she was he would never have got involved. But then trouble seemed to follow Josten around like a stray dog.

When he was sure no one was following, he pulled Livia further into the wood. The thick undergrowth didn't make the going any easier and they both found themselves tripping over roots and bushes. But he had to keep going despite the rough ground, had to put as much distance between them and the town as possible.

Eventually they came out into a clearing. The moon was bright enough to see and he sat Livia down, kneeling beside her. In the light he could see she still stared blankly. Josten took her by the shoulders and shook her, digging his fingers into her arms. She looked at him quizzically and he shook her again.

'Livia?' he said.

'Where are we?' the girl asked.

'The middle of nowhere. But we're safe,' he said, relieved that she was coming to.

She glanced around the clearing, gripping her arms against the chill of night. He had nothing to give her to keep her warm; building a fire would be difficult but not impossible. There was a risk it would give away their location but what choice did he have? He hadn't come this far to freeze to death in a shitty wood in the arse-end of nowhere.

It took him a while but he found enough dry wood to make a tinder bundle. Lighting a fire with sticks wasn't easy, and it had been a while, but eventually he managed it. Josten breathed hard after, his hands almost raw from the effort. Livia watched him from the side of the clearing. She wasn't in shock any longer, just a little bewildered at what she'd been through.

After piling more wood on the smouldering bundle, Josten told her to move closer. Soon the fire was crackling and he was relieved by the warmth. It did little to make him feel better though. Mullen was dead and nothing was going to make up for that.

As they sat in the light of the flames, Josten stared at the girl. What she'd done to those tallymen was inhuman. She'd kept the power she had a secret all this time and he had to admit it scared him some.

'What are you?' he asked, unable to stay silent any longer.

She looked up mournfully, then shook her head. 'I don't know,' she answered.

'If you could do that, if you had that power, why not use it earlier? Why let the tallymen take you? Why let me and Mullen?'

'I… It's not something I can control. It's like I'm… in a dream. It's like I'm someone else.'

'That's why Gothelm wants you so badly.'

'I imagine he wants the power I can bring him.'

'He won't be the only one.'

Livia stared at him over the fire. 'What do you mean?'

'I mean that every duke, king and warlord between here and the Ramadi Wastes will want you now. After what you did tonight, to those men, everyone is going to want a piece of you. There won't be anywhere you can go this won't follow you.'

Livia looked down. Her hair falling over her face, her shoulders trembling as she sobbed, still holding herself against the cold.

Josten felt sorrow and guilt creep up on him. He was partly responsible for this. Maybe he'd done the right thing letting her join him and Mullen, but then what good had it done her now? Mullen's blood was on his hands and now this girl – this child – was weeping and alone in the night because he was such a selfish bastard.

'Don't worry,' he said, sitting down beside her. 'We'll find a way out of this.'

'We?' she said, looking up with tear-streaked eyes. 'Why would you help me?'

Josten had to think. He was no hero. No bold knight

saving the damsel in distress. And from what he'd seen tonight Livia could more than save herself.

Deep inside though, there was a part of Josten that needed to help her. He'd never killed any babies, never hung any old women, but he'd committed evil acts and he knew it. Maybe Livia was his way to redemption; a way to wipe all the dirt of his past away. But there was no way he could tell her that.

'It's what Mullen would have wanted,' he said finally. 'I think he saw you like the daughter he never had. Well, maybe a niece. A favourite one…'

'And what about you?' she asked.

Josten smiled. 'I'm a mercenary. We make terrible fathers.'

'Then I'll hire you,' she said. 'I'll pay you to take me somewhere safe.'

Josten had to stop himself laughing. 'Two problems with that: firstly, you've got nothing to pay me with. Second, there's nowhere safe. For either of us. Everyone I know wants to kill me. And you don't seem to have friends in abundance right now.'

She stood, a stubborn look fixed to her face. 'Then we're stuck together. You and me against the world.' She held out her hand.

Josten looked down at it, then back to her face, full of determination.

'I guess we are,' he said with a smile, grasping her hand and shaking it once.

Livia flinched.

She stared at him as though he'd just slapped her and Josten wondered what the hell was happening until he noticed something protruding from her neck. She fell, and he caught her. As he lowered her to the ground he could see her eyes glazing over.

Josten plucked the thing from her neck, holding it close. A dart.

There was a shriek of triumph from the woods. Josten couldn't see from which direction it came; the light from the fire made it impossible.

'I told you Randal was right!'

Josten span at the voice. He recognised it – one of the tallymen who'd given him a beating.

'Poisoned fucking blowdart?' Another voice Josten knew. 'I don't believe it worked.'

Josten spun again, expecting the tallymen to rush him from the dark at any moment. With no weapon he wouldn't stand a chance, whether he could see them or not, but he wouldn't go down without a fight.

He needn't have worried. They walked out slowly and calmly. Two came out at first, smiling widely, then more, until half a dozen tallymen stood around the fire.

Josten looked at Livia lying on the ground. So much for being stuck together.

The first tallyman hit him from the side. Josten went down on one knee. He was more badly hurt than he'd realised. No way he should have been taken—

A kick to his ribs knocked him on his back. The wind was blown from his lungs and he tried to breathe, humiliated at the gasping noises he made.

'Just do him quick and let's get back to town,' one of

them said. 'It's fucking freezing out here.'

'Fuck that,' said another – was his name Deren? 'I've been waiting ages for this.'

Another sharp kick to the side of Josten's head and he rolled over onto his front. He could see the edge of the trees and the darkness beyond. In his stupor he wondered if he'd be able to make it, to slink off into the dark before these cunts kicked him to death. As he started to crawl he heard the tallymen laughing at him.

This was how he'd die. Being laughed at by a bunch of nobodies, crawling on his belly in the cold dark. All of a sudden he missed Mullen. He could only think of how much he needed his friend right now.

Then the laughing stopped.

Josten looked up groggily as another man limped into the firelight.

He stopped beside Josten, staring at the tallymen. For a second his eye twitched, and Josten could see a pattern of scars on the left side of his face, running up beneath the scant hairline.

'What the fuck do you want?' Deren asked the stranger.

The man regarded each tallyman in turn before pointing at Livia. 'Give me the girl.'

Josten had forgotten his plans of escape. This was the dumbest thing he'd ever seen. If this idiot cripple didn't limp away, and soon, Josten wouldn't be the only one getting kicked to death.

Deren walked forward. 'Are you insane? Fuck off before I make you sorry.'

'Give me the girl,' repeated the cripple.

The tallymen were finding this funny. Josten couldn't bring himself to join in with their mirth.

'I don't think we will,' said Deren. 'So, what the fuck are you going to do now?'

The cripple regarded them all matter-of-factly. 'If you do not give her to me I will have to kill you.'

More laughter.

'And how are you gonna do that with one good leg and no weapon?'

'I will take yours,' said the cripple, his eye twitching in the night.

Deren laughed again. 'And kill us all with it? Like fuck you will.'

'Then, so that you may witness,' said the cripple, like he was talking to an idiot, 'I will kill you last.'

Not all the tallymen were laughing now. Some of them looked nervous, like the joke had all of a sudden turned sour.

'Just fucking do him,' said one of them.

Deren drew his sword and walked forward. The cripple made no move until Deren raised his blade and brought it down with a grunt.

Josten barely saw him move, could barely track him as he stepped aside on his one good leg, hand striking out to pluck Deren's sword from his grip and spin, using the weight of its momentum to strike. The cripple swept the blade across Deren's gut, opening it up to the night.

Deren squealed, falling on his back, trying to staunch the blood and guts spewing from his belly. The other tallymen drew their weapons.

Josten watched as they rushed in. The cripple moved at the last second, effortlessly anticipating how each of them would attack. He cut a tallyman's head from his shoulders, stepping aside to avoid a strike from another, the cripple's blade sliding in and out of a ribcage so fast Josten could barely follow it. A third tallyman barely had a chance to scream as his arm was lopped off at the shoulder, his last cry cut short by the blade slicing across his throat.

Despite the cripple's limp, his form was flawless. Josten had never seen its like. He parried blows from the last two tallymen, countering with such grace Josten barely registered the horror of one man losing a leg at the knee and the other his head.

Alone now, the cripple turned. Deren still floundered on the grass, staring in disbelief at the grievous wound in his gut.

'Please,' he said as the cripple limped slowly toward him. 'Please don't—'

The cripple finished him with a deft thrust, his free hand pushing the pommel so the sword ran Deren through, pinning him to the ground.

Then silence.

Josten felt panic suddenly grip him as he saw the cripple turn his attention to Livia.

'Wait!' he shouted, trying to get up off the ground. The pain in his ribs and hip meant he could barely get up on all fours.

The cripple crouched awkwardly on his bad leg, lifting Livia onto his shoulder.

'Wait,' cried Josten again, as the cripple walked past,

not even deigning to glance in his direction.

All Josten could do was lay there as the cripple carried Livia off into the dark.

30

JOSTEN had been blindly wandering this freezing wood all night, and the rising sun brought some amount of relief. His ribs felt like they were poking out of his side and he could just about fill his lungs with air if he stopped and concentrated for long enough.

He leant against a tree, face resting against the damp, cold bark, feeling its roughness on his cheek. Just a moment's respite. That was all he wanted. Just a few moments to rest and forget about how much his body hurt.

Someone shouted in the distance. Josten couldn't see anyone through the trees but he knew they must be after him. Maybe more tallymen. Maybe Canio's mercenaries. Either way it was unlikely they'd give him a big friendly hug when they found him.

Josten pushed himself off the tree trunk and moved. Every step was agony – down his hip, in his back, in his chest and lungs. His neck still burned from where they'd strung him up and his jaw and cheek ached from being beaten in the grain store. He was in a sorry state. But he was damned if he'd be caught out here in the woods like a snared rabbit.

Half a dozen tallymen lay butchered not too far back and

there weren't any witnesses to who had done the butchering. It was likely that Josten Cade was being blamed for the massacre right now. Not that it mattered anyway. Josten and Mullen had got away with more than their share of butchery over the years; it would be a fitting irony if he ended up being fingered for killings that weren't his to claim.

Josten tried to put as much distance between him and the voices as he could but he wasn't having much luck. In the state he was in he couldn't cover his tracks, so it wouldn't take a bloodhound to follow him through the dense woodland. Any fucker could follow his trail.

'This way!' The cry was only yards behind him.

In the dawn light he thought he could make someone out through the trees and he quickened his pace as best he could. Another glance behind reassured him there was no one too close, but with not watching where he was going his foot slipped out from under him.

He stifled a cry of alarm as he reached the edge of a ridge, realising he couldn't stop himself. The fall was brief... and painful. He buffeted his shoulder, feeling his ribs scream at the impact as he rolled down the hill. Something sharp stuck in his leg.

Josten stuffed a fist in his mouth, biting down on muddy, bloody fingers and screwing his eyes up tight at whatever was embedded in his thigh. He braved a glance, seeing the branch of a thorn bush clinging to his leg.

Wheezing as quietly as he could he shuffled close to the ridge he had just fallen down, hearing his pursuers above. They were talking in whispers, like they knew he was close.

The branch stung his leg and Josten felt tears well in his eyes. He had to get it off.

His hand shook as he grasped the branch and with a sharp tug he pulled, feeling the thorns tearing him open. He opened his mouth to scream, clamping his hand over it and letting out a muffled cry before the darkness enveloped him.

Josten fought against it, trying to stay awake, but it was too much.

His next moments flashed by in dark glimpses. Voices shouting in alarm as his hiding place was discovered. Someone taking his arms, and him too weak to resist. Being dragged, legs trailing in the dirt.

He realised he'd been caught but there was nothing he could do.

By the time they'd dragged Josten back to Canio's camp it was dark, the stink of campfires and the waft of meat hitting him as he drifted in and out of consciousness.

They laid him on a bed. Through the fug of his stupor Josten felt tender hands treating his wounds until he finally lapsed into the blessed arms of sleep.

Freezing cold water dragged him out of a pleasant dream.

Josten sat up in a wide tent, wincing at the pain that wracked his body. Canio's face was the first thing he focused on. It didn't look pleased to see him.

'Always a fucking problem, aren't you, Cade?' Canio said. Josten thought about replying with a smart-arsed comment but the look on Canio's face kept him silent. 'Lucky for you my men found you when they did or you'd be rotting in the woods somewhere.'

'My gratitude knows no depths, Canio,' Josten replied.

'Don't thank me yet. I took payment for you. We both know that means I'm bound to hold up my end of the bargain.'

'If any of those tallymen were left alive that would worry me,' said Josten, unable to suppress a painful smile. 'But they're all dead if my count's right.'

Canio stared at him. 'Confident of that, are you?'

Josten had a familiar sinking feeling he'd grown used to over the past few years.

The flaps to the tent opened at one end as though on cue. Randal limped in, clutching his left arm close to his body. He looked exactly how Josten felt. He'd look a lot worse when Josten had finished with the little cunt, but as he tried to rise he felt the ache of his wounds. Two of Canio's men pressed him back down to the bed, one half-drawing his sword.

'Where is she?' demanded Randal.

'Fuck you,' Josten spat. 'I'll cut your fucking throat.'

Canio stepped in between them. 'All right, calm down,' he said.

'Fuck you, calm down,' Josten replied. 'This bastard is why Mullen's in the dirt.'

'I know,' said Canio, raising his hand. 'And I'm sorry. We all liked that big fucker, but right now you should be worrying about yourself.'

'What have you done with her?' Randal repeated. 'I know there's more in your crew. You must have had help to kill all my men. Where have they taken her?'

Seeing Randal so upset was truly satisfying, though it didn't dull the ache he felt at the loss of Mullen.

'It was one man,' said Josten, the memory of it hitting him hard. 'He cut through your boys like they were nothing. He was a cripple too. Limp, twitch, the whole show.'

'Utter shit.' Randal turned to Canio. 'I paid you for delivery of the girl. You owe me.'

Canio was unmoved by Randal's petulance. 'And I delivered the girl. What do you expect me to do about it now?'

'He knows where she is.' Randal jabbed a finger toward Josten. 'Make him tell you where they've got her.'

'And how do I—'

'Fucking cut his balls off for all I care. Just find out.'

Canio glanced over at Josten as though he was considering it, then back at Randal. 'No one is getting their balls cut off.'

'Is that right?' Randal said, drawing the knife at his belt.

He stalked towards Josten but before he could get close enough to geld him, Canio grasped Randal's wrist.

'I said no.' Canio had never been a man to ask a thing twice.

The tallyman backed down, moving away and reluctantly sheathing his blade. Arrogance fell like a mask over his face. 'All right,' he said. 'We'll find their trail. But I need to borrow your men.'

'You must be kidding,' said Canio.

'Do I look like I make jokes? I've paid you handsomely for delivery of the girl. I want my money's worth. You've been paid for services that weren't delivered. I think that will tarnish your reputation among the mercenary companies when it gets out. And I know what you're thinking, but making me disappear won't solve anything. My men are dead; there's an entire village that saw us arrive. As soon as word gets back to Gothelm that you're responsible for the deaths of his tallymen, half the duchy will be sent to wipe your company from the face of the earth.' He paused, letting his words sink in. 'Five men should do it.'

Canio considered Randal carefully, as though he was wondering if it would be too much bother to kill the little shit. 'You can have four,' he said, finally.

Josten felt himself suddenly gripped by panic. He was wounded, but not incapacitated, and there was no way he was letting this situation get away from him. Livia was out there, frightened and alone, and he remembered well the bargain he'd made with her before the tallymen arrived. Deep inside he knew it was a bargain that had to be honoured.

'I'll make up the five,' he said, struggling to stand.

Canio glared at him, then his expression softened. 'That sounds like a good idea to me.'

'Are you insane?' said Randal. 'This man wants me dead.' He eyed Josten warily.

'Right now he's not the only one,' said Canio. 'You've got four of my men. They'll take you north. Josten goes with you. I suggest you grab your supplies before I change my mind.'

Randal opened his mouth to argue, then thought better of it, surrounded as he was by Canio's men. Without another word, he left.

'Thanks,' Josten said as Randal stalked from the tent. 'I'm sure you think you're doing me a favour,' he said. 'But Randal will kill me the first chance he gets. And given half the chance, I'll do the same.'

'Then don't give him the chance.' Canio shrugged. 'And there's no need to thank me. The sooner you're both out of my hair the better.'

'Don't worry. I won't feel bad about leaving this shit hole behind me.'

'Then good luck.'

Josten couldn't tell if the words were sincere or not, but right now he didn't care.

As Canio left him alone, Josten gave silent thanks his luck was holding out. But only by the most frayed of threads.

✝

I am the hallowed legacy that stands the test of aeons,
Raised and anointed in his eternal name,
My faith is the cloak that protects me in the dark,
My will is the robe that shields me from the burning sun,
In suffering so do I find my strength,
For the blood of conquerors runs through my veins.
I am the terror in the night,
I am vengeance on the wind,
I am Sword Saint.

— Credo of the Sword Saint

The winds of the Ramadi blow devils from Shem
    to the Gargamere,
Dust of uncounted bones, memories of uncounted souls,
The Seven Deserts calling myriad names.
Calling thy despair.

✝   — Lament of the Ramadi

31

The Cordral Extent, 92 years after the Fall

THEY were heading north. Kaleb knew this because he'd heard Bolan and the hostler talking back at the inn at Farcove.

'These boys are bound north on the Scrimshaw Road,' said Bolan.

Kaleb had seen the look on the hostler's face, like the man had just vomited in his mouth. There had been silence between them after that, like the hostler no longer trusted Bolan. Kaleb understood that. He'd only known Bolan a few days and already it was clear he was an easy man to hate.

That night, the six boys had slept under the cart, chained together, while Bolan slept inside the inn. Kaleb had spent the night imagining Bolan in his warm room and his comfortable bed. Some of the other boys talked about how they'd like to slide a knife across his throat, but without a knife to hand it was just a flight of fancy.

The next day, as the sun beat down and the gulls screeched their morning chorus, they carried on the trek north. It was a dull journey, the sea lapping the cliffs to their left, the cart rolling along the endless Scrimshaw Road and Kaleb's stomach grumbling in constant complaint.

Still, all this had to be better than where they'd come from.

Kaleb's earliest memories were of his sister. Her dark hair and her sweet voice still came to him, in the days when his belly had not been empty and the nights hadn't been cold. But she was long gone.

After she'd died, he'd grown up on the streets. The city of Tallis was huge – big enough to get lost in, which had come in handy more than a few times – but filled with the worst scum imaginable. Food had been scarce, and Kaleb spent his time robbing what he could. Bolan and the Seawatch had come for Kaleb as he slept in an alley. Before he could fight or run he was in irons alongside a group of other boys he didn't know, headed to Halbor knew where.

Over the past four days he had learned what he could of his travelling companions. There were the twins, Tem and Rulf, who said very little to anyone but each other. There was Jodeth, who had spent the first two days weeping until Bolan had beaten that out of him. Olivar was always trying to make jokes, despite the hardship, and he often made the other boys laugh when Bolan wasn't looking.

Then there was the last boy. Kaleb didn't know his name for he never spoke to any of them. His eyes were dark, his hair long, and he had a constant look, something like a wolf, about him. Kaleb was even more scared of this one than Bolan, though he did his best to disguise it. Any sign of weakness would be pounced on, by Bolan or the other boys, and he wasn't going to be anyone's victim.

As the sea crashed against the rocks, covering the

Scrimshaw Road with a fine spray, Bolan pulled his cart over.

'Off,' he ordered. The boys duly obeyed, climbing down from the cart and lining up.

'Piss if you have to. No talking,' said the slaver as he fished in his bag. None of them needed to piss.

He walked along the row of boys, offering them a drink from a waterskin and tearing off a hunk of bread for each of them. As they stretched their legs Bolan took himself off to piss over the edge of the cliff down onto the Ebon Sea. Olivar whispered a joke about Bolan struggling to find it beneath that gut of his. None of them dared to laugh out loud.

They journeyed on. Out to sea the horizon turned dark, black clouds rolling across the sky, and by the afternoon the rain hit the coast. The boys hunkered in the back of the cart, cloaks drawn around them. It did little to stop the rain seeping through and soaking them all to the bone. Kaleb noticed Olivar still had that shit-eating grin on his face all the while, but he didn't have the energy to ask him what was so funny.

As the evening turned to night, the rain continued to beat down and Bolan pulled his cart over. The boys crawled beneath it once again, pulling their damp cloaks around them as Bolan hastily erected an awning for himself from a canvas sheet. They sat shivering in the cold as Bolan pulled what looked like a chicken leg from somewhere within his sheepskin cloak and began to devour it in front of them.

When he'd finished he threw the bone off into the dark and lay down on his bedroll for the night. Kaleb saw the other boys settling themselves to sleep. All but Olivar. He simply sat and waited. The last thing Kaleb saw before his eyelids drooped was Olivar's face in the half-light, still grinning.

They awoke to commotion. The rain had stopped and the dawn light was beginning to illuminate the Scrimshaw Road as Kaleb opened his eyes.

'Little. Fucking. Bastard.'

Kaleb heard each of Bolan's words punctuated by a loud thud. The boys crawled out from beneath the cart to see Bolan atop Olivar, smashing the boy's head into the dirt. Olivar didn't move. He certainly had nothing funny to say.

Bolan stood, wiping blood from his neck, and Kaleb could see a knife on the ground nearby. As the boys stood watching, Bolan turned on them, his face a mask of fury.

'And if the rest of you get any fucking ideas, you'll get the same.'

Somehow Olivar had slipped his chains.

Bolan had the boys load Olivar's body onto the back of the cart before they all climbed aboard. Kaleb noticed the boy was still breathing, despite the beating he had taken and the blood covering his face.

'What do we do?' Jodeth asked, as Bolan urged the horse onwards once more.

No one had an answer for him.

It took almost the whole day before Olivar stopped breathing. Bolan checked him in the evening, then when he realised there was no profit to be made, unceremoniously dumped him in the ditch at the side of the Scrimshaw Road. If any of them needed a warning that escape was a stupid idea then seeing Bolan dump that body served well enough.

There was more silence and much less to eat over the next few days as they travelled further north. The Scrimshaw Road eventually led them to a city, similar to the size of Tallis. As Bolan's cart trundled through the gates, Kaleb could see the folk who walked the streets were a fearsome bunch. He'd heard tales of the northerners – pirates and warriors all – but he was no more scared now than he had been the first day he was taken. The only thing that awed him was the vast bridge Bolan took to cross the waters that split the city in two.

Kaleb and the other boys watched with open mouths as a ship sailed right beneath them, traversing from one sea to the other. Then, as quick as they'd arrived they were over the other side and the shining waters were replaced with endless sands once more.

Their road became more dust-strewn with every mile until it was almost impossible to see. Kaleb couldn't understand how Bolan knew where he was going; he seemed to be leading them into empty wasteland for all they could tell. No one had the courage to question him. All they could do was sit in chains.

When Rulf spied something on the horizon and began to make a fuss, Kaleb couldn't help but feel relieved. Through the haze appeared a massive fortress on the horizon and it was nothing like Kaleb had ever seen. The outer walls were white and sheer, the towers within rising like spear points, reaching toward the sky, twisting into the blue as though they were trying to claw their way to the heavens.

The closer they got the more Kaleb's unease grew. Jodeth looked on the verge of tears and Tem and Rulf grasped each other's hands in fear. Only the nameless boy seemed unperturbed by their journey's end. Kaleb tried his best to mimic the boy's blank features, even though his insides roiled.

When they reached the huge gate Bolan pulled on the reins, bringing the cart to a stop. Kaleb could see up close that the fortress walls looked hewn from a single block of white stone. Within them stood a vast metal gate, which looked sturdy enough despite the rust and wear that gnarled it. Atop the walls flew a score of fluttering pennants displaying a black skull on a red background.

Bolan sat and waited until, with a deep grinding sound, the massive gate began to open. It creaked, painfully slow, revealing a little of what was within the fortress.

'Out,' ordered Bolan, as he climbed down from his cart to greet the man who walked from within the fortress.

He wore a plain grey robe from neck to foot. His face was pale and slim, and his dark hair was cropped short to his scalp. He approached Bolan without a sound.

'Well, here they are,' said Bolan.

'Only five?' asked the man in a quiet voice after looking the boys up and down.

'One of them didn't make it. But I'm sure you'll make do.'

Without a word the man pulled a purse from within his robes and handed it to Bolan. The slaver nodded his thanks then turned to the boys.

'Been nice knowing you,' he said, before climbing aboard his cart and steering it back towards the south.

The boys stood in a row, the sun beating down on them.

Silently the man approached, unshackling each of them with a key he produced from his robe. When each of the five boys was freed and their manacles dropped to the floor he stood back and assessed them. No one spoke for an age, and for a moment Kaleb missed Olivar's smart mouth.

'I am Gerval,' said the man. 'Hierarch and master of recruits within the great city of Kragenskûl. You should know that each of you is free to go.' He paused, letting his words sink in.

The boys looked at each other quizzically. Only the silent one with the dark hair held Gerval's gaze.

'But you should also know,' he continued, 'there is desert in all directions. Pick the right way and you may find water in a day. Pick unwisely and you will find only sand, snakes and carrion birds.' He glanced at them each in turn. 'Or you can come with me.' He gestured back toward the rusted gate and the fortress beyond.

Jodeth was the first to move towards the gate. Gerval asked his name as he passed and Jodeth told him before entering. Then Tem and Rulf did the same, leaving Kaleb and the dark-haired boy standing outside.

Kaleb knew he had little choice other than to die in the desert, but something in him wanted to be the last to enter – wanted to show a little defiance, to demonstrate he did have some kind of choice.

Gerval stood and waited for the boys without a sound. Kaleb could not see inside but he knew there would at least be food and some kind of shelter.

He glanced at the other boy. Kaleb couldn't tell whether

or not he intended to enter the fortress or strike out into the wasteland that surrounded them.

Defiance be damned.

Kaleb walked past Gerval, giving his name as he did so. Almost immediately he heard the last boy follow.

'Dantar,' he said as he followed Kaleb inside.

In all the days they had travelled together it was the first word he had spoken.

32

THAT first night they ate and drank their fill. As Hierarch Gerval led them to a solid circular tower the smell of food wafted from within, luring them like moths to a candle. Kaleb had little time to appreciate the buildings that towered around them within the walls of the fortress city. His only thoughts were of filling his empty belly.

Inside they sat at a long table, one of many within the hall. Other boys sat around them in silence, too many for Kaleb to count and of such different races and colours he could barely recognise their origins. There were dark-skinned boys from Shem, brutish-looking boys with almost full beards who must have come from the lowlands of Gargamere, and dozens of others, with skin as pale as the moon, or hair so black it shone, or eyes so blue they resembled ice.

But all this faded into the background as the food came out. Kaleb barely noticed the looks from the boys surrounding them as they were served first. Didn't care that they ate their fill as the rest of the boys in the hall looked on with hungry eyes.

When the five of them had eaten, Gerval came to stand at the end of their table. Still there was silence within the hall.

'That will be the last time you eat without first earning the right,' he said. 'The Qeltine Brotherhood will feed, house and clothe you all. But this benefaction will not come without a price.'

Kaleb looked around, noting that not one other boy within the hall was looking their way. Whoever the Qeltine Brotherhood were, he was grateful for the food and could only hope he could afford whatever price needed paying.

As Gerval left, two cauldrons were brought into the hall. In silence the rest of the boys began to line up, taking a bowl and filling it with whatever stew was inside. Kaleb didn't envy them – the smell of it was vile – but none of them complained. In fact none of them said a word as they took the bowls back to their benches and began to eat.

Kaleb hardly slept that night. The bed, though simple, was more comfortable than any he had ever slept on, and the night was silent, but Kaleb lay awake staring at the ceiling, listening to the quiet breathing of the twenty other boys who shared the room. He had a dread feeling about what the next day might bring, and it seemed that by the time sleep took him the dawn light was already beginning to encroach on the room.

The door opened. Kaleb didn't hear a word ordered or anyone step inside but immediately there was a commotion all around as the other boys rose quickly from their beds to stand like statues in the half-light.

Kaleb had never been a fool, and he rose too, standing to attention before glancing towards the door to see a tall dark figure framed there. He noticed Dantar was already on his feet. Tem and Rulf were the next to rise but Jodeth looked up sluggishly from his bed.

The figure in the doorway walked forward, his footsteps clicking ominously on the stone floor. Kaleb tried not to look at him, seeing the other boys staring straight ahead, but he could not resist. Instantly he regretted it, as he looked upon the most fearsome figure he had ever beheld.

The man's bald head was huge and horribly scarred. Some of the gouge marks looked like they'd been hacked there with an axe, others looked like they'd been carved into his flesh on purpose. Veins stood out on his neck and arms and the leather that adorned his body seemed to fit like a second skin, showing the thick muscle beneath.

He grabbed Jodeth's foot as he lounged in his bed and dragged him out. Jodeth landed on the ground with a thump, wearily protesting, still half asleep. Kaleb watched with growing horror as the scarred giant unhooked a whip from his belt.

The first lash brought such a scream from Jodeth that Kaleb almost had to cover his ears. Only fear stopped him, keeping him transfixed where he stood. At the second lash Jodeth screamed again and tried to crawl away but his torturer stamped down hard on his bare leg with a thick leather boot and continued to go at the boy with his whip.

Jodeth's cries seemed to recede with every stroke until finally he grew silent. The bald brute secured his whip back to his belt and silently walked back past the row of boys and out through the doors. In his wake, the boys filed out of the room.

Kaleb looked down at Jodeth as he passed. Seeing his flesh torn and bloody. He still breathed, albeit weakly, and his body shook in convulsions. Without medical attention it was doubtful he would last long, but no one looked like they were coming to his aid. Kaleb followed the rest of the boys out of the chamber.

Outside was a vast circular courtyard. There must have been hundreds of boys arranged in ranks from the youngest at the front to older youths in their teens towards the rear.

Surrounding them on all sides were high buildings built from the same smooth white stone as the rest of the city. Carvings had been cut into the surface of each, creating friezes that seemed to rise up in the shape of vast animals and beasts of legend. Kaleb could barely comprehend how long it must have taken to hew such things.

No words were spoken as the brute with the whip stood in front of them, regarding them from beneath heavy brows. With a crack of that vicious scourge, they began.

The boys surrounding Kaleb and his fellows moved into a strange stance, their legs spread wide, hands placed in front of them, in a similar manner to how a pugilist might stand before a fight. Beside him, Kaleb saw Dantar adopt the stance almost exactly, and quickly he did likewise. Tem and Rulf weren't so fast to catch on, and he heard one of them yelp. An older boy with a stick had struck one of them on the arm to raise it to the right position. With another quick crack of the cane he struck his thigh to move him into the correct posture.

As soon as the boys had mastered the first stance it

suddenly changed. This time it was Kaleb's turn to make a mistake, his body clearly too far forward, and without any words spoken he was struck in the back, straightening his stance, the cane then nudging his chin upwards.

This went for most of the morning, with Kaleb's legs shaking more violently from the strain every passing moment. It wasn't just the newcomers who were subjected to the lash. Further back the older boys were put through more complicated and strenuous routines, their punishments all the more harsh if they made an error. Kaleb noted more masters wandering the rows of boys, none too shy about using their whips.

When he thought he could take no more, the silent signal was given for them to finish, and the boys filed back inside for food. Kaleb realised what Gerval had meant by them earning the right to eat.

As they sat in silence, Kaleb leaned in close to one of the older boys.

'Is it like this every day?' he whispered.

The boy shook his head almost imperceptibly. 'No,' he whispered back. 'Most days it is worse.'

That night Kaleb stared at Jodeth's empty bed until exhaustion took him.

†

The next weeks and months were an endless routine of sleeping, eating and exercising in the Circle. Every morning they were awakened in the same way by their grim taskmaster, by the man Kaleb came to know as Dominus Morghil. He was one of many such men set to training and disciplining the younger recruits.

Had Kaleb known what this place was months earlier perhaps he would have accepted Gerval's offer of the desert. Now he had no choice but to stay.

Other than the harsh physical discipline they endured, the recruits were quickly indoctrinated in the ways of their order. Every third morning was dedicated to prayer in the temple. The boys would sit in silent reverence before being lectured in the doctrines of their new master – Blood Regent Seferius.

They never saw him, but they learned enough to be afraid. Every one of their masters, even Gerval, seemed to hold the man in reverence, fear even, and that was enough to instil the same respect in Kaleb.

He learned that Seferius ruled in the stead of the Blood Lord, who himself was an avatar of Qeltine, a being of sorcerous might who had perished almost a century before when magic had been excised from the lands of men. Kaleb was taught to observe the rites and sacraments of the Brotherhood, and soon he began to accept the dogma as though it were a part of his own soul.

Not only were these rituals designed to praise the Regent Seferius, but they also taught the boys the honoured history of the Qeltine Brotherhood. It was an ancient order, steeped in war and death and valiant deeds. He learned that the Brotherhood was ancient and powerful, until that power was stripped away during the Fall. Now it served to uphold the tenets of Qeltine until such a time as its followers could bring back magic to the world and serve their god once more.

†

After more weeks than Kaleb could count, he and the other boys – Tem, Rulf and Dantar – were brought to the main temple alone. It was a vast white tower, its walls adorned with carvings of snarling demons and ancient wyrms. Gerval awaited them, surrounded by several other priests, their dark robes hiding any detail of the men beneath.

The four boys were made to kneel in the centre of the temple. On the floor beneath them Kaleb could see sigils carved into the marble, each groove encrusted with something he couldn't identify.

The priests surrounding them were chanting in low voices in a language that Kaleb could not comprehend. Weeks earlier this whole scene would have unnerved him, but not anymore. This seemed normal to him now – despite what he had been put through since his arrival he had learned to trust his mentors, no matter how harsh his treatment.

As the priests chanted, Gerval came to stand before each of them, holding a chalice.

'You have all proven yourselves worthy. Once anointed you will stand a Brother of the Qeltine, granted a new name and a new life.'

Gerval came to stand before Tem and dipped his thumb into the chalice. It came out slick and red. As Tem looked up, his eyes closed, Gerval wiped the blood across his eyelids leaving a crimson line.

'Rise, Tem Kol,' he said.

Tem obeyed silently, and Gerval repeated the process

until the boys stood as brothers – Rulf Hark, Dantar Rus. When finally Gerval came to the end of the line Kaleb could feel his heart fluttering. For the first time since he had come to this place he now truly felt like he belonged.

The blood Gerval spread across his eyelids was warm.

'Rise, Kaleb Kharn.'

Kaleb rose to stand alongside his brothers and the chanting of the priests stopped.

Now they truly belonged to the Qeltine.

33

*T*here was a comfort he took from feeling that sword in his hand. Four feet of honed and tempered steel. Leather binding at the grip that had left calluses on his palm from years of use. The sword felt like it belonged. It was a part of him, and he was naked without it.

Kaleb Kharn had excelled. While still a neophyte he had mastered all forms – Mantis, Spider and Scorpion. Had learned how to overcome the defences of the fighting styles practised by other cults – Raven, Bear, Wolf, Falcon, Viper, Lion.

But even after becoming a formidable swordsman, Kaleb still tried to cling onto some semblance of compassion. Despite the ministrations of Kragenskûl's priests, he was still the Kaleb of old; only he buried it deep, keeping his humanity protected like a taper in a storm.

On the outside no one would ever have suspected.

In the Circle there were few who could stand against him, and certainly no other sword brother. None other than his brother Dantar. It seemed inevitable that they would rise to become Sword Saints. Nothing could stop them.

Of the thirty he had trained alongside in his first year, only four remained. The others had fallen during training or been sent to other parts of Kragenskûl to become priests, Bloodguard, or Silent Sons, if their failure in duty was deemed ignominious enough.

Soon the last four would find out whether they were worthy. Soon they would be put to trial as never before. Though Kaleb didn't know the nature of that trial he was sure he would be worthy. Neither he nor Dantar had reached their place by doubting their abilities. The only question was when that trial would come.

The histories of the Sword Saints had been written in blood and martyrdom. There had been a hundred wars fought for the glory of the Blood Lord and for Qeltine. With each escalation came fables of the bravest and most deadly warriors.

Faergan Ap'Ra was said to have single-handedly held back one thousand Maidens of Mandrithar at the Battle of Black Tarn Pass. During the Age of Penitence, Dulchus Ap'Krul cleaved the head from the Blood Lord of Katamaru, sending him back to his hellish plane for a thousand years. After the Fall, Cestius Ap'Gral travelled alone into the heart of the Gargamere, defeating the Bone Chieftain and returning with his rotting head.

The Sword Saints had always been an order of renown. Always balancing its reputation on the edge of a silver blade. For that reason only the most dedicated, only the most stalwart, could ever pass into their ranks. It was with sacrifice that the Sword Saints would carve their names in history. And so it was with sacrifice they would begin their lives.

Brother on brother was the ultimate test. Men who had trained together as boys now had to prove their devotion to an eidolon they had never seen by slaying one of their own. It was seen as the last sacrifice for men who were to become avatars of death. If Kaleb was worthy, he would survive. If Qeltine smiled down upon him he would advance into the most trusted and respected sect in the Ramadi Wastes. If not he would be buried out in the wilderness, *no marker on his grave, never mourned, merely forgotten.*

The day of the trial was one they had come to fear, to yearn for. When the trial was upon them, each brother would face it with solemn reserve. Expecting victory but accepting defeat if it came. For such was the will of the Blood Lord. The will of the Qeltine Brotherhood.

The Ramadi Wastes, 102 years after the Fall

KALEB stood in the courtyard. Dantar was to his left, then Tem and Hocka. Dominus Morghil paced impatiently, his hands gripped behind him, knuckles white, the muscles of his arms tensed and bulging. His jaw was set as he walked up and down as though he loathed the wait, but he suffered it in silence.

Each brother held his steel in his hand. Soon that steel would be stained red and four would become two. Kaleb gripped his sword loosely, feeling its reassuring weight. As confident as he was with the blade, he knew not to be too sure of victory or to underestimate his brothers. If he was picked to fight opposite Dantar he knew his life would be in the balance, his chance of victory small. Still, he would not let doubt turn to fear. If he was to die it was the Blood Lord's will.

There was movement across the courtyard. A figure appeared in the distance and Morghil ceased his pacing. He let out an impatient breath as he waited for the figure to approach.

Kaleb could see the man was of average height. Though physically he looked nothing special, his gait told the tale of a warrior: tread light and balanced, shoulders set. As he drew closer Kaleb recognised the black robe of a Sword Saint. His hair was dark, falling about his shoulders, and his face bore two deep scars: one across the forehead, one from cheek to chin.

The Sword Saint stood before them, ignoring Morghil as he addressed them.

'I am Jaegor Ap'Han,' he said. 'And I am here to preside over your final assessment.' From within the red sash at his waist he produced a black felt bag. 'Within are four stones: two white, two black. They will determine who you will face in this last test.'

Kaleb drew in a breath as Jaegor walked forward, approaching him first. The Sword Saint held out the bag and Kaleb reached within, feeling the stones against his fingertips. He picked one and held it tight within his palm. Jaegor moved along the row and Kaleb's brothers took their own stones.

'Show them,' said Jaegor.

Each of the brothers held out his palm. Kaleb's stone was shining black and he saw, with some relief, that Dantar's was white. Hocka held out his hand showing white. Kaleb glanced across, first at the black stone on Tem's palm, then at the look of reservation in his eyes. They glanced at one another for the merest moment but both knew their fates were entwined.

'Very well,' said Jaegor, taking a step back. 'Whites, begin.'

Dantar and Hocka stepped forward to face one another. Dantar slid a foot backwards, bending his front knee, sword held high, point down in the Mantis stance. Hocka spread his legs wide, resting his weight on his thighs, sword held to his side, blade down in the Spider.

Kaleb watched, feeling the tension mount as they stood facing one another. He was keen for this to be over, but neither Dantar nor Hocka seemed ready to begin.

Morghil seemed even more impatient, glaring at Dantar as though he had failed in some task, but the dominus said nothing. Jaegor Ap'Han watched in silence and Kaleb began to get a sense that Morghil was cowed by the Sword Saint.

As Kaleb pondered the power Jaegor held, Hocka made his move. Kaleb barely saw Hocka's attack, his blade moved so blindingly fast. But Dantar was swifter, stepping forward into Hocka's attack, his own sword cutting the air faster than Kaleb could see it. One attack, one counter and Hocka shuffled forward, the blade dropping from his fingers. Crimson spilled from his neck across his white tunic. He made no motion to stem the tide.

Dantar stood, sweeping his sword in an arc to flick the blood from the blade then wiping it on the sash at his waist before sheathing it. Hocka fell forward as blood pooled around him.

Before Kaleb had even had a chance to acknowledge the loss of his brother, Jaegor said, 'Blacks, begin.'

Kaleb and Tem silently took their positions facing one another. Tem adopted the Mantis – after all it had been successful for Dantar. Kaleb shifted his stance to stand square, sword back and wide over his head in the Scorpion.

This was it, Kaleb's final test, but as he looked at Tem's

determined expression he felt doubt creep into his thoughts. He and Tem were brothers. They had travelled here together from Farcove, trained together, suffered every trial side by side and now, in this courtyard, one would be forced to kill the other. There was no justice in this, but justice did not matter here in the Circle. Only the will of the Blood Lord. Only obedience.

As Tem raced forward, sword ready to strike, Kaleb expelled any doubt. It almost cost him, as he brought his blade down to parry and Tem anticipated it, sweeping upwards to score a strike at Kaleb's shoulder. The blade was so keen Kaleb suffered no pain, but he could feel the sleeve of his tunic split and the warm spread of blood on his flesh.

He turned, stepping back, sword rising to counter the next strike of Tem's Mantis, but his brother had already adjusted his stance to the Spider.

Despite his brother's change of strategy, Kaleb advanced. Tem's blade thrust forward, but Kaleb made no attempt to parry. Instead he allowed the blade to strike, tearing at his tunic again and scoring a flesh wound at the hip. Kaleb did not step away, letting the strike pierce his flesh so he could gain the advantage.

His own blade struck forward – the Sting of the Scorpion – taking Tem above the hip and into his innards.

Tem stopped, realising he had already lost. As Kaleb swiftly pulled his blade from his brother's body, Tem fell to his knees. He stared up at Kaleb, resigned to his fate as blood spilled across his groin and thighs, turning his white tunic red.

This was the time for the killing blow. It was a mercy

– Tem must have been in agony though his face did not show it. Kaleb lifted his blade to strike but paused. Though their fight had been brief, Tem had fought well. He deserved better than this.

But Kaleb had no choice.

His final blow was swift, piercing Tem's heart and halting his last breath. In a single motion Kaleb slid the sword free and cleaned it on the sash at his waist. After sheathing his blade he walked back to stand beside Dantar.

'Kneel,' Jaegor commanded.

Kaleb and Dantar immediately dropped to one knee. Kaleb felt the sudden sting of his wounds but gave no complaint.

'You have both been chosen, by the grace of the Blood Lord. From this day, until you die in service to the Qeltine Brotherhood, you are Sword Saints. You will bear the title without pride, but so that others might fear your name. Stand Dantar Ap'Rus. Rise Kaleb Ap'Kharn.'

They stood, facing Jaegor. No emotion was shown, despite the thrill filling Kaleb like an elixir.

Jaegor made to speak, but Dantar stepped forward before he could. 'Him,' he said, sword raised, pointing at Morghil. 'I want him.'

A grim smile crossed Morghil's face at the same time a frown creased Jaegor's brow. 'Brother?' said Jaegor. 'This is not—'

'I have waited long enough.' Dantar stepped forward.

Morghil picked up Tem's fallen blade, testing its weight in his right hand as he unfurled the whip from his belt.

'Fear not, Jaegor,' Morghil said. 'This pup has wanted to

test his mettle against me for a decade. It's just a shame you'll only have one new brother to take to war.'

Before Dantar could adopt a stance, Morghil's whip flashed through the air, catching Dantar about the neck. Morghil pulled Dantar towards him, sword raised. Dantar's blade flashed, slicing the whip in two before coming up to parry. Another swift strike and he hacked a furrow in Morghil's bicep. The sword fell from the dominus's hand and Kaleb saw his confidence fade.

Dantar stepped to the side, his swift blade hacking off Morghil's whip arm at the elbow. The dominus gritted his teeth in pain, but he was not as accepting of defeat as Kaleb's brothers had been. He opened his mouth to bellow one last time, just as Dantar swept the head from his shoulders.

Dantar cleaned his blade and turned back to Jaegor. Kaleb could see his face was impassive as he pulled the whip from about his neck, letting it drop to the ground. Jaegor seemed unperturbed by the dominus's demise.

'Brothers,' he said. 'Shall we?'

With that, he led the Sword Saints from the Circle.

34

*T*he Ramadi cults had been in a perpetual state of war for centuries. Even before the Fall they had battled one another for every last league of territory, sacrificing teeming hordes to their dark gods, turning the once verdant lands into a wasteland. Heroes had fought and died and been committed to the histories over those centuries, their deeds becoming legend. And now, gods be willing, Kaleb Ap'Kharn's would be among those hallowed names.

As was tradition, Kaleb, like all fledgling Sword Saints, had been apprenticed to a veteran. Having known nothing but Kragenskûl and its surroundings since he was a child it was only practical that he have someone to follow, to aspire to. Someone to teach him the way beyond the cloistered shelter of the great city in the desert. It was Avenor Ap'Wroch who had been given that task.

He was a solemn and brooding warrior, but then he had a solemn duty. Defeating the enemies of the Blood Regent Seferius was a task only the most dedicated could accomplish. And it was only through war that such a deed could be achieved.

Though Kaleb had been forged within the walls of Kragenskûl, he was to be tempered on the field of battle.

Of all the cults of Ramadi he could have faced, the Hand of Zepheroth was the most ferocious and the most hated. Gortanis, their *vast hive of a city, lurked a hundred leagues across the desert and after ten years of uneasy truce they had decided to break with the treaties and encroach upon the territories and hunting ground of the Qeltine Brotherhood. Such an insult would not stand, and the Blood Lord had sent his armies to strike back with ruthless efficacy.*

For Kaleb Ap'Kharn it would be a deadly trial. During it he would ascend or die; the only choice for a Sword Saint.

With eagerness, he went to war.

The Ramadi Wastes, 103 years after the Fall

THE armoured wagon trundled eastwards along the desert road. Within it, the air was stifling, and Kaleb felt the sweat trickling down his neck, his tunic sticking to his back.

Avenor Ap'Wroch sat opposite. He didn't seem to feel the heat, despite being clad in his black leather warjack. His blade lay across his knees, his hand lightly brushing the sheath as though he were lulling it to sleep.

Kaleb held the grip of his own blade, standing as it was between his legs. He could barely wait to unsheathe it. Avenor glanced across as though sensing his eagerness.

'There will be time aplenty for that,' he said, his deep voice resonating within the wagon.

'I'm sure,' said Kaleb. 'I only hope the Hand know what they are about to unleash.'

Avenor laughed. 'Your confidence serves you well,' he said. 'But never underestimate the enemy. Nor underestimate the need for tactics and diplomacy. Swordplay will save your life in a fight. Negotiation and planning will remove any need for it.'

'We have come far,' said Kaleb, feeling the stifling interior of the wagon more keenly than ever. 'Surely we haven't spent so long travelling in this oven to just negotiate.'

'So eager to whet your blade. I remember when I was like you. I doubt it's what you're expecting.'

'I am ready,' said Kaleb.

'Of course you are,' replied Avenor, closing his eyes, a wry smile on his face.

The veteran's words stung, but Kaleb said nothing. He wasn't so confident that he would disregard such a man. Avenor had fought a dozen campaigns – it would be foolish of Kaleb to dismiss him.

Eventually, the wagon rumbled to a halt. The doors swung wide at the rear, the heat just as oppressive outside. Kaleb stepped out onto the stony ground, squinting against bright light. They were greeted by a single rank of Bloodguard, red armour dusty from the desert, spears held aloft in salute.

Avenor stepped down beside him, almost a head taller, looking as though he were dressed for some kind of parade rather than having just been encased in a sweaty box for the past fifty leagues.

Below them a slope ran down onto a shallow flat plain. The battle camp of the Brotherhood was a sprawling mass of tents, pennants flying the black skull on red everywhere they looked. Immediately Kaleb heard laughing as the warriors of the Bloodguard rested between battles.

Strung up about the perimeter were around a hundred bodies, their sickly sweet smell wafting across the camp. They might have presented a stern message, but leaving corpses to rot would only lead to disease.

Kaleb and Avenor were approached by one of the Bloodguard, his helmet in the crook of his arm, sword by his side. His jaw was square, hair dark and closely shorn.

'Avenor Ap'Wroch,' he said, dropping to one knee and bowing his head. He stood, ignoring Kaleb. 'I am Adjutant Kreese. I have been sent to bring you before General Xanti.'

'Lead on, Adjutant,' Avenor replied.

Kreese walked them down to the camp. Kaleb could see a flat plain stretching beyond it, the detritus of war scattered across its wide expanse. Dead men and horses rotted in the sun, and the ripped and burned pennants of both the Brotherhood and the Hand fluttered in what little breeze there was.

They saw the command tent in the centre of the camp and its guards bowed in reverence as Avenor and Kaleb were led inside. Kreese stood to one side as they entered and Kaleb could see someone reclining in the corner, a damp cloth over his face. Kreese noisily cleared his throat and the man sat up. Kaleb could see he was old, grey hair rising into peaks at his forehead, his face scarred and careworn.

'General Xanti,' Avenor said, regarding the man sternly.

The general stood, a little flustered, before regaining some of his composure.

'Avenor,' said the general.

They regarded one another for a moment, before Xanti smiled and stepped forward. The old veterans clasped arms.

'It's been years,' said Avenor.

'Too long, old friend,' Xanti replied, clapping Avenor on the shoulder.

Kaleb glanced at Kreese, who seemed as uncomfortable with the overly familiar exchange as he was.

'This is Kaleb Ap'Kharn. My brother.' Avenor gestured to where Kaleb stood.

Xanti bowed. 'An honour, my lord,' he said, before turning his attention back to Avenor. 'I wasn't expecting you for days.'

'The hierarch thought it best I come with all haste.'

Xanti's smile quivered at the edge of his mouth.

'I agree, things haven't been progressing as we'd hoped. We are sorely outnumbered. I need more men. But you're here now, Avenor; the tide is about to turn, I'm sure.'

Avenor's smile had faded now. 'Sorely outnumbered? When has the Blood Regent ever accepted that as an excuse, General?'

Xanti frowned. 'Avenor, come now. When does the Blood Regent ever accept anything other than the total annihilation of our enemies? You know as well as I that his expectations can never be met. Remember Black Tarn Pass? Remember how we were expected to hold it for three weeks.'

'I remember we did hold it, General.'

Xanti shook his head. 'And what did it cost us? You are experienced enough to know we cannot sustain such losses. Our wars have gone on long enough.'

'So you and the Hand are just sitting here, waiting...'

'We have agreed on a truce. Until—'

'Until what?' Kaleb could sense the menace in Avenor's voice.

'Until one side becomes bored and returns to their homeland?'

'There will be victory—'

'Yes there will, General. That is why I am here.'

Whatever these two had shared in the past, whatever loyalty or friendship they bore one another, seemed to be gone now.

'I can assure you, there is no need for—'

'Discipline has been allowed to slip. Your men live in squalor. They have grown slovenly. You have bodies strung up rotting in the sun. How long before disease spreads? If left up to you, there would be no Bloodguard left to fight. Then what? The Hand of Zepheroth stroll over the plain to piss on the bodies?'

'I have done all I can,' said Xanti, panic rising in his voice. 'Those corpses send a message. This war is—'

'One we must win,' said Avenor. 'Our light cannot be seen to fade. The glory of the Brotherhood must be preserved. But it seems you are no longer up to the task, General.'

'Avenor, please...'

'Adjutant, have the General clapped in irons.'

'Avenor, we are friends. We have fought together, shoulder to shoulder. We trained together...'

Xanti's words were worthless. His fate was sealed.

Kreese returned with three Bloodguard. Xanti was silent as his hands were manacled and he was led from the tent, leaving the two Sword Saints behind. Avenor stood for some moments in silence.

'I know what you're thinking,' he said finally. 'One moment I speak of diplomacy and tactics. The next I clap an old friend in irons.'

'I'm thinking nothing,' Kaleb lied.

'The truth of it is I wasn't sent here to help. I wasn't sent to add my blade to this army. I was sent here to *lead* this army.'

Killing its general seemed an odd start, but Kaleb would never have dared say it. Avenor was a veteran of the Brotherhood and Kaleb kept a respectful silence.

Later, as the sun fell, bathing the broken battlefield in an ominous red light, they strung General Xanti up. The rest of the corpses had been pulled down and burned, the stench of the fires almost as bad as their rotting bodies.

Twenty men had been chosen at random and were being mercilessly flogged as Xanti was hoisted aloft. Avenor had decided to make an example of more than just their general. No longer were the men slovenly. Each had cleaned his armour and weapons. Each stood with rigid discipline.

For his part, Xanti made no sound as they stretched him out for all to see. It was his one final attempt at dignity. Kaleb admired him for that.

Avenor strode in front of them, silhouetted by the fires.

'Warriors,' he called, as the flogging went on. 'Brothers. Tomorrow we cross the field. Tomorrow we take the fight to the enemy. None of you will fail the Blood Regent. You will make the Brotherhood proud. I will show you the way.'

Kaleb watched from the sideline, admiring the respect Avenor commanded.

'General Kreese,' Avenor spoke to the former adjutant. 'See the men are fed and rested. Tomorrow will be the hardest day of their lives.'

'Yes, my lord,' Kreese replied, and the men fell out.

Kaleb came to stand beside Avenor as he glared out over the plain.

'What do you think of my methods, Kaleb?' he asked.

'I am learning much, brother,' Kaleb replied.

Avenor nodded grimly. 'I hope so. For tomorrow it won't just be me the men will look to for an example.'

'I am ready.' Kaleb meant the words, despite the trepidation within.

Avenor glanced at him, but Kaleb couldn't make out his expression in the shadows.

'Of course you are,' he said, before stepping away.

Over the plain, the ambient light from the camp of the Hand was glowing in the desert sky.

He *was* ready.

35

*W*ord of him spread quickly. Kaleb Ap'Kharn became a name
to fear for the Hand of Zepheroth. That had always been
his intention: to write his reputation in blood across the sands of the
Ramadi Wastes. To become a legend.

It was not an easy road. The battle across the plain had spread,
and quickly. The Bloodguard were slaughtered by the score, but for
every one of them to die Kaleb had made the Hand pay threefold.
His sword was anointed with the blood of a hundred enemies before
he lost count of his tally, and he wore his scars with pride.

In response, the Hand of Zepheroth escalated the war, attacking
on several fronts, enlisting their entire army to destroy the Qeltine
Brotherhood. And for every phalanx they brought forth, the
Brotherhood matched it with one of their own. The Blood Regent
would not be outdone, and his lust for slaughter and sacrifice only
blossomed in the face of the Hand's defiance.

Kaleb revelled in the slaughter. His enemies no longer
bore faces — they were only meat to be cut down for the glory of
the Qeltine.

Avenor rose to become supreme commander of the Brotherhood's
armies and had little time to guide Kaleb in the subtle ways of
warfare. As a result, Kaleb was taught by the blade in his hand,

schooled on the battlefield in the merciless art of slaughter. He was feared and admired in equal measure.

But as the weeks turned to months and the war seemed to stretch out ahead of them, other cults came to see the advantage the Brotherhood and the Hand had gifted them. With their warriors depleted, the two cults, whose former power was unrivalled, had become weak.

The Lords of Byzantus added their own warriors to the slaughter. From the east came the Daughters of Mandrithar, bringing their screaming, frenzied warriors to lay waste to what remained.

Badab Endyr had entered the fray heralded by chariots of bone and skull-helmed berserkers. He was High Lord of the Legion of Wraak, a fierce warrior of the northern wastelands. He also threatened Avenor's crusade, having slaughtered a thousand Bloodguard at the Bridge of Souls. There was nothing to stop him rolling across the wastes on his chariot and levelling Avenor's entire force. Unless he was killed before that could happen.

Avenor knew that soon there would be no army left to lead, and so he had to act. One deft strike in the night to cut the head from the beast. And what better weapon to slay the enemy than one tempered in blood.

The Ramadi Wastes, 104 years after the Fall

THE Legion of Wraak were notorious for their lack of discipline. If their High Lord was slain the entire cult would be in disarray, fighting within its own ranks until a new chieftain could be crowned on a throne made from the skulls of his enemies.

Word had reached Avenor that the Legion was encamped at the base of Kyba Tarn. Scouts had reported that Badab Endyr was housed in one of the ancient watchtowers beside the Cestus River. One swift strike and Kaleb could end the Legion's involvement in this conflict, allowing Avenor to concentrate on the Hand.

Tonight Badab Endyr would die.

Kaleb crouched in the dark across the river. Beside him were four of the Bloodguard's best, elite amongst the Brotherhood. Under different circumstances they would have made Sword Saints, but for one reason or another they had not been deemed suitable. Now was a chance to prove their worth.

Fierdun crawled forward as they made their way to the riverbank. He seemed the most eager to prove himself. Kaleb remembered back to his first battle against the Hand of Zepheroth. He remembered his own eagerness and how it had fuelled him; and how it had also made him complacent. Kaleb still bore the scar on his back to prove it.

He tugged at the tunic bound tightly about Fierdun's torso. The warrior looked back, nodding at the Sword Saint's unspoken order. Silently, Kaleb, Fierdun and the others – Haleg, Vardick and Netan – crawled to the edge of the riverbank.

The river ran past sluggishly, the smell rising, pungent and ripe. Nevertheless, Kaleb led them into the water, holding his weapon aloft as they waded across.

He scanned the far bank as they approached, but there didn't seem to be anyone on guard – for who would be mad enough to brave a camp of fanatics in the dead of night? Surely that would mean only death?

The five warriors crawled up the bank at the other side, feeling the chill of the desert night on their wet bodies. Kaleb listened in the dark, watching the side of the tower for any sign they had been spotted. Nothing.

And then Kaleb was up and running, his four warriors at his heels. They stepped into the shadow of the wall, leaning against the tower, listening as the sound of revelry and combat rose from the enemy encampment. There were screams, loud and shrill, as well as laughter, but whatever foul rites were being enacted was none of Kaleb's concern. Eagerly he began to climb the tower.

A window on the first floor revealed only darkness. Kaleb slipped in, crouching in the dark as his eyes adjusted to the gloom. There was no sound but that of his men following him inside.

Kaleb moved to the edge of the room. The corridor that ran parallel was silent. He paused, straining his ears, trying to catch any kind of sound. There was nothing.

He moved into the corridor. At one end was a door, light lancing out from beneath it. Badab Endyr had to be here somewhere. If it was not him in the room then at least it would be someone who knew where he was hiding.

The four Bloodguard stuck close to Kaleb as he approached the door. When he reached it he stopped and listened again, but there was no sound. He had a brief feeling of unease, that this seemed too easy, before he dismissed it and opened the door.

Candles were lit and mounted on an iron chandelier, illuminating the room. Skulls were piled in every corner and the place stank of raw meat. A door stood at the other side, and Kaleb could suddenly hear a constant knocking from beyond it.

Gripping his blade he crossed the room, his four fighters close behind.

Before he could reach the door, the skulls erupted.

From within the piles of bone that surrounded them, Legion berserkers burst forth, screaming in rage as they raised their axes. Vardick was cut down before he could even move, a plume of blood spurting as an axe cut him shoulder to sternum.

Kaleb had no time to wonder how the Legion had managed to set an ambush for them or who was responsible for the betrayal. He ducked an axe, before cutting down two enemies in quick succession, turning in time to see Haleg take the head of one berserker before his own was lopped from his shoulders.

More berserkers flooded into the room, and Kaleb realised flight was the only option. To stand and fight would be to die.

The way to the door ahead was clear, and as Fierdun and Netan fought furiously behind him, Kaleb darted forward, kicking it open. More light from beyond, dim and red.

'This way,' he barked as he ducked into the room.

He could still hear the knock, knock, knocking as he entered, but had no time to work out its source. He turned briefly, seeing Fierdun and Netan enter, before the look of shock on Netan's face made him turn back.

From the shadows came a giant, bedecked in armour of black bone, his greataxe held aloft and ready to strike.

Kaleb span, dodging the scything blow but Fierdun was not so lucky. The axe came down, splitting his skull and hacking him in two to the waist.

Kaleb struck at the giant, his sword striking the warrior's midriff and shattering his bone armour, but the giant grasped his blade before he had time to pull it free.

The huge warrior stood to full height, eyes staring down with amusement as he pulled the blade free of his body and flung it into the corner of the room.

Kaleb took a step back, barely registering Netan's plight as he was cut down by the clamouring berserkers, their axes hacking at him until the warrior was nothing more than bloody meat.

'You have come for me, Sword Saint?' the giant rumbled. 'Well here I am.'

Kaleb realised this was Badab Endyr, High Lord of the Legion of Wraak. For the first time in a long time, he felt fear well up within him.

The berserkers waited in the doorway. Kaleb could hear them grumbling in their battle lust, but their fear of Badab kept them at bay.

The High Lord placed a foot on Fierdun's body and wrenched his axe free as Kaleb glanced around for an escape route. A flight of stairs led upwards from the room, most likely to the roof and a dead end, but what choice did he have?

'I wonder if your master, Avenor, will learn his lesson when I send him back your head.'

With that he swung the axe, the speed of it belying its size, but Kaleb was faster. He ducked, dodging past the gigantic warrior and heading for the stairs. The axe crashed down again as he raced upwards, splintering the wooden steps behind him.

Kaleb leaped through the hatch at the top of the staircase, finding himself on the open roof of the tower. The noise from the camp below was cacophonous, the light from the fires killing any starlight. The sky was black and there was nowhere to go.

Badab Endyr climbed out of the hatch, his bloodstained axe resting on his shoulder.

'There is nowhere to run, Sword Saint,' he said.

Kaleb already knew the truth of that. 'Give me a weapon,' he said. 'And we can end this.'

Badab's sonorous laugh bellowed into the black night.

'You think me so stupid?' he said. 'I have no need to prove myself against you. All I require is your head.'

He took a step forward. There was nowhere to run. No escape other than leaping from the roof. This had only one way of ending, but at least Kaleb would not be thwarted in his mission.

He ran forward to meet Badab, ducking a swing of that axe before bowling into the huge warrior. It was like hitting a rock, the bone plates of his armour cracking as Kaleb's shoulder impacted against the High Lord's chest.

There was a clatter on the rooftop as Badab lost his grip on the greataxe. Off balance, Kaleb managed to shove him backwards. It was like lifting a bull, but he would not be stopped.

With a cry of rage on Kaleb's lips he and Badab toppled from the roof.

The fall was brief. Wind rushing like a hurricane in his face. Kaleb heard the snap of bone as Badab's body cushioned the impact. He felt pain in his head and shoulder as they both lay crumpled in a heap at the base of the tower. When his head had quit its spinning he looked across to see Badab staring blindly at the sky.

With his one good arm Kaleb tried to crawl away from the High Lord's lifeless body. If he could make it to the river perhaps he could—

Before he had made it five yards, the Legion were on him.

36

*K*aleb's earliest memories were of the streets. He had grown up in a city where opulence and indulgence lived alongside poverty and strife. Both sides of the same city, existing in symbiosis, feeding off one another like a roiling wyrm with two vile heads.

In the years since he'd been taken, Kaleb had tried to suppress his memories, curbing the emotions he had for the place. They had been hard years of hunting for scraps, of huddling from the cold. Years in which he had made and lost many friends, too many to remember the names. His rise to Sainthood within the walls of Kragenskûl had been no harsher than his fight for survival in Tallis. It was a time he was happy to forget, and over the years thoughts of the place had faded to almost nothing.

But there was one memory he tried to keep and hold onto; an ephemeral thing he was desperate to grasp but which would slip through his fingers more often than not. Kaleb Ap'Kharn could barely recall his sister – they had been separated at an early age – but he knew one thing beyond doubt: she had loved him.

He had known that when he was finally beaten, when he lay on the cold ground staring up and waiting for the sunlight to fade, his final memory would be of her. One final image. And as he took his last breath he would see her face, his sister's smiling face, beckoning him home.

Kaleb's eyes opened. The left felt heavy, swollen shut from his fall. His shoulder ached and it took him a moment to realise his hands and feet were manacled.

He was naked and strapped to a chair of heavy oak, hands secured to the arm rests, feet secured to the legs. A hole had been cut from the wood beneath him so it was as though he sat on some kind of sadistic privy. His head had been strapped into position by steel rings at forehead and neck. There was no escape.

Surrounding him was shadow and a small brick room. From beyond it came the sounds of violence, as though a battle were raging all about him. Weapons clashed and voices were raised in bellowing war cants to create a cacophony.

The room was dark; candles burned to his left and right, but Kaleb barely noticed them. He was more focused on the man who sat opposite him. A grey robe hung loosely off his shoulders and a bald tattooed head watched him from the dark.

As Kaleb's vision began to focus he could see the tattoo was of some kind of lizard or great sand wyrm, curled about the man's deep-set right eye. As Kaleb came to, the man smiled.

'Ah,' he said. 'You're still with us.' He took a step out from the shadows and Kaleb could see his gaunt face as though it had been whittled from a rotted tree. 'I was worried you might not regain consciousness. That would have been most unfortunate.'

Kaleb stared back, working his jaw, loosening some of the blood that had settled in his mouth after the fall from the roof. He spat it at the man's feet.

Ignoring the gesture, the man's smile still beamed out those white teeth. 'I am Byram. I hold a somewhat senior position amongst the Legion of Wraak. You might call me "Hierarch" though there is no official term for it within the Legion. They're far too savage to give much credence to titles. You, however, I know are the Sword Saint Kaleb Ap'Kharn, if I'm not mistaken.'

'How did you…?'

'As I said,' Byram continued, 'I hold an elevated position within the Legion. You could say I am its beating heart. Its mind and mouth. Why do you think this rabble does not destroy itself? Can you not hear them? Already they are about to indulge in their savage ritual of slaughter just to find another High Lord.' He paused, as though listening to the baying outside the room. 'Without me this would be an everyday occurrence. Then where would we be?'

He came closer, looking at Kaleb with concern. 'I'm not sure how long you'll last. I'm surprised you survived the fall, but young Badab was quite sturdy. I imagine he was quite the cushion, despite the distance you fell. Still, it's unlikely you'll be with us long. So I will be brief… Where is Avenor?'

Kaleb shook his head. For almost a year now Avenor had moved around regularly to fool the assassins of rival cults. And even if Kaleb had known the answer he would never have told this cur.

'Go to hell,' he said.

'Mmm,' Byram looked disappointed but not surprised. 'That's what I thought you'd say. So I have made arrangements. You will be tortured, Kaleb. It will hurt. You will resist because of your considerable training and the natural power of your will. But eventually, when we have ruined your body and your mind, you will tell all you know.'

A door opened, letting in a little more light and noise from outside. Kaleb could hear that the bawling and shouting from outside had changed to the sound of clashing steel and cries of the dying.

A figure entered and for a moment Kaleb got the impression of a giant snake, head bobbing from side to side in a hypnotic manner. Then the door closed, shutting out the light and noise.

The figure stood beside Byram, the light from the candle illuminating her.

'This is the Carpenter,' Byram said. 'You'll get to know her well. Now I must leave; a new High Lord is hard to find, and it sounds like a lot of potential candidates might be lost before the right one rises to the top of the pile.'

Byram left the room, but Kaleb could not take his eyes from the woman. She was dressed in leather, her clothes sealed with buckles as though she had been strapped in, rather than dressed. Her hair was shorn, sticking from her head in blonde tufts, and her eyes were rimmed with dark shadows as though she had been imbibing a cocktail of drugs for many years.

'Hello, Kaleb,' she said, and again he got that serpentine sense from her voice. 'I am here to ask you some questions.' She turned, walking to a table in the dark before returning with a hammer in her hand. 'But before that I will first show you there is no hope. That resistance is pointless. To do that I must take away what is most precious to you.'

She walked forward and Kaleb felt panic grip him. The Carpenter paused, drinking in his fear. Then she raised the hammer and brought it down on his right hand.

Kaleb spat the pain through his teeth as the first of his knuckles was smashed. She raised the hammer again, another knuckle shattered beneath the hammer's ministration, and this time Kaleb couldn't quell a yelp of pain. Twice more she brought the hammer down until all that remained was a bloody ruin at the end of his wrist.

He stared at it for a moment. His sword hand. No surgeon would ever be able to repair such damage. Of course he could fight with his left – he was a Sword Saint after all – but it merely made the weapon sing. With his right hand he could compose a symphony. And now it was gone.

He breathed erratically as she walked back to the shadows. His head was muddled from the pain and his whole right side had begun to shake.

The Carpenter stared down at him, allowing him to register the damage she had done. Slowly she reached behind her and produced a nail from her belt. It shone in the candlelight, six inches of polished iron.

'Blunt pain hurts, I know. But to get the most from this I will have to stimulate your nerves. That will mean damaging the surrounding flesh and bone… an unfortunate side effect. I would avoid such crudeness if I could, but there is no other way. My apologies.'

She knelt before him. Kaleb felt the panic begin to wash over him once more but he was not afraid of the pain. It was the damage he was afraid of – the prospect of her ruining his body, making him less of a man.

As she positioned the nail against his knee, Kaleb tried to struggle against his bonds but he'd been secured to the solid oak chair with utmost precision. He could not stop what was happening.

The Carpenter struck the head of the nail. Again Kaleb tried to grit his teeth against the pain but he could not quell it. She struck again, this time a light tap, and the nail hit whatever nerve ending she had been aiming for.

Kaleb screamed as the pain seared up his leg. It was as though someone were stripping his muscle from arse to ankle. He had never felt anything like it – not even on the battlefield or in the Circle of Kragenskûl.

Eventually, when he had stopped screaming, she produced another nail.

'Where is Avenor Ap'Wroch?' she asked.

'Go to hell,' Kaleb said. He tried to shut out the pain, tried to draw on all his courage.

The Carpenter positioned the iron nail against the side of his head. Kaleb breathed heavily as she paused, allowing him to savour the prospect of what was about to happen. He gave a little gasp of laughter as she raised the hammer. He had no idea what was funny.

As the hammer came down driving the nail into his skull he felt his throat becoming sore. Another strike and he felt something break in his head. His ears began to throb, and it took a moment to realise that it was his own screams he was hearing.

Beneath him he heard the slosh of his bowels evacuating into a bucket, and it was a weird feeling of satisfaction to suddenly know why they had carved a hole in the seat of the chair.

'Where is Avenor Ap'Wroch?' the Carpenter said.

'I don't know,' Kaleb screamed.

It was the truth; he had no idea where the Sword Saint was.

The Carpenter produced another nail.

37

Iron nails became his life. The resonant sound of the hammer as they were driven into his body. The scything agony as every nerve seemed to be stripped bare and torn free.

Kaleb could not tell how long he suffered; in the dark of the room there was no way to know where day waned and night began.

He tried to hold onto his sanity, to his memories, but with every nail that pummelled into his flesh, with every crack of his bones, he seemed to lose his grip a little more. His life at Kragenskûl became a distant dream. Avenor's crusade was just a memory, Kaleb's victories on the field becoming nothing more than a vision beyond his grasp.

The one thing he had always tried to hold onto, the memory of his sister, faded into nothing. That had been the hardest part for him — trying so hard to hold onto something that slipped out of his hands and fell away into the deep black agony his life had become.

Only one thing mattered anymore. The Carpenter.

Eventually she stopped asking him where Avenor was. It was as though she didn't care, or she realised that Kaleb didn't know, but was still happy to ply her trade, to torture him into madness.

She became the only thing he had. Her and the nails…

†

He sat in the dark. The room was cold but he could still smell the bucket of shit and piss beneath the oaken chair. There was nothing but his breath to keep him company and the perpetual noise of battle outside.

Kaleb had no idea if the sound was real or just another fleeting memory. He could no longer discern between what was real and what was imagined. Where the Carpenter was he had no idea. Neither did he know how long he had been alone. Every time he moved he felt the nails that protruded from his body tease his nerves, filling him with spasmodic pain, making him flinch, causing him endless agony until he willed himself to be still once more.

He tried to concentrate on the noise, on the sounds of battle and death. It was the only way he could stop himself thinking about his body, about the constant pain he was in. Even when he willed himself to be still, his muscles twitched, his left eye fluttering and weeping as tears rolled down his cheek.

The clashing of steel seemed to grow louder. Angry voices screamed in an unknown language. Raging at one another, the battle echoing down myriad corridors.

Kaleb was sure the noise was creeping nearer, louder with every imagined death. The voices became clearer, their gurgling death cries sounding as though they were right outside the room.

The door burst open.

Kaleb flinched, feeling the searing agony course through his body. The light from beyond the room was blocked out by a figure that Kaleb first thought must be the Carpenter.

But the intruder was larger, bulkier. His gait was that of a fighter, confident rather than serpentine.

As the figure came into the light, Kaleb thought he recognised the face. It leaned in, and a memory began to coalesce along with a name... Avenor.

'What have they done to you?' whispered the Sword Saint.

This could not be real. It could not be him; that was impossible. This was merely another trick of the Carpenter's. One more torture.

Kaleb began to laugh. He could hear it in his head, long and loud and raucous.

The man masquerading as Avenor did not share Kaleb's mirth.

'We are leaving this place,' he said, looking over Kaleb's broken body, as though he dare not touch any of the nails sticking from it.

Avenor's expression turned from sympathy to determination, and he gingerly reached for one of the nails. As he pulled out the first one, Kaleb's laughter turned to screams. It was as though Avenor were wrenching free his brain, pulling out what little thoughts and memories were left. Kaleb felt a line of drool spill from his lips, his breath coming long and fast.

One by one, Avenor pulled the iron nails from Kaleb's body. Each one seemed more painful than the last, and of all the tortures he had endured, Kaleb seemed to suffer most under this one. There was a final jolt of agony as Avenor slowly pulled the last nail from Kaleb's knee, before unbuckling the leather straps that held him to the chair.

The Sword Saint stood back. Kaleb was free, but he couldn't move; the pain in his head and limbs was burning like fire. The sounds of violence from outside had erupted once more and seemed closer than ever.

'We have to go,' Avenor said.

Kaleb shook his head, feeling the pain lance through his spine. 'I don't believe this,' he said. 'It's a trick.'

'Stand, boy,' Avenor demanded.

Kaleb trembled in the chair. 'I can't.'

Avenor drew his sword. 'You can and you will. You are a Sword Saint. You will follow me and we'll bloody well walk from this place together.'

For so long he had been at the Carpenter's whim. He would have done anything to obey that snake of a woman. But Avenor would not be denied.

Kaleb pressed his hands against the arm of the chair, feeling the smashed right hand groaning in pain. As he pushed himself up his left leg collapsed beneath him.

Kaleb gritted his teeth as Avenor let him rest the weight of his body against one broad shoulder, and together they walked from the room.

The tower was in disarray as they moved through it. Bloodguard and Legion warriors lay dead and broken, their blood and entrails spread throughout the dark corridors. Avenor carried Kaleb down the twisting staircase that ran through the centre of the tower until he reached the rotted wooden door at the bottom. He kicked it open, revealing the hell that lay beyond.

Vast skeletal beasts, raising weapons of blazing iron, fought one another on a field of molten lava. Among them teemed giant insects, their red carapaces glinting in the light of a thousand fires. They attacked the giant skeletal warriors en masse, mobbing them with their steel blades, cutting them down and consuming them beneath a swarm of death.

Avenor's sword was in his hand as they made their way across the infernal battlefield. Kaleb stumbled along beside him, eyes wide in terror as he took in the scene of carnage.

A skeletal warrior, wreathed in fire, came screaming at them from the throng, axe raised high. Kaleb saw his end approach and faced it as best he could, but Avenor had other ideas. His sword flashed in the night, smashing the skeleton into burning shards. He never missed a step as he dragged Kaleb along beside him.

War raged around them as they picked their way through the nightmare. Kaleb could only watch wide-eyed as he limped through it, smelling the stench of fire and blood. When they eventually reached the far side of the battlefield there was only the black of the waste ahead of them.

Kaleb glanced over his shoulder. It seemed the horde had seen them now, as though their attempt at escape had spurred on the skeletal masses and now they were hell-bent on pursuit.

'You must go,' ordered Avenor. 'Across the desert. Follow the furthest star.' He pointed with his blade and Kaleb squinted with his one eye, seeing a baleful red orb in the sky.

'I can't,' he said, trying to put weight on his right leg and feeling it buckle beneath him.

Avenor pulled him close. 'You are a Sword Saint,' he growled. 'You are Kaleb Ap'Kharn. You will walk.'

Kaleb felt Avenor's words fill him with strength. A part of him remembered who he was, the victories he had achieved, and for the briefest moment he saw the battlefield with clarity. Legion warriors in armour of bone fought against the red-armoured Bloodguard.

'Go,' said Avenor, turning back to the battle.

Kaleb paused long enough to watch Avenor march back towards the charging Legion berserkers, before he turned and stumbled into the dark.

Every fibre of his body screamed as he walked. He could still feel the phantom pain of the nail through his knee, grinding and twisting through the joint as he put weight on it. Kaleb gritted his teeth against the pain, but he could not quell a moan as he took step after agonising step into the darkness.

With every yard he heard the sound of battle recede behind him as he put distance between himself and the raging demon armies. At any moment he expected some figure of bone, wielding serrated iron, to come thrashing and hacking at him out of the dark. His sense of urgency made him want to run but he could manage little more than a stumbling limp as his feet scraped across the hard earth.

The pain became more unbearable but Kaleb weathered it as only a Sword Saint could. Vague memories of who and what he was saw him through, as he focused on that red star in the sky. He had to keep going. Had to survive.

As the sun began to rise he was surrounded by silence.

Kaleb was on his hands and knees now, wounded leg dragging, his ruined right hand screaming as he pulled himself along. The morning brought the cawing of carrion birds and he knew they called out for him, watching eagerly as his slow stumbling flight had turned to a crawl. Every time he thought he could go no further Kaleb dug deep, searching for the reasons. Avenor's words seemed distant now. There was only one thing – the face of a woman – but he could not place her. Kaleb just knew he could not stop. That she would not have wanted him to. That somewhere she was looking for him.

A bird fluttered down beside him, head bobbing, filthy feathers splayed. Its beak dripped with black, a beak that would soon tear through his dead flesh.

Kaleb wanted to laugh but his voice was gone.

'Die,' said the bird. 'Die, die, die.'

But he would not die. Not yet.

Through a distant haze someone was coming. Kaleb tried to shield his eyes from the sun but he could still not make out what he saw.

'Die, die, die,' said the carrion bird.

The figure in the distance approached. Kaleb knew not to trust his eyes. This could be a trick, just like the words of the bird.

If he could stay conscious just a little longer…

Someone crouched beside him, uncorking a waterskin. Cool life trickled over Kaleb's lips and he managed to force some down his parched throat.

He looked up, seeing a face from a distant memory. A

face he knew, but one that had changed; one marred by years, grown gaunt and scarred.

'Kaleb,' spoke the memory.

Kaleb smiled, a name coming to match the features of that face, features that had changed so much.

'Dantar?' he replied.

'Die, die, die,' said the bird.

Kaleb succumbed to the dark.

38

KALEB woke to blinding light and a room of white marble. Columns rose, entwined in bright green vines and drapes of white silk blew in the quiet breeze. At first he thought he had been taken to the Halls of Qeltine to stand forever beside the other Sword Saints. It was the pain and noise that made him realise his mistake.

He could hear troubled cries and weeping from other parts of the room, beyond the billowing silk. When he tried to move to see the source of the noise his body was wracked with agony. Every inch of him was in pain, but he refused to add his own cries to those of the white hall. Kaleb had cried enough. No more.

Raising his right arm he saw that his smashed hand was tightly bound. He tried to flex his fingers but they would not respond. Lifting his left hand to his face he realised his head was likewise tightly bound, his left eye covered, the sickly sweet stench of salve thick in the air around him. As for his shattered knee, any attempt to move it sent lancing pain up from his ankle to buttock.

Before long, silent figures came to minister to him, checking his bindings, applying more salve. The figures were wrapped in white, only their eyes visible. Kaleb tried to speak to them, imploring them to tell him where he was, but they remained silent.

This continued for days, and slowly Kaleb's pain receded. When he asked the white figures for information they continued with their silence.

One morning, still in delirium, he reached out with his left hand, tearing aside the white mask only to see a gaunt face, its mouth sewn shut with metal thread. It was a horrific sight, but one Kaleb was unmoved by. He had seen these 'Silent Sons' before and knew they served the Brotherhood faithfully.

Eventually his bandages were removed and the Silent Sons made him rise from his bed. They supported him as he attempted to walk but Kaleb was weak, only able to limp on his damaged knee. Likewise, his sword hand would never be the same, and he could barely even clench a fist.

The dizziness when he stood gradually receded as he was made to walk every day, but there was a searing pain that would sporadically cut through the centre of his head. His left eye wept uncontrollably and his vision was constantly blurry.

Along with the pain came a lack of memory. No matter how hard he tried to remember his recent past he could only grasp fleeting moments.

There were no answers from the Silent Sons. They continued to minister to him, until finally he could limp unaided, and it seemed he had healed as much as he ever would.

They led him through the halls of white, through the silken drapes, passing the sounds of the dying and the vine-wrapped columns. The Sons walked with him to an open door, then stopped. Kaleb paused for a moment before continuing out into the bright day.

He found himself in the Circle, feeling the familiarity of its wide expanse. The memories of it came flooding back. And though they were not all welcome, Kaleb still cherished them, held onto them like precious gems.

There was a solitary figure standing in the centre of the Circle but through his blurred vision Kaleb could not quite make out any details. He wanted answers, and something told him this lone figure at the centre of the Circle would hold them.

On he limped, pain flashing up his leg and through his skull, the ruin of his right hand clenched and useless. As he drew nearer the figure, Kaleb recognised the man standing there. The Sword Saint stood rigid, black robe tied with a red sash at his waist, blade at his side, dark hair falling over his shoulders. Dantar's face was a blank mask. He gave no smile of welcome.

Kaleb stopped several paces before the Sword Saint, staring into that face he barely recognised.

'Brother?' he said.

'Kaleb,' Dantar replied.

'Why am I here?' asked Kaleb. 'Why was I saved?'

Dantar looked Kaleb up and down, taking in his smashed and ruined body.

'Despite what has happened, you still have value to the Brotherhood. You are a Sword Saint no longer, that much should be obvious, but we can still use you. Seferius is dead. We have a new Blood Regent now. One chosen by prophecy, and it has been foreseen he will raise us up to our former glory. He has deemed it wasteful to cast you out merely because you have become weak.'

'Weak?' said Kaleb, feeling himself flush with anger. 'Give me a blade and I will show you weak.'

Dantar shook his head. 'Look at yourself. Can you even hold a blade?'

'My left hand will work just as well.' Kaleb flexed his left hand, his palm itching for a sword.

'We both know that is not true. And your left leg will never be the same; your lack of balance will never allow you to fight the way you could. Your eye is likewise impaired; you cannot judge distance. We both know you are no longer Kaleb Ap'Kharn.'

'I—' Kaleb wanted to argue, but he knew the truth of it.

'The Brotherhood has no room for cripples,' said Dantar. 'But you have been given a chance at redemption.'

'Redemption?' Kaleb could barely quell his anger. 'Look at me. I am a cripple because I served the Brotherhood faithfully.'

'And you failed. Avenor is dead. His obsession with freeing you from the Legion led to his rash attack. One in which he and hundreds of his best warriors were slaughtered.'

Kaleb felt the news pierce him like a lance through his chest. Avenor was dead because of him, and the guilt of it gradually began to dawn.

'The Silent Sons have done all they can,' said Dantar. 'The Brotherhood has accepted you back within the fold. Now you have a chance to repay that mercy.'

Kaleb began to understand the chance he had been given.

Avenor had sacrificed himself, and for what? To rescue a broken man? They should have let him die. This was more than he deserved.

'What would this new Blood Regent have me do?' Kaleb asked.

'Word has reached us from agents in the Suderfeld. A farm girl has been discovered who could aid us. Who could be the answer to what we seek.'

'What we seek?' Kaleb mulled over the words. 'And what is that?'

'The restoration of the Brotherhood to its former glory. The return of the Blood Lord. To once again commune with Qeltine through blood and sacrifice.'

'And this girl?'

'Could be blessed with the gift of magic.'

Kaleb shook his head. 'After a hundred years? Magic returns to the land in the form of a peasant?'

'I know how it sounds. And I also know how many pretenders there have been over the years. It is a small hope, but one that must be explored.'

'And you are so convinced of the truth in this that you would send a cripple? Why doesn't the Blood Regent send you?'

'No Sword Saints can be spared. We are a dying breed.' He looked Kaleb up and down once more, as though his crippled body made the point for itself. 'Just travel south. Learn what you can. If you return with the girl there will be a place for you among the Brotherhood. You will be given a rank.'

'Given my rank?'

Dantar shook his head. 'Kaleb Ap'Kharn is dead. You will never be a Sword Saint again. But the Blood Regent has promised to reward you.'

Kaleb looked around the Circle, and more memories came flooding back. His knee twitched, his right hand hanging flaccid and useless. But perhaps there was still life in his left.

'Where do I find this girl?' he asked.

✝

The Age of Penitence brought a period of deep division, of conflict and war, throughout the lands of men. Nowhere was this typified more than in the realm of the Seven Deserts – the Ramadi Wastes.

Death cults emerged, worshipping the ancient gods; the lost eidolons who had left the world bereft. The harshness of the land cultivated a brutal culture of perpetual conflict and the disparate tribes evolved into factions dedicated to one god or another – idols to which endless rivers of blood were to be bequeathed in an orgy of blood sacrifice.

In the beginning there were twelve factions, warring in the desert, fighting over scraps. As the centuries unfolded they would develop into their own singular entities – unique organisations with their own creeds and traditions, fashioned for but a single purpose... total dominion over all the lands of men.

But first they would have to overcome one another.

Amidst the ranks of each cult a Blood Lord rose – an avatar of their eidolon's power on earth. Imbued with unparalleled sorcerous power, and unspeakable lusts to match, these beings ruled the Ramadi with an iron fist. But their rivalries were to turn what could have been a glorious conquest into a petty dispute over a wilderness empire.

The Seven Deserts soon turned into a charnel pit. A wasteland of ash and blood. In those distant days of war, three of the cults were wiped out altogether, their adherents left in the desert to rot, the names of their progenitors lost to the desert winds. The remaining nine have remained locked in mortal conflict ever since, honouring their dead gods with slaughter on the battlefield.

With the cults' constant lust for violence and sacrifice, fortune smiles on the rest of the continent. For if the wars of the Ramadi Wastes were ever to cease, and the cults united under a single banner, they might turn their eye to the south and the rich lands that reside there.

†

39

The Cordral Extent, 105 years after the Fall

THE landscape had turned from green to brown, then barren, and it seemed to stretch north forever. If Livia thought she'd been in trouble with Mullen and Josten, there was no doubt she was in trouble now.

The memory of them cut her deep. Seeing Mullen so cruelly butchered haunted her every step. And just when she thought she had found a friend in Josten they had been torn apart from one another.

Her new travelling companion made Josten Cade seem like a court jester. He had not spoken a word to her since she'd woken by a campfire two days previously. Livia had felt fear welling up inside her as he regarded her with cold, dead eyes, but if he was going to do her harm she was sure he'd have done it by now. Instead he had not touched her, not spoken, merely led her forever north and, with little choice to do otherwise, she had followed.

Of course she could have run – he was a cripple after all – but where would she have gone to in this dead land? Livia wouldn't last a day out here, and despite his ailments he seemed to know how to hunt. Each morning she had woken there was a fresh spitted rabbit, though where he had caught such an animal in this desolate place she had no idea.

Livia's body still trembled on occasion from conjuring the power she held within. The thrill of it was wearing off slowly but she could feel the essence of it inside her. Try as she might, Livia could still not repeat her actions with will alone. It was clear that she could only manifest her power when under stress. Clearly being kidnapped by a silent cripple was not stressful enough.

He moved ahead of her, his limp pronounced, left leg heavy under his stooped gait. His clothes were rags, and though Livia knew she must have smelled awful herself, she found herself almost gagging when she got close to him.

And that face. She found herself trying to avoid his gaze, to skirt any need to look at his scarred visage. His hair was unkempt and the scalp beneath the left side was visible in patches. There were scars on his face and neck that looked old, but fresh lesions marked the flesh of his skull. His left eye twitched sporadically and would occasionally weep until he dabbed it with his sleeve.

It made Livia wonder how long this man had been a cripple. She guessed there was only one way to find out, but so far she had remained silent on all matters. But then how did you start a conversation with a man like this? A man who was leading her relentlessly onwards to gods knew where.

'Have we got much farther to go?' she asked.

Her captor said nothing.

'Where are you taking me?' she said, trying her best to sound conversational rather than just plain desperate. 'It's only polite to let someone know their destination when they're on a journey.'

Polite? Livia raised her eyes to the grey skies. *Polite?* This man could kill her at any moment, or worse, and she was rebuking him for his lack of manners.

'At least tell me your name,' she demanded, stopping in the road and folding her arms.

The man shuffled on a few more steps before stopping. He let out a sigh, as though his patience had run thin, but he did not turn around. At least she had got some kind of reaction from him.

Slowly, she took a pace forward. 'My name is Livia Harrow,' she said gently.

He turned slowly to face her and she almost took a step back in revulsion. In the sunlight he was pallid, left eye glassy and moist. It twitched as he regarded her and a tear broke free and ran down his scarred cheek.

Though it pained her she held out her hand for him to shake. He glanced down at it, then back to her face.

'You must keep walking,' he said. 'We still have far to go.'

His voice was warm, the only thing about him that did not fill her with revulsion. And at last he had spoken – it was a start.

Livia quickened her pace to move up beside him.

'Please, tell me your name.'

He glanced at her nervously, as though this scant human contact made him anxious. As though her demonstrating she was a person with thoughts and feelings was unnerving to him.

'You said we still have far to go. I need to call you something if we're going to be together for much longer.'

He glanced at her again, then back to the road before saying, 'Kaleb.'

Livia felt her heart race that much faster. This was progress.

'It's nice to meet you, Kaleb,' she said, trying a smile. He didn't seem to notice that. 'Do you have a second name? A family name?'

Kaleb's eyes scanned the ground for a brief moment as though searching for an answer. Then he shook his head.

'No. Just Kaleb.'

'Okay. Just Kaleb it is.' She tried another wide smile with that but he didn't seem to have one to respond with. 'Where are you taking me?'

'We are travelling north, to Kragenskûl.'

'Why?' This was like pulling teeth, but Livia's smile was fixed and she persevered.

'Because the Qeltine Brotherhood demands it.'

Kaleb spoke as though reciting litanies rather than having a conversation.

'And what do they want with me, Kaleb?'

He shook his scarred head. 'You do not need to know why.'

'But—'

'Enough questions. We must walk now.' With that, he limped on.

Livia watched him go. Wondering if now was the time she should try to escape. If she ran, surely he would never catch her. But then he had found her in the middle of nowhere. In the middle of a wood even she didn't know she was headed to. Even if she could escape him now would he simply hunt her down, limping relentlessly on until he tracked her once more?

She continued after him, glancing around at the bleak terrain, still trying to work out whether it would be best to take her chances in the wild.

The sun had begun to creep through the grey sky as they came to an ancient bridge. Kaleb stopped, looking as though he expected something to come charging along its ancient stone walkway. Livia saw that would be impossible; the bridge had collapsed halfway across. It was a beautiful thing among its bleak surroundings – ancient carved stone that would once have stood white and majestic, traversing a dried riverbed. Perhaps in the past, before the Fall or maybe centuries before that, it might have been a wondrous experience to step across that bridge as the fast waters flowed beneath. Now it was just a crumbling relic in a desiccated valley.

As they stood in silence, Livia was sure she heard the fleeting ring of a bell in the distance.

Kaleb suddenly grasped her arm with his right hand. Briefly she looked down, noticing his knuckles, knobbled and broken. He dragged her to the side of the bridge, pulling her down next to him as he hunkered behind the stone bulwark.

The ringing grew louder. Livia could feel her heart beating like thunder as she wondered what kind of monster could have spooked Kaleb so. It was approaching along the dried riverbed. Unable to contain her curiosity she moved, glancing through an eroded section of the bridge to see what it was. The sight almost made her laugh out loud.

An old tinker was leading his mule behind him. The beast was over-laden with wares and looked none too pleased, though it followed its master obediently. The tinker looked old and wretched, his only redeeming feature the jaunty cap he wore atop his head on which sat the ringing bell that heralded his arrival.

Livia relaxed and made to stand. Kaleb tightened his grip, forcing her to remain hidden behind the bridge.

'What we got here?' The voice echoed up from the narrow valley below.

The tinker was no longer alone.

Four men had appeared from nowhere; all of them looked like they'd been in the wilds for days. They dwarfed the tinker, who smiled a toothless grin back at them.

'What's your name, old man?' asked one of them, as another began to rifle through the pack mule's load.

'I'm Jachino Sand,' the old man replied. Livia could still see that grin but hear the uneasiness in his voice. 'Purveyor of trinkets. Traveller on the great road of—'

'All right, grandpa. We don't need the spiel.'

'Apologies. I have been on the road for many days. I haven't seen fellow travellers—'

'What have we got?' said the bandit, ignoring the old man's rant.

'Fuck all,' said the one checking the mule. 'Few pots and pans. No silver.'

'Where is it?' asked the bandit leader.

Jachino shook his head. 'I – I have nothing. Times are hard, as I'm sure you kn—'

'I said, where is it?'

The old man held his hands up. 'I am a member of the

Penitent Order. I have been given dispensation to travel this road by the Lords of Byzantus. I come under their protec—'

The bandit leader took a step forward. Livia saw there was already a knife in his hand, which he shoved into Jachino's gut.

She opened her mouth to scream. Despite all she had seen, the sudden brutality still filled her with horror. Kaleb's hand clamped over her mouth before she could utter a sound.

He pulled her away from the gap in the bridge, hand still silencing her. Livia could only listen as the bandits cut the old man to pieces. His cries of pain were mercifully short.

She and Kaleb hid behind the bridge for what seemed an age as the bandits tore Jachino's possessions apart, searching for their silver. When they had finished she heard one of them say, 'Fuck all. The old fart wasn't lying.'

They laughed after that. Livia could hear it echoing along the dried riverbed as they moved away.

When it was silent, Kaleb moved his hand away from her mouth.

'Quickly,' he said, taking her arm and leading her down the riverbank and into the valley.

Livia couldn't help but look down at Jachino's body for a fleeting moment, wondering how desperate the old man must have been to come and ply his trade in this dangerous country. His mule was gone. The bandits had even taken the old man's hat with its annoying bell. So much for the Penitent Order and its protection.

As Kaleb pulled her up the other side of the riverbank

her horror at Jachino's murder was already waning.

Livia didn't know what troubled her the most – the fact that she had no idea what fate awaited her to the north, or that it no longer frightened her.

40

THE Cordral Extent was imbued with its own savage beauty. In the main it was a vast desert of dust and sharp stones, but every now and again there was a copse or a tree blown into a theatrical pose by the incessant winds, branches clawing at the sky. Sometimes there would be a solitary flower blooming within the carcass of the tree, defiant and vivid against the desolation.

Half a dozen times Kaleb had spied a monument in the distance, stark against the bleak horizon. Crumbling ruins that were a testament to a glorious past, lost to the ancients. On rarer occasions there were definite signs of civilisation – a well-worn road or distant crops – but the further north they travelled the more desolate this place became.

Livia was keeping pace with a quiet resolve that Kaleb would have admired were she not so troublesome to him. It wasn't just her defiant spirit. Every time he looked into her face it sparked a memory from the distant past. It was difficult to hold her gaze, and he found himself avoiding it as often as he could. That task in itself was made all the more difficult by her incessant noise.

'How much further?' she asked. Kaleb had lost count of

the times he had heard that question and it was beginning to try even his patience.

'We are almost there,' Kaleb lied. The same lie as always. He did not want her to lose heart by telling her the truth of it. This would be a gruelling journey neither of them might survive. Livia fell quiet but he knew it was only a brief respite.

As they walked he was conscious of her looking at him. He knew he must have looked pitiful – even frightening – but to her credit she simply seemed curious. Despite that Kaleb still felt self-conscious – a sensation he was unused to. No matter how he tried to mask his limp or his withered hand or the weeping from his eye, he knew his ailments were all too obvious. The only way to distract attention from his broken body was to lead them on apace, but still it did not subdue Livia's enquiries.

'What happened to your face?' she asked again.

Memories came back in a flood. A dark room. Not knowing if he was awake or dreaming. A serpent. Pain.

Kaleb glanced at her briefly but did not answer for the half-dozenth time.

'Only, the scars look like they were made intentionally,' she continued. 'I just wondered what you've been through.'

Why would she ask him such a thing? What purpose could it serve if she knew how he had been given those scars?

Kaleb turned his attention back to the far horizon, but his silence only seemed to frustrate her.

'What about the hand?' she asked. 'Some kind of farming accident?'

He stopped and turned towards her. No, there was no

subterfuge there. She was not enquiring to gain some kind of advantage. It was genuine curiosity born of… concern? But why would she care? He was her captor. She owed him nothing and yet…

Kaleb turned his head so she could clearly see the wounds on his face. Her brow furrowed at the sight, and Kaleb knew full well the hideous visage he bore.

'Carpenter,' he said, feeling his left eye twitch, water pooling beneath his left lid. The memory of it haunted him, just the mention of the name on his lips raising the hairs at the back of his neck.

Livia's hand moved, her fingertips reaching towards Kaleb's face as though she might touch his scars. Panic gripped him and his left hand came up on instinct, grasping her wrist. He held it there as they stared at one another. A flicker across her cheek made Kaleb realise he was holding her too tightly, though she tried her best to hide the pain.

He released her wrist and turned, moving on. This time Livia followed in silence.

The path led them on for another half day until Kaleb finally spotted the monument up ahead. Livia noticed it too, and he heard her intake of breath as she took in the sight.

It would once have stood tall, but now the towers that surrounded it were crumbled and fallen. The relic was perched just on the edge of a huge crevasse that seemed to spread as far as the eye could see to east and west.

Livia suddenly increased her pace, as though eager to reach this semblance of civilisation. Kaleb held out an arm, stopping her as she attempted to move past him.

'Wait,' he said. 'Someone could be waiting. Or something.'

'What?' she replied. 'Nothing's lived in that place for centuries.'

'There are dangers everywhere in this land,' Kaleb replied. His words were true enough, and they had not yet reached the Ramadi Wastes. The dangers in that war-torn land were tenfold compared to the relative safety of the Cordral Extent.

He approached with caution, conscious of his limp, aware that his senses weren't what they once were. His eye constantly twitched, ruining his peripheral vision, his ear throbbed with a low hum, hampering his hearing, and he bore no weapon. Now more than ever he felt vulnerable as they approached the entrance to the ancient place.

Before he stepped over the threshold, Kaleb paused. There was a slight breeze that carried no aroma and all he could hear was Livia's breathing as she stood close by him. Through the archway was a crooked tree next to a small stagnant pool.

'What are we waiting for?' Livia whispered.

Kaleb had no answer for her.

He stepped forward into what had once been a spacious courtyard, now eaten away by sand and dust. The walls that surrounded the place had crumbled, the eroded heads of ancient statues lying in the dust as though victims of a mass execution.

'Please tell me this means we can rest,' said Livia.

Kaleb nodded, moving forward toward the pool. He stood at the edge, peering into the dank water. If the stories he had heard of nomadic traditions were true there may well be a lifeline for both of them here.

He examined the base of the crooked tree, brushing away some of the dust at its base and finding a rope secured to it. Brushing away more dust, Kaleb saw the rope ran into the pool, and he grasped it, pulling firmly. From beneath the surface rose an animal bladder secured with twine. The corner of Kaleb's mouth twitched into a smile and he turned to Livia, showing her his prize.

She raised an eyebrow. 'That looks disgusting,' she said. 'But if it's brought a smile to that face I'm very pleased for you.'

When Kaleb ripped open the bladder Livia's raised eyebrow became an expression of joy. Inside were dried meat and a skin of fresh water.

'Traders and messengers in these lands leave hidden caches for one another,' he said. 'It is the code of the desert.'

'Thank the gods for that,' Livia replied, eagerly taking the waterskin he offered and unstoppering it. She glugged a long draught, then reached for the meat.

'Not too much. Who can say when we might find another.'

Livia did as he said and they both ate sparingly.

As night drew in, Kaleb constructed a fire at the edge of the courtyard, beneath the shadow of one of the shattered towers.

Livia was silent as they sat and Kaleb was thankful for the temporary respite. Still, he found his eyes drifting towards her as they rested in the firelight. There was something familiar about her. Something that stirred a memory from his long forgotten past, before Kragenskûl. Before the Circle.

'What is it?' she asked. 'You've been staring all night.'

Kaleb had tried to be discreet with his glances. Obviously he had failed.

'You remind me of someone,' he confessed.

She looked at him, the light of the flames dancing on her features. 'Someone else you kidnapped?'

An attempt at humour. He ignored it. 'No I... Someone from my childhood. She was...'

He struggled to find the words. Struggled even to picture her face, but something about Livia made him remember those days with his sister in Tallis.

'Well I hope you showed her a better time than you've shown me.'

Kaleb shook his head. 'It was not like that. It *is* not like that. I am not your captor.'

'You're not my... Well you're doing a pretty good impression.' Livia stood and brushed the sand from her skirts. 'Does that mean I can go?' She turned and walked towards the dark.

Kaleb stood as quickly as his painful leg would allow.

'Don't worry,' Livia cast back. 'I'm not running. I'm taking a piss. If I'm allowed to do that alone.'

Kaleb stood and watched her march into the shadows, before letting out a long sigh. He had been set a seemingly impossible task – one he had grasped eagerly to prove he was still worthy of the Brotherhood – but now doubt was creeping into his mind.

He was a warrior born – an exemplar of his craft, reduced to the status of abductor. It was beneath him, he knew that; a task with little honour or distinction. As he stared into the flames the fleeting thought of allowing Livia her freedom cast its shadow over him.

The flames crackled and Kaleb heard a faint jingling in his ear. There should have been no doubt – this was his task. He had no will of his own. All he knew was how to obey.

As he chastised himself, the jingling sound grew louder, until Kaleb realised it was not his damaged senses that caused the noise.

'Hello there,' said a voice, faintly familiar in the dark.

Kaleb took a step back from the flames at the sound of the intruder, silently cursing himself for his inattention.

'Woah there, stranger. We mean you no harm.'

Three men emerged into the light. One was small, with jagged teeth so yellow Kaleb could see their sickly colour even in the wan firelight. The other was skinny but with a ridiculous paunch indicating a man whose diet consisted of nothing but ale. The third was tall, overconfident, wearing a cap with a bell on it.

The tinker's cap. These were his murderers.

Kaleb stood silently, weighing up their fighting capabilities from their stature, their expressions, the weapons they carried.

'Looks like you're lost out here,' said the one with the yellow teeth. The leader. 'Us too. Just wanted to get warm by that fire.' He pointed at the flickering flames.

Kaleb didn't take his eyes from the man but he was

conscious that somewhere in the dark Livia was hiding. She must have heard them. Kaleb could only hope she had the wits to stay out of sight.

'You don't mind us getting warm, do you?' said the leader, taking a step forward.

Kaleb didn't take a step back but he adjusted his stance to face the man side on. What once would have been a sure transition was now a clumsy movement as his damaged right knee almost buckled.

'He's a fucking cripple,' said the one with the paunch. 'What we waiting for?'

With that he pulled out a knife, striding forward.

The leader shrugged, pulling a club from his belt. 'Sorry,' he said. 'Looks like we do mean you harm.'

Kaleb set his weight on his good leg. As he expected the first attack was clumsy, the one with the paunch striking high, signalling his intent as though he'd written it on parchment. Kaleb hardly moved, turning the man's elbow with his crippled hand and redirecting the attack with his good one. In an instant the knife was sticking in its owner's throat and he stared as though he had no idea how it got there.

The leader came in yelling, waving the club like he was scaring birds away. Kaleb turned his head a few inches, allowing the club to pass him by. His good hand smashed the man's throat.

As the leader fell back clutching his crushed windpipe, Kaleb heard the tinker's hat jingling. Its wearer was drawing a short sword, but Kaleb moved in; even on a damaged leg he was faster than the draw. As the blade left its scabbard,

Kaleb grasped the man's wrist, fingers of his crippled hand redirecting the blade towards its owner's belly. He shifted his weight, pressing the blade home. The man stared at him for scant seconds before pitching back into the dark, the bell jingling as he fell.

Kaleb turned, already sensing the presence of a fourth assailant, already making ready to attack, but he was forced to stay his hand.

From the darkness shuffled the last bandit, his eyes wide with fear. He had Livia about the neck, a knife pressed to her throat.

'Don't come any closer,' he said. 'I'll kill her, I mean it.'

Before Kaleb could think what to do, a lancing pain struck his side. His knee buckled and he stumbled to the side, his hand reaching down to pull out the knife. The bandit with the paunch was on his knees. He'd dragged the knife from his own throat and struck in a last-ditch attempt at vengeance.

'Don't fucking move!' said the one holding Livia.

Kaleb glanced down. His attacker was lying prone. After pulling the blade from his own throat the blood was running free, his last ounces of life seeping into the dirt. Kaleb held that knife in his hand, the red blade shining in the firelight.

'I'm taking her, and I'm walking away,' said the man, dragging Livia toward the archway.

Kaleb's side felt cold. He had to do something quickly; he would pass out soon.

Before the man could back away any further, Livia grasped his wrist, pulling the knife away from her throat and biting the arm he held around her neck. The man squealed, releasing her.

Kaleb flung the blade.

His aim was off, only hitting the man in the cheek where it stuck and quivered.

As he fell to one knee, all he could hear were the man's screams.

41

KALEB was on the ground, three corpses surrounding him, but one of the bandits was still very much alive. He stared at Livia, the knife sticking out of his face as he let out a strangled cry, eyes so wide she could see the campfire dancing off the whites. It turned her stomach. She backed away a step as he came forward, hands held out toward her. He stumbled and let out another garbled sob. Livia was transfixed by the hideous sight.

Slowly, with one shaking hand, he reached up and grasped the handle of the knife. A screeching sound came from his throat as he drew the blade from his cheek, blood running down his face and neck. When it was free of his cheek, the bandit's look of shock furrowed into anger. He spoke again but the open flap of his face made the words unintelligible.

When he came at her, Livia knew she had to move or die.

She turned, instinct taking over as the man's footsteps made clumsy stamping sounds in the dirt. For a moment Livia thought about hitching her skirts and running off into the night, but something stopped her – a voice at the back of her mind, a devil inside telling her not to be such a coward.

The fire was waning, its light a dying beacon in the night. Livia rushed to it, grasping a branch of wood that lay half in the flames. She cried out as the blackened branch burned her palm. A cry that turned to a scream of rage as she span, raising the fiery brand high.

He was coming at her, eyes hungry for vengeance, his mouth a bloody ruin, and his knife blade glinting black. She brought the flaming branch down and she saw his eyes widen in surprise. The branch struck with a sparking thud, the bandit's unintelligible babble turning to a whining cry of pain. He staggered back, the knife dropping from his hand.

The searing pain of the burning branch coursed up her arm but still she held on, determined not to back down. She expected him to come at her again, spitting blood, thirsty for her end. Instead he turned and fled into the night.

She was breathing heavily, her legs shaking. It took a moment for her to let go of the branch. Then the pain hit her, like she had been branded.

Livia grasped her wrist and opened her mouth to scream but nothing came out. The darkness closed in…

Mist enshrouded her. All she could see was her burned and blackened hand, flesh cracked, skin seared. It was a hand that had dealt death aplenty. And given life.

The power coursed from deep within, a light that started as an ember growing to burn like a sun. It glowed beneath the black flesh, seeping out through the cracked skin like the sun, blinding, healing.

She closed her eyes against it, blocking it out, and when she opened her eyes the pain and the black flesh were gone. So was the mist, so was the darkness, and all she saw was a meadow of corpses, each face staring at the too-blue sky above...

It was dawn. Livia awoke to the four bodies lying around her. The fire had burned out. As she lifted her head from the floor she spat, and wiped away the dust that had crusted about her lips. She examined her hand to see it was healed, like new.

Livia had barely enough time to acknowledge the miracle before her eyes darted to where Kaleb lay. She picked herself up, stumbling on unsteady legs as she rushed to his side. Blood had ebbed from the knife wound in his side, drying around him in a pool, turning the sand a dark, sickly colour.

Her hands shook as she reached out to him, turning him over. His eyes were closed, face pallid. Bowing her head to his chest, she let out a sigh as she heard the weak beat of his heart.

Then she looked at the archway to the south. She could escape now. Grasp her freedom and take the long road back to the Suderfeld. Back home.

But even if she survived the journey alone, what was home anymore? The people there wanted her dead. Her only chance at survival lay dying in the dirt next to her.

Livia lifted Kaleb's ragged shirt, now caked with dried blood. The wound beneath had clotted but he had bled profusely before that happened. She grabbed a knife, cutting a strip from her skirt to bind his wound, but try as she might she could not lift him to wrap the cotton around his waist.

Kaleb moaned as she moved him.

Livia moved her face close to his, seeing his half-opened eyes. 'Kaleb?' she said.

His lips moved but all he could do was mumble.

344

'I don't know what to do,' she said to him. To herself. To no one.

A shadow moved across the dusty ground. Vultures were wheeling above the ancient monument, keen to claim the carrion that lay strewn below.

Anger welled up within Livia. Those bastard birds could feast on the dead as much as they wanted but they would not claim Kaleb. She needed him. He was hers.

One of the birds landed, black and fetid, a hooked dagger of a beak protruding from its corpse face. It looked around with baleful eyes before hopping toward one of the bodies, stabbing in with the beak and tearing off a strip of cloth and flesh.

Another landed even closer, taking a long, lingering look at Kaleb's prone form before creeping towards easier meat. Then another, closer still, craning its head towards Livia and screeching a challenge.

'You can't have him,' she spat, grabbing Kaleb and dragging him away. He was heavy but she found the strength, pulling him across the dirt, away from the foul birds and toward the stagnant pool.

As she did so more vultures swooped down, as though unleashed in a feeding frenzy. They mobbed the other bodies, ripping and tearing, consuming the fresh meat hungrily. A bell jingled as one of them grabbed the tinker's hat, shaking it angrily in its beak when it found no meat inside.

Livia pulled Kaleb further from them until she was ankle-deep in the pool. One of the birds stalked forward, pecking at Kaleb as she pulled. Anger boiled up within her, and she screamed at the creature with a primal yell of hate. The beast was startled, having the good sense to hop back a pace, as Livia pulled Kaleb further into the pool. Deeper she went, cradling his head, feeling the anger burning within her. She looked down at his face, his lips moving wordlessly, his eyes glazed.

Around her the water of the pool began to bubble as she laid her hands on him, feeling his life pulsing weakly against her palms…

Fields of wheat stretched to the ice-blue sky, billowing like a cloak in the wind. Her hand brushed their ears as she walked between the yellow stalks, breathing in their fresh aroma as the breeze cooled her cheeks.

Respite from the endless war filled her with a glow that radiated from her stomach, up through her chest and into her throat. She let out a sigh, breathing onto the ripe crops, filling them with a virulent glow. Her hair began to billow around her, the white silk shift she wore undulating as though swept by the tide.

The land breathed once more after a millennium of warfare…

Something hit the dirt beside her head.

Livia looked up to find herself submerged. Her vision was blurred and she blinked away the fug to see the carnage filling the courtyard. Dead vultures lay all around, eyes of glass staring, beaks reddened with blood and flesh gaping silently at the blue sky.

She turned in panic, seeing steam rising from the pool. Kaleb floated atop the surface and she rushed to him, sloshing through the warm water and grasping his shirt, pulling him to the side of the pool.

'Kaleb?' she said. 'Kaleb…'

It was then she noticed his face had changed. Though still scarred, his eye no longer drooped. The wounds on his scalp no longer looked livid but were faded as though years old.

His eyes opened and he moved with a start, floundering in the water until he managed to regain his senses and pull himself out.

Livia could only watch as he found his feet, at first stumbling, then walking on steady legs, no longer limping like a cripple. Slowly Kaleb raised his once shattered hand to his face, flexing fingers that had been crooked and broken. He clenched his fist in amazement.

'What has happened to me?' he asked.

Livia pulled herself from the pool, careful to avoid the dead bodies of the vultures lying all about.

'I… I think I did this,' she replied, unsure if she spoke the truth.

He turned to look at her, then at the scene around them.

'They were right about you,' he said, raising his once crippled hand again and flexing his fingers.

'Good for them,' she replied. 'So exactly who are *they*?'

'The Brotherhood. They said you could hold the key.'

'The key? The key to what?'

Kaleb shook his head. 'I have already said too much.'

'Really?' She could feel her anger burning. 'Because from here it doesn't feel like you've said much at all. But none of that really matters as long as you take me home now.'

'Take you back home?' he said. 'I cannot take you home. We must reach Kragenskûl. Now more than ever. You must be delivered to the Blood Regent with all haste.'

'But... I saved your life.' She was feeling angry again, but this time her energy was all but spent. There was no power welling up within her this time, just ire. 'You'd be dead if it wasn't—'

'My life is not important,' said Kaleb, all emotion draining from him. 'The only thing that matters is that I complete my task. And that task matters now, more than ever. Before this no one knew if you really possessed any power, but now...'

She wanted to rail against him. Wanted to rekindle the power she had felt not moments before but all she felt was drained.

As he made his way from the ancient monument and the corpses within, Livia followed. If she ran or stayed she would die. But follow Kaleb and she'd live... and sooner or later she'd find a way out of this.

42

Her silence was the loudest thing Kaleb had ever heard. She wanted her freedom, and only he could grant it.

Yet she held such power.

The Brotherhood had been right about her. In a land where magic had been absent for a century, she was the firstborn. The start of a new breed. The Brotherhood had to have her. Had to harness her power for their own. It was the only way.

And yet Kaleb knew he was only alive because of her. Were it not for Livia's power he would be dead in the sand, rotting carrion for the birds. She had saved him. Restored him. He could only be grateful for that – but not grateful enough to grant her liberty.

'This will soon be over,' he said in a weak attempt to console her.

Livia glanced across at him, her mournful expression changing as her brow furrowed.

'By the gods, it speaks,' she said.

Kaleb couldn't hold her gaze, but instead looked at the northern horizon, toward which they were travelling.

'I understand why this must be difficult for you.' In truth

he had little idea. 'But when we arrive at Kragenskûl you will understand. The Blood Regent can offer you a position of great reverence. You will no longer need to run. You will be protected. Exalted.'

'That all sounds so nice,' she said, and at first Kaleb thought he had put her at ease. 'My uncle often told me stories of the northern desert cults. Reverence sounds great. Will you sacrifice babies to me on the hour or just every tenday?'

'Many tales are told,' he replied. 'I'm sure they are worse than the truth of it.'

'Whatever the truth of it I will still be a captive,' she said. 'Still held against my will.'

'What are your other choices? If I set you free you will only be captured by someone else. Someone who might not offer you the same benevolence as the Brotherhood.'

'At least I'd have a chance to be free.'

Kaleb was about to answer. To tell her that freedom was a myth, a fanciful idea told to children, when he saw the distant spires of Bathusala in the distance.

'We are almost there,' he said, suddenly eager to change the subject.

'Almost where?' Livia squinted her eyes at the distant city.

'Bathusala. The Forlorn City. First port of Devil Sound, where the pirates of the Ebon Sea trade slaves for precious gems and ore. It means we have reached the Ramadi.'

'You make it sound so welcoming,' said Livia.

That seemed a curious thing to say. Kaleb had not meant that at all. 'Welcoming it is not. Slavers and pirates are all that lie within those walls. We must be on our guard or we could end up in shackles.'

'Forgive me if I'm not filled with confidence, but I'm already a slave as far as I can tell.'

'No,' said Kaleb, 'you are no slave.'

'A prize then? What's the difference?'

Kaleb could have tried to tell her how important she was. Of the honour that awaited her, but he did not have the words. Instead he continued walking, done with the conversation. If Livia was not ready to accept her potential he was not about to try and persuade her. Perhaps the Blood Regent would be more up to the task.

It took most of the day to reach the city-port. The salt smell of the sea wafted across the sands as they made their way closer, though it seemed an age until they saw any coastline. Darkness was falling as they reached the southern gate. The entrance stood open, and from what Kaleb could remember the gates were rarely closed. Bathusala was a city where the secretive cults of the Ramadi met with outsiders to trade. This was sacred ground. Neutral territory intrinsic to the survival of all the disparate cults. Neither they, nor the savage pirates of the Ebon, would dare spark the wrath of their fellows by upsetting the balance of peace held here.

As though in stark warning, four bodies hung above the entrance. Two were clearly slaves; one bore the blue and yellow tattoos of a mariner while the third looked to have been a brutal warrior in his time. Which cult he served was impossible to tell, but Kaleb could only surmise his crime had been dire indeed for him to suffer such a fate.

He and Livia made their way through the gate, the guards lazily waving them along. Livia stuck close to Kaleb's side as they made their way in, the warm night air bringing the sounds of revelry and the stench of hot food and pungent drink.

'What is this place?' Livia asked, warily eyeing the waifs and vagabonds that lurked in every corner.

'It is the gateway to the Ramadi. This city stands at the mouth of Devil Sound and from here we can sail to anywhere in the wastes. If we can charter a ship it will shorten our journey to Kragenskûl by many weeks.'

'And how are we supposed to pay for passage on a boat when we have no money and we both look like we've been walking across the desert for a week?'

It was a fine question.

'I'll find a way,' he replied.

Three hulking warriors strode past them. Kaleb recognised them as devotees of the Eye of Honoric. Had they been anywhere but within the walls of Bathusala Kaleb might have been wary of attack, but here was neutral ground. All the cults were bound by truce on pain of execution.

Livia did not share Kaleb's confidence, and she clung to him as they passed, grasping his hand tightly. Kaleb's first reaction was to release her grip, but something about it was comforting to him. He couldn't remember if anyone had ever held his hand before, but there was something about it he liked.

They moved on through the crowds of mariners and cultists, northward towards the dock. The city was built across an inlet that led from the Ebon Sea to the vast Devil Sound. From here they'd be able to get a ship, any ship that might take them to one of the small supply ports on the northern shore. If they could find a captain willing.

As the two of them passed through the central square Kaleb glanced at the myriad wooden platforms erected in a vast circle. Here slaves were traded by pirates to the highest bidder. If those slaves were lucky they would be sifted out to be trained as warriors in one of the cult armies. Those who were less lucky would be sent to the mines of the Ramadi to dig for ore and jewels. Those too sickly to work would be traded as sacrifices to the gods. Kaleb could only take solace in the fact that there was no trade being carried out as they moved through. He doubted it would have done Livia's spirits any good.

The dark waters of the Ebon Sea spread out before them as they left the square. A long cobbled parade led to the dock where sea turned to sound. Across the inlet was a vast bridge linking the northern half of Bathusala to the southern. It was a magnificent construction, big enough to carry ten carriages abreast and high enough to allow a fleet to sail beneath. Kaleb doubted it could have been erected by any human hand. It clearly dated back to a time of gods and magic.

There were boats aplenty in the bay, their sails furled, crews busy on their decks. Kaleb watched, trying to judge which would be best to approach first and how to secure passage with no coin or anything to trade.

'Are we stuck? Or can you see a friendly face?' Livia asked.

Kaleb shook his head. 'I have no friends here,' he replied.

Before he could think what to do there was a jangle of bells. He turned to see a group of penitents moving along the dock towards them. Their heads were bowed and shrouded, the one at their lead swinging a smoking thurible in time to their walk. As he passed, Kaleb could smell the incense. It stoked memories of prayer in the chapel of Kragenskûl.

Livia watched them with open-mouthed wonder, and Kaleb could understand her curiosity – a group of religious men would naturally seem at odds with the brutal nature of this place. For Kaleb, it held no mystery. Penitents were rife across the Ramadi, held in esteem by most of the cults as representatives of a time long lost – a living, breathing representation of the old gods.

Before he could turn his attention back to the ships, the last penitent stopped as the group passed them by. The white-robed figure peeled back his shroud with filthy fingers, revealing an old and withered face, with a lank matted beard. He stared at Livia, who took a step back toward the dock.

'Be on your way, old man,' Kaleb said.

The old man ignored him, holding out a withered hand toward Livia.

'It's you,' he said in a dry voice not used to speaking. 'You have returned to us.'

The rest of the penitents had stopped, turning to see what their fellow had been distracted by. Other folk on the dock were also taking an interest.

Kaleb reached out to take Livia's hand and pull her away when the penitent fell to his knees, arthritic fingers grabbing at her skirts.

'You have returned to us,' shrieked the old man.

More penitents moved forward, dropping to their knees. Some sobbed, others chanted canticles in an ancient tongue Kaleb couldn't understand.

He grabbed Livia, dragging her away from the penitents, hearing the tear of her skirts as they desperately grabbed at her. They were drawing too much attention. They had to escape this place and worry about passage across the sea later.

As they ran along the dock, someone shouted for them to stop. Kaleb glanced over his shoulder and saw the penitents following, but also a number of others, curious to know the source of the commotion.

'Up here,' Kaleb said, dragging Livia up a flight of stairs away from the harbour.

He glanced over his shoulder again, seeing they were still being pursued. It would be impossible for them to gain passage on a ship now. Their anonymity was their greatest ally but they had been marked by the penitents. The whole city would want to know why.

As they came out onto a narrow street, Kaleb stopped. The way was blocked by a group of warriors, bedecked in desert wraps. Every hand was on the hilt of a sword.

'This is bad, isn't it?' Livia said.

'No, this is very good.' Kaleb allowed himself a sigh of relief. These warriors he recognised – Bloodguard of the Qeltine Brotherhood.

They moved past Kaleb, barring the way behind, and as the penitents and pirates caught up they stopped short at the sight of the menacing warriors. Kaleb barely paid them any heed. He was too busy staring at the warrior left standing before them, his hair long and dark, face lacking emotion, immaculately attired in a black robe, crimson sash about his waist.

'Hello, Kaleb,' the warrior said with the slightest bow of his head.

'Hello, Dantar,' Kaleb replied.

✝

Luckily for the people of the Cordral and Suderfeld, the old gods of the desert still hold sway among the disparate cults of the Ramadi. The memories of Byzantus, Qeltine, Mandrithar, Wraak, and the rest will not die so easily and, while they remain, the Ramadi will always be a feasting ground for carrion. For the warlord who could unite such a bloodthirsty and fractious place would have to be the mightiest the world had ever seen.

– A History of the Ramadi Wastes, Sebastius Hoight

✝

43

IT had been an uneventful journey north but hotter than a demon's dick. Josten had put up with the discomfort, not least because Canio's men hadn't complained one bit. Josten wouldn't show an ounce of weakness in front of them.

Randal had not felt the same.

He was a whiner and no mistake. For miles, he complained about the heat and the hunger and the thirst and the ache in his feet. Josten couldn't think of any man he wanted to silence more. If he'd had the opportunity to close his hands around the little bastard's neck he could have done it too, but he never got the chance. Canio had briefed his men to keep Josten and Randal alive, and that clearly meant keeping them apart and unarmed. Not that lack of a weapon would have stopped Josten.

He knew deep down keeping Randal alive, at least for now, was for the best. As much as he'd have liked to see the tallyman buried and gone in vengeance for Mullen, Josten realised they had strength in numbers. Though their journey through the Cordral Extent had been relatively incident free, who knew what awaited them the further north they travelled? No point killing Randal when he could be useful.

Besides, there'd be plenty of time for a reckoning later. Murder could wait.

Josten was reassured by the presence of Canio's men. They were all in their thirties, grim-looking veterans with hard faces and missing teeth. The kind of men you wanted at your shoulder in a fix. Josten could only give thanks Canio hadn't sent them off with green young lads.

Not that the journey had been particularly hard. Apart from the odd band of roaming brigands, the Cordral Extent was trouble free. The same couldn't be said of the Ramadi. Josten had been wishing they'd catch up to Livia and the cripple long before they got within a hundred leagues of that place, but it didn't look like he'd get his wish.

Their trail was easy enough to follow. Livia and the cripple weren't trying to hide their passing and their sign was plain to see: she had a light tread and he had a limp. Anyone could have followed them across the dry earth if they'd wanted, and they led a trail straight north from Arethusa all the way across the Cordral. A trail that was uneventful, until the fifth day.

It led them to an old monument, some kind of crumbling fortress. They'd approached it warily, a couple of Canio's men going in first to make sure no one was waiting for them with ill intent. When they gave the all clear, Josten came closer. The smell of rot hit him first, then he saw the sight inside. Three dead men, killed quickly as far as he could see. From the trail, another had run off bleeding. It was normal enough for a place like this, finding dead men in the dirt, but the bird carcasses lying about the place were strange, like they'd dropped dead out of the sky. The weirdness didn't end there.

From the trail that led north from the place Livia hadn't left with a cripple. Whoever she travelled north with now walked straight as an arrow, their footsteps measured and even, but there was no sign of the cripple's body.

It wasn't something any of them could explain and Josten wasn't too concerned with the whys and wherefores. All he knew was that Livia still lived, and he had to find her.

They moved on quickly from that ruin. None of them admitted it but there was a sense of unease hanging over the place like a putrid stink.

As they made their way further north, Josten began to get an anxious feeling deep inside. He'd not questioned why he was doing this, and now he had time to think on it he had to admit it was because he'd made a promise to Livia. He was all that girl had, the only one looking out for her. It was a strange and unusual feeling for Josten Cade, and one he welcomed. He couldn't remember the last time he'd acted out of loyalty to someone other than Mullen. Now Mullen was gone he was free of any allegiance, but there was something about this girl. Something that made him want to walk to the ends of the earth to make sure she was safe. Though he'd never have admitted it, he felt responsible for Livia Harrow.

On the sixth day, the vista of endless sand was broken by a city. It was nothing like Josten had ever seen in the Suderfeld, where everything was constructed in blocks and triangles. Here minarets soared with twisting steeples and curving annexes, and pennants flew from every tower. As they drew closer they were met by the distant salt-stink of the sea. After all this sand he couldn't wait to see open water.

The sight of the city quickened their pace and the six men reached the gates by the time the sun was at its zenith. Black gulls cawed their welcome but the city guards seemed none too pleased to see them. Despite the grim looks, Josten was surprised when they were allowed entry without question; he guessed the bodies hanging from the gate lintel were there as a reminder to behave once you were inside – they served as a warning all their own.

No sooner had they passed the threshold than Canio's men stopped.

'Here's where we leave you,' said Picket, the oldest of the veterans.

'Here's where you what?' Randal replied, eyeing Josten cautiously.

'Canio told us to take you as far north as the Devil Sound. If you hadn't found the girl by then we were to turn back. Besides, there ain't enough gold in the whole of the Cordral would make us want to venture into the Ramadi. Once we buy supplies we'll be heading straight back. Good luck.'

With that the men headed off into the throng. Randal opened his mouth to shout after them but thought better of it. Josten just stared at him and the two men weighed each other up.

What now? A fight in the street? Claw at each other like animals? Josten couldn't get the image of Mullen out of his head. Couldn't help but grit his teeth in anger.

'I know what you're thinking,' said Randal. 'But trust me, it's a bad idea.'

'You've got no idea what I'm fucking thinking,' Josten replied, but truth be told it was obvious he was thinking about murder. The only thing stopping him were the bodies hanging from ropes on the way into the city. If he'd been certain he could have got away with throttling Randal in the middle of the road that's what he'd be doing. But he didn't fancy being strung up for murder in the arse-end of nowhere because he couldn't control his thirst for vengeance.

'We have a difficult task ahead of us,' Randal continued. 'We both want the girl. It would serve us well to work together. Once we have her we can think about fighting it out. Until then I suggest we put our differences aside.'

Josten felt his fists unclench and he let out a long slow breath, grasping the sense in what Randal was saying. He wanted this bastard dead more than anything, but if there was even a chance he was to get through this in one piece he knew he'd need help. And Randal was the only one around who'd be watching his back. It wasn't much, but it looked like there was no other choice.

'Livia,' Josten said.

'What?' Randal replied, still looking uneasy.

'Her name is Livia. And you're right, if we've got any chance of finding her and getting out of this place alive we'll need to do it together. Who knows, once we've found her maybe I'll even let you live.'

Randal gave a curt nod of the head. 'And for that I'm sure I'll be grateful.'

Josten looked around the bustling city. The streets were busy with men and women of all creeds and colours but there was still an oppressive taste to the air, as though they were in constant danger.

'So, what now? The trail's gone cold,' he said.

Randal nodded. 'It's cooled, I'll admit. But I'm not willing to give up just yet. Are you?'

There was no way Josten was about to give up now.

'Whoever's brought her to this place may have had a mind to sell her on the slave market. I think we should check there first.'

Randal nodded. 'Good suggestion. Let's hope we don't end up on the ledger.'

Josten hadn't considered the state they were in. Both men looked like they'd been dragged most of the way across the Cordral Extent rather than walked.

'Maybe we should get cleaned up first?' he suggested. Randal agreed.

It took them a little time and a lot of hand-waving and talking loudly to foreigners before they found themselves at a market. With a little reluctance, Josten pooled what coin he still had with Randal and they managed to purchase clean clothes. Yet more bargaining and they found a washhouse close to the docks where they could clean themselves.

Josten hadn't realised how much he needed a bath. The water was cool, if not completely fresh, but it was still cleaner than anything he'd drunk in the past week. As much as he wanted to make the most of it, he couldn't shake the feeling of foreboding that plagued his mind.

Finding Livia was going to be tough. Rescuing her from whoever had taken her even tougher. This would be the last bath he took for a while.

Any attempt to relax was shattered as the sound of

wailing drifted in through the window. Josten lay in the bath suffering the din for as long as he could before he climbed out to see what the commotion was about. He stood there dripping, looking down onto the dock below.

Hooded men were kneeling in a circle, chanting. It was an odd sight, made that much stranger by the fact that passers-by seemed to pay them little attention. Josten was about to leave them to it, but before he could one of them stood up, arms to the sky.

'She has come to us,' said the figure from beneath his hood. 'The White Widow returns like a herald from across the stars. We must purge ourselves, for absolution is near. Our time is near, brothers.'

Deep in his gut Josten knew there was something more to this. Somehow he knew this had something to do with Livia.

He pulled his fresh clothes on over his sodden body, hopping as he headed toward the door of the bathhouse while pulling on his boots. Out on the street the robed men were still kneeling, chanting quietly to one another as the crowds wandered past. Josten stood to one side of the men, suddenly feeling foolish, unsure of what to say.

'You heard them too?'

Josten turned to see Randal standing beside him – close enough to have stuck a knife in his side if he'd wanted to.

'I guess I did,' said Josten. 'Good to know I'm not going mad. You think they mean Livia?'

'Only one way to find out,' Randal replied, taking a step forward. 'Holy brothers,' he began. 'We are pilgrims from a far-off land. And we too seek this White Widow.' A couple of the hooded men looked up but didn't reply. 'We are simply seeking enlightenment. Perhaps you could tell us where she might be found?'

The men had stopped their chanting now, every hooded head pointing toward Randal. It was clear his line of questioning was falling on deaf ears.

'Fuck this,' Josten said, grabbing the nearest of them around the neck and hauling him to his feet. 'Where is she?' he shouted, pulling back the hood. The head beneath was old and liver-spotted, bloodshot eyes staring in fear. 'Southern girl? Hair black as pitch? Is that who you mean?'

The old man nodded. 'Yes,' he said. 'She was taken.'

'Taken by who?' Josten demanded, giving the frail old man a shake.

'By the Brotherhood. The Qeltine Brotherhood.'

'Where?' Josten barked.

The old man shook his head. 'We do not know. If we did we would follow.'

Josten dropped the old man and turned to see Randal smiling at him.

'Crude but effective,' said Randal. 'We might make a good team yet.'

Josten thought about answering. Instead he walked away from the praying old men before they drew too much attention. Whoever this Brotherhood were, they were bound to show their faces sooner or later.

44

LIVIA stood in a dusty old storehouse that stank of fish and years of ill care. The masked warriors stood around like silent golems, lurking in the dark. She couldn't even hear them breathing in the quiet of the ancient building. Kaleb and the one he had called 'Dantar' were the only voices. Their greeting had been curt, and now they were in the relative privacy of the old dock building they seemed no warmer to one another.

'We leave in the morning,' said Dantar. 'There is a ship waiting to be supplied in the dock.'

Kaleb seemed confused. 'Supplied? For a journey across the Sound?'

'We are not heading across the Sound. We will sail beneath the Bridge of Ancients onto the Ebon.'

'We are not bound for Kragenskûl? But the Blood Regent—'

'Instructed me to wait here for you,' said Dantar. 'It seems this girl is more important than we first thought. Seeing you confirms that.' He regarded Kaleb's restored body as though a miracle had been performed. 'The Blood Regent waits in Kessel. That is where we will go.'

'Kessel? But—'

'No more questions, brother. We have all been given our duties to perform. And you have performed yours admirably.' Dantar glanced across at Livia. She almost shook under that animal gaze. 'Now you should rest. Your journey is almost at an end.'

Kaleb said nothing, seeming to crumble at the mention of 'duties'. It appeared he was as much a slave as she was.

Livia was led up a flight of rickety stairs to the highest level of the old storehouse. There, a bare platform looked down onto the rest of the building. She could see Kaleb and the other warriors resting in the darkness. Above her she spied a window open to the night.

As she lay her head on the bare, dusty boards she looked up at the stars beyond, her dreams of escape evaporating as she once again realised there would be nowhere for her to flee to, not even if she could sprout wings and fly from the roof.

She closed her eyes, and for the first time since this had all begun she wished for dreams of bloody spears and howling demons, anything to take her away from this hell. Instead, Livia slept soundly for a time, settling into a deep and dreamless peace until eventually her eyes flitted open in the dark.

It was silent in the storehouse, but she could tell someone was there. As she sat up, her shoulder throbbing from the hardness of the floor, she expected to see Kaleb sitting in the dark, watching her as she slept, her silent protector. Or was it captor?

It was neither. It was a woman's shape that hunkered in the shadows.

Livia stared into the dark for as long as she could at the silent shape. All she could make out clearly were the woman's steel-blue eyes which almost glowed in the blackness. When she could stand it no more, Livia opened her mouth to speak, but the woman raised a hand for her to be silent.

Like a phantom the woman moved forward, silent as death in the dark. Livia could see the details of her face now. She was lean, almost gaunt, her hair shorn close to her scalp, but there was still a strange kind of beauty to her. Her clothes were dark like the shadows, plain and tight-fitting. She wore a single blade strapped to her side.

'We must leave,' she said.

Livia's heart leapt. Escape at last. She moved to follow the woman but then stopped.

What was this? Yet another rescue by someone who wanted to use her? Was she to flee the hands of one captor to fall into the grip of another?

The woman stared at her with those cold blue eyes. 'You must come now. There is no time.'

'Who are you?' Livia whispered.

'I am here to help. Now you must come with me, before it is too late. You do not realise what is at stake.'

'How do I know I can trust you?' Livia asked, desperate for some reason, any reason, she could flee with this woman.

Those blue eyes glanced down at the storehouse below. No one had stirred yet and the woman continued. 'We are bound, you and I. We are of the same ilk. You must know that. Look inside and ask yourself. You will know you can trust me.'

Livia stared at the woman, the contours of her face seeming to solidify in the dark. There was something overwhelmingly familiar about her, as though they had shared a past Livia had somehow forgotten. Try as she might though, Livia could not conjure the memory.

'What is your name?' Livia asked.

'I am Silver,' said the woman. 'But the time for questions is later. For now, we must go.'

Silver rose to her feet, taking a step back as Livia stood up beside her. The woman wasn't tall but there was an aura of power that surrounded her. She was dangerous, of that Livia had no doubt.

The woman climbed out through the glassless skylight, nimbly pulling herself onto the roof. Quietly as she could, Livia followed, struggling out onto the rickety tiles. The city seemed oddly subdued as Livia stood on the roof, looking across the distant towers and out onto the sea. The sun was rising over the distant horizon, bathing the buildings in an ominous red hue.

Silently, Silver led her across the roof, but as Livia followed she heard one of the slates crack beneath her foot. Half the tile slid down the face of the rooftop. Livia stared at it in dismay, until it tipped over the guttering. There was silence for a moment. Livia held her breath in anticipation until the smash of slate made her gasp.

Silver didn't hesitate, moving swiftly across the roof, and Livia took that as her cue to follow. The woman reached the end of the building and leapt, spanning the gap to the next building. Livia got to the edge and stopped.

'Come on,' urged Silver.

Livia looked down into the yawning darkness. A glance back and she saw a masked warrior already climbing up through the open skylight. Livia felt panic grip her and she turned, leaping before she could think.

Her foot slipped as she landed on the opposite rooftop, another loose slate moving beneath her foot. Livia felt her balance shift and she reached out for help. Silver stood back, just watching without emotion. Livia's hands grasped at the smooth slate of the roof and she managed to gain her balance, cursing her clumsiness, cursing this woman for not helping, cursing her pursuers for forcing her into this. But she had little time to rant, as Silver turned and moved on, forcing Livia to act on instinct and follow.

Silver led the way, her pace inhumanly swift, every step measured and perfectly placed. She was like a panther picking her way across well-trodden terrain. Livia stumbled after, her eyes wide as she tried not to trip in the morning light. Behind her she could hear her pursuers. As she jumped over a low wall, Silver was waiting.

'Don't wait for me,' said the woman, slowly drawing her sword.

Livia allowed herself another brief glance back, seeing three of the desert warriors pursuing them. Silver waited for them with sword drawn. It seemed a suicidal move, but Livia was too caught up in her bid for escape to care. She crested another low wall and dropped down to the street below.

As she hit the cobbles she heard the clash of steel. That was the only sound – no desperate grunting as swords met, no stumbling footfalls as the fighters tried to gain purchase – just metal striking metal in a rhythmic staccato.

Livia knew she should run, putting as much distance between her and the fighters as possible, but instead she remained in the alley listening to the ringing sounds above.

Almost as soon as it began the combat ended. Silver dropped down from the roof above to land beside Livia, barely making a sound. Her breathing was even, not a bead of sweat on her brow, but the blade she held in her hand was slick, her sleeve spattered with what looked like black oil in the morning light.

Silver didn't speak, just led the way once more. Livia dogged her heels as they ran through the narrow twisting passageways. Nothing stirred in the silent morning bar beggars and drunks as they threaded their way through the city. Excitement built within Livia as escape began to look like a real prospect. Whoever this woman was she surely offered a better option than enslavement to some Ramadi cult.

Silver led them out into a small courtyard, surrounded by high-sided dwellings. She stopped, raising a hand, and Livia came to a stumbling halt behind her. Slowly, from the shadows ahead, stepped a tall figure in a pristine red tunic, hunter's eyes focused on his prey.

'Run,' said Silver, pointing to an adjacent alleyway.

Livia just had time to see Dantar draw his blade slowly, moving into a defensive stance, before she obeyed Silver, running down the alley as fast as she could.

The city was starting to wake as she ran from the sound of swordplay. Faces peered from doorways as she sped past, half-naked figures stumbling into the half-light at the prospect of witnessing violence.

Livia was hopelessly lost in a city of strangers, her breath becoming laboured as she ran endlessly through the narrow streets. Her path came to an abrupt stop, the street ending in a low ledge that looked out onto the harbour. She peered over, seeing a long drop to the cobbles below. If she could make the fall without breaking something maybe she could make it to one of the boats. Perhaps there was someone in this godsforsaken place who might take her to safety.

'Livia, don't run.'

She turned to see Kaleb, surprised by the relief she felt at the sight of him.

'I can't stay here,' she said, edging back to the wall. 'I won't be made a sacrifice. I won't be used as anyone's pawn in some game.'

Kaleb lowered his eyes to the ground, his brow furrowing as he fought with whatever feelings roiled within him.

'Then you must flee,' he said, looking up at her. 'Far away where no one knows who or what you are.'

That had been the last thing she expected from him. So far all he had demonstrated was blind devotion to his brotherhood. Only now could she see the conflict within him.

'Come with me,' Livia said.

Kaleb stared at her, considering the words. 'I cannot,' he said finally.

'Yes, you can,' she replied. 'We can go together. Far from here. We can be free. You have a choice, Kaleb. Stay and be a slave, or run with me and be free.'

She could see he battled with the choice. It was clear he yearned to be as free as she did. Eventually he nodded his head as he realised there was nothing to stop them.

'Very well,' said Kaleb. 'I choose freedom.'

45

THROUGH the window Josten could see the sky had turned from black to grey. He had no idea how long he'd been lying there staring into the dark but there was no chance he'd sleep now. He should have been exhausted, should have slept for a week, but there was no time for that. Sleep was an indulgence he couldn't afford.

They'd spent the day searching for any sign of this Qeltine Brotherhood but with little joy. It seemed Livia and her captors had simply disappeared. The chances of them finding her now were all but gone.

Randal was snoring in the opposite bed. Josten rose, bending his neck to one side and hearing the sinews crack within. All the while he couldn't take his eyes off the tallyman. Again, he asked himself why he shouldn't kill the little fucker right now. It would be so easy – just creep across the room and clamp hands around that throat. It would stop the snoring at least. But Josten knew he couldn't. Randal was the only ally he had in this place, maybe even in the whole fucking world. Even an ally he wanted dead was still an ally.

A noise from outside prompted him to move to the window. As he listened he heard the unmistakeable sounds of violence. Josten wasn't surprised that in a city such as this there'd be a fight when anyone with any sense would be asleep.

He leaned against the lintel, squinting out into the gloom. There was a grey haze hanging over this place to accompany the stale smell rising from the streets.

It was just bright enough for him to see her run below his window, her hair a dishevelled mess, bare feet clapping against the cobbles.

Livia.

'On your fucking feet, Randal,' he shouted, racing across the room. As much as he hated to admit it, there was every chance he'd need Randal's help if Livia was fleeing from someone.

'What?' Randal replied, rising from his bed like he'd been bitten by a snake.

'She's here,' was all he had a chance to say before he ran from the room and down the stairs.

The ground floor of the bunkhouse was a mess of drunken, slumbering slavers and warriors in outlandish armour. Josten had the sense to strip a sword from the scabbard of one sleeping warrior as he moved past, heading out of the front door before its owner could wake. If Livia was running, then most likely someone was after her. Josten wasn't about to face them with nothing but his dick in his hand.

Out on the street he turned left, following in Livia's wake, his own bare feet clapping on the cobbles. He could still hear the sound of fighting, but it was a distant echo along the narrow alleyways.

Josten raced along the path, feeling excitement grip his

gut as he ran until the cobbled street ended abruptly, the dock appearing just beyond it. Livia stood at the end of the street, her face flushed in the morning haze. Josten stuttered to a halt as he saw the man beside her.

A man he recognised.

The cripple stood tall, the scars that had once marred his face now faded. Livia stared at him, this man who had abducted her, but there was no fear in her face.

She looked up as Josten came into view and the man she was with turned. The three of them regarded each other until Josten said, 'Livia, come with me.'

He expected her to rush forward and take his outstretched hand, to flee from the man who had stolen her away, but she paused.

'I—' was all she had time to say before Randal came running up behind Josten, huffing breath coming quick and heavy.

'Livia, come on,' said Josten.

'What are you doing with him?' she said, staring with hate at Randal.

'It's a long story. But you have to trust me.'

She shook her head. 'No. I can't—'

It was all she had a chance to say before the cripple walked forward. Whatever had ailed him before was most definitely gone, and he strode confidently.

'You must leave,' he said.

'Like fuck I will,' Josten replied, stepping forward, his stolen sword held low and ready.

His thrust was true. The cripple stepped aside as though

Josten were shoving the sword through tar. Almost too quick to see, the flat of the cripple's hand struck Josten in the jaw.

Next thing he knew, he was lying on the ground. Everything span, the cobbles cold against his cheek.

'Get up!' shouted Randal.

Josten staggered to his feet, seeing the sword lying useless on the ground. 'Where?' he said, seeing through his groggy vision that Livia and the cripple had fled.

Randal pointed toward the low wall. 'That way.'

Josten picked up the sword, stumbling as his head cleared. When he reached the wall, he saw Livia and her cripple running to the dock. He looked down, head spinning at the drop. It was a long way down but an awning was spread across the bottom. It must have broken their fall.

Without thinking, Josten flung himself over the wall. The awning was surprisingly solid as he hit it. A crack and a tear and he hit the cobbled ground below, all the air shooting out of him. The sword went spinning from his grip, clattering to a halt a few feet away.

Josten hauled himself to his feet once more. His shoulder was aching from the fall, his head still spinning, but nothing would hold him back. He'd come too far to be stopped now.

Livia was in the distance, the cripple pulling her along toward a waiting ship. Josten lurched to the fallen sword, his foot catching a loose cobble and sending him sprawling to the ground. His hand reached out for the weapon, but a red-booted foot stamped down on it before his fingers could close around the handle.

Josten looked up in time to see a face regarding him, dark

brows over an animal stare. The warrior held a naked blade in one hand and his arm was wounded, blood running slick down his crimson sleeve. He raised his blade dispassionately, a butcher at the block.

Before the blow could land a second blade stopped it mere inches from Josten's neck, the ring of their clashing almost deafening his left ear. As his wits fast returned, he rolled aside and rose groggily to his feet.

With his head clearing, Josten saw he'd been saved by a woman. She stood in a defensive stance, weapon locked with that of the red warrior. The two stared at one another, weapons crossed, unmoving.

'Josten!'

He turned, seeing Randal standing behind him, pointing out towards the wharf. In the distance, he could see Livia aboard a ship, the mariners on deck unfurling sails, oars being raised by burly rowers.

Josten ignored everything else. He had to reach the ship.

As he sprinted toward the dock, more warriors came rushing from the shadows, faces covered by masks, their torsos wrapped in leather bindings, swords at the ready. They were barring his way, but as much as he wanted to smash his way through them and get to the ship he could see they meant business. There was no way out of this other than being hacked to death on the dock.

The woman who had saved him didn't feel the same.

She came charging past him, throwing herself into the fray, taking on every one of the masked warriors like a demon.

Josten would have liked to help – he had a debt to

pay after all – but instead he dodged through the fray, determined to reach the ship that was already pulling away from the jetty.

The red-robed warrior who had tried to decapitate him was sprinting for the ship too. Josten's legs were pumping, his feet splashing along the wet dock, but there was no way he could match the warrior. He watched in vain as the man leapt the gap to the ship, clearing the bulwark and landing on deck with feline deftness. All Josten could do was come to a stuttering stop at the edge of the harbour, watching helplessly as the ship pulled away.

Livia stood at the prow looking at him, her brow creased in confusion. Josten could only watch as she disappeared into the distance, the ship cruising beneath the huge bridge that linked the two halves of the city.

Josten turned, remembering the woman who had saved him had run headlong into a group of swordsmen. He expected to see her corpse lying in the street, but instead she stood tall, not even out of breath. At her feet were three corpses, and Randal stood to one side with a look of stunned amazement on his face.

Josten approached them, unsure of what to say. This woman had saved his life but she had a wild look to her, as though she might just as easily turn that blade on him.

'We have to find her,' said the woman before either of them could speak. 'We must follow, before it's too late.'

Josten shook his head. 'What's all this "we"? I appreciate the help, but we don't even know who you are.'

She looked him in the eye. Josten wouldn't have wanted

to admit just how unnerving that was. 'You need my help, Josten Cade.'

The fact she knew his name was even more unnerving. 'Look, I don't know who you are, but—'

'We could use all the help we can get,' said Randal.

'No one asked you!' Josten jabbed a finger at the tallyman, who raised his hands in surrender.

'All right, you're the one with the sword. Though I didn't see it do you any good when you were being beaten by an unarmed man.'

Josten had no reply to that.

He turned back to the woman.

'What's your name? And how do you know mine?'

She sheathed her blade. 'I am Silver. And I know many things. Things that will help us find Livia before it is too late.'

'Things like what?' asked Josten, wondering just what he was letting himself in for.

Silver turned back to him. 'For one, I know where they're taking her.'

That one made him think. Josten knew time was against them. He could spend all day weighing up the whys and wherefores.

'All right,' he said. 'Let's get moving.'

†

For twenty days and twenty nights did I wander the desert. As my body deteriorated in the searing heat, so did my mind. My eyes began to play tricks on me as thirst plagued my every step.

On that twentieth night, twelve moons appeared in the sky, each a different hue, each imbued with symbols in a language I could not comprehend. But I was grateful for their illumination, for it laid a path in the night to my salvation.

A ziggurat of desert-worn stone loomed from the dark. It was a foreboding place, all alone amidst the endless sand, but I was too desperate to be wary of it. Half-dead from exposure I stumbled inside, wondering if this place would deliver me from the clutches of the Reaver, or become my eventual tomb.

Within was only blackness and I lurched blindly through corridors for what seemed an age. Eventually, just as I was ready to give up my journey and curl up in the dark to die, I came out into a giant chamber. The roof lay open, allowing the bright moonlight to illuminate a stone well in the centre of the room.

Words cannot express how I felt as I staggered towards it, delirium teasing the frayed edges of my consciousness. I drank long and deep. Soon I succumbed to the fugue, and my body sagged beside the life-giving well. It was then I was blessed with my vision.

I knew him only as the Nameless. I neither saw his

*face, nor even heard his voice, but I knew there was truth in
the things he revealed to me.*

    *He showed me of the time before the Age of Penitence.
Of a land ruled by the Twelve. A race and creed known
unto themselves as the Arkaons. Immortals all, who would
perpetually battle one another for the right to rule over the
hearts and souls of men.*

    *I saw their banishment to the land of Delnak, a vast
plane they would eventually bring under their heel. I saw
how some of them rose to become exalted, how others fell to
become twisted things, and how fine the line was between
those two extremities.*

    *All this and more I was shown by the Nameless, and
when he had finished I was forever a changed man. For to
know the truth of things is the only way to enlightenment,
but with such forbidden knowledge will also come damnation.*

           – An excerpt from the *Archaeonomica,* by the Mad Priest
        Amzan Fahoud El'Hazir, First Scribe of the Scorchlands

⁜

46

'ARE you all right?' Kaleb asked.

She looked up, eyes boring into him. Kaleb took a waterskin given him by one of the Bloodguard and offered it to her. She glanced disdainfully at it then snatched it from his hand, gulping down the fresh water.

'Are you all right?' he asked again.

She stared at him, the sea wind whipping her hair into a fury.

'Am I all right? What do you bloody think?' she replied. 'I was almost free... *we* were almost free. Then you decide to drag me aboard this ship. I thought we were going to leave all this.'

Kaleb felt a sudden shame, both for letting Livia down and for almost abandoning his mission.

'It is my duty,' was all he could manage to say.

'To hell with your duty,' she replied, rising to her feet. 'And to hell with you. To hell with all of you.' She turned to stare out at the dark waters of the Ebon Sea.

'I had no choice,' said Kaleb, trying his best to sound comforting. 'But you should rejoice. You are truly blessed. When we reach Kragenskûl you will be revered. The Blood Regent himself will honour you. There is—'

'I don't give a shit about your regent or your Kragenskûl or any of that. I just want to be free.'

He saw hate in her.

'You will understand why you need to come with us soon. The honour—'

'Fuck your honour!'

He had no idea how to deal with this. Diplomacy had never been his purview. Kaleb was a fighter... a weapon. This was not his strength.

He turned and left Livia at the ship's prow, wishing he had the words to convince her this was the only way...

But was it the only way? For a fleeting moment back at the dock Kaleb had been ready to run away with her. And for that solitary moment he had experienced his first taste of true freedom.

Dantar was aft, dark hair billowing in the sea wind, eyes staring ever northwards. Kaleb came to stand beside his brother, seeing the look of satisfaction on his face.

'You have done well, Kaleb,' Dantar said. 'I am ashamed to say it but no one really thought you would succeed. Me least of all.'

'Thank you, brother. It was my duty,' Kaleb replied. He felt little satisfaction in what he had done.

'You have carried it out with distinction. And you have been rewarded in the process.' Dantar glanced down at Kaleb's renewed body. 'Surely a gift from the Blood Lord himself.'

Kaleb clenched his fist, feeling the restored muscle and sinew. He knew it was not the Blood Lord, but Livia, who had granted him this gift.

'How did you know where we would be?' Kaleb asked. 'How did you even know I had the girl?'

'The new Regent foresaw your arrival. He is young but oh so powerful. Never before has the Blood Regent been able to commune with the gods, but we are at the door to a new age. And that girl is the key.'

Kaleb couldn't bring himself to look back at Livia.

'But why the keep of Kessel?' he said, trying to change the subject. 'Why would we not simply cross the Devil Sound and head to a port near Kragenskûl? Surely if Livia is to be revered it should be in our holy city. Not some forgotten outpost.'

'Kessel is no mere outpost,' said Dantar. 'It is an ancient temple of the Qeltine Brotherhood. A place of holy sacrifice. A place of power. A conduit to the outer realm.'

Kaleb felt panic suddenly rise within him. 'A place of sacrifice?'

'Of course.' Dantar seemed to relish the prospect. Kaleb had never seen him so animated. 'When she is gifted on the altar, the Blood Lord will rise anew. Kessel is a gateway, and that girl is the key.'

Dantar stared across the ship at Livia, his wolf eyes hungrier than ever. Kaleb felt his heart sink watching Livia staring out to sea, oblivious of the fate that awaited her.

He had brought her to this. He was the one who had told her she would be safe, revered even, and the truth was that she would not be treated as some new messiah, but as a sacrifice to the gods.

Kaleb moved away from his brother, gripping the

385

bulwark, unable to take his eyes from Livia, who stood silently at the prow.

Why hadn't he run with her when he had the chance? Why hadn't he taken her hand and fled? If they hadn't been interrupted by the man Livia knew then they would be gone by now, both of them free to go wherever they wanted. But that opportunity was gone, along with any fleeting ambition of freedom Kaleb might have harboured.

For the rest of the voyage north, Kaleb could not bring himself to speak to her. What good would it have done to warn her, to tell her of her fate? Better she was ignorant of what awaited her. It was a burden he would gladly spare her.

It was with dread that Kaleb awaited the sight of Kessel on the horizon. But when the headland finally came into view it was not the imposing black walls of that ancient citadel that made him balk.

From the sea, the ship's company could see the flat plain that rolled up to the coastline, and on it fluttered a thousand pennants. Filling the field were warriors in heavy bone armour, pushing siege machines and carrying their spears and axes aloft.

Kessel was under siege.

Dantar, Kaleb and most of the crew gathered on the deck, looking out over the grim sight. It seemed their entry had been barred by an army, and Kaleb felt a brief glimmer of hope. Perhaps Livia had her reprieve.

'How do we enter?' asked one of the Bloodguard.

Dantar's eyes scanned the battlefield in front of the great citadel. Arrow-peppered bodies lay rotting on the ground and the distant winds carried the sounds of men barking orders.

'There is a way,' he replied.

Kaleb turned to him. Then saw what he was looking at. From the side of the citadel, two vast chains, each link as thick as a man's waist, ran down into the sea. Kaleb knew the ancient tales of Kessel and its orgies of sacrifice. He knew the chains were connected to a vast platform within the body of the citadel. Centuries before, those chains would lower the platform with dozens of souls chained upon it, into the sea where the beasts of the Ebon would feast on the bounty of human sacrifices.

'Brother,' Dantar said, turning to Kaleb. 'The honour should be yours.'

Kaleb looked at Dantar but could not hold his gaze. Then he saw Livia, still at the prow, staring out to sea, no doubt dreaming of her freedom.

What could he do? Refuse? Spurn his duty after they had come so far?

'Very well,' Kaleb replied, watching as the ship sailed closer to the chains.

He silently stripped off his rags and with one last glance toward Livia, he slipped over the side of the boat and into the dark waters. The salt of the sea stung his lips but soon the cold of it had numbed him all over. Kaleb kept his strokes even and gentle, doing his best not to thrash in the water and attract every predator within a mile.

He finally reached the nearest of the two vast chains, grabbing it, taking in deep gulps of air. Looking up he could see the black silhouette of Kessel on the cliff edge above. He had to climb perhaps a hundred yards of chain to reach it.

Kaleb gripped the thick link, the iron rusted by seawater, making the surface rough and easier to climb. Inch by inch, link by link, Kaleb began to make his way towards the citadel. When he reached the top of the chain, he paused, breathing hard.

Inside the citadel there was no sign of life. Kaleb slipped in through the massive opening, past the vast mechanism that controlled the chains. Two huge cogs, each the size of a horse, stood side by side. The wheels that controlled the chain stood beside them. It took a hundred men to turn each vast wheel – bulls of men built of muscle, bred specifically for the task. Yet those wheels had not turned for a hundred years, and the men that turned them were long dead.

In ancient times this chamber had been devoted to sacrifice and bloodletting. Hundreds would have been chained to the platform, their veins opened while ancient rites were observed and the gods revered. Before the victims' lives seeped out through their open wounds, the platform would slowly be lowered, gifting the blood and souls to the sea. A feeding frenzy would then take place as every predator would make its way to the bounteous offering. It was why the coast around Kessel was so rife with sharks and other beasts.

Kaleb moved further into the vast sacrificial chamber, onto the slabs laid out in their thousands – a vast pavement of man-sized granite, manacles at each corner. Each one was a testament to the thousands sacrificed, each one the scene of myriad horrors. Kaleb tried to put it out of his mind but he could not disregard the ancient signs of their use, for each slab bore the teeth marks and gouges from bygone beasts of the sea. The marks of their frenzy were clear to see in the dim light.

An onyx stairway, worn smooth by the passage of time, led up from the chamber. Still there was no sign of life within the tower, and Kaleb began to wonder if the place was abandoned, if the army outside were battering at the iron gates in folly.

The way ahead was suddenly illuminated, and any doubt was expelled from Kaleb's mind. Two warriors walked forward bearing torches in one hand, naked blades in the other. Kaleb let himself breathe out when he saw they were Bloodguard.

'Who goes there?' said one of them.

Kaleb stood to full height, naked in the torchlight. 'I am Kaleb Ap'Kharn,' he replied, using his full title for the first time in what seemed an age. 'And I have brought a gift for the Regent.'

The two warriors regarded him without suspicion, as though they had been expecting his arrival, then they moved aside. A small figure walked forward from the shadows. When he moved into the light, Kaleb could see he was little more than a child, hair shorn close to his scalp, body encased in a dark robe. He regarded Kaleb with curiosity before he slowly smiled.

'A gift for the Blood Regent?' he asked in a tiny voice. 'Then show it to me, Kaleb Ap'Kharn.'

47

THE sail was blood-red, the hull painted in pitch, and Josten stood at the black prow as they cruised across the sea called Devil's Sound. The three of them had scraped together enough coin to pay for their passage, Silver seeming the most eager of them for this journey to be underway. Josten knew he should have questioned her further, but Randal was right – they needed all the help they could get.

The ship bearing Livia away had headed out on the Ebon Sea on a northern bearing. As much as Josten wanted to follow, it seemed that was impossible. Silver made it clear that if the Qeltine Brotherhood were heading north along the coast they could only be going to one place – a citadel known as Kessel. Not a single reaver captain would dare approach the place, so the best they could do was charter passage across the Devil Sound and continue their way on foot.

Despite not being out on the open sea, they had lost sight of land some time ago. The waters that had once been calm began to churn and roil at their passing. More than once Josten spied things moving just beneath the surface as though an underwater predator were tracking the ship.

'Do you think we can trust her?' Randal asked as the day wore on.

Josten looked across the deck at the silent woman. She sharpened her blade with a stone, staring at it as though it held the answer to everything.

'What choice do we have?' he replied. 'You were the one who said we needed all the help we could get. Trust her or not, she's still coming with us.'

Randal peered over towards her, then shrugged, before looking back at Josten.

'And can I trust you?' he asked.

Josten turned to look at him. 'I think we'd be foolish to trust each other,' he said. 'We want each other dead and we both know it.'

Randal smirked at Josten's honesty. 'You know, you're not as stupid as you look,' he said.

'If I'm not stupid what the fuck am I doing here with you?'

'You're a good man, Josten Cade. That's what you're doing here. You're a hero.'

Josten almost laughed at Randal's sarcasm. He'd never done a good thing in his whole damn life until now. And now he'd started it was most likely going to get him killed.

'We're neither of us heroes,' he said.

Randal looked out at the sea, like he was remembering his own past misdemeanours. 'You're right about that,' he replied.

A cry from the crow's nest told them that a port was sighted up ahead. Men began to work feverishly on deck securing rigging and hoisting halyards.

The ship's red sail was furled and oars used to guide the ship into a small port. The place looked grim, a hive of dark domed buildings. Pennants were flying, but they were tattered by the wind and sands, their sigils barely visible. A sullen hush hung over the place, and all that could be heard was the ringing of metal as smithies made their wares.

Silver was the first to debark, eager to leave the ship. Josten and Randal followed her, moving up the jetty and away from the pirates. Once on land Josten could see the smithies weren't crafting horseshoes or weapons. Half a dozen shopfronts lay open and a row of burly metalworkers crafted chains and manacles of all shapes and sizes. Josten started to feel grateful the pirates who'd brought them here hadn't just sold them straight into slavery.

Silver led the way through the nameless port as though she already knew the way. Josten and Randal glanced at one another briefly before following her. She led a quick pace and Josten lengthened his stride to catch up.

'Do you even know where we're going?' he asked.

'Yes,' Silver replied, not breaking her stride or offering him so much as a glance.

'Should we not rest first?' he said, looking towards the edge of the port, seeing only endless sand stretching as far as the horizon. 'Looks like a long way.'

'There is no time,' Silver replied.

'What about supplies? We at least need water.'

Silver stopped, turning to him as though he'd asked something stupid. He could see the thought process on her face: annoyance, anger, understanding.

'Very well,' she said. 'Food and water. But that is all. We must not slow our pace. Time is against us.'

'Yes,' said Josten. 'You've made that pretty clear. But we're no good to anyone if we all die in the desert.'

Silver nodded, seeing the sense in it, and for the briefest of moments losing a little of the zeal in her eyes.

It took no time to find supplies, and they paid with what little coin they had between them. As soon as they were stocked with food and water, Silver led them off into the desert.

They soon lost sight of the port and Josten found himself completely disorientated. Silver seemed unperturbed by the lack of any landmarks, leading them briskly across the arid plain.

As night fell they made a rudimentary camp. Randal was asleep first as Josten sat across their tiny fire from Silver. She stared intently into the flames, lost in thought. Josten was wary of the woman but it didn't stop him questioning her.

'You seem intent on finding Livia,' he said. 'What is she to you?'

Silver was silent for some moments, and Josten started to wonder if she'd even heard him.

'She holds great power within her,' she said finally. 'More than she could ever know. If that power is unleashed she will be in great danger. We will all be in great danger.'

Josten had seen firsthand what Livia's power could do.

'How do you know all this? What is she to you?'

Silver stared back into the flames. 'We are bonded in blood,' she said.

393

'What does that even mean?' he asked.

A smile crept up one side of Silver's mouth. 'You would not be able to comprehend it if I told you. Ancient forces are at work here, Josten Cade. A war has been raging for millennia, it rages still, and if we do not rescue Livia Harrow this world will be in peril.'

There was a glint of madness in Silver's eye. Josten didn't know whether to take her seriously or dismiss her as a wild woman from the wastes.

'How do you even know where we are going? You seem sure of the direction we're headed.'

'I was born here,' said Silver. 'This is my home.'

'You're from the Ramadi? So, you're a cultist?' Josten grew even warier now. 'The war you're talking about is the one between the cults.'

Silver shook her head. 'No. There are battles fought in other places that are even more savage than those of the Ramadi cults. Best you are ignorant of them.'

'Ignorant of battle is the last thing I am.' Josten tried to give it the old mercenary's bravado. Silver seemed unconvinced.

'I'm sure you're right, Josten Cade,' she replied.

With that she rolled over as though to sleep. Josten doubted if she even needed sleep, but he took the hint and kept his peace for the rest of the night.

The next morning Josten was woken by a sharp kick. He sat up, hand on his sword, to see Silver had already struck the camp. Even Randal was ready to go.

'Time to move,' said the tallyman with a wink.

Josten didn't offer him anything back. He'd have liked to

offer the little shit a good kicking of his own, but that would have to wait.

They began their trek through the wastes once more. Josten knew they were heading north from the position of the sun, but if he was honest with himself they could just as easily have been retracing their steps.

It was a monotonous journey, with few landmarks but for the odd blasted tree to show they were making any progress. Josten was starting to think this a fool's errand until they crested a rise, and he saw a sight that lifted him. The Ebon Sea stretched out, calm and black, towards the distant horizon.

'Not far,' was all that Silver offered them as they struck north along the coastline.

'She's as talkative as you,' said Randal.

The last thing Josten felt like doing was proving Randal wrong.

The day wore on, with the sea breeze doing little to stifle the growing heat. Just as Josten began to wonder how much longer they would have to walk the jagged coast, Silver raised a hand in warning. At first Josten thought she was hearing things on the wind; the deserts of the Ramadi were fabled to drive travellers mad. But as dusk began to cool the heat of the day, they heard the unmistakeable sounds of war drifting on the wind.

'Doesn't sound good,' said Randal.

'No?' Josten replied. 'Sounds like we're nearly there to me.'

As they crested the headland they saw the distant tower

of Kessel perched on a cliff like a grim monument to death.

At its feet was an army.

Josten realised the scale of the task ahead. Kessel would have been all but impossible to break into, even without the ravenous horde of warriors assailing it.

'What the fuck do we do now?' he said.

'We could always ask to enlist in their army,' Randal replied. 'See if they'd let us join in their little siege.'

Josten was about to tell him what a stupid little bastard he was, when Silver took a step forward.

'That's exactly what we are going to do,' she said.

The two men watched her go, then looked at one another.

'It was only a joke,' said Randal.

'Well, no one's laughing,' Josten replied, before stepping forward to follow.

48

Livia had heard tales of vast dining halls. The lavish banquets held in the castle of Duke Gothelm were legend, and Livia knew the rumours of their opulence and debauchery. Her imagination had run wild with those stories. So much so that a tiny, sinful part of her had wanted to attend one.

She had never imagined her first experience of such a banquet would be quite like this.

Kessel was a grim place, all brooding dark corridors and hideous statues. Its dining hall was no less ominous, the ceiling disappearing into darkness to make it appear open to a starless night, the long, dark table polished to a black sheen, each chair high-backed and intricately carved. Crimson candles burned in sconces, wax having dripped and congealed to make it appear like the walls were weeping blood.

More candles burned in a dark iron candlestick at the centre of the table, illuminating the dinner set before her. Silver forks and knives were lined up precisely – though why she'd need more than one of each, Livia had no idea. The handle of each piece was made of carved bone in the shape of a writing demon. Three long-stemmed glasses, each a different shape, stood before her.

Livia took a deep breath. This was far and away the most uncomfortable she'd felt since that bastard Randal had come for her. At least she knew where she stood when she was being kidnapped and marched from one end of the land to the other. What the hell was this?

The only consolation was that she didn't stink anymore.

Kaleb had scaled the vast chains in the dark. Though she did her best to hate him for not running away with her, she still felt concern for him. She had sighed in relief as the chains had begun to move, grinding and whirring, churning up the sea as they lowered a massive platform from the side of the citadel. At first, she had marvelled at such a magnificent feat of engineering, and as they left the boat and stood on the platform she felt thrilled, as though she were walking on the sea itself. But when the mechanical cogs and chains began to turn once more she had noticed the platform had manacles attached to it. Places where people had been strapped. From the gouges and rents in the dark stone she guessed they had not come to a good end.

When they reached the top, Livia was shown to a small windowless chamber. In a side room had been a hot bath and perfumed soap. It was fit for a duchess, and she had peeled off her filthy clothes and bathed. The heat of the water had lulled her to sleep and when she woke someone had come and taken her mucky rags, replacing them with the dress she now wore, along with a brush for her hair. An offer of dinner had been too much to resist.

The satin gown was soft against her skin and it glowed red in the flickering light. Her hair was still damp but for the first time in weeks it was no longer a tangled mess. Something about this whole thing made her feel a little like a fatted calf before the cull.

Across the table the boy smiled.

'Hello, Livia. I am the Regent. Lord of the Qeltine Brotherhood, and you are my guest. Wine?' he asked.

Livia stared across at him, wondering what this creature was. This thing that looked like a boy but spoke like a man.

'Not for me,' she replied, trying her best to remain as defiant as she could.

Two figures walked from the dark, skeletally thin and bearing brass jugs. One filled the glass in front of the child. When the second began to pour Livia's wine she glanced up, unable to subdue a gasp as she saw the mouth in his gaunt face was sewn shut with copper wire.

'Don't mind the Silent Sons,' said the boy. 'They are quite harmless. Consider them servants, here to do your bidding.'

Livia looked back to her glass and the black liquid within. Quickly she took it and drank, all thoughts of defiance fleeing as she felt the rich, sweet wine coat her tongue and warm her throat. Before she knew it, she had drained her glass. The thrall filled it once more before she had a chance to put it down.

'Of course, you must be thirsty,' said the Regent. 'My apologies. And hungry no doubt?'

More Silent Sons entered the room through some shadowed doorway, heralded by the most delicious aroma

Livia had ever smelled. Her stomach rumbled, reminding her of how hungry she was, as one of the thralls placed a platter before her. On it were slices of white meat alongside mashed root vegetables, all lathered in a rich gravy.

Livia stared at the platter, then looked to the boy. There was no food for him. Clearly, he didn't have an appetite.

'Eat. Please,' he said.

She grasped one of the forks, ignoring the knives, and skewered a slice of the meat, stuffing it into her mouth. She closed her eyes at the delicious taste, breathing heavily through her nose as she chewed, savouring the warm succulent gravy.

She must have looked a sight, shovelling her food in like a savage, but she was past caring. This place might have been like a sepulchre, and they may well have brought her here to die, but if she found out who ran the kitchens she was determined to give them a huge kiss.

When she'd eaten her fill half the platter was taken away. Livia glanced up to see the boy looking at her with an amused smile. She patted her chest and burped.

'This must all be very frightening for you,' the Regent said. 'And I apologise for what you've been through. If I could have spared you any of it I would have.'

'How thoughtful,' Livia said, then took a sip of wine, swilling it around her mouth. She realised everything had gone a little fuzzy around the edges. The wine had gone to her head and she placed the glass down as gently as she could.

'You must be wondering what all this is about.'

Livia stared at the boy across the table. 'I know exactly

what this is about. You're a religious fanatic and I'm here to be sacrificed to your god like a lamb at solstice.'

The Regent's smile widened. Then he stood, his chair scraping behind him. He walked around the table to stand beside her.

'Please, come with me,' he said, holding out his hand.

There was no point in being defiant now. She was trapped in this place and she knew it. Best to play nice until there was a chance for her to make an escape.

Livia ignored the offered hand and stood. The Regent led her from the dark dining room and out into an adjoining hall. It was peppered with carvings on plinths, black onyx dioramas depicting battle scenes and bloody sacrifices.

'This place, this citadel, is an ancient conduit,' the boy said, as though he'd explained this a thousand times. 'Battles have been fought over the location. During the Age of Archons, Sicaria raised beasts from the sea to claim this place.' He gestured to one of the dioramas depicting a vast sea monster rising to crush an army on the land.

'In ancient times,' he continued, 'it was just a wooden fort, but the warriors of all twelve cults killed and sacrificed to own it. The wooden walls were rebuilt in stone, the fort made into a vast stronghold, all to protect what it held.' They reached a plinth on which two warriors fought atop a pile of corpses. 'This place was born from blood. And he who covets its power must bathe in blood to keep it.'

'That's all very pleasant,' Livia said. 'But what has any of it got to do with me?'

The Regent led her onward toward a dark staircase. He

took a burning torch from the wall and led them down.

'When the Age of Archons was over, the Blood Lords could only commune with their masters from a few chosen places. This is one such place. The last Blood Lord, Korvus the Red, kept it as his home, shunning Kragenskûl for the solitude of Kessel.'

They reached the bottom of the stairs and walked out into a long chamber. In the middle of it stood an altar, shining black in the dimness. At each corner were chains, in its midst were carved gutters, and Livia had no doubt what they were meant to channel. She couldn't withhold a gasp.

'It must seem savage to you.'

'You're going to offer me up as a sacrifice? You're going to use my blood to raise your Korvus from the grave?' Her voice echoed in the small chamber. The boy just stared at her with lifeless eyes.

'There will be a ritual, yes. And you will be at its centre. It is a great honour. The greatest the Brotherhood can possibly bestow.'

Livia didn't believe what she was hearing. It was almost as though she had a choice in this.

'That's a lovely offer,' she replied. 'And as flattered as I am, I'm afraid I'll have to politely decline.'

The Regent's childish laugh resonated in the cramped chamber. Livia winced at the sound.

'You misunderstand me, Livia. Your blood will not resurrect Korvus the Red. He is dead and gone.'

'Then why the hell am I here?' she demanded. She was done with this now, and done with these fanatics.

'I have not brought you here to bring back the Blood Lord. I have brought you here to *become* the Blood Lord. You will be the new avatar of Qeltine. You have power. A gift not seen for a hundred years. You are the one, of that there is no doubt.'

'You're insane,' she said. 'I'm no one. I don't have power.' Even as she said it, Livia knew that wasn't true. But she was certainly no one's Blood Lord.

'We will see,' said the boy, his hand tracing a line across the smooth ebony altar. 'Tomorrow we will perform the rite. Tomorrow we will see how much power you truly have.'

'And what does this rite involve?'

'As you said. We will cut out your heart,' the Regent replied nonchalantly.

Livia felt the walls closing in around her.

Silently she followed the boy as he led her from the sacrificial chamber and back up the stairs. They walked in silence, Livia barely noticing the route as they moved up through the citadel.

'Sleep well,' he said to her as they arrived back at her room. 'Do not look on this as an ending. It is a beginning. A new beginning for us all.' Livia wanted to spit in his face. 'Oh, and in case you feel you might want to avoid your destiny and perhaps fling yourself from the window during the night, I have left someone to watch over you.'

Livia saw someone walk from the shadows. It was the long-haired warrior, his left hand resting on the hilt of his sword. His stony face reminded Livia of the figures in the dioramas she had seen in Kessel's great hall.

'Think of Dantar as your protector,' said the Regent. 'Until tomorrow.' With that he closed the door.

Livia turned to Dantar. 'Where is Kaleb?' she asked.

He said nothing.

Livia took a step closer. 'Are you going to stand there all night? Because I may need to make water and I don't think there's a chamber pot.'

Still no response.

'Fair enough. I get it, not one for conversation. Which surprises me because I couldn't shut that little boy up. He's a smug little shit, isn't he?'

If Dantar had any opinion on the matter he didn't express it.

Livia left him standing in the corner as she undressed and lay down in the bed. The pillows were the softest she'd ever felt. As she lay there she stared at the dress, hung limply over a chair. It was the most beautiful thing she'd ever worn.

If she was going to die in the morning, then her one consolation was she'd at least look good as they ripped the heart from her chest.

49

THERE were no sentries at the camp's perimeter. Josten didn't know whether that made him feel any better. No sentries meant this army was either confident in its might, or they were an unruly rabble who'd kill intruders as soon as look at them.

That question didn't seem to bother Silver any. She strode right into the camp, past the fires and the wounded and the sleeping bodies as though she knew exactly where she was going.

Randal was on edge, that much was obvious. The simpering shit didn't say a word as they walked through the camp, past the demon head banners, and Josten was glad of the silence.

Beyond the camp the huge citadel rose up, illuminated by the trebuchet fire and flaming arrows that battered its walls. If Livia was inside, Josten was determined he would find her. How they would escape was quite another matter, but he guessed he'd have to figure that one out when he got there. Living out tonight was a more pressing problem.

The three of them managed to reach the centre of the camp before they started to receive attention. Several injured warriors glared at them as they walked past, and Josten did his best to look like he belonged.

'I hope you know what you're doing,' Josten said, as some of the wounded warriors began to limp after them, murmuring in disquiet.

'Trust me,' said Silver.

What other choice did he have? If all else failed there was a blade at his side, and he knew he could still run like fuck if the need arose.

It was with a little relief they reached the central tent. Josten had been in enough army camps to recognise a command post when he saw one, although this was the grimmest he'd ever encountered. Dark pennants flew from it, bearing an ancient Ramadi sigil, surrounded by skulls and feathers. The hide covering of the tent looked suspiciously like tanned human skin.

Unperturbed, Silver walked straight up to the scary-looking sentry guarding the entrance.

'Where are you going?' asked the huge warrior, his accent thick as his neck.

'I seek audience with your leader,' Silver said. She looked tiny next to the guard, but she faced him down, not showing any sign of fear.

The warrior's face creased into a grin. 'How about I give you an audience with my cock,' he said, reaching for his blade. Josten reached for his own, but Silver was quicker. Her sword was drawn and at the warrior's throat before he could even grasp his weapon's handle.

She pushed the brute back through the flap of the tent

and he duly backed away, hands up, eyes crossed staring at the blade to his neck. Josten drew his sword and followed them inside, knowing this might be the end. Behind he could hear Randal quietly whispering the word 'fuck' to himself over and over.

Inside there were three men in intricate bone armour, hulking over a table. Josten had lost count of the times he'd seen this scene – armoured men standing around maps planning the deaths of other armoured men. He'd never made quite such a dramatic entrance before though.

As they saw Silver leading the sentry with a blade to his throat, the men took a step back.

'Who is in charge here?' Silver asked.

The warrior wearing the most ornate armour, his dark hair tied in a topknot about his white-painted face, addressed her.

'I am Kraden. Known as the Fist. High Lord of the Legion of Wraak. Have you come here to kill me?' The notion seemed to amuse him. 'You should know, it won't be easy.'

Josten had just about had enough of being led through this by the nose. 'We've come to join you,' he said. 'To offer our swords and help you take the citadel.'

Kraden looked at them. Then the huge warlord burst out laughing.

'Offer your swords?' he bellowed. 'You tiny whelps? I have warriors aplenty. Men willing to die for me so that Kessel will fall. What could you possibly offer?'

Josten felt panicked at Kraden's reaction and not a little stupid. 'You're turning down willing swords?'

'If you are lucky I might let one of you clean the gore from my armour when I have crushed this citadel and executed every man that stands against me,' said Kraden. 'For now I have enough swords.'

Silver's blade flashed and the sentry she had been holding hostage fell. Josten moved out of her way as she stepped towards the warlord, her weapon cutting the air twice more. The two warriors that flanked Kraden fell clutching their throats.

There was silence in the tent. Kraden wasn't laughing anymore.

'Now you have three fewer,' she said to him. Her blade was poised at his neck, her jaw fixed.

The grin that had temporarily fallen from the warlord's mouth slowly returned. His chest quivered as he bellowed with laughter once more.

'I like you,' he said to Silver. 'You can fight. And you don't fear death. I value that more than anything.'

'Then we fight for you?' Silver asked, the blade she held not moving an inch.

'Of course.' Kraden opened his arms out wide as though about to embrace them all. 'You have the word of the Fist on that. And your arrival is most fortuitous. The gate to Kessel will fall tonight. The Brotherhood will be slaughtered where they stand and the citadel will be ours.'

Silver slowly lowered her sword. Josten wasn't sure whether trusting the warlord at his word was the right idea, but they had no choice. They were waist-deep in shit now, and nothing was going to get them out but to keep wading through it.

'We need armour,' said Josten, unwilling to leap into the breach dressed in rags. Then he looked at his rusted blade. 'And weapons.'

'Yours,' said Kraden. 'I have enough to spare – my dead are piled high. But before you go, I must know one thing...'

'What's that?' Josten asked.

'Why would you join with us? Do you hate the Qeltine so much that you would give your lives?'

No one seemed willing to speak.

'A long story,' Josten replied, to break the silence. 'Do you care as long as we kill your enemies?'

Kraden needed no time to consider his answer. 'Of course not! Kill my enemies and you will be hailed as heroes among the Legion of Wraak.'

'Then kill them we will,' Josten said, trying his best to sound as though he was born to it. Right now he didn't feel born to much at all. He was tired and he stank and more than likely he was going to die attacking some fortress in the middle of the desert, but he did his best to hide all that.

Kraden looked the bedraggled trio up and down. 'Come, I will see you are dressed more fittingly for battle.'

Josten couldn't help but think they'd be dressed more fittingly for their funerals as Kraden led the three of them from the tent. If the men Silver had killed meant anything to the armoured giant he didn't show it, leaving them behind in pools of their own blood.

They were led to an armoury of sorts – a huge hide tent housing a pile of arms and armour most likely stripped from the dead. At any moment Josten expected Kraden's warriors to come rushing from the darkness, but it seemed the Fist was indeed a man of his word.

'Dorcus!' the warlord yelled as soon as they entered the tent. From the shadows limped an old warrior, wispy grey hair hanging limply around his battered face. 'New meat for the horde. See that they are well prepared for the final assault.'

The old veteran nodded as his leader left. Josten was still wary that this could be some sort of trap, but as Dorcus led them towards the weaponry he realised if Kraden wanted them dead it would have happened already.

With the warrior's help, Josten and Randal managed to bundle together enough bone-embossed plate and mail to look the part at least, but Silver favoured the battered sword she had brought with her.

When they were suitably equipped, the old veteran led them from the tent. Josten wondered if he was leading them straight to the siege, but instead they were taken to a fire, upon which sat a cauldron of boiling broth.

'Do you think this is fit to eat?' Randal asked, screwing his nose up at the dubious stench.

'I'm too hungry to care,' Josten replied. 'Besides, I don't fancy dying on an empty stomach.'

As they helped themselves to the foul-smelling broth, Dorcus left them to it. Josten couldn't help but notice the sadness in the old warrior's eyes as he went, as though he would have much preferred flinging himself at the walls of Kessel than acting custodian to the arms and armour of his dead brethren.

Josten girded himself before digging into the bowl of broth. Two mouthfuls and he'd stopped caring how bad it was. Randal managed his own bowl, but Silver seemed to forego any food. She simply stood staring at the fortress in the distance, watching as the Legion of Wraak beat themselves against its stalwart facade.

When he had eaten his fill, Josten moved to stand beside the woman. In the firelight her face took on an eerie, almost otherworldly hue.

'We are almost out of time,' she said. 'I can feel it.'

Josten looked out at the army in front of him. 'All I feel is a knot in the pit of my stomach.'

'You will not die here, Josten Cade,' Silver said, still staring through the night. 'That is not your fate.'

'I wish that was as reassuring as you think it is,' Josten replied.

'I am not trying to reassure you. You will die. Just not here.'

'Thanks,' said Josten. 'That makes me feel so much better.' He had never been superstitious, and put no store by the mumblings of any old seer, but he had to admit, Silver put him on edge. 'And just how do you know all this?'

'You would not be able to comprehend—'

'You've already told me that,' Josten said, losing patience. 'I've had enough of your cryptic prattle. Who the hell are you?'

Silver turned to face him and he realised his mistake. For a moment Josten felt like a child caught in her gaze, as though she were looking into his soul and could see every bit

411

of him, from his birth to this very moment. All his secrets, all his evil deeds.

'I have many names,' said Silver. 'And I have lived many lives. I have been beggar and queen. I have seen the start of things and I will see the end.'

'Enough,' said Josten, mustering as much strength of will as he could. 'Just give me a straight answer.'

Silver stared, her features hard in the dim light. Then she seemed to soften.

'Patience, Josten Cade,' she said, and as she spoke all the fight seemed to leave him. 'You will see the truth of things soon enough.'

With that she walked off into the darkness.

As he watched her go, Randal came to stand beside him, also watching Silver as she disappeared.

'What was that all about?' Randal asked.

'Not a fucking clue,' Josten replied. 'But apparently we'll soon find out.'

'If we live long enough,' said Randal, glancing towards the imposing sight of Kessel. 'Chances are we'll be dead tomorrow.'

And despite Silver's reassurance that he would not die here, Josten couldn't help but think Randal was right.

50

KALEB had never put much store by vanity, but he had always taken pride in his appearance. That was something he had learned from Avenor.

'Look impressive,' the Sword Saint had told him. 'Intimidate the enemy with your presence and half the battle is won.'

They were useful words. A tenet Kaleb had lived by. He remembered the fear in his enemies' eyes when he entered the battlefield. Avenor had never guided Kaleb wrong in those hard years of campaigning.

How Kaleb missed his mentor now. How he wished the warrior stood beside him. As it was he had to make do with a few Silent Sons, their mouths sealed shut, eyes mournful as they ministered to him.

He stood in a bare antechamber, the walls dancing in the red candlelight. In front of him was a mirror showing him a man he had not seen for what seemed like years. His hair was cut short, his stubble shaved, body washed and treated with perfumed oils. The thralls had bedecked him in robes befitting his status. He looked every inch the Sword Saint – black tunic embroidered in gold, red sash at his waist, boots polished to a sheen.

A thrall brought forth a new blade. Four feet of straight steel sheathed in a plain black scabbard. The thrall made to tie the belt about his waist but Kaleb stopped him, taking the sheathed sword from his hand, barely noticing as the thrall retreated into the shadows.

Kaleb held the blade in his hand, taking a moment to appreciate the craftsmanship. It was not as ornate as other blades he had seen over the years. There was no adornment. It was a weapon for killing. Plain in the making but expertly forged.

He should have been proud. Should have felt like his former self, but Kaleb knew he was irreparably altered. Livia had shown him something different to his old life. Before her he had been a slave. Now that he had tasted freedom, had dared to hope he might have another life, his regalia meant nothing to him. The weapon in his hand was more burden than gift. Yet still he buckled the belt about his waist, feeling the weight of the sword at his hip. Where before it had filled him with strength and pride, now it just felt like a heavy lump of metal.

Kaleb stared into the mirror. The warrior that looked back was a stranger to him, a peerless exemplar of the blade, but inside all Kaleb felt was uncertainty.

Livia had offered him a future away from all this. He could have fled with her. Lived a different life, but he had turned his back on that. Now the regret of it weighed on him more heavily than anything he had shouldered before – more than the Circle, the Carpenter and all the wars in the Ramadi.

Kaleb tore his gaze from the reflection and walked away,

ignoring the Silent Sons, who watched with desolation in their eyes.

As he escaped along the dark corridors of Kessel he found his head filling with a fug, his legs buckling. He held out a hand to the cold wall to steady himself. This was unbearable. All the hardships he had endured and now he was brought low by doubt. Kaleb fought the feeling, reciting the credo of the Sword Saints, squeezing his eyes shut against the nausea that assailed him.

A few quick breaths and he had gathered himself. Though gripping the hilt of his new blade did not fill him with the pride he had felt in times past, it still steadied him enough to walk out of the main barbican and into the waning light of dusk.

His ears were filled with the sound of the attacking army. It echoed from the plain beyond, the noise rising up and crashing down into the courtyard of Kessel like a tidal wave. Its fury galvanised his thoughts for a moment, filling him with a renewed sense of purpose. Best he focus on that. Best he concentrate on fighting the men who were set on murdering him and everyone in this citadel. That was what Kaleb knew – how to fight. How to kill.

He mounted the stairs to the rampart, passing by the vigilant Bloodguard, seeing the respect in their eyes upon seeing his vestment. It did nothing to allay the feeling that he was a fraud. That he was merely playing a part and that any moment he would be found out.

As he looked out over the battlements he saw the army below, a seething mass of armoured hate assaulting the walls. Their attack looked futile as they smashed themselves into the huge gate but Kaleb knew that there was no futility here. Even water could erode a mountainside given time. With enough strength of will, one man could achieve almost anything. And these were no ordinary men but the Legion of Wraak. They would not stop until Kessel was left in ruins.

The scene reminded Kaleb of days gone, when he had fought against warriors such as these on the battlefield. He realised he no longer regarded them as he had in days past. They were no longer the scum of old, to be trodden in the dust and forgotten. Back then he had been filled with righteous fury. He had faced the enemies of the Brotherhood and destroyed them without mercy. Now the hate he should have felt was replaced by pity. The anticipation of battle was consumed by his apathy. These warriors were slaves, as he had been. Their zeal was born of indoctrination, not choice. Whether they knew it or not they were being forced to besiege this place. Kessel had been built as yet one more testament to every man enslaved in the Ramadi.

In that instant, Kaleb could not have cared if this place fell around his ears.

Let it burn.

A figure approached along the walkway. Kaleb saw his brother Dantar walk with all surety, at peace even in the face of such an assault from their enemies. Kaleb was not surprised – Dantar had never been one to show emotion, even when faced with the most extreme hardship. He seemed to thrive on adversity, to own it and bend it to his will. He was a true servant of the Brotherhood. The epitome of a Sword Saint.

Dantar stopped beside him, looking down at the

advancing armies. The light of the fires below illuminated his face, making his animal eyes dance with light. It was the most life Kaleb had ever seen in them.

Though he was reluctant to break the silence, Kaleb could not help himself. He had to know.

'What has become of Livia?' he asked.

Dantar did not turn to look at him. 'Your concern for her is curious, brother. I have spent a brief time in her company and must admit... I was eager to depart.'

'I can see how she might have that effect. Her language is... coarse.'

'Indeed. And yet the Blood Regent would have her treated like a dignitary.'

'Then she is safe?' Kaleb asked, failing to mask the concern in his voice.

'For now,' Dantar replied.

Kaleb felt something grip him inside his chest. His hand tightened on the hilt of his new blade. 'So the Blood Regent plans to offer her as a sacrifice?'

'I do not know the Blood Regent's plans,' said Dantar. 'But if the gate falls she is as doomed as the rest of us.'

Kaleb let out a sigh. Perhaps there was hope. Perhaps she would not be offered as a sacrifice after all. 'Some of us might be deserving of such damnation,' he said.

'Why would you say such a thing, brother?' Dantar turned to look at him now, his brow furrowed.

Kaleb regarded his brother. It was odd to see him so confused. 'We were bred for this. For war. We were always destined to die in battle. Do we not deserve such a fate?'

Dantar shook his head. 'We are servants of the Brotherhood. We are no more deserving than—'

'No. We are not servants. We are slaves, Dantar. Do you not see that? We were raised to die for the Brotherhood. Given no choice. No free will to choose our fate.'

Kaleb's emotions were getting the better of him but he didn't care. As he spoke the words he realised they had been a long time in coming.

'And what would this free will have given us?' said Dantar. 'An ordinary life. To live like the cattle and sheep of the south. We would never have lived for the glory of—'

'We would have had a life worth living!' Kaleb barked the words, instantly regretting it. He should have kept his emotions in check. Especially now, when he was talking to a man who had shown no emotion in all the years Kaleb had known him. Yet Dantar did not chastise him. Instead he lowered his gaze, staring thoughtfully at the ground.

'You are not alone, Kaleb,' Dantar said. 'I too think about what could have been. I too remember the past...'

Those few words were the last he had thought to hear his brother say. Dantar had always borne an air of confidence and surety. He above all others had been a faithful servant. Unwavering in his devotion.

'And you too are troubled by it?' Kaleb asked.

Dantar looked up, fixing him with those eyes that had always seemed feral but now bore more humanity than Kaleb had ever seen.

'I am haunted by it, brother.'

They regarded one another as the noise of the siege raged

below. Dantar seemed to battle with his emotions until he wrestled them back under control. He raised his head, his mask firmly back in place.

'I experienced it too, Dantar. I was there, remember? I was with you—'

'Not for everything,' Dantar said, staring out over the plain once more. 'There are things I have been forced to bury. But nothing stays buried forever.' When he said the words it was as though he were talking to someone else. Someone distant.

Kaleb was suddenly reminded of the Circle. Of a day that seemed a lifetime ago when Dantar had challenged…

'Morghil?' he asked.

Dantar glanced at Kaleb as though he had uncovered some forbidden secret.

'I said it is buried,' Dantar replied. 'It should stay there.'

'Tell me,' said Kaleb. 'Perhaps I can help.'

'There is nothing you can do, Kaleb Ap'Kharn. There is nothing either of us can do but serve.' It seemed Dantar's armour was back on. 'The Blood Regent has said that tomorrow we will know the truth. That tomorrow the Brotherhood will ascend. I know you have feelings for the girl. That you want to protect her. For your own sake, bury those feelings. It is the only peace you will ever have.'

With that he turned his back on Kaleb and made his way back down from the battlements.

Kaleb watched him go. He could only imagine what horror Morghil had enacted upon his brother. But then they had all faced horrors in Kragenskûl.

As he looked out at the attacking army, Kaleb knew that there would be more horrors to come before the night was out.

51

JOSTEN could anticipate the slaughter to come. He could hear it, smell it, feel it in his gut, the fear and excitement building. Activity in the camp had reached a frenzy. Even wounded men had risen from their torpor, gingerly donning armour, moving towards the citadel as though the gate were about to fall right before their eyes.

At the edge of the camp, High Lord Kraden stood staring wild-eyed at Kessel. Beside him was a smaller man in a plain robe, a serpent tattoo entwined around his right eye. He was speaking to Kraden in what looked like a constant diatribe, as though reciting litanies into the warrior's ear. Josten was too far away to make out the words, but whatever he was saying seemed to fuel Kraden as he looked on at the siege.

As Josten watched, he got the impression this robed man was more than a mere advisor. It was almost as though he were instructing Kraden, dictating to him even. Kraden nodded at the smaller man's words, like he was acquiescing to his instruction. It looked ridiculous from where Josten stood.

When the robed man had finished, Kraden moved toward the warriors amassed for battle. Josten was still watching as the robed man turned to regard him, his hairless face and serpent tattoo giving him an unsettling demeanour. Josten couldn't draw his eyes away, until the man nodded at him, his lip curling into a knowing half-smile. Then he was gone into the night.

To the north, High Lord Kraden bellowed. A wordless war cry of pure hate. This was it. Josten knew they were about to make their final attack.

He turned, seeing Randal sitting staring at the ground. 'Let's move,' Josten said, feeling the hairs rise on the back of his neck.

The expectation of battle began to fill him. The knowledge that this could be his final night.

Randal moved up beside him, eyes wide as he stared at the army before them.

'This is really happening, isn't it?' he said.

'It really is,' Josten replied. 'Scared?'

'Aren't you?' Randal seemed surprised at the question.

'Shitting myself. And I can't wait.' A smile crossed his face at Randal's bemused expression. There was no way the tallyman would ever know how he felt. This was another battle, another siege in a long line. This time though, he was fighting for something worthwhile. He'd come a long way to find Livia and to honour the promise he'd made. If he met his end, at least it would be for a cause worth dying for.

Silver joined them and the three walked forward to join the rest of the attacking army. Ranks of warriors looked on as trebuchets battered the walls of Kessel.

High Lord Kraden bellowed at his men, raising their ire. He spurred them on with canticles of hate and promises of glory as in the distance the gate was being battered by a huge ram. From the parapets of Kessel arrows were flying, but for every warrior that fell another stepped forward to take his place, the ram never halting in its relentless assault on the gate.

Kraden pushed himself forward through the crowd of armoured men. As he passed by he seemed to infect them with his own zeal, and their war cries turned into a cacophony. Every eye was fixed on the gate as it trembled beneath the relentless ministrations of the ram. Every warrior desperate to see it fall.

Josten's thumb strayed to the hilt of his sword, flicking up the cross-guard, loosening it in the scabbard. The wait was always the worst part. Josten scanned the crowd. He knew there were no allies here, no one he could rely on. Usually before a battle you were surrounded by friendly faces – men you'd lived and eaten and slept with. There were no friendly faces here.

He turned to Randal, who was staring down at Josten's thumb as it flicked the cross-guard as though it was the most annoying thing he'd ever seen. It made Josten all the happier.

Silver just stared at the gates, sword in hand like all she wanted was to leap into the fray. Josten still didn't know her story and didn't care. He could only hope that when it came to the killing she'd remember whose side she was on.

The ram kept pounding out its beat and Josten had no idea how long they stood waiting. He marked each long moment with another click of that cross-guard, feeling the steady thrum of his heart beating in his chest and the churning of the tight knot in his gut.

Finally, the great gates cracked.

It was like wood hitting onyx. Shards fell from the gate and the massive iron hinges buckled. A roar went up from the warriors at the foot of the wall, and the men surrounding Josten began to bellow all the louder.

Silver was motionless, but Josten could see Randal begin to quiver.

'Never been in a siege before?' he asked, knowing full well the answer.

Randal shook his head. 'Never been in a battle before,' he replied.

Josten had no advice for him, even if he'd been inclined to give it. *Don't die*, was about as good as it got. There'd be confusion and blood and screaming. In the middle of it all Josten had to find Livia and get out. That was all he knew.

As thoughts of Livia spun in Josten's head, the gate fell. A horde of screaming cultists surged forward, and Josten was jolted into focus. The sword came ringing from its scabbard, shield gripped tight.

Silver was away, sprinting with the rest, a tiny figure amongst armoured giants.

Josten didn't know if Randal was with him, and he didn't care as he began to run with the horde. The ground was churned and broken beneath his feet but he kept his legs pumping. *Don't pause. Don't take a backward step.* That was the only way.

Past the sea of armour before him, Josten could see into the citadel and the open gateway. Several structures towered within, gigantic statues leering down at the warriors as they surged through the gateway.

The roars were deafening. There had been a time when Josten would be roaring right along with them, but now he had to think. Finding Livia was all that mattered.

The vanguard funnelled through the open gate and Josten was swept along. He lost sight of Silver ahead of him and soon the sound of screaming was joined by that of clashing steel.

As he reached the opening the press of armoured men became a crushing throng. Josten could barely breathe, but he kept his legs moving, fighting to keep his head above the mob lest he fall and be trampled to death.

Through the gate, the press of men spread wide to fill the courtyard. He kept moving, no time to feel any relief as he almost lost his footing, stumbling over corpses, desperate to stay on his feet.

In the courtyard the scene was of carnage. The chaos of battle hit Josten like a wave, almost drowning him with its intensity. Memories came flooding back of a dozen times he had faced similar horror; but it had never been like this. Where previously men had screamed in anger and fear, now there was frenzy and zeal. Bloodied and battered warriors fought with insane smiles, grinning maniacally as their limbs were hacked off or they were battered to the ground under a tumult of blows.

Josten found himself watching in awe at the barbarism, at the insanity of it all, before he was brought into sharp focus by someone screaming in his right ear. He dodged as a bone-armoured warrior fell down dead beside him, his face cleaved open, but the teeth still gnashing in a rictus grin.

Another warrior surged past, yelling for vengeance, gladly throwing himself into the fray.

From out of the press ahead a masked cultist came at him, sword raised. Josten had time to lift his shield before the blade could cleave his head in two. The impact jarred his arm and he staggered back, losing his footing on a corpse and sprawling backwards. The cultist bore down on him, silently, efficiently. Not a move was laboured as he raised the blade again.

Josten could only watch. All he had done, his valiant journey, had come to this – to die at the hands of a madman in this damned place.

Randal cut in, his sword coming down hard, slicing the cultist's arm off at the elbow. The warrior had a chance to regard it curiously before Randal dug the blade into his neck. Blood sprayed black in the half-light as the mad eyes dulled and the warrior fell, another corpse on the pile.

Josten could only sit there on his arse watching. Randal watched too, unable to quite believe what he'd done, before turning to Josten and offering his hand.

Reluctantly Josten took it and allowed Randal to pull him to his feet. The battle still raged around them and Josten looked about for any sign of where Livia might be.

'Does this mean you owe me?' asked Randal, as Josten spied movement atop the vast pyramid that lay in the centre of the courtyard.

'We'll see,' he replied, moving towards the huge monument.

There'd be time to pay debts later.

For now, he had to find Livia.

52

Hot wind whipped the summit of the ziggurat. The monument rose from the centre of Kessel's vast courtyard and Livia could only watch from it as the two armies battled below, butchering one another now the gate had fallen.

She had seen battle in her dreams. Demonic beasts and winged seraphs slaying one another under dark skies, but it had been nothing like this. These men were real, human, and their death cries were haunting. In her dreams, she had fed on the violence, yearned for it. Now it filled her with disgust.

The Blood Regent sat on an onyx throne. He watched proceedings with a gleeful look in his eye and for the first time he seemed like the child he was, delighting at a circus spectacle.

To the left of the throne stood Dantar, hand at the hilt of his sword, face expressionless as ever. On the opposite side was Kaleb, now dressed in black, a fine sword at his hip. He was far from the broken cripple she had first met, but a man born again. Just like Dantar, he stood proudly, but every time Livia caught his eye he looked away as though ashamed.

'Do you see?' said the Regent, his lips slick where he'd

licked them in hunger. 'The slaughter! All for you, Livia Harrow. They die for you.'

She shook her head. 'I don't want this. I didn't ask for this.'

'No, you didn't. But the immortal inside you lusts for it. Surely you can feel it within, writhing for release?'

Livia laid a hand to her belly, but there was nothing malevolent in her gut. It was her head that felt the rush. She knew the violence was feeding something deep in her soul. Her disgust was turning to something different entirely... hunger... desire.

'No,' she gasped, fighting the feeling. 'I don't want this.'

'You have no idea what you want,' said the boy. 'But the one that waits inside you does.'

'There is nothing inside me,' she cried. 'I am Livia Harrow. I am Livia Harrow from...'

But she had forgotten. She could not remember that small detail. It seemed so far away. Insignificant.

'Your past is meaningless,' said the boy. 'It is not who you are. There is greatness inside you. Let it out. Let it win. Give in to it.'

'Never!' she turned on him, hands twisted in rage. All she wanted to do was scratch the little wretch's eyes out. To claw his hair from his head. To sink her teeth into...

'You see,' he said, smiling up at her. 'Feels good, doesn't it? It feels right.'

'I am Livia Harrow,' she said quietly, trying as hard to convince herself as the evil little shit in front of her.

She looked down at her hands, still curled into claws,

but now they no longer belonged to her. It was as though she were looking from behind someone else's eyes. As though she were an imposter in her own body.

Wings spread, bearing her aloft on scented air – a rich perfume that tasted of victory. This body was hers. She owned it as she would soon own this land and all the mortals that dwelt within. It could be hers if only she would accept it. Taste the blood of the kill. Consume her victory in a crimson flood.

'Enough!' Livia opened her eyes to see Kaleb standing before her. 'I'm sorry,' he said. 'I should never have brought you here. But you must fight this. You are still Livia Harrow. You can win.'

Before she could answer, the boy pushed himself up from the onyx throne.

'Dantar,' he cried angrily, as though Kaleb were ruining his sport. 'Kill your brother.'

'No!' Livia cried, but two of the Bloodguard had already seized her, pulling her aside.

Kaleb's blade rang from its scabbard as Dantar slowly drew his. Livia struggled in the arms of the warriors but she was held fast. Both Kaleb and Dantar seemed more resigned to the fight than determined to win it. They were like slaves forced to fight for the sport of their master. Both reluctant. But fight they must.

Kaleb give an almost imperceptible nod, which Dantar duly returned.

Then the men went at each other faster than she could comprehend. Their blades flashed twice, ringing loud above the sound of battle below. Kaleb darted past Dantar, blade sweeping down in a final flourish. Then both fighters came to rest, statues locked in a fighting stance.

Livia gasped as the blade dropped from Kaleb's grip. She cried out as he fell, but the sound was lost on the hot air. Dantar moved to his brother's side, catching him before he could hit the ground. As the warrior cradled his brother, Kaleb stared up, whispering something she couldn't hear.

Rage. A crimson rage, burning from her core. A fire that could no longer be quelled.

Livia gripped the arm of one of the Bloodguard, steel fingers crushing flesh and sinew. He cried out as she flung him aside. The second she took by the throat, raising him high before throwing him over the side of the ziggurat.

The Blood Regent smiled at her from his onyx throne. Even as she bore down on him she could tell it was a smile of victory. The boy closed his eyes as she reached forward, grasping his head in one hooked hand and lifting him from where he sat.

A voice inside her cried out in triumph. It was a voice she had kept chastened for so long. Too long.

The boy's neck cracked as Livia wrenched it to one side with inhuman strength. Her mouth opened and she bit down on his throat. The first taste of his lifeblood was luscious, as though she had been starved of it for decades.

Then the light hit her.

It was as though she could see her own body, as though she were witnessing her actions from several feet away. Livia could only watch as she dropped the child like a half-eaten hunk of meat, mouth dripping red. Her eyes were black now, solid pools of night. From the roots, her hair began to change, the colour draining, white strands creeping over the black.

Through the eyes of a stranger, she saw herself. She was Livia Harrow no more. Now she knew what had consumed her. What had infected her like a disease. A larva growing inside her, thick and rotten, now bursting forth like the darkest butterfly...

⸸

They were at the summit of the Blue Tower. Innellan, Armadon, Siff.

Innellan could not take her eyes from the Heartstone. So much had brought her to this moment. So many years of planning. Of dealing and scheming. Now everything was coming to fruition.

The Heartstone had been all but restored. It sat on a giant plinth in the centre of the tower's summit, its surface playing with both light and shadow, each facet of it reflecting a different hue. It showed every scratch and imperfection, but aesthetics were not Innellan's concern. She only cared whether the stone still functioned. Whether she could walk through it to another world. Whether she would rule as the goddess she was.

Siff held out a hand toward the Heartstone. The air grew thick as though the burgeoning clouds outside were growing heavy.

'Durius has not fled,' Siff said. 'He has not gone through.'

'And the gate?' Innellan asked. 'Is it repaired?'

'It is imperfect,' breathed Siff, clearly distressed that the stone had been wrought anew. 'But it could still provide a pathway. We must destroy it. Armadon. Smash this thing to pieces.'

When Armadon did not move, Siff turned to face her fellow Archons.

'Sweet Siff,' Innellan said with a smile. 'Gentle, caring, gullible idiot that you are.'

Siff shook her head. 'What have you done, Innellan?' she said, panic rising in her voice.

Innellan walked forward, staring into the Heartstone, feeling its burgeoning strength. 'What have I done? I have restored our power. I have forged the Heartstone anew. Now we can cross into the mortal realm once more. Now we can rule as we once did. Feel the power we used to hold in both worlds, not just this broken land.'

'But Durius…'

Innellan laughed at her sister's stupidity. 'You think Durius had a hand in this? He was the one who tried to stop me. Why do you think you were brought into this? Your desire to keep the Heartstone forbidden was just what I needed to defeat him. He was the last thing standing in my way. And you helped move him from my path. I did this, Siff. I have restored the source of our power. Now nothing can stop us.'

'No.' Siff's voice was filling with rage. 'You have damned us. You have condemned us to centuries of endless war.'

'Don't be so dramatic, sister. This is what we were created for. Things are now as they should be. Now and forever.'

'I won't let you—'

'And how will you stop me?' Innellan moved towards the Heartstone. 'Do you think I have not prepared for this day? Even before the Heartstone was fully restored it allowed me to commune with the mortal realm. A sacrifice has already been prepared, for both me and Armadon. Can you not feel them? Can you not sense their devotion? My acolytes are ready to accept us. The sacrifices ready to host our bodies. To give us form in another world. All we have to do is pass through.'

'No,' said Siff again. 'I will not let you.' She stood barring the way, her spear held defensively.

Innellan could only admire her sister's single-minded devotion to keeping the Heartstone from them. She looked at Armadon.

'Kill her,' she said.

Armadon hefted his huge blade, the only thing he took any degree of pride in, and stomped toward Siff. She was tiny next to that huge frame, and Innellan licked her lower lip in anticipation of the slaughter. But her sister was quick. No fragile flower was Siff.

As Armadon's blade swept down to cleave her in two, Siff span, her spear twirling. It skewered Armadon's thick, meaty thigh as his blade came down, shattering the tiled floor. He gave a howl, grasping the spear shaft and wrenching it free of his thigh and Siff's grasp.

Before he could attack again Siff leapt at him, hands outstretched, nails set to rake his face. Armadon took a step backwards, wounded leg giving way on the blood-strewn floor. As Siff's hands closed about his face they both toppled back, falling against the Heartstone.

Innellan could only watch in horror as the power of the stone consumed them both, swallowing the Archons as though they had been cast into the sea.

She was left alone.

Her howl consumed the tower, the thunder outside rumbling in sympathy at her defeated plans.

Lightning flashed as Innellan rushed to the Heartstone. She could sense the waiting sacrifices; feel Siff and Armadon consuming their bodies on the other side of the portal. Slowly she realised that *no one was waiting for her in the mortal plane. There was no longer a host for her to dominate.*

Innellan resisted the temptation to cross over regardless. If she were to enter the mortal realm with no willing vessel prepared for her she might be consumed by a dominant mortal mind. It might be centuries before she had the power to overcome the host and by then her rival Archons might have built empires of their own.

She closed her eyes, hand straying toward the Heartstone, palm facing the glimmering facets. Power oozed from the stone, faint but still tangible. There was still worship there, despite the fact the Archons had been cut off from their source of power for a century. The mortals still believed. She just had to find one worthy.

Her mind reached out, probing forth into the mortal realm, scouring the lands for a suitable host. She needed a mortal of strength, of pedigree, but also vulnerable enough to be manipulated. Young, malleable, yet with the strength of a warlord in the blood...

There.

A girl. Innocent but strong.

She was an unwitting host. It might still take Innellan weeks to take control, but take control she would.

Opening her eyes, Innellan saw the girl, asleep.

With a smile crossing her lips she stepped forward and let the Heartstone consume her.

Beyond the portal, Livia Harrow waited, unknowing...

53

The Ramadi Wastes, 104 years after the Fall

*H*era waited in the tower. It was an old chamber, long unused, one of many within the fortress city of Mantioch that had been left to ruin after the Fall. From its window, she could see out over the city, over the slate rooftops, mostly broken and dilapidated.

They said, before the Fall, Mantioch was the most vibrant city within the Ramadi. A beacon of glory and prosperity. A bright lantern in the gloom of the wastes; richer than Kragenskûl, more industrious than Gortanis, more beautiful than Isinor.

Now it was a relic, like all the cities. Like all the cults.

Hera shook that last thought from her head. Such heresy could not be allowed to infect her thoughts. She was Justiciar, Honour Guard to the Set, and as such held in a place of esteem. She had to be an example to others. Such doubt would not be tolerated. Questioning the glory of Katamaru's Faithful would only lead to her demise.

And yet here she was. Waiting for him again.

To think sacrilegious thoughts was one thing. To engage in such iniquity was quite another. But Hera had long since stopped scourging herself for her lust. After all, what was the point? The Blood Lords were gone, and they would never return. Their magic spent. Now all that remained were their priests, adhering to ancient rites and poring over meaningless scripture. Where did such observance get them when the Fall came? What had their exalted tomes done for them when Tauri the Mighty died in a torrent of his own blood, blown away on the breeze like so much ash?

The door opened behind her with a creak. As he shut the door behind him she could smell his musk, and she closed her eyes, savouring it for a moment.

Mandrake said nothing, and Hera continued staring out of the window – a game they played every time. Sometimes he would give in first, coming to her, wrapping himself around her and kissing her neck. Other times she would weaken, turning and running to his arms, kissing him fully, her hands scrabbling at the buckle of his belt.

This time their desire was simultaneous. She turned just as he was making his way across the chamber, his bare broad chest gleaming, his hair oiled back, beard twisted and braided into three forks. They met in the centre of the chamber and Hera grasped him around the neck. Mandrake reached down, grasping her buttocks in his huge hands and lifting her, grinding their loins together as he kissed her hard. She could hear his breath, the deep moan in his throat. It stirred her within.

His beard was soft against her face. Mandrake had already unbuckled the belt at his waist, allowing his kilt and sword belt to fall to the floor. Hera took him in her hand, feeling him quickly swell, her own excitement growing as he moaned at her touch.

He dragged the leather hauberk off her torso and her own kilt fell to the ground. Grasping her buttocks, he raised her up, his mouth devouring her breast. Hera's breath came short and sharp as she tried to quell a moan of her own. They were lost up here, far from the rest of the fortress, but her voice might well carry from the open window. Cries of ecstasy would stand out starkly in this dour city.

With her legs wrapped around him she could feel the flesh of his powerful thighs against hers, the end of his manhood teasing her quim. Eagerly she eased him inside her and they both bit their lips, staring into each other's eyes as they felt their long-subdued lust finally given free reign.

Mandrake pushed himself slowly inside her, his brow furrowing, his mouth open in a silent moan of rapture. Hera gasped a shallow breath with every stroke, faster and faster until she was riding him as he plunged deeper and deeper.

All too quickly Mandrake closed his eyes, biting down on Hera's shoulder as he came inside her. She pressed her cheek to his as he breathed deeply, a sheen of sweat having gathered on his rough flesh.

When he had recovered, he laid her down on the cool floor of the chamber, kissing her breasts, her stomach, down to between her legs until she had to bite her own palm to quell a cry of joy.

Afterwards, as the evening began to cool, they lay in each other's arms. And as she did every day, Hera fought with her guilt. She knew it was forbidden for temple guardians to consort, but it felt right. They were risking everything – capture would mean execution – but as much as she wanted to tell Mandrake that this should be their final tryst she could not bring herself to say the words.

Hera knew he must have felt the same, but he too could not say it. That was Mandrake's way – words were not his strength.

'We should leave,' Mandrake breathed as the sky darkened.

'Just a little while longer,' she said. It sounded pathetic on her lips, but she could not resist just a few more moments in his arms.

His grip on her tightened and he kissed her forehead.

Then the door burst open.

Six temple guards stormed the room. Mandrake looked to where his sword belt lay but Hera put a hand of warning on his arm before he could try to reach for it. They were caught — there was nothing either of them could do now.

Each of the guards held a drawn weapon. Each of them Hera knew by name. She had grown up with them, trained and fought with them. But none would show her an ounce of mercy if she resisted.

Hierophant Grimald entered the chamber after his men. He wore a scant loincloth, bronze bands covering his arms, neck and thighs. Around his shaven head was a circlet of gold and in its centre an emerald jewel through which it was said he could commune with Katamaru himself. Hera had never believed that was true. Not that it mattered now.

'You were given every opportunity,' said Grimald. 'Granted every privilege. And still you spurn us.'

The temple guards were already clapping irons to Mandrake's wrists. Hera felt a sudden swell of panic as they approached.

'It was me,' she said to Grimald. 'I seduced him. It was all me.'

The hierophant shook his head. 'You are both complicit in this. Temptation is no justification.'

They clapped the irons around her wrists. Perhaps she should have resisted. A feeling of helplessness overcame her with the manacles on and she suddenly regretted not fighting back.

But what good would it have done? To die here rather than on the pyre? Besides, deep down she had always known it would come to this. Her fate had been ordained, creeping nearer every time she had come to this place to meet her lover.

Hera glanced to Mandrake one last time as they were dragged from the room. Neither had a chance to speak.

⚔

She hung from the ceiling, her toes barely touching the cold, damp tiles. A grate was set in the floor just beside her feet, draining whatever fluids were shed within the torture chamber. Hera's back had long since stopped stinging from the ministrations of the lash. She was just numb now. At first, she had tried to brave the pain as she had always been taught, trying her best to quell her screams. Eventually, caught up in the delirium of agony, she had cried to the heavens.

In the periphery of her blurred vision she could see a figure. Squinting through the haze she saw Grimald watching. He made no sound, but his eyes gave away everything. He stared at her naked body, hungry, eyes alive with need. How he wanted her; that much was obvious. Perhaps her pain had been that much harsher because of the hierophant's jealousy. If it had been him in that high tower with her, and not Mandrake, it was doubtful she would be suffering so.

'I know what you're thinking,' Grimald said. 'You're thinking that this is a huge waste. That you were a faithful servant. That your prowess in battle was all but peerless.'

That wasn't what Hera was thinking at all, and she would have told him had her lips not been swollen and gummed with blood.

'But you will not be wasted,' Grimald continued. 'You will be revered. More than you deserve, I know, but you and your lover will bring about a new era. Our eidolons restored.'

'What are you talking about?' Hera asked, speaking through numb jaws.

'Our seekers have heard the call,' Grimald replied, moving to stand before her. With one finger, he wiped a trail of blood from her mouth. 'The path to the gods is opened anew. We have an opportunity to bring them back. To welcome them, so that they might walk among us once more. For that we will be rewarded.' He raised the finger to his mouth and licked Hera's blood from it. 'Your sacrifice will be remembered for all time.'

As though the taste of her were not enough, Grimald leaned in. Hera could not move away from him as he breathed her in deeply, then licked her from chin to temple.

All she remembered as he left was how his breath stank of raw meat.

†

They were both shackled to the floor of the sacrificial chamber. Its low ceiling was oppressive, as though it might fall and crush them at any moment.

Hera glanced across at Mandrake, his face a bloody ruin. Metal plates had been screwed into his face and skull – a crude homage to Tauri the Mighty. She wanted to speak, to tell him how she felt, that if this was the punishment they had to endure for what they had shared then she would have endured it a thousand times.

Hierophant Grimald stepped forward. He was naked but for the bronze rings on his arms and thighs. The jewel in his golden circlet seemed to glow brightly as though it was ablaze with anticipation of the sacrifice.

In the background the seekers chanted their perpetual prayers in a language few understood. Grimald smiled as though this were a feast day, as though Hera and Mandrake should have been appreciative of the tribute they were to receive.

In his hands, Grimald held a huge jewel. Inside it Hera could see something roiling with life. The Stone of Katamaru, an artefact that for a hundred years had lain dormant, was now alive with energy.

Hera could feel it filling her with something inhuman. She tried *to quell it, but despite her efforts it was consuming her body and soul.*

Mandrake made a sound, crying out from behind the iron screwed to his face. It was something more than human, an animal bellow that filled Hera with dread, despite the fear she harboured for her own life.

'Yes,' said Grimald. 'Come forth! Return to—'

Mandrake's chains shattered. He rose, somehow larger, more muscular than he ever had been, his head scraping the ceiling. Before Grimald could say any more Mandrake grasped his face and hoisted him high. Hera could hear the hierophant make a high-pitched squeal as his skull cracked in Mandrake's bestial grip. The Stone of Katamaru fell to the floor of the chamber, rolling towards Hera, but she barely noticed.

Mandrake smashed Grimald's head into the ceiling, dashing his brains out and shattering the brickwork. He roared. It was deafening, filling the chamber like a flood, silencing the seekers, who staggered back, their emaciated features showing only fear.

Hera could still feel her insides being torn apart, every sinew burning with apotheosis. Mandrake took a step towards her, but now it was her turn to roar.

Her body burst into flames. The metal that bound her melted in an instant. Heat consumed the room as she rose, screaming. Wings of fire sprouted from her back as the sacrificial chamber was consumed in an all-encompassing conflagration.

The sky was on fire as she staggered to the huge window at the north end of the chamber and took flight...

⸸

She fell burning from a crimson sky...

54

THE blade rang in her hand as the battle assailed her senses. There was a roaring in her ears like the crashing of waves, the stench of blood and sweat pungent in her nose. She scanned the battlefield, this charnel house, for more enemies to slay, but they hung back. Breath came swift and hot to her lungs as armoured men backed away. But it was to be expected. How could they face her? How could they match the battle fury of a god?

Siff saw the fear in them. *Or was her name Silver?* She was an Archon walking the soil of the mortal plain after so many centuries, but Silver was still there, still fighting within her. They were one – all Siff's benevolence and hope, alongside all Silver's fury and hate.

That night in the valley seemed an age ago. How she'd slaughtered the bandits, enacting a bloody revenge for the death of her boys. Of course Siff knew they weren't hers. She knew she shouldn't have cared, but Garvin and his sons had been close to Silver – she had loved them with all her heart – and something inside Siff loved them too. Ripping the last bandit asunder and drinking of his blood had not just been necessary to bring her forth... it had been her pleasure to take. Silver had still been in control then, her rage and grief manifesting in violence. That act of bloodletting allowed the Archon residing within her to rise and take control.

And now Livia Harrow was about to do the same. The blood of a single mortal and the Archon within her would be unleashed.

Siff looked up at the ziggurat. A monument to the Archons, erected by misguided mortals as a place of worship. She could see activity at its summit. Men fighting as Livia watched. A boy on the throne.

Ranks of warriors stood in her way but Siff knew she had to be swift. Any compassion she might have felt for them was gone. She could let nothing stop her – if Livia was to succumb to the Archon inside, all would be lost.

Her blade cut a furrow through the fighting men on both sides; they fell away from her path as she hacked her way through. All the while she was focused on the summit of the ziggurat.

As Siff burst through the melee, something screamed in her ears. A primordial cry as though the very fabric of this world were being torn apart. The screams of a million souls. The death of an entire population. The end of a continent.

She was too late.

Innellan had won.

Livia Harrow had succumbed to the Archon inside her. Innellan had taken hold of her host. How she had tricked the girl into killing and consuming the blood of her victim, Siff might never know, but Livia Harrow was lost. All Siff could do now was stop her immortal sister from wreaking any more harm on this world.

The stairs ran up the side of the ziggurat. No one stood in Siff's way as she mounted them.

When she reached the top of the pyramid, Innellan was waiting, eyes black and hair pure white. Her mouth was rimmed red with the blood of a boy, dead on his throne. To one side knelt a dark-haired warrior cradling a corpse in his arms.

Innellan smiled, teeth stained red. 'Sister,' she said in greeting.

'You do not belong here,' Siff replied, feeling the raw power emanating from Innellan's newly adopted form. 'None of us belong here.'

Innellan laughed, throwing her head back, hair falling in white tresses about her shoulders. 'Do not belong here? This land was meant for us. These... apes were born to serve. Accept it, Siff. This world is ours.'

'Never,' said Siff. 'I will never accept that.'

'Don't be a fool.' Innellan's black eyes bored into Siff. 'We can rule this place together. You and I. Queens atop our dark thrones. Nations at our feet.'

Siff shook her head. 'You know I would never allow that. I fought too long to end the misery we wrought upon this land. I will not let you spread your poison upon it again.'

Innellan suddenly looked sullen. 'Then, fair sister, you will die.'

The air roiled about Innellan's head, as Siff leapt.

They had fought many times over the millennia in different guises. On occasion, they had slaughtered enemies side by side. More often they had opposed one another on the battlefield. Siff had forgotten how often each of them was the victor, but that was a distant memory. All that mattered was that Innellan was stopped.

Siff's sword cut through the air, aimed at Innellan's heart, but before it could strike her sister held out her arm, a discarded spear flying to her outstretched palm. Their weapons rang against one another, and Siff could see a smile of ecstasy cross her sister's face.

Siff's sword sang again, a high-pitched hymn of unrestrained violence.

It was not enough. She could not match Innellan, and her sister's spear parried every blow.

'You inhabit a fighter,' said Innellan, as their weapons locked once more. 'That much is easy to see. But Livia Harrow carries true power within her.'

Innellan thrust her spear forward, pushing Siff back. She could feel the strength there. The power Innellan spoke of.

Innellan parried Siff's final blow, the spear countering, thrusting, impaling.

Siff gasped, the blade dropping from her hand to grasp the shaft of the spear that ran through her chest.

'We will enjoy conquering this land, this girl and I,' Innellan said. 'I can feel her inside, raging against it. This child has a good heart... but it will not stay that way.'

Siff saw the black of Innellan's eyes flicker for a moment. They were suddenly brown, innocent, pleading for release. Then Livia Harrow was gone.

The spear burned inside Siff. She could feel the pain radiating from it, filling her essence. Her head tipped back and she screamed as fire consumed her from within…

†

A plume of flame ignited on top of the huge pyramid. Josten staggered back from the fight, his shield a heavy lump of battered metal, his sword like lead in his hand. In an instant the battle was over, every fighter now glaring up at that pyramid.

The fire soared into the dark of night like a shooting star, impossibly high until it disappeared into the black.

When it was gone, silence fell over the citadel.

Something was coming – they could all feel it. Something terrible and dark.

As the two armies watched, a figure descended from the summit of the pyramid. White hair floated about her head as though she were submerged in water, and her black eyes scanned the battlefield. Dried blood surrounded her smiling mouth, and it took Josten some time before he realised it was Livia Harrow.

Two warriors rushed forward, bone-armoured demons desperate for the slaughter to begin anew. Livia flung a spear at one, knocking him back across the battlefield. The other she let come, his sword raised high. He screamed as he brought the massive blade down, but Livia merely raised a hand and caught the blade, stopping it as though it had just struck a stone block. With her other hand she grasped the warrior's face.

His head exploded in a crimson gout.

Men began to fall back at witnessing the murder. Josten stood his ground; he had come so far to rescue Livia he could not abandon her now. Despite how much she had changed, even though he could see this was not the girl he'd travelled so far to save, Josten could not turn back.

She walked among a bed of corpses, red dress trailing through the blood. Josten took a step towards her and her eyes fell on him. He was a lone figure, defiant amongst the cowering mass.

'Livia,' he said.

That thin, red smile wavered on her lips. The piercing black of her eyes softening for a moment.

'Josten?' she replied, as though seeing him for the first time.

Then Livia disappeared, her eyes turning to black pits. All that remained was the white-haired witch.

'Kneel,' she said.

Josten felt a pull, compelled by an irresistible force. Behind he could hear armoured men dropping to their knees, weapons falling from their grip. Stubborn as he was, Josten remained standing but his grip loosened on his sword and it clattered at his feet.

'Kneel!' the woman repeated.

Josten could not defy her.

As he fell to his knees, she moved forward, eyes scanning the prostrate hordes before her.

'I have returned for you,' she said, her voice echoing around the silent courtyard. 'I have come to unite you under a single banner. Whatever allegiance you held before is now gone. Your loyalty now is to me. I am Innellan. The White Widow. In the kingdoms of the Suderfeld I am the songbird

Frith. In the Cordral I am Lilith the Masked. All you need know is that I am your queen. Now and always.' Silence infected the citadel. No one moved as the witch surveyed her army. 'What say you?'

As one the two armies rose to their feet. Every man in unison bellowed her name. 'Innellan! Innellan! Innellan!'

Over and over they chanted until the noise of it made Josten's ears ring. They had lost their souls to this creature. A god that had stolen the body of Livia Harrow.

Josten was powerless but to add his voice to theirs.

55

LIGHT lanced into the cell through a tiny hole near the ceiling. Despite the shade it was still hotter than a Bedouin's shoe in the cramped chamber. Josten had been sitting for hours in the same spot, but still was drenched in sweat.

Randal sat opposite, hugging his knees, face hidden. They were going to die, and it was pretty clear the tallyman had given up all hope.

Josten couldn't blame him; he knew there was little point in either of them making any long-term plans, but Josten had been here before. Locked up and waiting for the axe man was something he'd lived through once already. He knew there was always a chance, no matter how bad things appeared.

No need to tell Randal that though.

Despite what they'd been through together, that bastard was the reason Mullen was dead. He was the reason Livia had been taken and the reason Josten was in this cell right now. Who cared if he was suffering? Josten had his own woes, and the main one was the two feet of chain securing him to the wall. If only he could find a way of loosening it he'd be in with a fighting chance at least. But if there was a way to loosen a chain with nothing but hope and a whispered prayer he didn't know what it was.

Before he could think more on it, a creak of ancient hinges heralded yet more light cutting through the shadows of the cell. Josten braced himself. It seemed there would be no time for him to formulate any plan of escape.

Footsteps echoed through the chamber, but they weren't the stomping footfalls of any jailer. This tread was light, bare feet padding softly on the stone floor. Josten felt something snatch at his insides as the hem of a red dress came into view. Without thinking he gripped his own knees, as much to stop his hands shaking as to guard against the sudden chill that crept over his moist skin. Clamping his eyes shut wasn't enough to quell the feeling of dread as she stood in the centre of the cell. It was all he could do to not piss himself.

'Look at me,' she ordered.

Josten was powerless against her will, and slowly he raised his head. This was Livia no more. Her features seemed twisted somehow… corrupted. Where before had been an innocent girl now stood a cruel and heartless mistress. And despite himself, Josten felt only the urge to serve her.

Her black eyes regarded him without pity. Behind her, at the foot of the stairs, stood a dark-haired warrior, hand on the hilt of his sword as though this woman might require protection. Josten knew how laughable that notion was.

'Traitors,' said the woman. 'You came here to kill me. To banish me. You are servants of that cunt, Siff.'

'No,' said Randal in a panic. 'We came to save you. We don't even know that woman.'

Innellan's smile was cruel, made all the darker by her lifeless eyes. 'Save me? From what? Ah…' She tapped the side of her head with an outstretched finger. 'The girl.'

Innellan squatted down beside Josten.

'She is still in here,' she said in a low voice. 'I can feel her rattling around inside. It's confusing for me. When I look at the both of you there is great affection. But also great hate. I think she wants to kill one of you. Who could it be, I wonder?'

Josten looked at Randal. They both knew which of them Livia wanted dead, but Josten still said nothing. It was only his word against Randal's.

'This is difficult,' the woman said, rising to her feet. 'I should kill you both. But she is still in here.' Sharp fingers teased the side of her temple. 'Still a part of me, however small. So there will be a mercy.' She turned to the swordsman, who seemed disinterested in proceedings. 'Dantar, you will take both of these traitors out into the desert. There you will slay one of them, and release the other. Never tell me who you decide on. Do you understand?'

'Yes, my queen,' Dantar replied.

The snow-haired witch turned to leave, but her dark eyes lingered on Josten's for just a moment.

Was there a flash of humanity in that look? If so it was gone as soon as it appeared, and she swept from the room, the tresses of her red gown whipping up the dirt as she went.

Dantar watched them both closely as a hunched jailer entered the cell and unlocked their chains. Josten and Randal stood, looking at one another while they rubbed the life back into their wrists. One of them was about to die, and it was up to this warrior, Dantar, this killer, to decide which he would execute and which he would set free.

Josten led the way. If this was going to be it, he wasn't about to tarry. He'd been here before when Harlaw's men walked him into the woods that day. But there was no Mullen here now to help him. He had no weapon. There was every chance he'd be marched off and murdered, and all on the toss of a coin.

The sun was blinding as they walked out into the courtyard. A path had been cleared, bodies piled to either side, making a road through to the gate and out into the desert.

Josten walked on, with Randal right behind him. No one paid them much mind as they passed through the smashed archway. Once outside, Josten spared a glance over one shoulder. Dantar was following behind them, eyes watching with no emotion. It was clear this was a man with little compassion. There'd be no bargaining with that one.

They took the path south, out past the camp of High Lord Kraden and so far that the tower of Kessel disappeared. They were so deep in the desert Josten couldn't tell which way was north and for a moment he missed Silver. He could have done with the woman's fighting prowess now, but it was doubtful he'd ever see her again.

'This is far enough,' said Dantar, finally.

Josten stopped. He'd been dreading those words.

He and Randal turned to face the warrior. Dantar still didn't seem interested, though his hand lay firmly on his blade.

'You don't have to do this,' said Randal.

Josten had expected that. Some men took their execution with a stubborn silence. Others begged. Josten had spotted Randal for a whingeing shit right from the start.

'I just wanted to save her,' the tallyman went on. 'He was the one who wanted her dead.' He pointed an accusing finger at Josten.

Any other time he'd have been angry at the injustice, but not now. Livia was gone. Whatever that thing was back in Kessel it wasn't the girl he'd come to save. If he was the one to die then so be it. Josten didn't care anymore.

Despite Randal's lies, Dantar didn't seem particularly swayed either way. His eyes remained fixed on the ground as he slowly drew his blade.

Randal looked around desperately, as though there might be somewhere for him to run to in the open desert. Josten took a deep sigh, waiting for his fate, whatever it might be.

Dantar skewered his blade in the ground and it quivered a little as he looked up at them.

'To hell with it,' he said, his eyes now filled with tears.

Without another word he walked past them both, leaving the sword wavering in the ground.

Josten turned back to Randal whose eyes were desperate. Neither of them spoke, but neither of them needed to. Randal was first to move, but Josten was quicker. They both scrambled across the desert floor towards the sword and Josten's hand closed around the hilt first. Randal's hand slammed on top of his, stopping him drawing it from the ground. Josten smashed his forehead into Randal's cheek and he fell with a grunt.

As the tallyman foundered, Josten yanked the blade free. There was no cross-guard, and it was straight as an arrow to the tip. Josten had never held a blade so exquisitely balanced.

'Wait,' said Randal, as though he was going to talk his way out of this one.

'Close your fucking mouth and get on your feet,' Josten replied.

Randal slowly rose, his cheek fast reddening. He held his hands up defensively, as though somehow they might stop the thrust of a sword. It was obvious he wanted to start pleading all over again but fear kept his simpering mouth shut.

'One of us had to die, either way,' Josten said. 'You knew we weren't both going to make it through this.'

'Then do it,' said Randal, his voice cracking at the end.

Josten felt the sword in his grip. Four feet of perfect steel. It would have been so easy.

He should have done it for Mullen. Should have done it for Livia and however many others, but Josten was tired. The taste for vengeance had withered on his tongue.

'You saved my life,' Josten said, remembering the warrior bearing down on him in Kessel. Remembering Randal hacking off his arm. 'Consider us even.' Randal stared in disbelief. 'Now piss off.'

The tallyman paused, as though Josten were tricking him. When the death blow never came, he shuffled away.

'Thank you,' he said as he went.

'Save it,' Josten replied. 'Next time one of us will die.'

Randal took off at a run.

Josten watched him disappear into the haze.

Dantar had already disappeared and Josten was left alone in the desert, with nothing but a sword and a shitty sense of direction. He'd travelled so far, risked his life for nothing, and now it looked like he'd end up dead and rotting under a foreign sun.

'Well,' he sighed, wondering which way to go. 'Everyone gets what they deserve.'

EPILOGUE

The Ramadi Wastes, 105 years after the Fall

IT was the blackest night Hansi Alek had known in years. He and his brother Salann walked with torches held high along the northern shore of Devil Sound, the flickering light barely penetrating the dark as they travelled.

It was dangerous for them to be out at this hour. As traders and members of the Penitent Order they were in good standing with a number of cults, but there could be bandits or worse lurking out here in the dark, lying in wait to prey on the vulnerable. And the Alek brothers were no warriors.

'This had better be worth it,' whispered Salann.

'The *umma* has deemed it necessary, brother,' Hansi replied. That light in the sky was more than a mere shooting star. The omens have been divined. The entrails have been read—'

'And we are the fools sent to investigate.' Salann's voice quivered, the torch in his hand unsteady in his boy's grip. 'This is an errand for warriors. Not merchants.'

'The holy light was seen, brother. This is an honour we would have been foolish to refuse.'

'Foolish? Because the *umma* would have had us whipped? I would gladly have taken a flogging to avoid this. A flogging

I will survive. The Ramadi at night I may not.'

Hansi ignored his brother's whining. The *umma*'s word was law and the caravan obeyed without question. She had not seen them brought low yet and years under her guidance had only seen them prosper. Even the strongest cults valued the wares traded by the Alek and it was for that reason Hansi had not argued when bidden to find the source of the strange light in the sky. To risk his life on a pilgrimage that was more than likely a fool's errand.

The pair walked until the mercy of dawn began to creep up over the horizon. Their torches were beginning to gutter as the dim light showed them the endless expanse of the desert to the north and the grey waters of Devil Sound to the south.

'What's that?' said Salann, pointing across the flat waste.

Hansi squinted over the stony ground, his eyes nowhere as keen as those of his younger brother. He could see movement in the shadows, about a thousand yards off.

Salann made to move towards the shape, but Hansi held out an arm.

'Wait,' he said. 'We should approach with caution. We have no idea what we face.'

Salann nodded, seeing the sense in his brother's words, and they both moved carefully, the fire of their torches their only defence against what they faced.

As they moved closer Hansi could see that a creature was fussing something on the ground, and he momentarily wished they had better weapons than torches.

Something barked at them as they drew closer and both

men stopped. As his eyes began to focus, Hansi could see a jackal staring at them, eyes reflecting the morning light. At its feet lay the carcass of something... or someone.

'Away from there!' Hansi shouted, but the jackal did not move.

As though suddenly possessed, Salann rushed forward, screaming from the bottom of his lungs and waving his torch around his head as though it were the sword of some ancient hero. Hansi was relieved to see the jackal did not stand and fight for its prize, and instead ran off into the desert.

Salann turned with a smile.

'Very good,' said Hansi. 'Perhaps you should consider pursuing the way of the warrior.'

Salann's smile faded at his brother's sarcasm.

Gingerly they approached the carcass on the ground, each of them slowing as they drew closer. Salann's previous bravery seemed to fade the closer they got.

'What is it?' he whispered as they reached the corpse.

'Dead,' Hansi replied, staring down at the blackened lump of meat.

From what he could see it was human in shape but the extent of its burns were so horrific there was no way to tell any more than that.

Salann gave an audible sigh as Hansi crouched beside the figure. Heat still radiated from it, along with a burnt-meat stink.

'How did it get here?' Salann asked.

Hansi looked up. 'Clearly it fell from the sky.'

'This is the burning star seen by the *umma*?'

Hansi almost laughed at the thought. 'Of course not. How would that be poss—'

The lump of burned meat took a haggard breath.

Hansi jumped back as Salann squealed in terror.

Both men watched transfixed as the charred body slowly rose to its feet, burned sinews cracking in the silence of morning. Salann gave the sign of the Cup Bearer to ward off evil, before falling to his knees and touching the ground with his forehead.

Hansi could only watch as the blackened body raised its head to the sky and cried out to the dawn.

The *umma* had been right. The prophecies were complete.

Gods walked the earth once again.

ACKNOWLEDGEMENTS

As always I have to give a huge thanks to my agent, John Jarrold, for his expert guidance. He will forever be the Obi Wan to my Luke (and occasionally the Vader).

Cath Trechman and all the staff at Titan deserve my undying gratitude for commissioning the novel in an embryonic form, and for being very patient after I decided to completely change the third act... six months before its original publication date. Particular recognition should also go to Gary Budden for his meticulous editing and for not cutting out any of the bad language!

And thanks to everyone who has read and reviewed any of my books. Your contribution means more than you know.

ABOUT THE AUTHOR

R.S. Ford originally hails from Leeds in the heartland of Yorkshire but now resides in the wild fens of Cambridgeshire. His previous works include the raucous steampunk adventure, *Kultus*, and the grimdark fantasy trilogy, Steelhaven.

You can find out more about what he's up to, and download free stuff, here: http://richard4ord.wordpress.com.

And follow him on Twitter here: @rich4ord

DUSKFALL
Christopher Husberg

Pulled from a frozen sea, pierced by arrows and close
to death, Knot has no memory of who he was. But his
dreams are dark, filled with violence and unknown
faces. Winter, a tiellan woman whose people have
long been oppressed by humans, is married to and
abandoned by Knot on the same day. In her search for
him, she will discover her control of magic, but risk
losing herself utterly. And Cinzia, priestess and true
believer, returns home to discover her family at the
heart of a heretical rebellion. A rebellion that only the
Inquisition can crush... Their fates and those of others
will intertwine, in a land where magic and daemons
are believed dead, but dark forces still vie for power.

"A great new fantasy epic."
Library Journal

THE PAGAN NIGHT
Tim Akers

The Celestial Church has all but eliminated the old
pagan ways, ruling the people with an iron hand.
Demonic gheists terrorize the land, hunted by the
warriors of the Inquisition, yet it's the battling factions
within the Church and age-old hatreds between north
and south that tear the land apart.

Malcolm Blakley, hero of the Reaver War, seeks to
end the conflict between men, yet it will fall to his
son, Ian, and the huntress Gwen Adair to stop the
killing before it tears the land apart. *The Pagan Night*
is an epic of mad gods, inquisitor priests, holy knights
bound to hunt and kill, and noble houses fighting
battles of politics, prejudice, and power.

"A tale of religious conflicts and cleverly drafted
characters, a must for all epic fantasy fans."
Starburst

For more fantastic fiction, author events, competitions,
limited editions and more

VISIT OUR WEBSITE
titanbooks.com

LIKE US ON FACEBOOK
facebook.com/titanbooks

FOLLOW US ON TWITTER
@TitanBooks

EMAIL US
readerfeedback@titanemail.com